mw 350½

Other Avon Bard Books by
Susan Fromberg Schaeffer

ANYA

Avon Books are available at special quantity discounts for bulk purchases for sales promotions, premiums, fund raising or educational use. Special books, or book excerpts, can also be created to fit specific needs.

For details write or telephone the office of the Director of Special Markets, Avon Books, 959 8th Avenue, New York, New York 10019, 212-262-3361.

FALLING

SUSAN FROMBERG SCHAEFFER

 A BARD BOOK/PUBLISHED BY AVON BOOKS

FOR
Lester Schwartz,
who let me back into the house.

AVON BOOKS
A division of
The Hearst Corporation
959 Eighth Avenue
New York, New York 10019

Copyright © 1973 by Susan Fromberg Schaeffer
Published by arrangement with Macmillan Publishing
Company, Inc.
Library of Congress Catalog Card Number: 72-87159
ISBN: 0-380-59006-9

First Bard Printing, June, 1982

BARD TRADEMEARK REG. U.S. PAT. OFF. AND IN
OTHER COUNTRIES, MARCA REGISTRADA, HECHO EN
U.S.A.

Printed in the U.S.A.

WFH 10 9 8 7 5 4 3 2 1

Contents

Prologue: The Old Country   1

The New Country   11

Falling   229

Family Tree

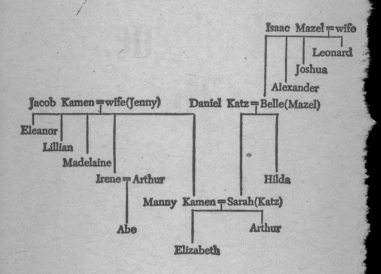

Prologue:
The
Old Country

It was a time of inexplicably happy marriages. Elizabeth's grandparents had arrived, penniless; their first wealth was their children. Her grandfather, Jacob Kamen, spoke Yiddish and Russian, her grandmother, only Yiddish. They had come from Russia to England. There, Jacob visited one of his brothers; he saw the great rolls of brown paper, the cardboard forms for the patterns, the soap chalk for marking the fabric of suits. Isaac expected him to stay, but Jacob shook his head. "A little country, what is it?" he said. "You don't watch your step, you fall off and drown." "So swim," said Isaac. "You swim," said Jacob, "I'm no water rat." "America has no streets paved with gold, Jacob," Isaac said with tears in his eyes. "So long as they're paved," said Jacob. They packed all their things in two stiff paper boxes and got on the ship. "Where are the boxes?" Isaac asked, stuffing his hands viciously into his pockets. "I'm sitting on them," said Jacob. Then he said, "Some suit. One pocket higher than the other. You can swim in the air here, you don't need the water." Isaac said nothing. Twice a year, Jacob would get a letter from Isaac, written out by his daughter; like Jacob's wife, Isaac never learned to write in English. In America, Jacob would answer twice a year; one of his daughters would type the letter so Isaac could read it; handwriting had to be read to him. Any letters concerning business were typed by their sons.

In America, Jacob Kamen had one boy and four girls. "Enough arms and legs for a factory," he would shake his head over breakfast; outside, it was still dark. He would walk across the kitchen for his challah and tea, making a wide circle around the dog. He was terrified of the dog, but his youngest daughter had asked for it. "Frisky," he said to himself, "a name for a pair of teeth." The dog was lying with its head on its paw, but managed a growl as he passed. "Too early for you?" Jacob inquired to the air. He drank his tea from an empty jelly glass. He drank it more quickly after he reached the halfway point. "Almost five," he muttered to himself, and began patting his pockets, starting with his shirt, then his jacket, then trousers. Cigars, keys, wallet, fare. At five thirty, he was in the factory. At precisely five thirty every morning, he opened the door, sounding the alarm, turned off the alarm, turned on the lights. By six, he was raving: "This is a tailor? What are you cutting, meat? We should call the Rabbi; he'll kosher it." The tailor would point to the chalk markings; in Yiddish, the tirade when on. "So what are you drawing, the Sistine Chapel? Uniforms, these are *uniforms* the army orders. They all look the same." His voice rose to a shriek. "Bankruptcy at five in the morning! For this I need relatives! Strangers from the street! Goys!" The third cousin holding the square flat piece of chalk mumbled something about blood; it was thicker. "Blood! I'll show you blood!" shrieked Jacob; he ran around the table, demented. "Your head, that's the only thing that's thick! Blood! We'll see about blood!"

At night, he and the five children and his wife sat around the polished oval table; it was a mahogany table, and in it their faces wavered and shone among the frail reeds of grain. It was very important that they eat; it was very important that no food go to waste. From behind her glasses, thick as magnifying lenses, their mother watched with the eye of a hawk. The filets were breaded, the bread was buttered, huge mounds of potatoes and potato pancakes and beets and spinach, and cold pitchers of milk. Tzimmis. Kugel. More than obedient, they ate. By the time they reached adolescence, the four girls were solid and heavy as atlantes. Only the son, Manny, was graceful and slender, "a movie star." He ran in track meets; girls followed him home. He was over six feet. Jacob was short and round. When they put a picture of Manny alongside their own wedding portrait, Jacob was astounded. All week, a little planet, he gravitated to the mantle. He looked at himself and his wife. "Shrimps!" he muttered to himself. "They could hire us to stand on a cake!" Then he would look at his son, and as he looked, it seemed his son grew and grew until his head touched the rim of the picture, and the sun was a gold earring in his ear. "So long as they're paved," he said aloud to himself with satisfaction. "Sugar, they're rationing sugar," said his wife.

Jacob had every man in the place buy two pounds of sugar. His wife went from store to store, buying sugar.

4

All of the children could not come home from school until they had stopped at the store, for sugar. Finally, they had to move the pots and pans out of the cabinets under the sink, and the dishes, and they filled up the dark cupboards with package after package of sugar. Then Manny read in the paper that "agents" were arresting anyone found to possess more than ten pounds of sugar. "Hoarders, they're after hoarders," Manny said. Jacob's wife was frantic. She pleaded; she wanted to throw it down the sink. Jacob was adamant. He had five children. "If the agent comes," he told his wife, "give them each a few spoons; he won't find a thing." She would not be calmed: "They'll come. They'll find it," she wailed, pushing back her chair. It tipped over and fell against the sill where it stood, suspended in midfall, its arms up and imploring. "Sugar!" Jacob said with scorn; "Sugar! Hitler's sinking ships, they worry about sugar!"

The sugar never ran out. The agent never came. Frisky continued to growl at the hand that fed him. One day they found that all the sugar had hardened; it was solid, like rock. "So what now?" demanded his wife. "We could carve statues of Uncle Sam," suggested Irene, the youngest. "We could fill up the bathtub with coffee and pretend it's a cup," suggested Eleanor as she stared into hers, coffee and sugar, a caramel-like sludge. "Show some respect!" shrieked Jacob, jumping up from the table, knocking over a chair. "A war, they think it's funny!" "What did we do?" Irene asked. "What did we do?" Eleanor echoed. "Eat," said their mother. It was the remark that closed all discussion. Later in the week, they spent an afternoon carting the huge packs of sugar up to their parents' bathroom, watching them dissolve under the hot-water tap, pocking with corridors and hallways, like stone, "like the beginning of the world," said Madelaine. "Like the end," said Manny.

A few days later, they heard their Aunt Frieda's only son had been killed; Frieda had worshipped her Michael, and her Michael was a doctor. Michael had been on a hospital ship, marked with a red cross, painted red on its deck, and the Germans had bombed it. After that, Frieda never was the same. Her caughter, Lenore, was also studying to be a doctor, and Frieda, who was afraid of everything now, would run into Lenore's room, where she was melted over her books like a candle, and scream, "Fail! You're going to fail like a dog! You'll wind up

5

selling ribbons in Macy's!" Lenore began to spend more and more time at Jacob's house. Frieda sat in the kitchen with Jacob's wife. His wife peeled potatoes and carrots. Frieda cried. One day Frieda began peeling potatoes. "So how is she now?" asked Jacob, "better?" "She peels," said his wife. When Lenore went to medical school, Frieda followed her to Boston. When Lenore married a man, a millionaire, Frieda moved in. Twice a year letters arrived, written on expensive paper in Lenore's precise hand. Every year, the handwritten letters got smaller and smaller. "By now Lenore should be able to hide behind the walls," said Manny. "Don't be so smart," said Jacob.

Mrs. Kamen had never said much, and once she left Russia, she said less. When she got to America, her eyes got worse and worse, as if the very act of setting foot on the strange earth had fogged her eyes as thoroughly and completely as glasses fog when worn into a room from the great outside cold. Her children had the feeling that she never saw through them; true, when they looked at her, they could see themselves reflected on the twin sheets of glass; the room was reflected on the two tiny panes, the stuffed couch, the crystal, the cupids, but she lived somewhere behind them, behind all this, behind the furnished rooms, in empty rooms with bare planks on the floor where people screamed at her, do this! do this! Where she cleaned and scrubbed and cleaned and polished and scoured, and not a thing was her own. Lillian, who was the oldest girl, wanted to know what kind of life her mother had had "over there." She never got tired of asking; she asked again and again. Her mother would say only, "I met your father. He came to our village, he had a pushcart." At, last, Lillian went to Jacob. "She cleaned," said Jacob. In later years, the children would ask themselves again and again, did he love her? did she love him? They would remember the fights, the fights over money, the fights over food. Their mother thought Irene should have more money, she was plain, no one would marry her. Then Jacob would shout they were all spoiled, it was her fault. The children would close their doors and pretend to study. When it was over, their mother would tiptoe in, take a look, go away. Then their father would come, open the door, and go on, a watchman, making rounds. The procession ended with Irene's room, to the left of the stairs. Later, they would take a long walk, two miles, to Marine Park, or farther, to Coney Island; they would see whatever movie was playing; they never called in advance. They did this two or three times a week. "Manny will watch," Jacob announced, as he slammed the front door. When they came home, Madelaine had locked Irene out on the back porch. Jacob locked Madelaine in her room. Then he got out the strap, and, tiny, enraged troll, he went after Manny. "You were supposed to watch," he said, cornering his son.

One day, all five of them were sent to the movies. Manny had the money for candy; Eleanor had the money for the bus. When they came back, queasy and sticky, their parents met them at the door like conspirators. From inside, they heard a deep gong. Then it chimed five more times. When they rushed into the dining room, they saw it standing in the corner, still wet with lemon oil, shining like a knight, standing taller than Manny, the faithful soldier of the house, the guardian angel, the great heart of brass. They had never seen their mother so happy. "When I was a girl," she said, so many words together, they were a necklace, bright stones, "I cleaned them." Later, Jacob told them, once she had pushed the handles around to hear the chimes; they were beautiful; she was impatient, and the woman had come in and hit her across the head with the flat of her hand and beaten her with the broom. That night, all of them, even Jacob, stayed up until midnight to hear it strike twelve times. By the next night, they thought they were used to it. But that night, when the clock struck twelve times, they all woke up and rushed into the hall; they had forgotten. From her room, their mother called out, "Go to bed. You have school." But she didn't get up to check; she sounded pleased.

A week after the clock began marking the hours with its thin hands of brass, Manny decided to marry. "Who is this girl?" Jacob asked. "Is she Jewish?" "I met her at a dance," said Manny. "What kind of dance?" asked Jacob; he saw blonde hair, blue eyes, disgrace, the end of a career, his only son, his tall son. "A *temple* dance, Poppa." The next day, they met the girl. She had no accent. Jacob and his wife agreed she could not be a Jew. So she went down to talk to the girl's father; the girl's father, Mr. Katz, was a pharmacist, and when she got there he was behind the marble counter, making ice-cream sodas for the Catholic school children in their blue jumpers and white blouses and gold pocket insignias and leather strap-bound towers of books. She asked for some aspirin.

7

While she was looking in the dark places of her purse for the coins, she said, "Tell me, Mr. Katz, you're a Jewish man?" "Naturally," Mr. Katz said, smiling. "You have children?" Mr. Katz said he had two children, two girls. They were named Sarah and Hilda. "And you?" he asked. Mumbling something, she fled without answering. Jacob and his wife agreed it looked suspicious; the father was blond and had blue eyes, but eventually the Rabbi convinced them Sarah was Jewish, and then it was just a matter of waiting until they had enough money to marry. After that, the brass hands of the clock went around faster and faster; there was no need or desire to push them, and soon all of the children were married. Manny had the first grandchild, and they named her Elizabeth. She was everyone's darling. Her hair was dark black and curled in little springs, and her mother had to watch her or children would pull her hair in the park to watch the curls spring back against her head, and then she would cry. "Monsters," muttered Sarah's mother, who came along to supervise. Soon they all had children, except for Lillian, the oldest girl. Everyday, her mother would say a prayer for her, and everyday she would tell Lillian not to worry, "time, it takes time." But to her other children she admitted her belief that Lillian would never have children, while she had too many, the others had so many, it was not right, God was not right, she could not understand. At night, she would wake up and go through it all: the bare feet? She didn't eat? And then the clock would strike, four, five, six, and she would fall asleep, decapitated.

The whole family gathered for the holidays. The children now ate at a separate table in the living room: "Communist Russia," said Irene, "we don't want any spies," as she sent her oldest one back. There were mounds of chicken liver, and potato pudding, and noodle kugel, and the old gefilte fish, yellow and heavy as a rock, "a dangerous weapon, you could be arrested," Manny commented, eating his third. Irene's husband shoveled his food onto his plate. "The great sugar scare," whispered Madelaine, nudging Lillian. "He's a good eater, God bless him," said Irene from the other side. But no one said anything out loud, for Irene was plain, very plain, and no one could believe their good fortune, that Irene was married, that Irene had children, and what did it matter that her husband was a good-for-nothing with no manners and could hold a job as long as a greased pig. Irene was

8

happy; it was Irene that mattered. In silence, Jacob said the blessing. "Now we can eat!" said Irene's husband. Madelaine nudged Lillian again. Lillian ignored her. "Ma," she said. Her mother looked up at her through her glasses; now they were thick as clam shells. Bifocals, they gave her a perpetually astounded look, an octogenarian Orphan Annie, Manny called her. Lillian looked at her: the glasses reflected the chandelier like to suns. "Ma," she said, "I'm going to have a baby. In April." The silence was thicker than the bread. The noise of the children came from the other room, sounds under water. Then they all began to scream. Lillian began to cry. Her mother began to cry. Big tears rolled out from under her glasses, catching the light, and splashed down onto the yellowish fish, heavy on her plate. "Ma, it's salty enough," Irene said hoarsely. Jacob didn't say anything. Manny didn't say anything.

Afterwards, when they remembered those days, they remembered their mother fitted into her silences like one of their father's customers into his suits, their father's threats, he would cut them out of his will, he would cut out their children, they remembered the beatings, the locked doors, the silences, the little black book Jacob kept to reckon their sins, its black simulated leather binding peeling from the cardboard backing like cheap veneer on a bad coffin, they remembered the sugar, and the clock, and the happiness, and they remembered with wonder, how their lives, and their characters, and their morals and their fates had always hung there like long clothes in the closet, waiting for them to grow into them, and now they were grown, and they perfectly fit, and they were happy, and when holes appeared in their garments, they mended and sewed and darned as if they had always known how.

The
New Country

Chapter 1

After Mark finished shaving, he came out to look for Elizabeth; she was lying under her crescent-shaped stained glass window, curled up, muscleless. For the first time, Mark began to feel some alarm. Lying there like that, limp, with no muscle tone, she perfectly resembled the little white rats he anesthetized daily, and it was this comparison, finding himself making it, that caused him to pick up the phone and call their friend Robert, one of the interns assigned to Student Health. The hospital switchboard had to page him. Mark listened: he could hear the automatic voice: *Dr. Hart, Dr. Robert Hart, Dr. Craig, Dr. Phillip Craig, Dr. Hart, Dr. Robert Hart, Dr. Hart.* While he waited, he straightened his tie. Later in the morning, he had a lecture and a lab section; after that, they would have to make up a departmental exam. The exams were difficult to make up; when the students handed them in, the grades had to fall into a precise curve, or all concluded something had gone wrong with the exam. So for hours they would sit around the square wood table with pencils, and blank sheets of paper, and stock room stopwatches, composing an exam that was too long for any student, including problems that most of the students, those who had done their work, could solve; others that only those with some ability to generalize about what had not been covered, could solve; and still others that none of them, theoretically, could solve. This was the educational process: it was necessary, Mark took it very seriously. For several weeks in advance, he would compose problems, classic ones with a new twist, imagining the expression of the students, the good ones, coming up to them and stopping, stark still, like race horses faced by a frightening gate. He never thought of the despair of the students—of most of the students—who had stayed up all night, who had studied until they fell asleep watching violet equations complicating themselves in the night light; good, conscientious students who would not know, unless they, or some of their friends, were dating these assistants

13

who made up the exams, that some of the problems were not meant to be solved, who would not know, as they strained to finish, skimping on time, riveting their full attention on the clock, that they were not meant to finish at all. Elizabeth, who was a pre-med major, had told him that the medical students did not take exams this way, that when they were all seated in the giant amphitheater, the instructor on the stage, tiny in the pit, looking up at the pale heads, the pale tiers of balloons, students who knew each other would divide up the work; the one on the left doing the even-numbered problems, the one on the right, the odd. When they were finished, they would change sheets. This was easily done. One of them would pretend to knock his paper to the floor; the other would pick it up. The assistants, relying on the proverbial competition among pre-meds, had assumed there would be no help among the gladiators, no risks taken which might raise the curve. It seemed to Elizabeth that higher mathematics were useless to them in real life; the students did not care how high the curve spiraled, provided they were on top, climbing the beanstalk, collecting the golden eggs, the medical acceptances, the gallstones in jars.

Mark was shocked. He had spent some time inventing a plan to prevent the undermining of department exams. Finally, he came up with a partial solution everyone accepted. They would grade the papers, and mark them with a penciled X invisible in white light. If a student protested the grade, they would hold the paper under ultraviolet light; then, if there had been any erasing, the X would also be erased, the culprit would be caught, branded. But then Mark realized that this would only eliminate cheating after the fact. They tried A series exams, B series exams, giving the two sets to students in every other seat. This made passing exams back and forth harder, but not impossible. The students had not taken calculus for nothing. They arranged themselves in the appropriate patterns. The curve continued to rise, a demented balloon, the instructors hanging on by a loose rope floating out over the rough, unpredictable land of emotion, out of the calm shoals of reason and order. It had always annoyed Mark that Elizabeth took these courses. She was not serious. She had come to his lab and worked under a red light while he flashed lights in the rats' eyes, writing out themes, literary analyses, logical as a machine, but when she looked at a pendulum, she saw it with personality and

14

will, slicing the air, slowing down, not with friction, but weariness. And she was not like everyone else. There was a reason to things. There was a reason for wearing stockings downtown. Elizabeth could not be bothered. One winter, she had worn bermuda shorts and knee socks through March. Robert Hart had told her that if she wore them to Thanksgiving dinner in the dorm, he was leaving the table. "You're the one who'll be hungry," she told him, barely taking note. She wore shifts she made herself, out of upholstery fabric. When Mark asked her why, listing all the perfectly good stores he passed on his walk to the school, she said hers had better colors. She reminded him that his mother made his shirts, but he did not think this was the same thing at all: his mother made him *shirts,* not monk's hoods, or capes. "A monk's hood or a cape might be a very good idea," Elizabeth told him, and Mark had a momentary vision of himself in a black cowl and cape, a flash of scarlet disappearing around the gray granite wall of the gothic lab, and then he was angry. "I'm going to the lab," he informed her. "When will you be back?" she asked; she wanted to know when to make dinner. "Whenever the experiment's through"; this was the ritual answer. "Try not to start a long one at five," she said, knowing perfectly well this would happen, seeing with perfect clarity the two pork chops solidifying in the refrigerator like an exhibit in a wax museum, the broccoli beading with little white drops of wax, worn out by the wait, the obscure disease.

At eight o'clock, Elizabeth ate alone. Mark's dinner was sitting on the bottom shelf of the refrigerator next to the half-rotted apple. She no longer bothered wrapping anything up. She no longer got angry enough to put dinner, plate and fork and knife, in the freezer, where it froze to death in rigid attitudes of reproach. At six-thirty, she had watched "Bullwinkle and Rocky the Flying Squirrel." She tried to think of what she could do to Mark to make him regret this new assault on her patience; all she could think of was withholding information about the latest installment in the adventures of Bullwinkle's Boris and Natasha; but this wasn't much; tomorrow's show would begin by recapitulating. Elizabeth thought this must be a clue: everyone led such disorganized lives. Thinking about it, she realized that one third of the show was a flashback, one third coming attractions. In between, the action ran back and forth like a frightened rat in a cage. The beginning

15

was a lifeline to those who had gone under the wave the day before, the coming attractions a rope for those who feared going under with the dawn.

When "Bullwinkle and Rocky the Flying Squirrel" had sounded its last, Elizabeth turned off the set. The walls took a giant step in. At night the living room curtains looked muddy, their brown background dominating the big blue and yellow and red Gauguin flowers that shimmered during the day like stained glass. Elizabeth had made them out of hopsacking, lining them, sitting under them; they weighed pounds, for three days one hot summer, thinking, why was she trying to make something glamorous out of a cloth with a name that made you think of potatoes sprouting damp white limbs from blind brown eyes.

All of the furniture returned her stare. "You get up, I'm tired," Elizabeth told the couch. She wondered why she tended to talk to inanimate objects. She wondered whether she was living with an inanimate object. She noticed her notebook, watching her from the center of the rug like a square black eye. She had been ignoring *Othello,* and there would be hell to pay in Humanities Three if she did not scrape him out of the musty grave into which he had fallen behind the over-stuffed cushion of the couch. She was to discuss whether or not the eavesdropping scene, in which Othello sees Cassio with Desdemona's handkerchief, was absolutely essential to the action of the play. She wondered who made up these exams: surgeons? On the whole, she preferred *Hamlet* and *Macbeth.* There was something in *Othello* that disturbed her; she could not write this paper. Finally, she decided to pretend she was taking an exam. She set the alarm to ring an hour and a half later, and began to write. When she finished, she still had ten minutes left. The paper obscurely upset her, and she thought that the faster she typed it up and got it out of the way, the better off she would be. When she was finished, she would try to answer a long list of questions she had assigned herself: Why did she go out with men only six feet and over? Why wouldn't she date a Jew? What was she doing here, watching someone's dinner congeal? Who was she jealous of? Mark's lab assistant? The blonde next door the neighborhood called Miss Easy Crotch? How seriously did she take her own threats to a) jump off the roof, b) take forty-five tranquilizers, aspirin, anything she could lay her hands on, Dramamine, c) go next door and steal that woman's gun and shoot them both? One day, that woman, her neighbor Emily Reid, had had company, and her daughter had wandered out on the landing where Elizabeth found her holding a real gun, a gun, a long piece of dust, like a nightmarish roach, dangling from the trigger. The child, who looked pleased, was dangling the gun by the barrel. Then her mother called her: "March!" and the child smiled at her, turned around, and went in. They took the gun away from her, and Emily was sorry; she promised never to leave it under the bed like that again, but Elizabeth was sure it was there.

Still, she was the only one she was annoyed with, annoyed to death, with her weird notions that she and Mark were fated to share the same life, like two characters in a bad Platonic dream; by her cowardice, her inability to decide what to do with the engagement gifts: the sheets, for instance. Should she take them off the bed, wash them, iron them, and send them back to her grandmother's friend Bertha? And she was attached to Aunt Irene's salad knife and fork, all the way from Italy, cherubs among the lettuce. She was greedy. Nor did she want to admit she had failed, or if she had not failed, what was worse, made a mistake. The whole family would blame it on the difference in religion: "Sooner or later, in the end, they turn on you, they all turn on you, they're all the same," her mother had said. She was in no hurry to hear all that again. And, then, supposing this came to an end, what would come next? This is where she always stopped, picturing the next life, the life past this, a gray place where the stars ran out, where a heart beat, tremendous, behind the black sky, black as paper, and every night was a burnt-ash copy of the night before. Mark was handsome; he looked like a Marlboro ad. He was intelligent; she had never known anyone so intelligent. But more and more, he could not follow anything she said; he would not follow. He would spend hours calculating the probable path of a stone, but when she asked why his mother fried fresh fish in old bacon grease, she was a heretic; she was cut off. And yet he seemed to get satisfaction out of what she said; her tongue sliced at the bread; she ate the slices. Furtively, he ate the crumbs.

Finally, Mark came to a decision. He did not love her. He did not love someone who would not wear stockings, who made her own clothes, who thought his sister looked like a flat-chested rockinghorse neighing on her hind legs. To underline his decision, he decided to sleep with Miss Easy Crotch. He walked off with her, right under Elizabeth's window, while she watched. Shaking, Elizabeth waited ten minutes, then called the girl's new apartment. She asked to talk to Mark. She told him if he wasn't back in twenty minutes, she would send his things to him in a cab. He was back in ten minutes, and he wanted to sleep with her. Elizabeth wanted him to take a shower; she was quietly hysterical. They made love, woodenly. When they were finished, she said to his ivory back: "I don't even feel like a woman anymore." But Mark was already asleep.

After that, they constantly fought. Mark, whose family thought of itself as a miniature Kennedy clan in the Middle West, who never tired of telling the story of how he had fallen out of a tree and landed on his back and bit his tongue almost in half, how Mark's younger brother, Sam, had slashed his arm on the mailbox door as they rode by and he reached his arm out of the window, the tendon exposed; Mark wrapped the arm in *The Post;* they drove to the hospital in the family calm; Mark's family dispatched his older sister, Margaret, to see what she could do in a land where tongues were obviously slashed, arms obviously bitten off at the wrist. Several times that day, Elizabeth saw them, walking, always walking, the car waiting useless at the curb, Mark gesturing like a character in an Italian comedy, Margaret, sage, blonde, older, and wise, nodding. The next morning, she left. They went back to sleep. Elizabeth woke up first. The room was dark except for one blinding shaft of light, brilliant yellow, cutting diagonally through the air from the top of the window to the floor. Elizabeth half expected to see someone walk down it, a tiny angel, a fledgling, a trainee, useless. It would trudge all the way back up, to give its gruesome report. It would get no cookie for lunch. Elizabeth began to feel sorry for it, but then she realized it was herself she felt sorry for: there was only that blade of light, cutting the air, clean, surgical, but when she looked closer, she saw bits of dust dancing in the light. "And the patient died," she said to herself. "And the doctor lived happily after."

She woke Mark up. "Well," she said, "what did the two of you decide? Are we going to get married? Do you love me?" "I don't love you; we are not going to get married,"

18

Mark answered her. His voice sounded pompous; Elizabeth realized she had never heard how pompous it sounded before. The syllables lay on her pillow like stones. "You have failed the exam; you cheated; you had help; you ruined the curve," she said. She turned on her side, resting her cheek on the knob of her elbow. It was hot. "Juvenile arthritis," the doctor had said, after some blood tests. "Rheumatoid, it will get better," and it had. She had no time to cry. "Are you sure? You won't change your mind?" "I'm sure, I won't change my mind." Elizabeth turned over, propped herself up. "Your sister, your beautiful blonde gentle sister with her flat chest and her big bottom and her hair shorter than yours so it never needs setting, and her two beautiful blonde children with their beautiful blue eyes who keep her from studying Chinese, your sister slept with her husband's brother on the rug in front of her couch, in front of the Christmas tree, last Christmas, 1959." Mark didn't say a word. "Your ex-roommate told me, he told me last week, over coffee, when he took me out." Mark got out of bed. She looked at his back. Now she had done it herself. Now he would never come back. She heard him take out the familiar pot and put it on the stove to boil the water for the Ralston he had eaten every morning since he was old enough to eat by himself. When she heard him turn on the shower, she went into the kitchen and took down a bottle of pills she kept in the canister of coffee. Mark never drank coffee. Then she took out the bottle of pills she kept in her bag. Thirty-five yellow ones, forty white. She divided them up into pairs, a white one, a yellow, couples. "One for you, one for me," she said to herself, as if feeding a baby, swallowing the first two. Then she swallowed them by the handful. She lay down on the bed and looked at the ceiling. She wanted to remember the cracks; she wondered if there were people you could call in to read the patterns in ceilings; she wondered if ceilings had life lines, times to fall in. When her lips began to get numb, she went in to the bathroom and told Mark what she had done. Then she went into the dining room, and lay down in front of the stained glass window Mark had fastened to the building's sill. "He takes a long time to dress," she thought to herself, stretching out an arm, then a leg.

When Elizabeth was very small, she had constant trouble with her ears. When the pain began, and she began to heat up her clothes, they would put her to bed. She would lie in the bed, fingering the rumplings at the ege of the pillow, imagining they were mysterious letters, tracing them endlessly with her fingers; they were reassuring, like grandmotherly skin. Later, the pain in her head would get worse, and she would begin to heat up like an iron, and when she got up out of bed, there would be a hot patch, in the shape of her body, pressed flatter than the rest. Finally, she would begin wandering around the house, always coming to rest in the bathroom, and her grandmother would tell her she had just been to the bathroom. She would get confused because she could not remember. The bathroom wall was white, made of small white, octagonal tiles, held together by some substance of black. The floor was made of the same thing. They always were cold. Even in the summer, they were cold. When her ear hurt, she would rest her head against the wall until the pattern had impressed itself on her cheek; by that time, the patch of wall had begun to warm up, and she would move her head to where it was cool. When she got up, her face was crisscrossed with wrinkles on one side and she liked to look at it, imagining this was what she would look like when she got old. She liked the idea of being old, and wearing a rustling slip. Then she would get back into bed and wait for her parents. She would keep the light on and stare at the ceiling, with its cracks, like a map. She began to feel friendly toward these patterns, the bathroom tiles, the cracks in the ceiling, the tracings on the pillow. She would lie there and wait for her parents who always brought her a piece of doll's house furniture when they went out and she was sick. Tonight they were supposed to bring her a grand piano with shiny white keys and a lid that raised up and could be propped open with a stick. She heard them come in. Her grandmother had fallen asleep on the couch, her head propped on her fist. When she lifted her head, her cheek still kept the marks.

Elizabeth appeared in the doorway. Her father said she shouldn't walk around in bare feet, not when she was sick. She asked about the piano. Her mother said they were sorry, but the stores were closed; they couldn't get it. Elizabeth went back to bed. She traced the pattern of her pillow a long time before she fell asleep. When she woke up in the morning, her ear felt better.

A long time later (was it years?) the doctor appeared. The doctor looked triumphant. He gave her mother a grainy yellow powder that was oily and smelled like half-rotted fish. "Mash it up in applesauce," he said, "and give it to her." Her mother explained that this powder would go straight to her ears, and fix them, and she could go back to school. "What a stupid idea," she thought to herself; the powder went straight to her ears; she went back to school.

They decided it was time for her to learn the piano. She liked the idea. She pictured herself turning into some kind of machine, spinning out music; she pictured herself reaching down deep and finding the black, round disc, the silver thorn. When she got to the teacher's, the teacher wouldn't let her near the piano at all. "First you have to learn to play the xylophone," the teacher said, "it will train your ear." Her mother bought one for her. They brought it home in a black box, like a coffin. Elizabeth would not go near it. They offered to find another teacher, but Elizabeth said she didn't want to learn.

The next time her ears hurt, everyone looked worried. They took her to the doctor. Elizabeth was terrified of shots. The doctor remembered the last time he had come to the house. She had hidden under her bed, and wrapped her arms and legs around the slats and, to get to her, they had to lift off the mattress, then the springs. She had been dragged out screaming. "This is not good for your ears," the doctor said sternly. The doctor said he couldn't see much because of the scar tissue. He took something cold and poked it way in. She screamed. The doctor looked grim. "Another infection," he said. He asked her if she would like to play with a little plastic duck. It was a yellow duck, with a red plastic beak. He had the duck nibble at her arm with its red beak: "The duck is hungry," said the doctor, smiling. Then something jumped out of the duck's beak and into her arm. "That wasn't so bad, was it?" he said, wiping his forehead with the back of his hand. In the back seat of the car, watching the sky come and go in the back of the alleys, falling on her faster and faster, like bullets, she screamed all the way home.

It was Easter. Her grandfather brought her three baby chicks the color of lemon meringue. Her mother insisted they keep them in the bathtub. Elizabeth was worried that they wouldn't be warm enough; one of them died. Her mother and grandmother were at the sink, peeling carrot skin. They would take the orange curls, spotted with black, and drop them into the white porcelain can. When they stepped on the pedal at its base, its lid jumped up into the air like the jaw of a great snapping turtle. The orange peels kept mounting up over the stiff cold body of the Easter chick. She wanted to go out and bury it. They said she was not going out of the house, not with her cold. She started to cry. No one paid any attention. Then she couldn't stop crying. When the doctor came in the morning, he said "Grind it up in applesauce, and give it to her." Years later, whenever they went to a farm, her mother would point out two roosters and claim they were her Easter chickens. Her mother would say they were much happier here than home in a tub. Elizabeth was not really interested in these explanations.

She began to go everywhere with her grandmother. Her grandmother and grandfather were "separated"; she could not understand this; her father's parents lived in one place. Her grandfather was a nice man; he would take her out to lunch and feed her bacon, lettuce, and tomato sandwiches. She had never eaten bacon before. "I won't have it in the house," said her grandmother. Her grandfather worked in a pharmacy where he had indigo blue eyecups and a soda fountain and she could have any kind of soda she wanted. But when they went for walks, he would spit in the street. This made her ashamed. He would always give her a quarter "to spend on herself." Her other grandfather would give her a dollar, "not for clothes," and never spit in the street. She felt ashamed of this one. He did not have much money. Her grandmother did not like him. He spit in the street. When she came home, she was ashamed; she was a traitor: to her grandfather, for his quarters and spitting; to her grandmother, for liking her grandfather; to everyone. She was no good.

She wanted to know why they were separated. She asked this over and over. Finally, her grandmother told her that her husband, Elizabeth's grandfather, used to follow her all over all the time; he thought she liked other men; he was jealous. Elizabeth was astonished. Her grandmother told her this while they were waiting for a train. For years after, she turned around, expecting to see her grandfather, pale as a ghost, behind one of the rusting pillars, its paint flaking off in complex patterns while he observed the intricate pattern of his wife's strange, suspect life.

Always, she was trying to understand things. It seemed there must be a way. First, she decided to be a doctor. She wanted to know what went on under the smooth

22

skin, the smooth white skin that gave no clue. The doctors could read the truth in the patchings of the tongue, in the map of white coating the dry surface of pink. There were secrets in the marrow of the bone. The heart was complicated and full of rooms. She began to study. The first advanced course in her major was botany. She had taken chemistry and calculus and physics. Now, there would be lab exams: clear petri dishes filled with an amorphous brown substance would be numbered, and little flags stuck in various parts. At each ring of a bell, they were expected to name the part identified by the flag. The exam resembled a version of musical chairs and a smorgasbord lunch. When it was over, Elizabeth felt she knew everything there was to know about plants. She went to her advisor and began the complex ritual of changing her major.

She decided the next best thing would be to fall in love with a physicist. She had been interested in all the wrong things. The fifth one she met in the library where she studied looked just right: he looked like Abraham Lincoln stepped off the back of a coin. His was another religion, with its whole set of truths. He knew about antimatter, and studied with a man who caught neutrinos in acres and acres of sandbags. They would know when they had it by a disturbance on a delicate chart. When it was trapped, it would destroy another, tiny particle of matter. Then she began to notice how he would check to see all the lights were out, even when the room they were leaving was perfectly dark. He explained that the lights could be off because the bulb had burned out, but the machine might still be on. They could not decide whether to marry. One night, she threw a stone statue at him and missed his head by an inch. The door wore the scar until the building was torn down. After this, she did not know what to do. She had a stained glass window that inverted the buildings across the way in the colored globes embedded in its skin. She took to counting them like pills, swallowing two pills for each globe that she counted. After awhile, she told him what she had done. He went on with his shaving. Finally, he called a friend. She was saying goodbye to the window, and in no hurry to leave. She wanted to drive around the school once more. Later, all she could remember was the sensation of something in her stomach, cold. Much later, they told her she nearly had died.

23

One day, her mother came home very late, and she had no chest of drawers for the doll's house. Elizabeth began to whine. "Leave me alone!" shrieked her mother, "I've had enough for one day!" Elizabeth couldn't understand what had gone wrong. Finally, her mother screamed at her, "Your grandfather's dead, they shot him in his store!" "Who shot him?" she asked, but no one would tell her. Later, she asked her mother why the police didn't catch him. "Oh, the police," said her mother, "What do they care?" In the back of Elizabeth's mind a long parade of police passed, all of them giving her dimes when she was lost and had lost all her money, or spent it on candy or comic books, telling her which bus to take, how to get home, when to cross, to look out for cars. She used to take down their name and numbers, and later, put a dime in an envelope, and mail it to them at the police station with a note.

When she woke up in the hospital, her mother and father were there. They wanted to know why. She didn't have the slightest idea. When they tried to take the physicist's handkerchief away to wash it, she became hysterical. Many years later she read a clipping about him, syndicated. A woman downstairs had been knifed by an assailant and crawled up to his door at the University of Texas, one floor above hers. He had opened the door, and when he saw her, bleeding, he picked her up and put her in the tub so she would not bleed on the rug. Then he called the ambulance. Elizabeth read the clipping over and over. It seemed like a message, in code. Several years later, she met him and his wife. His wife had become nervous about life in the city, and seemed vaguely afraid. The woman greeted Elizabeth like an old friend; she told her she had studied her old pictures. When they left, Elizabeth looked after her a long time, and felt very sorry.

After several days in the hospital, she was told she would have to see a psychiatrist. She refused. They told her it was either that, or go to jail. She asked them what the hell they meant. They told her suicide was against the law.

As Mark drove Elizabeth to the Emergency Room, she would lapse in and out of consciousness, as if in and out of a dream. In her drugged state, she felt only a euphoria, as if all the pain of her life had become a vast salty

24

water, buoying her up, where she floated on the great blue waves of a vast, melodramatic sea. In this state, she and Mark were cheerful accomplices, playmates, doing something mischievous behind the hedge of the yard. Elizabeth, who could not get drunk, thought this must be what it was like to be drunk, the main elements of life remaining, a kind of a plot, the people acting the parts only characters, uninvolved, washing reality from their faces like makeup or paint. Her lips were numb; she loved the numbness of her lips. And her arms and legs moved with a kind of lassitude, full of that grace she knew only when she swam. Later, all she could remember of the first day and night in the hospital was a sudden, brilliant flash of the examining room where she was propped up on a couch; she knew it was the same room where she had been taken to give samples of blood, where the technicians had shaken their heads over the cultures that grew steadily from the drops of urine on slides, over the results of the tests, which showed she was resistant to the drugs, resistant to them all. After one of those tests, the doctor, an Argentinian, had told her that if she did not take her medicine, if she did not drink eight quarts of water a day, her kidney would shrink to a size "this big," and here the doctor made a fist, "and you cannot live with a kidney this big." But by this time Elizabeth was exhausted. She did not have the energy to tell the doctor, whose name was Dr. Sundquist, that doctor after doctor had diagnosed the infection as a virus or flu; that Mark had insisted her temperature, going up every day, like the sun, to 104, was psychosomatic; that he would demand she come with him downtown, shopping for shirts, and when she could not stand up, and took a cab home, how she had been lectured for leaving him there looking for her, searching the book department, taking a cab, when they had a perfectly good car. She did not tell the doctor that she did did not drink gallons of water because she was afraid of gaining weight; she could close her eyes, and her ears would open on her grandmother, standing in the kitchen, telling her not to drink so much, she would be puffy, bloated; she imagined herself drinking eight quarts of water, turning puffy and bilious, a frog one lily leaf away from the current, the black current, moving fast.

"So what shall I do?" she asked. Dr. Sundquist had finished listing the drugs she was resistant to, beginning with penicillin, gantricin, and others she had never heard

25

of, was sure she never had taken. "There is this drug, it is still experimental," he said, taking eight square white cards with plastic pockets shaped like small submarines, each containing a yellow pill. "Take one every six hours. Set the alarm, and wake yourself up during the night." At four in the morning, the alarm would go off, and Elizabeth would wake herself up, grope for the pill, grope for the water, and Mark, the martyr, would turn convulsively to the wall. After ten days, she began to notice a change in her vision; she would be typing, or staring, or typing and staring, when the whole spectrum would slide, as on ice skates, from technicolor, into browns and blacks. It was as if a filter had been drawn across her eyes. For the first time, Elizabeth was frightened. She told Dr. Sundquist; he insisted it was her imagination, but he took her off the drug, and prescribed Chloromycetin. "What's that?" Elizabeth asked. "An antibiotic," he told her, "you will have to come in for blood tests every ten days." When Elizabeth asked him why, he said it was just a precaution. Before she left, she stopped in the lounge and picked up a copy of the medical magazine and looked in the back for the index of drugs: Ortho-novum, Chlortrimeton, Chloromycetin. She read the description of side effects. Chloromycetin could destroy the blood marrow; this was noted under *adverse reactions*. Deader than a duck, Elizabeth said to herself, remembering the lamb chops on the chipped plate, remembering the marrow bones, sucking them dry. After ten days, a routine test showed the infection was gone, but Elizabeth still could not stand up without dizziness; she still felt perpetually flushed. They decided to take some tests "to be sure," "a cystoscopy, nothing, a way of looking at the kidneys directly." She was totally unprepared for the pain; she was told the pain was necessary—she had to tell them when enough fluid had been pumped into the kidneys. They found nothing; she got dressed; they sent her home. Late that night, she woke up agonized; she could not catch her breath. Mark drove her to the Emergency Room; she was given a shot of morphine. "A blood clot from the test," they said, "like a kidney stone." When the pain stopped, they gave her an envelope of pills and sent her back. Elizabeth was afraid to go back to sleep. The next day, she met Robert and told him what had happened. He looked away. "Butchers," he whispered, then louder, "They should have put you in the hospital."

Many years later, Elizabeth would pick up the same medical magazine, and look up the no longer experimental drug; she would find "photosensitivity" listed among the adverse reactions. She would say to herself, "I should have known its name, a pain should have a name."

Now, swimming into the light of the room opening off the lab, she felt the sudden cold flash in her stomach; she thought to herself, stomach, stomach pump. Next she saw Robert, peering anxiously at her, another pale underwater fish. She began to be aware that there were many people in the room, but she was conscious only of Robert; she wanted to tell him she was sorry, she was sorry to do this to him: "I'm sorry," she said, "I'm sorry," beginning to cry, and then the pills took over; she was gone.

She woke up in a gray place. She knew she was in a hospital bed from the feel of the sheets. They were white and tight and starched. There was only one pillow on the bed; it was a single bed, and it floated grayly in the center of the room, narrow as a stick. Elizabeth could not tell the color of the ceiling or the floor; she knew she and the room had been drained of blood; she knew that if anyone came in, in full color, they would be drained, faded, turning gray as they stood. Gradually, she became aware of the black, solid phone where it seemed to float toward the side of her head in the air. She thought for awhile, and then turned over, picking it up. "I would like to make a call," she said in her most authoritative voice. The operator connected her. There was no answer at the apartment. She called her friend from her Old English class, Paul. She asked him would he please keep calling Mark, and tell him to call her. She asked him to try and find out where he was. This was too much to bear, the abruptness, the change, the indisputable narrowness of the bed. Elizabeth got up, and explored the room. No shower. A window. A window set into the wall of an air-conditioned room. It did not open. The quadrangle spread out grayly, fifteen stories below. Then she got back into bed, and lay on her back, rigid. The doctor came in. He told her the hospital had called her parents; she would see them in the morning. She kept shaking her head, No, No, but there was nothing she could do. When he left, she tried dialing her apartment again.

In the morning, a famous doctor came to see her. He was surrounded by eight medical students. "Oh God, a teaching hospital," Elizabeth thought to herself. They

27

danced around the famous doctor like eight celebrants around a maypole. Elizabeth had a vision of them connected to him by ribbons and strings; she saw one circle about him, and the tape covered his mouth. "Has it ever occurred to you," the doctor was saying, "what a distance there is between people's idea of you, your success in school, your success in life with Mark, and your own sense of failure?" He looked at Elizabeth, and then at the eight students. Had they caught the significance of the question? Elizabeth was stunned. "It has occurred to me," she said. "Have you any idea of why you did this?" the doctor asked next. "I was unhappy," Elizabeth said. She wanted to say it was none of their business, and these eight students were no older than she was; she might meet any one of them on campus, but that morning, the consulting psychologist had told her that, depending on his recommendation, she would be discharged or sent to Ward Three, the psychiatric ward. She said nothing else.

Sarah and Manny arrived next. Her father sat at the foot of the bed, squat, and unhappy, and angry, not speaking. Her mother wanted to know what had happened; how she could have done this. Elizabeth stared at her father, sitting at the end of the bed, speechless with rage, silent with condemnation, like a footnote to the story in whose blank sheets Elizabeth was now wrapped, like a last, cryptic line. "I was unhappy," she said. Later, she admitted, at last, that she had been living with Mark for years, that she had once lived with Joshua. "I don't know why you're telling me this," her mother said. They lived through another long silence. "You've got to find a man who will put you on a pedestal," her mother said at last, "that's the important thing." She had a far-away look in her eyes, as if remembering something important; her voice sounded faint.

Every morning, Elizabeth would wake up and find the sun filling the room, slowly, like sand. Before the nurse came to take her temperature, her mother would arrive in the room, pull a chair up to the bed, and sit down. She would not say anything; she would only look. After some time, she put her chair at the foot of the bed, staring over the footrail. "You look like the Raven," Elizabeth said at last, "I wish you would not come before visiting hours." But still her mother would appear, as omnipresent as the paint on the walls. Elizabeth spoke to the doctor in charge of the floor; he promised to do something about her mother, but the next morning at seven, her mother appeared. Elizabeth decided the only way to put an end to this was to get out of the hospital. The psychologist decided she could not leave until she had an appointment for the next day with a psychoanalyst downtown. Days passed. Her mother sat at the foot of the bed; her father would come in, sit on the side, angry in his chair. Elizabeth felt her mother was getting heavier and heavier; the bed was a seesaw and her mother was at the other end, heavier, and soon the bed would spring into the air, catapulting her out, through the green sheet of glass. Finally, the psychologist came in and told her that she had an appointment with a Doctor Greene at ten in the morning. She would be able to leave early the next day. She asked if she could wash her hair. The nurse showed her the shower room. When she was finished, Elizabeth looked out the window; it was narrow, rectangular, and swung out from the wall. It led into a vast black shaft, fifteen floors to the tiles on the ground. Elizabeth looked down a long time; she was dizzy. "Careless," she said to herself, ducking her head, throwing her hair forward, wrapping it in a turban of towel.

That night, the nurse from Student Health materialized in her door, terribly upset. She kept telling Elizabeth nothing was worth this, nothing. Elizabeth listened to her, hard. She wanted to know more, but she knew she could not ask, and that the nurse could not say. When the nurse left, she started to cry. "Always crying," she muttered to herself, scrabbling under the pillow for Mark's handkerchief. Within minutes, Dr. Sundquist appeared in the same blank space. "Elizabeth?" he whispered. "I'm awake," she said, sitting up. "Elizabeth, I wanted to know what pills you took. I prescribed those sedatives for you last month; I was afraid this was my fault." "I didn't take any of those pills," Elizabeth said, "I had taken them already, a few at a time." "I thought it was my fault," he said again. "It wasn't your fault," Elizabeth said, reassuring, "you had nothing to do with it. I had an old prescription; I filled it twice." Dr. Sundquist stood up straighter; he was growing back into his doctor suit. "Come see me when you're better," he said, "we'll check on those kidneys." "They're getting a good rest here," Elizabeth told him. Kidneys! God, how she had worried! And then she had swallowed two bottles of pills. Adverse effects: death. She had not cared.

When he left, Elizabeth sat up a long time. She watched the geometrical beams of light arrive from the hall; she listened to the bells ringing faintly over the Head Nurse's desk. She heard the footfalls of rubber soles carrying the pill tray; she heard the feet enter the next room. "Nothing is worth it, nothing." Elizabeth would not believe this was true. She thought about Doctor Sundquist and his prescription for the little yellow pills, every one of which she had swallowed with the bottle of white ones, sugar-coated. She had told a lie. She had not told a lie for some time. She had told Doctor Sundquist he did not chop down the cherry tree, and now the branches were flickering with leaves, heavy with fruit, canopying her head. A chink appeared in the wall of her mother and father and Mark, and she could see vague shapes dressed in white; they were mysterious, they were beckoning, and with a precious new ember burning her eyes like a tear, she slept.

When Elizabeth came home from the hospital, Mark was still there; she still found his Ralston pot in the sink every morning, holding its fork and its spoon, but he was as irrelevant as a storage closet, filled and locked. Yet, occasionally, tendons would weave out from behind the locked door, twinging an arm, or a leg. When her friend Betty got engaged, a man named Raymond gave Betty's fiancé a bachelor party. Mark was invited. Elizabeth knew perfectly well Raymond was homosexual; she imagined everyone in the world knew Raymond was homosexual. That night, Mark did not come home. Out of habit, Elizabeth began to worry. It was easy for her to imagine his body, paling to white marble in the glassy moonlight, somewhere in a granite-filled lot on Drexel Avenue, while the police car circled the block, oblivious. It was easy for her to imagine this, because she had imagined this so many times. She remembered what Emily Reid had told her: that the only way to get a policeman to come in Chicago when you wanted one was to call the station and say someone was mugging a policeman under your window; then they would all come, the policeman, the sargeant, the mayor.

At five o'clock in the morning, Elizabeth fell asleep in her chair; at seven thirty she heard the sound of a key turning in a lock. She woke up as if she had been shocked. "Where *were* you?" she demanded, a parody of her neutral tone. "Talking to Raymond," said Mark, sitting down

30

on the couch, beginning to take off his shoes. "Until this hour?" Elizabeth asked. Then she was furious. This was Mark; this was just like him. In the six years they had lived together, he had asked her again and again, why he did not seem to make friends; it puzzled him that hers seemed to arrive mechanically, like junk mail, like something the government provided everyone; he could not understand why he was not on the list, and Elizabeth would explain, patiently at first, that friends did not necessarily want to discuss *Time* magazine, or the war in Asia, or recent advances in medicine, that every now and then, a friend liked to talk about Himself, or Yourself, and Mark would shake his head, puzzled; such conversation was, as far as he could see, a waste of time. He could not believe it was interesting. Every Tuesday, when *Time* magazine arrived in the mailbox, Mark would be waiting near the window; it was the only time during the week he volunteered to go down for the mail. Then he would take it into the bedroom and lock the door and, sitting on the unmade bed, would read it from front page to last, as steadily and seriously as a Bible is read by a priest. Every Tuesday at eleven, he would come out of the room, an evangelical light in his eyes.

"Mark," Elizabeth asked, ominous, "what the hell did you think you were doing?" Mark looked shocked; he had made a friend; he had had a *long* talk. Elizabeth could imagine what the subject had been. In the hospital, the two psychologists who interviewed her had asked her how she had expected Mark to react to her suicide. She had said she hadn't imagined it would bother him much; probably he would have felt guilty for a short time, but then his family would have persuaded him that such an attitude was unhealthy, and, logically and carefully, they would prove, more neatly and carefully than an *A* student a geometry theorem, how it had all been her fault, how he had nothing to do with it. Then they had interviewed Mark. They had asked him all the same questions, very scientific, very controlled. Mark had answered, "Not as sorry as she would have wanted me to feel." When they told her this, they looked quite pleased with themselves. They wanted to know what she thought. Elizabeth thought about her mother, Nevermore, sitting at the foot of the bed; she thought about the famous doctor; then she pushed back her hair with her hand: "*I* think," she said, "that when you work together, your mutual I.Q.'s are

perhaps twenty points higher than when you work alone."
The female psychiatrist glared at her; then the male said,
"Tomorrow you will see Doctor Greene." "Is he a good
doctor?" Elizabeth asked. "Very good," he told her, "very
experienced, you won't be able to pull the wool over *his*
eyes." Elizabeth wondered what on earth he was talking
about; she would give her life to anyone who could pull
the wool from hers.

"A good long talk, a good long talk, *all* night," Elizabeth
mimicked. She thought if Mark did one more thing to em-
barrass her before leaving the city, she would kill him on
the spot. In a flat voice she told him, "You really are
crazy, you really are something, everyone knows why
Raymond keeps people in his house for the night, you're a
tease, a disgusting tease." Mark's face crumpled like a
dirty tissue. But still he refused to leave, to move in with a
friend, to sleep in the car; every morning, he was there.

When Elizabeth woke up in the morning, Mark had already gone. She found a note on the table saying he would
be back in time to get her to the doctor. Elizabeth had
always been very independent; she had prided herself on
this, but now that she had given up looking happy, now
that she had seasoned herself with the suicide's pepper
and salt, she was ready to let the world take care of her;
Mark could drive her into the city. He could pick her up
afterwards. As far as she was concerned, he could carry
her up and down the stairs, over every threshold she
would ever have to cross as long as his shadow still fell
over hers like a thick black gas.

Doctor Greene. She would have to get dressed. This
was a new problem. In the hospital, she had put on white
gown after white gown; the nurses left them for her on
the chair near her bed. She had pulled back her hair
with a rubberband, and, when that broke, she tied it back
with the red and white candy-stripe string from the bakery
box of cookies on the window sill. But Doctor Greene,
now; he had an office downtown on North Dearborn; his
office was on the twenty-fifth floor. Already, Elizabeth
could imagine it, overlooking the Prudential Building, the
people below as comprehensible and as patterned as black
and brown ants, and beyond, the soothing blue stripe of
the lake. Elizabeth thought it was very important to im-
press Doctor Greene. She would have to look respectable.
Respectable. She looked in the mirror. Definitely, it was
true, respectability posed a problem. Her black hair was

32

down to her waist, unironed; her face looked like a moon caught in a wild tangle of branches and roots. She would have to do something about her hair. First, she tried a french knot. "Not bad," Elizabeth muttered to herself, but as she turned to look at the side view, it began dislodging itself, slowly uncoiling like a fantastic, black snake. She pulled it back with a rubberband: headaches and the Wizard of Ox. No good. Finally, she parted her hair in the middle, and braided it into two thick ropes. Then she wound them around the crown of her head, and pinned them in place. The bobby pins were bronze, the wrong color, and gleamed oddly, cheap jewels.

Now Elizabeth was faced with the rest of her body. The only clothes she wore were her shifts, her upholstery shifts, but she could not face the twenty-fifth floor in upholstery fabric. In the hospital, she had starved, trying to get back to a reasonable weight. Every morning, she would fill out a spartan menu card, until even the nurses began to be upset, and, when an ice cream was left untouched, they would arrive with it, nervously grinning in her blank, yawning door. She kept staring into her closet; the clothes seemed to stir darkly, like dregs of tea leaves. Finally, she took out a black skirt, a belt, and a bright, flowered blouse with a black ground. She put on the blouse. It was too tight across the bust, a familiar problem, but an old one, antique almost. Automatically, she went to her jewelry box and rummaged through for the safety pin she knew would be there, left over, a reminder of the days before she had stopped wearing clothes. She pinned the blouse shut, but the material still stretched across her breasts in little wrinkles, flattening her out.

Then she put on the skirt. The skirt was tight and too long. When she put on a belt, she looked like a well-filled Christmas sock tied with a ribbon. She had no stockings. She stuffed her feet painfully into high-heeled shoes. Their toes were very pointed, and their heels were very high. Elizabeth could not remember when she had last seen anyone wearing such shoes. She stepped back and inspected the result. A different person peered out of the mirror, bleakly, with fogged almond eyes. Respectable women wore makeup, Elizabeth told herself, and began poking about in her top drawer. She knew it was in there somewhere. Her brother had bought it for her when she was still in high school; he had gone to the drugstore and asked the druggist for a lipstick for his sister who had black hair and a white face, and it was the best lipstick she had ever had. When she found it, she was astonished to see it looked practically new. Putting it on, she remembered the family fight, how her father had insisted she was not to wear it, how finally her mother had interfered, and how she and her friends had prided themselves on being able to put it on, in a moving bus, and without looking in a mirror at all. This skill mastered, they could bend over their desks, pretend to be looking at a book, and restore their fading, caking glamor. Elizabeth put it on. Her lips were a red slash in her white face; her hair was still black.

By the time she found the doctor's office, Elizabeth was in a state of absolute awe. Anyone who could afford to pay for offices like this had to be some kind of genius, a god! She sat on a couch in front of the gold-foil paper printed with a tortoise-shell pattern, and, looking nervously around her, wondered what the other patients thought. They were all well-dressed; they were obviously rich. Her parents had agreed to pay for this. After ten years of swearing to the deaf heavens that they could not afford to send her away to school, that it was not important for her, a girl, to go away to school, they were now willing to pay four thousand dollars a year so no one would ever call them again to tell them their daughter was in the hospital, would they please come? The secretary instructed her in the workings of a little black box with a row of buttons next to the names of the five doctors who inhabited the suite. Whenever she came in for her appointment, she was to press the button, and the doctor would know she was there. Elizabeth thought it over, and decided she had better wait for him to come out.

When his door opened, and a man walked out and over to her, Elizabeth was afraid. He was very tall, and looked old. She thought he must be at least fifty-five. He did not look wealthy at all; he looked very serious. There appeared to be a coffee stain on his tie, and Elizabeth had a sudden compulsion to inspect him for crumbs. "Miss Kamen?" he said, and when she nodded yes, he said "this way," and she followed him in. She didn't know what she had expected—an electric chair, painted shocking pink? straight jackets hanging from the hooks on the walls? Instead, there was the Danish modern couch, which she instantly understood as archetypal; and the Danish modern chair, which reclined, and a matching ottoman; and a Danish modern rectangular coffee table with one large ashtray, and a distinctly more humble chair on its other side. The walls were lined with cast iron bookshelves; the metal looked like a great black exoskeleton climbing the walls. The floor was gray. Elizabeth was upset by the bareness of the room, at once bleak and rich. She noticed the neat hand-lettering on some kind of file filling most of one shelf. When she sat down in her chair, everything swam out of her mind like a school of fish. "Well," said the doctor, "where would you like to begin?" Elizabeth opened her mouth to say something about the hospital, how she did not really need a psychiatrist, and instead, began to cry. She was horrified. She never cried in public. She dug a fist into her eye, embarrassed as a child. "Why are you crying?" the doctor asked gently. It was the last straw. Uncontrollably, she began to sob. Sometime later, the doctor asked again, "Why are you crying?" Elizabeth made a convulsive effort and caught her breath. "I feel as if I ought to apologize." "For what?" He looked like a friendly, curious owl. His speech had a strange cast she could not place. Sinus? A foreign accent? She took a deep breath. She knew it would sound trite. She was tired of being sophisticated, of trying to cope. She knew her lipstick was too red, her blouse too tight, her skirt too long, her feet swollen and painful and naked in her ridiculous shoes. "For everything," she said, "for my life." When she stopped crying, most of the hour was gone. "I see your last patient smokes," she said. The doctor looked startled. She pointed to the ashtray; a thin wisp of smoke coiled gray into the air, rising like a tiny charmed snake, the last puff of smoke from the finished battle, the army of ants. The doctor nodded his head, hunching his shoulders slightly forward. It was a sign he understood what she meant. "Tomorrow at three-thirty," he said, looking at his watch, getting up. In the hall, her heels sounded like hammers. "Tomorrow I will have to bring sunglasses," she said to herself, "I will have to get something to wear."

After Elizabeth was relatively sure Doctor Greene intended to keep her on as a patient, it seemed they spent a great deal of time arguing about clothes. Doctor Greene felt it was part of her "symptomatology" that she would come downtown dressed as if she were going to pick apples in a blighted orchard, or clean out the hospital sewer. When she protested that everyone at the University dressed the same way, and that if she were crazy, so were they, he was unruffled. "Most of them are," he said. Then Elizabeth would start raving that he was a materialistic maniac; she started in on his ashtrays which looked, she said, like yellow amoebas, embryos of a race of blobby giants. If she was still angry, she would go on to the pale beige walls, "psychiatric soothing," and if really enraged, would begin on the books, the neatness and precision of their arrangement, the mechanical hideousness of the black brackets holding the *de rigueur* walnut shelves to the wall. On days of exceptional fury, Elizabeth would begin on Doctor Greene's secretary, Jane. Jane looked like a model, and made all her own clothes. She explained to Elizabeth that this was a perfect job for her; she didn't have much to do, and she was writing a mystery novel in her spare time.

Gradually, Elizabeth began to learn about Jane's husband, Edward, who also wrote novels, but worked for a medical advertising house to make a living, and drove motorcycles. Jane didn't like this much, and told Elizabeth how just last week someone had bought a motorcycle in the Loop, and as they were driving it out of the shop and across the sidewalk, had lost control of the machine, and flown into the side of the bus. He died while the ink was still drying on his check. "They really should be required to make sure people know how to drive those things before they turn them over," Jane told her, violent. Jane and Edward had a fancy townhouse which they were decorating together. They had bought a piece of stained glass which they put in their fireplace, and in back of it, they put a light. Elizabeth listened to these stories as if they were fairy tales. Jane began to be Elizabeth's source of information on makeup and clothes. Jane told her to get rid of the red lipstick and get one of the new, softer colors. She told her which stores had good clothes for reasonable prices, and which buses to take to get to them. Elizabeth found all this knowledge perfectly mysterious; it had never occurred to her, with her two courses in bibliography, that a real human being might read *Vogue, Glamour*, or *Mademoiselle*.

Elizabeth, who was new at living alone with her walls, wanted to know how Jane had met her husband. They had met in a Fine Arts program somewhere in Iowa. "Too bad," Elizabeth thought to herself, mentally reviewing, as in a police lineup, the males available in her course

36

of higher education. There was the Jesuit Monk who sat next to her in Old English, compromising himself, risking salvation, by whispering answers to her, patiently explaining the meaning of the parables, gardens with radishes, God knows what; every year, he sent her a Christmas card. There was a six-foot-four department character named Armand who would call her at three in the morning to say he had swallowed so many barbituates with a glass of vodka, and now wanted to discuss the fate of the world. No matter what they began discussing, they ended discussing his life in a concentration camp, how his parents had lost him, how the nuns had raised him, how he had lived in a convent, how he had forgotten how to eat; last year, when he weighed 100 pounds, the doctors had put him in a hospital. "That must have been nice," Elizabeth said, but he went on to the next disaster, the next insult, the next war. "Go to sleep, Armand," she said, and hung up. When the phone rang again, she turned over and stared out the window. The bird which appeared in the court of her building every spring was screaming its throat out. The man who coughed half the night in the other wing was giving him good competition through the open window. Spring, and the windows were wide.

Thanksgiving waddled over the horizon like a frightened turkey. Elizabeth considered going home, but the doctor made some ominous noises about her tendency to avoid responsibility, and when she protested, he clarified: "To yourself." When Armand called up and asked her to have dinner with him, she weakened and decided to go. They found an Italian restaurant in the Loop with colored, flashing lights, and animated colored window displays that reminded them both of Coney Island; it was at the top of a narrow flight of stairs that reminded Elizabeth of her old Brooklyn apartment on the second floor. When her grandmother had come to live with them, she remembered, and when her brother had reached a certain age, they decided to move her out of the room she shared with him and into what used to be the dining room, the room next to her grandmother's. Elizabeth used to like that room because it opened onto the porch, and when everyone was asleep, she would go out onto the porch in her nightgown, leaving the door to her room open, and stand there, barefoot in the snow. When she was chattering with cold, she would run in, slam the door, and pull the pillows up over her head. She thought that if she only had ice

37

cream to eat, or an ice cube to suck, the performance would be perfect. Elizabeth liked the idea of standing in the snow, swallowing ice, turning cold as the snow, growing paler and paler; she imagined she could see the buildings across the street through the bones and veins of her hand; she was growing invisible; soon she would be gone.

At the top of the stairs, they found more colored bubbles of light. The place looked like an undersea whorehouse, perfect. When the waiter came to their table, they both ordered standard Thanksgiving dinners. Everyone else was eating spaghetti, pizza, lasagna. They had this much in common, at least: perversity. While the waiter was taking their order, there was some kind of commotion; he looked startled, but went on with his ritual. When the spumoni arrived, two men rushed past their table, carrying something queer. Armand sat up straighter, a light in his eyes. "I think it's a resuscitator," he said, looking thrilled. A few minutes later, the two men came back, carrying a stretcher. An old woman lay on it, gasping for breath. They put the stretcher down next to their table, and began fastening the mask over her mouth. Armand was staring greedily and eating his ice cream without looking at his plate or spoon. "Merry Thanksgiving," Elizabeth said bitterly. All the rest of the way home, shivering in the blue-black wind off the lake, Armand wanted to talk about the old woman; it was as if he had known her personally; it was as if he had gotten personal satisfaction out of witnessing the probable last act of her fate. Elizabeth lapsed into what turned out to be a permanent silence. When they got to her house, Armand said, "I'll call you." "Don't," said Elizabeth.

The next day, she raved to Doctor Greene about Jane, how she had to be crazy, wasting her life as a secretary; she told him about the time she had worked for a publishing company in Boston, running their Medical Order Department; how, by twelve o'clock, she would be sick to her stomach, dizzy, and have to go home. It was her job to code orders for the IBM machine, to answer letters from irate doctors who wanted to know why they had a book on Epidemiology instead of the epidermis; to go upstairs and find the men in the shipping department and explain to them that they must send the *exact* title requested—these were *doctors* getting the books; if they wanted a book on smallpox, they probably had a good reason. She was dying of boredom. Mark had decided to spend a year in Cambridge, working with a man who specialized in his field. Elizabeth had decided to stay in Chicago and finish her Master's. For the first three months they were separated, each one of them had one hundred dollar phone bills. Finally, Mark decided it would be cheaper for her to fly to Boston. One night, she had to call him from the airport to say she didn't know if she'd make it; the airport was closed; there was a howling snow storm and planes were grounded. At last, the airport decided to open a runway for her flight, and Elizabeth, who was terrified of flying, was still more terrified of something else, and got on the plane, a zombie going to its last reward. For the whole four hours, she kept thinking, so what if it crashes, so what if it crashes, what difference would it make?

Once there, she stayed. She was fond of the cobbled, crooked streets; she hated the smugness of Mark's school. Mark hated the smugness as well, but liked the sound of its name. He was working with an impossible man, Dr. Fromm; his whole unit was working with rats, and Fromm was allergic to rats. Elizabeth would come to meet Mark at the lab, and the famous scientist would be ranting at someone, Mark, someone else, that they had obviously left a cage of rats in his room some time that day; why else would he be sneezing? After the famous man had seen Elizabeth in the lab hundreds of times, and invited them to one of his famous sherry parties, where they all sat on the floor rigidly, mice in a cage, eating cheese with plaster of paris smiles, he came over to her and said, "You're a very lucky young lady. You have a very intelligent man there." "Oh," said Elizabeth, "thank you."

The next day, when she got to the lab, Mark was still teaching his lab section. She went into his room. A baby rat was clamped by its paws to the plain piece of pine board. The clamps were non-rusting aluminum; it was still alive, and its breath whistled; it was pink; it looked like a fat pink spider. Its fur had not yet grown in.

Elizabeth, who was not supposed to be in the building, picked up the board. When she stopped crying, she marched down the hall, and into the office of Dr. Fromm. He started to say something, hello, but when he saw what she had, he said, "Take that thing out of here. I'm allergic to rats." "Oh, too bad," snapped Elizabeth, her voice rising helplessly, like a balloon torn from its string.

"You find out who did this, you find out who left this animal here overnight, you look at how its feet are clamped; who the hell do you all think you are, Adolph Eichmann? You find out who did this, and you do something about it, or I'll find out who did this. I'll call that number that accredits your lab and lets you use these damn animals; you do something about it now." Doctor Fromm looked terrified, repulsed. "Elizabeth," he started to say, getting up. "Get up," she said, "come with me." He stared at her. "Come with me," she said in the same hard voice. "You're going to inject this rat and put it to sleep. Now." Doctor Fromm got up and followed her, as if hypnotized. When he filled the syringe, Elizabeth saw it was long enough to go through the tiny pink body. When he injected the animal, his hands were shaking. He was not sneezing. "Thank you, *doctor*." Elizabeth said in a horrible voice she did not recognize as her own. "I go to school in Chicago; I have no manners."

When Mark heard about the incident, he was terrified. He mumbled something to Elizabeth about his career. She was making curtains for the kitchen. "Drop dead," she said, without looking up. After dinner, she told Mark that Doctor Fromm's spine was made of glass, and he could stop worrying. After that, Doctor Fromm often apologized when Elizabeth came to the lab and Mark was late. Years later, when she saw his picture in the paper, he had won some kind of prize, Elizabeth, an Associate Professor, took out her black ballpoint pen and drew mustaches over every picture of him she could find in the papers of the Faculty Lounge.

"And what does all this make you think of?" asked Doctor Greene. "It makes me think of rats," said Elizabeth, ever cooperative. She canceled a momentary temptation to begin raving about Jane, how she was wasting her life working as a secretary, for doctors, the work could hardly be more boring, what kind of idiot could like such a job ("You don't understand about marriage," Doctor Greene had commented the last time she did this). And indeed, now, in the silence, she saw the dust motes coming in the window, and landing on her feet in their new stockings and shoes, as tiny white rats, falling and falling. "The dust motes look like little white rats," she said out loud. "Is that how you feel, like a little white rat?" Doctor Greene asked. "That's a stupid question," said Elizabeth, whose main problem at the moment seemed to be her weight—

a little white Moby Dick might be more like it. There was a long silence. "When we had two pet white rats," Elizabeth went on, "Mark used to kill the babies by throwing them against the tiles on the bathroom floor. They were so tiny he could flush them down the toilet." Finally, she had made him take them to the lab and anesthetize them there, though he insisted the fright of the trip and the pain of the shot was worse. "Just do it," Elizabeth had commanded. "And?" asked Doctor Greene. "And what?" asked Elizabeth. She was irritated to death. The dust motes kept sifting, hallowing her shoe. Elizabeth had no idea a shoe could look so beautiful. "When I was a child, my uncle used to take me for shoes. They had a machine in the store, and you could put your foot in it to see how the shoe fit, and you could see the bones in your feet, they were green." The doctor didn't say anything. "I loved my uncle very much," Elizabeth commented, closing the book. "I'm sure you did," the doctor said, "which uncle was it?" "My Uncle Joshua," she answered, beginning to cry. If this went on, she would be mildewing the couch. "What became of him?" "He died. He never got married. He went out with a woman named Mary for most of his life, and then he stopped. I always liked her, but the family thought it was a disgrace. They wouldn't let him bring her to the house for Thanksgiving; they said it was because of the children, me, Arthur. My grandmother got worried when he didn't call up, and we went to his house. He was lying in the middle of the floor. They said he had a heart attack. There were bills all over his desk, and there was a paper knife the sun kept striking, like a sword." She caught her breath: why couldn't she talk about anything without crying? "My grandmother said that before he died, he talked to her about how he had wasted his life, and he cried. My grandmother couldn't get over that, that he had died like that, alone."

It was beginning to occur to her that she felt she had killed him; she felt she had killed her grandfather, everyone who had died was lying at her feet like so many rats. She told the doctor how her grandmother had told her, again and again, how she would kill her mother with her bad behavior, how her mother had told her she would give her father a heart attack if she went out of town to school; she had told herself she had killed her grandfather; she had adored her grandmother, and her grandmother

41

had left her grandfather alone, and finally, he didn't care about anything; he had gone to work in that neighborhood; he had been shot. She had been an accomplice in it all; everyone she loved died like that, horribly.

Next she told Doctor Greene that her friend Bob's psychiatrist had had a heart attack; they had all these patients; their sedentary professions didn't do them any good. Elizabeth suggested that Doctor Greene walk up the twenty-five flights to his floor. "Do you want *me* to have a heart attack?" he inquired in mock astonishment. Elizabeth started crying again. "Well, you should watch out about your health; it's serious," she said. She had a sudden hallucination of Mark doing his Royal Canadian Air Force exercises, at no matter what hour, until the downstairs neighbors complained. She saw him falling out of a tree, and hitting the earth, and getting back up, bouncing, like the legendary Earth god. She saw him walking again on the railing of the overpass of the Outer Drive, six lanes of traffic, speeding. He had feet like a cat. He never would fall. He had nine lives. In one small cell of her mind, a light snapped itself on. As far as she knew, Mark had no emotions, but he had no physical fears. He was all intellect, all intellect in a body, welded, like steel.

Later that afternoon, when Elizabeth left for the long drive to the school where she studied, she found her eye twitching again at the same stretch of road. It occurred to her that there was nothing wrong with her eyes; her car was simply facing into the sun. She would get sunglasses the next day. And so the problem was solved. After that, Elizabeth began coming earlier and earlier to Doctor Greene's office. She had exams to take. At home, it would take her hours to read a page; she would have to read the same paragraphs again and again. None of it made any sense. Mark Twain made no sense. Doctor Greene's office was the only place where she could read, take notes, study. She got there earlier and earlier; she and Jane began to be friends, exchange books. Doctor Greene disapproved on some obscure Freudian principles, but Elizabeth knew it was all right, even when she had to borrow thirty cents from Jane to get home, and Doctor Greene made a fuss; she ought to have known it was office money she had been lent; she was *acting out;* it would have to stop.

When Doctor Greene went off somewhere to give a paper, Elizabeth expected to get a great deal done. Instead, she stayed in the house and observed the little hard buds on the trees latticing the sun-porch windows like iron. She took to sleeping on the huge pillow in front of the window. Finally, she decided she needed company, and called Robert. Robert was busy; in the middle of a sentence, she started to cry. When she could stop, she told Robert to pay no attention, she didn't know what was the matter with her, she cried all the time. "I'll be right over," he said, and hung up.

When he got there, they had a long discussion of gram-negative and gram-positive bacteria; it was a matter of how they took the stain. The chemical composition of their walls was different; the negative were harder to kill than the positive. "I always wanted to know," Elizabeth said. She was remembering the yellow pills, the change in her sight. Then he told her about the Emergency Room, how last night they had brought in a suicidal woman, and the nurse had found razor blades hidden in the rat in her hair. There were women who came in and had babies and didn't even know they were pregnant. He told her about their friend Bill, who was a psychiatrist, and how he had a very compulsive patient who had an appointment at 4:10. Last week, when Bill had been running late, this patient had gotten up and walked in, and sat down in the chair, and began to talk about his problems with girls while the other patient sat up, electrified, on the couch. Robert told him about how Bill had trouble with this; he always had trouble with anger. Elizabeth began laughing. When he was leaving, Bob asked Elizabeth what she'd be doing now. She said she'd be studying for exams. "I have lots of time, now that the doctor's gone." "Oh," Robert said, drawing the word out like chewing gum, "so *that's* what this is about."

Elizabeth went back in, and sat on the couch. In the moonlight, the buds looked like little clumps of tight cast iron. They never would open. She thought about how she had asked Doctor Greene why they had done that, why they had all threatened her with each other's death, why they had tried to make her, a child, feel responsible. She could not understand it. She understood that the things she said had upset them, that she had not fit their idea of a child ("I never had a child until I had Arthur," her mother was fond of saying. "Elizabeth was born old," she said), she understood their need to shut her up. But

43

it did not seem enough. "They were only human," Doctor Greene said, "They were only human."

Chapter 2

From the beginning, Sarah Katz's life had been a conflict of allegiances, her mother, her father, her husband. Her mother, Belle, was born in America; she had long blonde hair, she spoke without a trace of an accent; she had clear, white skin, with high pink spots under her blue eyes; she was her parents' only daughter, and she was the youngest, the baby. Sarah's father, Daniel Katz, had also been born in America, and in a time when no one finished high school, had not only gone to college, but to pharmacy school. "A professional," Belle told her mother with satisfaction. But from the beginning, there was trouble, and when Daniel looked into Belle's eyes, he would see they were clear and brilliant as a summer sky, without even a trace of cloud. Daniel looked, and he was frightened; they seemed not quite human. But Belle's body and her hair were human; her blonde hair, worn in two thick braids which reached below her waist as she worked around the house, and the two pink spots on her cheeks.

In the neighborhood, on Carroll Street, where they all lived, Daniel Katz had the reputation of being a good-looking man, even a handsome man. His parents had died when he was a child, and he had raised himself in a household of strangers whom he called uncle and cousin and aunt. So it was not only Belle who attracted him, but the whole family in which she was set, a jewel in a renaissance ring. In Belle's house, the old country maintained itself, lovely and complete as a bubble rainbowed in soap. Belle's mother reigned like a queen; she was a fountain of recipes, of remedies, of advice. When Belle's brother had diphtheria, she sent for the doctor. The doctor came and set his bag down on the enameled shelf over the sink; he went in and looked at Joshua, and when he came out, he shook his head. "His throat is closing; he can't breathe." "So what must we do?" Belle's mother whispered. For the first time in years, they saw their mother still in her robe,

44

and the sun high enough to see from the window where they stood, her hair pulled to one side of her head and slipped under the rope belt of her robe. The belt was tied tight in a knot, and when Belle looked at it, she thought to herself, "She will never be able to get it out, she will have to cut it off." "Do?" said the doctor, "there is nothing to do." Belle's mother stared at him and said nothing. "Doctor, he will die?" "He may die," said the doctor. "How much?" she whispered hoarsely. "What?" the doctor asked; he looked disoriented, embarrassed, as if he had come to the wrong house, here to this woman with loose hair, dressed in a robe. "How much *money*," Belle said loudly. "No money," said the doctor, "I will come in the morning." "In the meantime, we wait," said her mother, "we wait." Toward afternoon, Joshua could no longer breathe. He would jerk up in bed, gasping, his face purple and blackening; they could hear the sounds of his strangling down the long dark hall, in the kitchen, where they waited, cold and clean as the scoured pots hung on the nails. "He is dying," said Belle's mother, "it cannot be." Silence fell through the air like snow; outside, the heat beat down on the cracked cement walks, on the facades of the identical brownstones, on the little trees struggling upwards in the square of earth in the little wells of cement. She went to the stove, she lit a match; a burner jumped into life. She went to the icebox and took out the heavy rectangular jar of milk; then she sliced off a thick slab from the rectangle of butter. She put the butter in the milk and turned the heat up high. When it was very hot, she began to stir it; when it was boiling, she poured it out into a mug. Her lips were compressed into a thin line, and the blood had gone out of them; they were thin and white as a scar. Belle watched her; the boys watched her; her husband watched her and said nothing. They had seen her do this hundreds of times; they could not remember when she had not gone down the hall, holding a mug, for the one who was sick, the one who was unhappy, the one who could not sleep. "Mother," Belle whispered. "Stay where you are," her mother told her; "Isaac, come with me," she said to her husband. He sighed and got up; he moved after her, never taking his eyes from her eyes, he floated toward her as if he were sliding down on invisible wire to the ground. Together they set off down the hall. "Will he die?" asked Belle. Joshua was her favorite brother. Joshua was tall, and had a mustache, and when he was young, had jumped from the top of a flight of brick stairs, and his appendix ruptured, there, on the spot. Her other brothers, Leonard and Alexander, had carried him home; their mother had taken a look, and without waiting for Isaac, they left for the hospital, the crowded room, the doctor shaking his head, but he had come out of it; he had been all right, and later, when his mother was scrubbing clothes on the ridged iron board, he had shown Belle his scar. It was jagged and angry. "The boy down the street died," Leonard said, "he was only three. Mrs. Rosenblatt's children have it now." Alexander stared into his tea. "Miss Greenbaum died last week," he said out loud, to himself. Belle could not believe her ears. Miss Greenbaum! A teacher! Teachers did not die; doctors did not die, what was he saying, how could he say this! "She's dead, Belle." Leonard was saying it too.

Isaac came back to the kitchen, and leaned against the sink, facing them. "He will be all right, I think; he may not sing in choir, but he will be all right." They did not know what to believe. "Your mother," Isaac said, "your mother poured boiling milk down his throat; it opened it up; he can breathe." They looked at each other in horror. "I go back now," Isaac said, "we will take turns." Five days later, Joshua was sitting in front of the stove in the kitchen wearing an old blue flannel robe. "He smells." Alexander complained turning his handsome Barrymore profile, the family trademark, aside in disgust. Joshua was smeared over in camphor; a mustard plaster covered his chest. "Better to smell here than to smell in a box," Isaac retorted. Two weeks later, Joshua was back at work, "ready to jump off stoops" Isaac remarked, grinning, but worried. Joshua was old enough; he should marry; instead, he had "girls," he ran around, he looked like John Barrymore. Belle adored him. She liked to feel his mustache tickle her cheek. When he stood with Alexander and Leonard, she could not believe these were her brothers, they stood so tall above her, they shut out the sun. But a radiance fell on her, and to them, she was the baby, the golden haired child; she was a queen. They took her with them to movies, to the zoo; they bought her popcorn, and spun cotton; they made her promise not to say a word, and if their parents went out, they let her stay up late; she sat on their laps, and they read her stories, in dramatic voices, a new one for each picture and part.

On Sundays they all would gather in their mother's room, on the great featherbeds; until the end of her life, they would do this. They would bring their mother chocolate, tea, sponge cake squares streaked with cherry jam. When they were done, they would take the featherbeds to the windows and shake them out, "for the robins," their mother said, with satisfaction. Isaac could not get her to trap a mouse; instead, one night, he found her leaving the corner of a stale hamantashen near the suspected entrance to its hole. They would tell each other jokes, they would tell each other about their dates; there were long discussions of jobs. Everyone took an interest in Belle and her typing, and they were all very proud. "Think of it!" said her mother. "Fifty words a minute, she doesn't even look!" The boys pretended to try their hands, but their fingers caught in the keys; then they would praise Belle to the skies. She was a genius! Somewhere in the middle of this was Isaac, an important planet in the constellation—but completely eclipsed.

When Belle's mother died, everyone in the neighborhood was sorry; after Joshua and the boiling milk, she had become a legend. Everyone on Carroll Street knew about her, and women, mothers she didn't even know, would stop her with tears in their eyes. People came to her for advice. She was said to have planned the family's arrival in America. In her good black dress and her black velvet ribbon and cameo pin, with her head bowed under the tight, coiled gray braids skewered in place with great iron pins, she governed the house. Everyone adored her, and later, her grandchildren adored her, and would sit on the bed on Sunday, until there were so many someone was always sliding off, onto the floor and the old patterned carpet, and Isaac used to tell her that was the trouble with a satin cover, it was like ice, it was dangerous, you couldn't get a grip. And Belle, who was the only daughter, and who looked like her mother, saw all this, and in her mind it grew fixed as an engraving from an old children's book. Her father was a gentle white hand among the green jungle plants, rioting; her love for him was gentle and detached; she could see only her mother, rising in the center like a great golden sun, while the children revolved in their orbits like planets, drinking in warmth. Isaac had brought the children; he had brought them as he brought the money for the groceries. But Joshua, now! And Alexander, and Leonard! They were

47

exciting, they made her feel like a character on a screen.

So when Belle married, she had her own ideas, and they were more fixed than steel. Daniel, the pharmacist, who the whole neighborhood thought handsome and remarkably intelligent, "self-made," was a good man, a kind man, but he would never jump from stoops; he would never have his throat scalded with burning hot milk, he would never be carried into a hospital by his brothers and have "an operation," go "under the knife," and jump again, on a dare. Belle had two children, Sarah and Hilda. Every morning, she would get them up early, make Daniel his breakfast, finish dressing the children, pack Sarah into her little wicker carriage, and with Hilda holding onto the handlebars, or her hand, walk down the street to her mother's. In her mother's house, nothing had changed. Belle was still the baby, the princess, the china doll. The two children took their places on the satin coverlet; Isaac was partial to Hilda, who was extremely bright, and would tell *him* stories, and he took her to the zoo. Sarah stayed with her mother, and her grandmother, and her uncles.

After they had been married five years, Daniel began to grow jealous. Belle had a way of treating him, he did not know how to put it, like dirt. One day, he closed the store early and snuck into the house. The house was empty as a waiting grave. He went down the street to her mother's. She was sitting on the shining purple coverlet, and her mother was brushing her hair, and she was laughing. Sarah was playing with old painted wooden blocks on the floor. Hilda was in the park with Isaac. When he came in, no one really said hello. They wanted to know what he was doing there so early, who was minding the store? Finally, Belle's mother noticed something, and said to him, "Daniel, sit, here on the bed." But he would not sit; he said he had to go back to the store. Later, Isaac could hear his wife talking seriously and steadily to Belle.

Now Daniel began to be tortured by jealousy. More often than he should, he left the store with his assistant, and began spying on his wife. He went down to the police precinct and explained to the sergeant how a man in his business, open all hours, he needed a gun. He got the license, and a customer of his, a shaigetz, told him where to get the gun. "Of course," thought Daniel, "they know all about these things: their women."

One day, Belle met a customer of Daniel's on the street. He drew back the coverlet and looked at Sarah. "She looks just like the pharmacist down the street," he said. "I should hope so!" said Belle; "he's my husband!" Later, the man went into the pharmacy for aspirin and an egg cream. While Daniel was getting his change, he mentioned that he had seen Belle; they had had a nice conversation. When Daniel went home, he waited for Belle to tell him about the conversation. When she didn't mention it, he went into the closet, and took out the gun. He came into the kitchen where she was making beef stew, quartering the potatoes, peeling the carrots, and waved it at her. "The truth! Tell me the truth! Conversations with men!" Belle was terrified; she started to cry. She swore she had never done anything wrong; she never would; she was a good girl; he could ask her brothers; she had just seen the man on the street, she was going to her mother's, he could ask Hilda; he could ask anyone. At last, Daniel put away the gun. But Belle would not stay. What kind of man was it that would point a gun at his own wife? She and the children moved into the house with her mother; then they found an apartment. She would not go back. She had her children; she was happy as she was. Hilda had to come to court and testify that her father had threatened her mother, called her bad names, thrown a bottle of milk at the wall, and boiling water on the floor. She was dressed up in her best navy coat and matching hat, and she kept looking up at the judge as if she thought it was some kind of test. Her father sat in the row in back of her mother, his face in his hands. Hilda looked at him, and some tears squeezed through his fingers. She felt she had done a terrible thing.

In their apartment, Daniel visited them continually. Sarah, the baby, was the one he took with him the most. Sarah loved her father, and loved her mother, but whenever she left the house with him, she was afraid; while they were at the zoo, or Sheepshead Bay, or going to the museum on a trolley, she would have sudden pictures of their house in flames, her mother burning up like a piece of paper, curling and crackling, blackening to ash.

When Sarah was old enough to marry, she told Hilda she would only marry a handsome man. One night, she met him at a dance. His father was wealthy and manufactured clothes. Manny Kamen was very tall and distinguished. He did not speak perfect English; he had an accent, and that was a ripple on the smooth surface of their love, but Sarah was in love, and she was old enough to marry, and she wanted children of her own; she was tired of being the only child on the block with a mother in one house and a father in another; she wanted a normal life. They were married when Manny graduated from school and went into business. A year later, they had their first child, Elizabeth.

Now Daniel came to see Sarah in her own home. On holidays, her family and Manny's came, bringing extra folding chairs, and card tables, and cardboard boxes full of cookies, but Daniel was always uncomfortable; he was never really accepted; he was "separated." Sarah began to notice that he did not look well. Also, he would have nothing to do with Belle's brothers, Leonard and Alexander and Joshua. When Joshua brought his "girl friend," Mary, to the house, and everyone said it was a scandal, Daniel said nothing. Sarah's eyes would travel around the room after him; she worried constantly.

In the middle of the night, the hospital called her to say he had been shot. Sarah rode with him in the ambulance, but he died before he reached the hospital. Before he died, he tried to sing, "I'm always blowing bubbles, pretty bubbles in the air," but Sarah could hear only the words, not the melody. *"Chasing* bubbles, poppa," she corrected him gently, thinking she was right. The police told her that a man, a colored man, had come into the store, pointed a gun and asked him for his money. Daniel had reached into the money drawer and pulled out the gun. Daniel had never fired a gun in his life. Before he had time to find the trigger, the man shot him twice and disappeared into the street. "A hero," said the policeman, "he should have known better." Sarah was crying: "It wasn't even his store. He sold his store so he could work all night in a bad neighborhood. A hero. Like in the movies." When she heard, Belle could not believe it. She called him a fool; he should have turned over the money. Joshua agreed.

But the bullet seemed to have passed through Daniel and into Belle. She aged. Sarah could not stand to think of her alone in her apartment, knowing no one. She spoke to Manny late into the night. She begged; she pleaded. It was agreed that Belle would come to live with them, in the little bedroom off the dining room, the little room with the window opening onto the porch.

When her grandmother Belle came to live with them, a subtle balance shifted. It was as if someone had pulled the cord on the venetian blinds; light still flooded the rooms, but it fell across the floor in bars. Before her grandmother came, her mother would leave for night-school every Wednesday night, and her father would baby-sit, and he would let her stay up until 11:30 to listen to "The Lone Ranger." This was a secret they shared and kept from her mother, who always saw to it that Elizabeth was in bed by seven. She would be so impressed with how late she was getting to stay up, with how lucky she was to have milk with a whole spoon of coffee in it, that she would go straight to bed the minute the last *Heigh-ho Silver!* sounded through the mesh mouth of the set. It was not until Elizabeth was a graduate student that she realized "The Lone Ranger," now a television program, was on at seven, and realized with a shock that "The Lone Ranger" had always been on at seven, that her father had told her it was on at 11:30, and she had never stayed up until twelve in her whole Brooklyn life. When she realized this, she was filled with a gentle radiance, a forgiveness for the whole adult world, a benefi-cence which she would not have thought possible.

And when her mother and father would get ready to go out, her mother rustling in the bathroom in her black taffeta slip, uncorking bottles, and powders, and creams, a young baby-sitter would come with a large white pad of paper and a box of pastel chalks, not crayons, magical strange chalks which drew in soft blurry colors, and she would draw furry animals for Elizabeth, and leave them for her to find in the morning. One morning, after the baby-sitter had come, Elizabeth woke up and could not find the picture of the rabbit or puppy. She began search-ing everywhere: in the silverware drawers; she took out every pot from underneath the stove, she searched the desks, everyone's chest of drawers, she picked up all the cushions on the couch, and when she went back to the closets under the sink, her mother mildly suggested that the baby-sitter might have forgotten the pictures this time, Elizabeth could not believe this. But then the baby-sitter came again, and there were more rabbits, and puppies, and skunks, and in the mornings, Elizabeth would care-fully tear out sheets of wax paper from the aluminum holder, and place them over the pictures, and add them to her fattening stack of pictures, and when she was finished, she would look at each one of them, one at a time, carefully arranging the wax paper so they would not smudge; they were immortal now, precious as gods.

Much later, when Elizabeth was married, and with children of her own, she would try to remember the baby-sitter, try to remember her name; she would describe her to her parents, but they would shake their heads, puzzled. "Mrs. Guilini?" they suggested, but no, no, Elizabeth remembered her; she crocheted little gray wool elephants for her, and when they visited her where she lived in the basement apartment under her grandparents' house, she always had bright green soda for them to drink. Then, one day, Elizabeth's father had a heart attack, and her Aunt Irene drove her to the hospital to see him where he was plugged into the cardiac monitor, looking for all the world like a soap-opera character in standard crisis. "This is not serious," Elizabeth said to herself, "he will get a good rest." She was very upset. When they were driving home, her aunt began to talk about the trouble she was having with her son, and Elizabeth made some suggestions. "You're probably right," Irene said. Then she began to reminisce about how she used to baby-sit for Elizabeth, how remarkable it was that Elizabeth could write things, rhyme things, while she had no artistic talent at all; she could only copy; when Elizabeth was a child, she would baby-sit for her, and bring a picture book and copy out the animals for her on big pieces of paper; she drew them very large so Elizabeth could color them in. Somewhere in Elizabeth's mind, two rope ends moved toward each other like snakes, tied, and were tight; another strand in the rope bridge over the chasm, the way to the lovely, sunny, glowing rooms of the past.

Her grandmother, Belle, had come into this world like a scissor. She, a Mazel, did not approve of the other branch of the family, the Kamens. They had no manners. They talked too loud. They were too fat. They had terrible accents. Elizabeth's father did not treat her mother right. She would repeat these accusations like incantations; then she would stop and tell Elizabeth if she drank another glass of milk, a cow would grow in her stomach; if she didn't wash, potatoes would grow behind her ears. Elizabeth, a city child, would lie awake at night, poking at her stomach, awaiting the fateful and expected horns, the deformity, disgrace. Her neck was stiff from twisting it to get a look behind her ears. While Elizabeth stood on a stool, her mouth full of pins ("Don't talk"), her grandmother pinning up the hems of her skirts, her coats, she would go on: "he's an animal, an animal, the way he talks to her, the way he hits you, look at the way he eats, the whole family, the whole family, what kind of family is it?" And Elizabeth would stand there quietly, swallowing pins, while her grandmother pulled one, then another, out of her lips, swiftly impaling the red hem, the blue hem, moving over buttons, pricking her flat chest through the cloth, saying, at intervals, regular as a metronome, "Don't talk."

The era of baby-sitters came suddenly to an end. Mrs. Guilini no longer appeared with a crochet hook and a ball of gray wool, and a paper bag of old stockings she would stuff into the finished animal, first the trunk, then the head, the body, the legs, the arms. She stuffed them with stockings, she explained to Elizabeth, so she could wash them when they got dirty. After that, Elizabeth gave her baby elephants baths once a week. The baby-sitter never came with her pad and her box of pastel chalks, and all Elizabeth had was the pink chalk stub she had found behind the blue plush cushion of the couch. Now there was much talk of cleanliness; the house had always been washed, and polished, and cleaned, but now there was to be "eating off the floor," though if Elizabeth so much as tried to eat standing up, she would be physically propelled back to her proper seat.

In the morning, she would be wakened by an alarm, and her grandmother would have breakfast on the table before she had time to get out of ged. On weekends, when the beds were not made by nine o'clock, her grandmother would stand in the hall and wring her hands, and lecture the floor and the hall and the walls that she was "killing" her mother with her sloppiness, her indifference, her neglect. Then she would go on to Arthur's room, and Elizabeth could hear her voice, higher and shriller for each unmade bed; they were killing her mother; it was not enough her mother had to live with that man, but two ungrateful children who could not even make their beds, who lived worse than pigs, who did nothing but fight, she did not know where it would end; they would all wind up in prison. In a short time, she would be back. She would peer critically at Elizabeth, her hair. "Sarah," she said firmly, "her hair is too long." Her mother went on with her cooking. "This afternoon, we'll take her across the street and have them cut it." Elizabeth's hair was her pride and joy; every day, she would stand up on the toilet seat cover to look at it; she was waiting for it to grow right down to the backs of her shoes; she had a secret vision of herself lying in bed, her hair falling over the edge of the bed like a black waterfall in waves; she could not imagine anything more alluring. She cried all afternoon. She begged. She pleaded. The more frantic she became, the more adamant they grew. "You always cry when we comb it," Sarah said reproachfully, as if that settled the issue. "I won't, I won't anymore," Elizabeth wailed at the top of her lungs. "Oh yes you will," Sarah said, "we are going at three-thirty, and that's the end of that." "Come over here and let me comb your hair," Belle ordered her. "I won't!" Elizabeth shrieked, jumping up from the table, knocking over her chair. "Come back here, you!" demanded Sarah, but Elizabeth had locked herself in the bathroom, and was sitting on the toilet with her cheek pressed against the wall, sobbing. "It will be worse for you the later you come out," Sarah warned her, ominous. "Come out now or you'll be sorry." Elizabeth decided she would stay there forever. "You'll get a good beating when your father gets you; he'll take off his strap; I'm warning you for the last time." Finally, it was quiet. Elizabeth could hear them working a knife point in the lock. After a long time, she opened the door. An arm grabbed her and then she was being beaten, across the arms, across the legs, with a black wire hanger. Elizabeth started to scream. Her mother ran over to the window and began closing it; Elizabeth ran over to it and threw it open. She wanted the whole world to know what was happening to her. "I hate you, I wish you would drop dead!" she screamed to the gaping black hole of the kitchen window facing the narrow alley. "That a child should say such a thing to its mother!" cried Belle, aghast. "I wish you were dead, you stinking old witch!" she screamed at her grandmother. Her mother picked up the hanger; without a word she advanced on her daughter. "A monster! A monster!" her grandmother was raving, apoplectic. Behind her, Arthur was watching, astonished. Her mother came after her, maniacal. "Go ahead, kill me, kill me! I'll call the police! I'll run away!" "To threaten her own mother with the police! Thank God Daniel didn't live to see this, his only

54

granddaughter!" Her mother cornered her near the stove. "I hate you, you lousy bastard!" she shrieked, and then her mother hit her in the face, hard. Elizabeth shrieked and ran back into the bathroom; she locked the door. When she blew her nose, there was blood all over the tissue. Terrified, she climbed up on the toilet and looked in the mirror. Her eye was swollen like an egg. She opened the door and walked out. "Look what you did," she sobbed to Sarah. "I hate you; you're not my mother." Sarah looked at her eye, and told her to put on her coat, they were going to the doctor. When they got there, Elizabeth caught sight of herself in the waiting room mirror, her black hair tangled, blood-caked. There were other little girls in the waiting room, other little girls with long hair. "Their mothers can teach them to fix their hair; why can't mine?" she asked herself. Some blood dripped down her cheek like a tear; it splashed on her blouse. The instant the doctor opened the door, Elizabeth began to cry. When the doctor wanted Sarah to hold her for the stitches, Elizabeth refused to let her mother near her. The doctor had to call his wife; Elizabeth was screaming at the top of her lungs. His wife pressed Elizabeth's good cheek into her bosom, and the doctor worked on the other side. Whenever her mother tried to come near her, she started screaming. After that, she had to go back to the doctor every three or four days. But it was some time before they cut her hair.

After her hair was cut, Elizabeth would climb up on the toilet seat fifty times a day, holding on to the molding of the wall with one hand, clutching a mirror in another, checking on its progress. Finally, it began to look longer. She gathered the little feathery bits together in a rubberband and called it a pony tail. When it finally reached her shoulders, her grandmother came in to brush it; the comb ran into a knot and Elizabeth's head jerked way backwards. "It will have to be cut," Belle said. Elizabeth said nothing, and the next day, they took her to the barber across the street, and it was cut off.

Now Elizabeth's father began to lose patience with her, to move away from her as if she were under quarantine. Elizabeth understood this had something to do with her grandmother; now, everyday, when Manny arrived home, there were long lists of her crimes, and Belle and Sarah would explain the intensity of the punishment she was to receive. Elizabeth, who had not seen her father all day, would see him for the first time when he advanced upon her with his leather belt. She gave up trying to hide; she no longer locked the bathroom door. She began to get up later in the morning, so she would not be there while he ate. Secretly, she had begun to agree with her grandmother that he was an animal, a miserable beast, he was not human at all. When he came home, she would be locked in her room with "homework" and the radio: the radio alone was too dangerous; she might be expected to come out and "talk." When she finished her homework, Elizabeth would play with her Toni Doll; it had very long hair. One afternoon, Elizabeth decided to dye the doll's hair brown. She went to the five and ten, and bought a box of brown dye. Then she went home and boiled the dye in a pot, and holding tight to the doll's feet, dipped her head in. Then she colored the roots with her paintbox brush. After she had done this three times, she took a good look at what she had done: the doll's hair had turned green. Elizabeth decided to cut the doll's hair short.

Now the days separated from the nights like a ship sliding silently out of the lit port into the dark. Elizabeth began to be afraid of the dark. At night, when the moonlight slid into her room, and into the kitchen, which she could see from her bed, it seemed to transform everything. She conceived a particular fear of the toaster, whose two long cigar-shaped slots seemed like two dark fangs; in the strange silver light, the toaster seemed transfused with sinister blood; Elizabeth was sure it came alive. At night, she would forget her grandmother's trespasses. She would lie awake listening to her parents' voices, rising and falling like a bad radio, and when she was sure they were asleep, would take her pillow, and creep to the doorway of her room, listening. Then she would steal off down the hall, terrified, through the dark kitchen, past the sinister toaster, the dining room, Arthur's room, and into her grandmother's room. Then she would crawl into the bed from its foot, inching up slowly toward its head like a worm, settling her pillow, and falling asleep like a stone into water. Her parents did not approve of this, and sometimes Sarah would hear her and call out, "Elizabeth! Elizabeth! get back into that bed. Immediately! Do you hear me?" And Elizabeth would answer dutifully, "Yes, mother," and get into bed so the springs creaked, and then she would wait. After some time, she would go down the hall and crawl into her grandmother's bed. Finally, Sarah spoke to her mother about it. Belle said she would tell the child to stop, but she was never awake when Elizabeth got into bed, so how could she send her back? Everyone knew she had no intention of doing anything of the kind.

What Elizabeth especially liked was waking up in the morning and watching her grandmother get dressed. She had very long hair, silky smooth, which never knotted, and which she wore in one long braid. She wore long flannel gowns printed with bright flowers, red ones with yellow flowers, blue ones with green flowers, and Elizabeth, who wore flannel pajamas printed to look like ski suits, thought she had never seen anything more beautiful. Sarah wore transparent nightgowns, and Elizabeth did not like to look at her in them, dressed and undressed at the same time, and she could not understand it; when she came out in her slip, her mother would get angry: "Go back! Put something on!" She was distinctly outraged with her. Her grandmother would brush her hair with a silver brush covered with flying cupids in diapers, and in the center of the mirror she used to measure her accomplishments, were three fat cupids with feathery wings wrestling with an enormous fish. The fish and the cupids rested on the silver waves as on a rumpled blanket; they were completely happy. At the top of the mirror, an adult face wearing a crown stared straight ahead, never looking down, knowing nothing at all. Her grandmother's hair fanned out over her shoulders and down. Elizabeth could not understand why she didn't wear it like that, loose. "Loose," Belle snorted, "next I'd be standing on streetcorners with a red leather bag." Elizabeth asked her what she meant. Her mother didn't answer either. Instead, she turned away from the stove and faced down the hall. "Mother!" she called in a loud, angry voice. There was no point in asking her father, who never spoke to her now.

When Elizabeth stayed with her grandmother, and her parents went out, they would fight endlessly. Elizabeth would make lists of her grievances, what her grandmother had done to her now. She would write down the names her grandmother called her, how she hit her, how she called her "just a Kamen," how she took after her father, how she would wind up in a jail, or worse, an institution.

57

When she showed this to her parents, her mother would say, "You must have done something to deserve it."

Sometime later, they were all given a test in school. No one told them what it was for. Then one of the teachers told her that she could enter a Special Progress class. "What is it?" she asked. "A special class for good students," the teacher told her. "Is it harder?" Elizabeth wanted to know. "Oh yes," said the teacher, looking very pleased, offering the student a challenge. Elizabeth told her parents. They told her that Tina Berlini was in a Special Progress class and did very well; her parents were always bragging about her. They said she would have to work very hard. They seemed unhappy about the test, the Special Progress class. Lately, they had been accusing her of being stupid; that seemed to explain the fights, the endless disagreements. "You will have to work hard, like Tina Berlini," her mother said. "I don't think I feel like it," Elizabeth said, spiteful. The next day she told her teacher she wasn't good enough in math for Special Progress; she would stay where she was. Elizabeth was enraged with them all, even her teacher. They should have told them what the test was for.

One day Elizabeth was sitting on the couch staring out the window, thinking about whether or not she ought to get an unlisted number; it was not Armand and his midnight calls giving her the recipes of his latest concoctions —fourteen Miltowns and a glass of gin, seven Libriums and a Löwenbrau dark; he was very meticulous in his descriptions, and, as he evaluated the relative potency of his sleeping concoctions, a true forerunner of Julia Child; it was not her friend, Benita, whose long phone calls reporting the progress of her divorce gave Elizabeth plenty of time to read the material for her classes between the proper noes and yeses; she was sure Benita never noticed which. Last week, Benita had called her up to tell her that her husband had come into the apartment, beaten her up, and thrown her out into the hall without any clothes. "What did you do?" Elizabeth asked with some interest, imagining Benita in her well-carpeted North Shore hallway, each apartment with its fancy fish-eye in the door, imagining her moving through the hall, a suddenly animated marble statue from the front entrance. "I knocked on the neighbor's door and borrowed a robe," Benita said in her sensible voice. It was that sensible voice, that sensible mind, Elizabeth thought, that had driven her to marry a maniac like Fred. She must have thought she was too normal to live; she needed a balance. Once, she had actually voiced this theory to Elizabeth. Elizabeth had not been impressed: "You can have a third world war over the garbage without looking for extras," Elizabeth said wearily. "We *never* fight over the garbage," Benita said smugly. "Good for you," Elizabeth said in a voice that sounded exactly like her grandmother's, "Fred must have a lot of it, what with his being an artist." "And then what?" Elizabeth asked. This was much more promising than discussing what color Benita intended to paint her walls after she moved out and in next week. "Then I called my mother, and she picked me up and took me back to Oak Park." "Oak Park," repeated Elizabeth, turning a page, and when Benita had finished the rest of the story, she had finished the rest of *The Mysterious Stranger*. None of these calls bothered her; they punctuated her life like episodes in a continuing drama that endeared itself to its audience through sheer continuity, endlessness, whoever the characters were, however bad they were. Elizabeth had a great need for continuity, and the black vein of the phone led deep into the well of the past, connecting her with her high school friend from her honor's English class, Mark's ex-roommate who kept her posted on his new romance with a flat-chested English girl, a friend in Cambridge who had gotten married after abandoning attempts to seduce a gay physicist; she used to hide in the clothes closet opposite his room in the boarding house they all lived in, and when she came out in her negligee, would knock softly on his door. "May I come in?" she would whisper throatily. He would take one look. "Go back to your room, little girl," he would say, soothingly, patting her on the head like a child, and the rest of the night would be punctuated by the slams of her door as she traveled to the kitchen and back, to the bathroom and back.

The phone calls that bothered her were from her mother; they were always the same. "What does the doctor *do,* Elizabeth?" "He gives me transfusions of black blood; before this I used to be a blonde." Then she would hang up. After that, the phone would cry every ten minutes, a baby in a crib; after it had rung, and stopped, and rung six times, Elizabeth would put on her coat and go out, "at night, in *that* neighborhood," and meet Armand at the delicatessen for a cup of coffee. "My analyst wants to rape me," Armand announced happily. The waitress stopped in her tracks. "He does?" said Elizabeth absently, wondering how she got into these things. "That's why I'm nervous about lying on the couch," Armand said, "I keep thinking he's going to leap on me." "Leap on you?" asked Elizabeth, picturing a perfectly plump analyst, holding a bust of Freud, hurtling out of his Danish modern chair and onto Armand's one hundred and four pound frame. "Leap on me, you know, from behind," Armand said, peevish. "Armand," Elizabeth said in her most learned, pedantic, scholarly voice, acquired for cocktail parties in Cambridge in the not-yet-distant past, "Armand, you, a scholar of romantic literature must know that, conventionally, the Dracula-figure, though admittedly drawn to characters pale and wan, rarely if ever pursues the man, but always reserves himself for the womanly one, the *female*." "Do *you* lie on the couch?" demanded Armand, petulant. "No, I lie on the window ledge, twenty-five stories up. That way, if the doctor should leap on me, he'll splatter himself all over the little boy scouts and girl scouts on their library field trips." "Do you know my friend Benita?" she asked, suddenly inspired.

When she got back home, purified by the cold, the furniture had the air of just having managed to make it back to its accustomed place; the apartment, empty, had a perpetually startled air. The phone was ringing. Elizabeth picked it up. ". . . right home, you'll have to come home, your grandmother, a fishbone." Little shards of sentences were spilling out of the receiver and into her lap. "What are you talking about, mother?" Elizabeth demanded. Then Sarah told her that her grandmother had swallowed a bone, and they had taken her to the hospital, and her throat had gotten infected from the breathing tube, and now she had pneumonia; they didn't know if she was going to live. Elizabeth was privately convinced that her mother and father and grandmother were indestructible, but it was Easter, she had no appointments; perhaps it was serious. "I'll come in the morning; don't bother to meet me." "It's cold here," said her mother, "dress warmly." The wind from the lake shrieked once more around Elizabeth's house. "Don't worry," she said, "I sleep in my coat," and hung up.

When she got to the hospital, she could barely recognize

her grandmother, lying under the oxygen tent, Saran-wrapped, like a sandwich. She was well-wrapped, she was spoiling. As soon as she saw Elizabeth, she started to cry. Elizabeth could feel her throat getting sore from trying not to cry herself. "All these years of telling us to chew ten times before swallowing a mouthful of fish, and you choke on a bone," she said to her grandmother, "fine thing." She remembered choking on a bone in a piece of smoked salmon and swallowing it. Her parents had gone into a panic. Her grandmother had called the doctor. The doctor had told them to give her some bread in sour cream, and that would wash it down. They brought it to Elizabeth where they had her sitting up motionless in bed; they didn't want the bone to "move" before the doctor got there. Obedient, Elizabeth ate. The bone dissolved into air.

Her grandmother kept looking at her and crying. Elizabeth held onto the hand that had crept out from under the sheet and the cellophane. She looked a hundred years old. Elizabeth suddenly realized that Belle's bridge was out "so she won't swallow it," Sarah explained later. Elizabeth thought that her grandmother looked, now, like all the death's heads she had ever seen in museums; she was horrified by this hurry on the part of the gods, taking back the costume before the actress had even finished the part. In the car on the way home, Elizabeth remembered the times when her grandmother had lived with them. She remembered the time she had taken a quarter from her grandmother's pocketbook and used it to buy a little pink plastic doll that came in a tiny wicker crib. When they found out she had taken the quarter, they had guessed that she used it to buy the doll. Sarah and Belle pried the doll out of her hands, and broke it in pieces, and using old bakery string, tied the arms and the legs and the body together, dangling, like rabbit's feet at the end of a ring. Then they had nailed the pink doll to the wall. "Every time you pass that doll," Belle said, "you'll think twice about stealing." The doll was nailed to the ironing board cabinet, and every time Elizabeth came into the kitchen for a drink of water, or a cookie, or a meal, the doll hung there in its pain. Elizabeth could not understand the cruelty of it. She could understand it less now than she had understood it then.

"I will have to go back tomorrow," Elizabeth said. "I have a lot of work to do. It cannot be good for her to cry whenever she sees me." "Of course," said her mother, bitterly, turning down the thin corners of her mouth. Her father glared at her, and then turned to his plate. The rest of the meal was the sound of the knife and fork, steel knives on bone. Suddenly, Elizabeth jumped up from the table. "What did you ask me to come home for?" she shouted. "Don't you think I'm unhappy enough without your help?" She ran upstairs and slammed the bedroom door; she locked it. Downstairs, she could hear her parents arguing. She didn't have to listen. They were accusing each other; they were trying to decide who was responsible, who should take the blame, whose fault it was; her mother would say it was because she took after the Kamens, the same old song. Her father would say it was because she and Belle and all the Mazels had spoiled her rotten. Elizabeth, lying in bed like a broken doll, thought they both were entirely right.

Her grandmother got better and left the hospital. She went to live with Hilda, Elizabeth's aunt. But now she had lapses of memory, and got dizzy, and tended to fall. She also nagged the children until Hilda's husband decided enough was enough. Sometimes, she thought she was still married to Daniel, and that he was threatening her with a gun. At these times, she would follow Hilda through the house and insist over and over that Daniel was insane, that they could not live with him, that they would have to move out. At night, when Hilda's husband came home, he would find his wife in tears, and the children sullen. Finally, they decided Belle would have to be put in a home. Everyday, Hilda would tour the nursing homes, trying to find one suitable, while Belle stayed with the housekeeper, who at night threatened to leave if Belle kept coming into the kitchen complaining about her cooking, her cleaning, the way she sewed seams. At last, Hilda found one which had a good staff, lovely gardens, good recommendations. Several other mothers from the block were in the home, and all their daughters told Hilda that it was not a bad solution; it was all for the best.

One afternoon, when Elizabeth was home from school, her mother insisted that she come with them to visit her grandmother in The ShadyRest Home for the Aged. Her mother and Hilda sat in the front of the car. After they had gone about three blocks, Sarah began to complain that they had not done the right thing; it was wrong of them to have put Belle in that home; she should live in an apartment at least. In a hard, hateful voice, Hilda said that Belle had lived with them for the last three years, and it could not go on; her family would be destroyed. "Then she could come to live with me," Sarah said. "Would Manny let her in?" Hilda asked, smiling bitterly. "She nearly broke up your marriage the first time. If she hadn't threatened Manny with a scissor when he spanked Elizabeth, you'd have her there yet; you wouldn't have him."

"She could stay in the room downstairs, in the den, and we could hire a nurse," Sarah suggested, desperate. "First of all," Hilda said, slowly, as if talking to an idiot, "Mother falls down. She needs a great deal of care. Would you want to be responsible for her starting a fire in the house? Where would you put the children after you found rooms for mother and the nurse?" "I still think it's wrong," Sarah said, guiltily. "You can feel guilty as you want," Hilda said, indignant, "I looked for the place; I know it's all right. If you had one ounce of sense, you'd know there was nothing else to do." "Hilda is right," Elizabeth said. Her aunt was staring rigidly out of the window; her mother was driving jerkily, her foot spastic on the accelerator; it felt as if they were being driven down the road by a demented jack rabbit.

When they got to The ShadyRest Home, Belle was not to be found. Then it turned out she was taking a walk with Martha, the nurse. "We're going on our honeymoon to Niagara Falls, aren't we, dear?" asked Belle, looking at Martha. "He comes from Texas; that's a long way," Belle continued. Sarah was beginning to cry. "Cut it out, mother," Elizabeth said flatly. Later, when Belle talked, she told them how she had been visited by this high school friend, and that high school friend, and how she lived in an apartment on Carroll Street. Every time, Sarah corrected her. "That was fifty years ago, mother," Sarah said. "Leave her alone," Elizabeth said, "what difference does it make?" When the Occupational Therapist came in to play the piano, and all the patients and the visitors sang "America the Beautiful," Belle kept nudging Elizabeth and smiling. She wanted Elizabeth to notice how the man in front of her was singing off key, and in a terrible accent, through his nose. She was still a snob.

When she came back five months later, Belle was firmly convinced she was engaged to Martha, whom she absolutely believed was a man. She kept asking Sarah and

Hilda to get her money out of the bank so they could buy tickets to Texas to visit his parents. "Mother, what difference does it make, she's happy," Elizabeth protested, frantic. When they left, Belle was absorbed in conversation with Martha, and barely acknowledged their departure. She did look up long enough to ask Elizabeth if she was going out with anyone "nice."

A few weeks later, Belle fell when she went into another woman's room whom she was sure was stealing her things; her own room had been changed, and she thought she lived in the old one, but every time she opened the drawers of the old room, nothing of hers was there. She broke her hip and in the hospital contracted pneumonia. Then the doctors discovered she had a serious aneurysm of the heart. "She could go any day now," one of them said. One morning, Elizabeth woke up and wanted to visit her grandmother in the hospital. The last time she had seen her, she had lain, shipwrecked between the sheets, the spars of her bones poking through her skin, whiter than the robe, her breastbone, sharp, lifted and dropped. Her mother was not going that day, but Hilda was. "Then I'll go with Hilda," Elizabeth said. "Why do you want to go with Hilda when you won't go with me?" her mother demanded. "All right," said Elizabeth. "I won't go at all." At three in the afternoon, the hospital called to say her grandmother had died.

At the funeral, the Rabbi kept talking about how Belle was symbolic, he said, of that heroic generation who had come here from the old country, and prospered, and nurtured children, in spite of all odds. "That man is an idiot," Elizabeth whispered angrily to Hilda's daughter, "You'd think the least he could do was get his facts straight." The only emotion she felt was anger. Her grandmother's coffin looked oddly small on the stage; she had gone back to childhood; she had sunk below that, she was in a doll's house, a doll in a box. She was a toy now; they would take her out of their china-closet memories and play with her, on holidays, after disasters, when the weather was cold. The rich cousin from Detroit gave them a poisonous look. She was crying copiously into her embroidered handkerchief. Elizabeth was trying to borrow a piece of Kleenex for her mother. She was thinking, in the end it had turned out all right, Belle had made friends; she had found out water, salt water, was thicker than blood; she had sunk below religion and sex and found the basic layer of time on the bottom of the rough sea; she had fed there at the last. "She was born in this country. That nurse, Martha, wasn't even Jewish," she whispered to Hilda's daughter, sounding spiteful. The two of them left, like accomplices, following the people out, down the aisle. The cousin from Detroit stared knives after them. "She thinks we don't care," Elizabeth thought to herself, astonished.

Elizabeth was very anxious to go to school. She already knew how to read. Her favorite story was *Bluebeard*, and there were pictures of the bodies Bluebeard hung on hooks in the attic. She loved to have her mother read the story to her, and she waited, holding her breath, for the part where the wife would steal up the stairs, and take the key to the forbidden attic, and find the blue bodies hanging stiffly on the hooks. As soon as the story came to an end, Elizabeth would forget how it had ended; all she could remember was the picture of the bodies hanging there, stiff on their hooks. Finally, her mother got tired of reading *Bluebeard* and wanted to read other stories from *The Book of Wonders* to her. And Elizabeth heard about Cinderella and the glass slipper, but she was not interested, and as soon as her mother finished, she would say, "Now read *Bluebeard!*" One day, she took the book down while her mother was trying to get her brother to sit up in his crib, and tried to read it herself. She knew the whole story by heart. She took the book over to her mother, and asked her: "What is this word?" Her mother pointed to it, and looked at her questioningly. *"That* word," Elizabeth said, pointing so emphatically that the stub of her finger entirely covered the word. "That word is 'one,'" said her mother, turning back to the baby in the crib. "One," said Elizabeth to herself, keeping her finger under the word; then there was a space. She moved her finger under the next word. "Day," she said to herself. Every now and then, she would take the book into the kitchen, and pull at her mother's apron, or her grandmother's apron, and ask, "What is this word?" "What word?" her grandmother asked. *"This,"* she said impatiently. "Wood," said her grandmother. After several weeks of this, Elizabeth could read the story to herself; she sat with the book, reading it over and over. Then she got another book and opened it up and some words jumped up at her from the page, like puppies. In the middle would be smudgy things, like puddles, like briar patches. Then Elizabeth would take the book into the kitchen and ask, "What is *this* word?"

One day, Elizabeth's grandmother was taking her to Macy's for a winter coat. "Are we going to buy it with my birthday money?" asked Elizabeth. "No," said her grandmother, "I want to get you a coat." When they got to the store, her grandmother looked for a ladies' room. "A ladies' room," Elizabeth murmured to herself. After awhile, her grandmother said they had found it. "Not in there, grandma," Elizabeth said, pulling her grandmother back. "What are you talking about?" her grandmother demanded. "The door," Elizabeth said "says *women*." One day, Elizabeth was sitting on a chair in the kitchen. Her mother was stirring something into the stiff batter in the enormous ceramic bowl. "What next?" her mother asked her. "You cream the sugar," Elizabeth said, moving her finger down a line. "Mother, what does that mean, cream the sugar?" In back of the door, there was some kind of commotion, and a hissing, and Elizabeth could make out the words, "Daniel," and a few minutes later, "don't make a fuss."

A few weeks later, everyone began to worry about her baby brother's health. "What's the matter with him?" inquired Elizabeth peering down at the cheerful pink slug wrapped in his blanket, ready to go out, a hat on his head, knitted mittens on his hands. "Nothing," her mother said. "He won't sit up," Belle told her. "Maybe he doesn't want to," Elizabeth suggested, thoughtfully. Her mother and Belle exchanged tragic glances. The next week, Daniel insisted that they take the child to the doctor, a neurosurgeon at the hospital. "What's the matter with him?" Elizabeth asked again. "Nothing," said her mother, glaring vindictively at Daniel; "he said he's lazy; he doesn't want to sit up." "He's a fat baby," Elizabeth said. "He certainly is," her mother sighed.

They decided to put Elizabeth in nursery school. Elizabeth went, to see. When she found out about the naps, about all of them lying still like dead fish, she refused to lie down. When the teacher punished her, she refused to go back. There was nothing else she could remember about it.

Later, it was time for Elizabeth to go to "real" school; the school had decided to take her, although her birthday "fell at the wrong time," because she knew how to read.

When Elizabeth tried to remember the first years of school, she could remember making an oilcloth cover for her mother's cookbook, she could remember punching the holes in the oilcloth for the woolen stitches which held it together, she could remember the bright red thread and the large blunt needle that dove through hole after hole like a bright leaping fish. She could remember making her mother a cotton apron with a pocket shaped like a heart, and embroidering her mother's name *Sarah* on the pocket in pale blue wool. She could remember the plaster of paris they poured into bowls, and how, when it hardened, they pressed in the shape of their hands. She could remember writing her name in the plaster of paris with a Good Humor stick. She could remember the class learning to read, the teacher calling on them one at a time, the children sounding out each word, or sounding out the wrong word, and getting it wrong. She remembered bringing her own books and reading them while the other children marched through the sentences as through a patriotic country defending itself from attack. But her clearest memory was of the schoolroom closet which was dark and filled with dark coat after dark coat, and under the rows of coats were rows of boots, boot after boot, falling against each other like Hansel and Gretel, and she remembered how she had thought about those hats and coats all day, waiting in the dark, like bodiless forms on hooks, waiting for the bright bodies in the chairs, and sometimes at night, Elizabeth would wake up thinking she could see them through the door, and they were beginning to stir.

Chapter 3

"Are we going to get there on time?" Elizabeth was hopping up and down at the end of Sarah's hand like a demented mitten held on by the five fingers of string. "Yes, we are. Hurry up, you're going to get caught in the doors." Sarah sat down on one of the basket-weave train seats. "I want to sit on another one, this one is facing the wrong way," Elizabeth told her. "What's wrong with it?" Sarah sighed, getting up, and sitting down on another one next to Elizabeth. "You can't see the building with the fountain when you're facing the other way," she told her mother. "You won't be able to see it anyway," Sarah said, "It's dark out." "They keep it *lit*, mother, I told you that last time; that's the best part," Elizabeth said severely. "There it is! There it is!" she jumped out of her seat screaming. "Sit down, for heaven's sake," Sarah scolded, "other people are looking; suppose the train should stop short?" "I'd fall," Elizabeth answered, uninterested.

"How many more stops?" she asked. "Three," said her mother. "How many more now?" *"Two,"* said Sarah, "keep quiet, we'll be there in a minute." "But suppose we can't see it," Elizabeth wailed. "We'll see it; they keep the shop lit up at night." "Suppose it's behind the part of the wire fence that's thick, and we can't see it?" "We'll worry about it when we get there," Sarah told her; "if we have to, we'll come back in the morning." Elizabeth brooded. "I don't know why we have to go to that damn dentist, anyway." "Do you want your mouth washed out with soap?" Sarah inquired. "Doctor Rothstein is a very nice man, he can't help it if you're such a bad patient and pull out parts of your braces so he has to put them back every week." Elizabeth inspected herself in the mirror. "I don't see why I have to wear them, I don't exactly look like Bugs Bunny." "You would in a few years," Sarah said; "enough of this already." "Besides, it hurts," Elizabeth complained. "So does falling down and cutting your knees, but I don't notice you stop skating," Sarah observed. "It's not just that it hurts, I think there's something wrong with the dentist," Elizabeth said. "There is nothing wrong with him." Sarah snapped. "He is just annoyed with you because you bit him last week." "I didn't," Elizabeth said. "You did, you did, let's not hear any more about it: do you want me to talk to your father?" "He told me to close my mouth," complained Elizabeth. "The injured innocent," Sarah mocked; "did he tell you to close it on his finger?" "Oh forget it," Elizabeth snapped back. "Don't you talk to me like that," Sarah said angrily. Elizabeth stared out of the window, or into her face: sometimes, the dark shape of a window of a house would settle and float over her, the two dark windows settling over her eyes like great cavernous squares, great hungry squares. There *was* something wrong with Doctor Rothstein; what did he want with those rows and rows of white plaster teeth lining his walls? Sarah had explained they came from old patients, but Elizabeth didn't understand why he couldn't throw them out after the patients left, or at least put them in drawers. "I think he likes to look at them," she meditated to herself. "How many stops?" she asked mechanically, feeling the slow pull and halt of the train. "This is it," Sarah answered; "get up, I thought you were in such a hurry." "I *know* it's going to be closed," Elizabeth predicted gloomily. "Don't run down those steps," Sarah called after her.

"Do you want a frankfurter?" Sarah asked her. This was the usual reward after a visit to the dentist. Elizabeth liked eating them: exciting, trying to keep the last piece from shooting out of the last bit of roll and onto the sidewalk; whenever that happened, she felt she had been cheated, as if she had had nothing at all. "I want to see the store." She tugged at Sarah's hand. "What about a Charlotte Russe? The bakery's still open." Elizabeth was tempted; she loved the sight of them in their jagged white cardboard circles, their little peaks of white whipped cream; she imagined they looked just like the white marble palaces in the Russia her grandparents had come from. "No," she said, "we're in a hurry." She thought Charlotte Russes would be nice, made out of plaster of paris, better to look at than to eat, you looked forward to them a long time and then they were gone. "Well, here it is," Sarah said; "I told you; they keep the light on." "*That's* the one, mother," Elizabeth shrieked, jumping up and down; she was out of her wits with excitement. "The second one, there in the back, that's the one." "What's wrong with this one?" Sarah asked her, "that one is very expensive." "That one's cardboard," Elizabeth was depressed to have to explain it at all. "The other one's metal and has a garage, and an upstairs, and a downstairs, and a patio with cobblestones. It comes with furniture for all the rooms. Look at that!" she pointed to it again. "At what?" Sarah peered nearsightedly. "It's got a *grandfather* clock in the living room." "I can't see it from here; it looks nice," Sarah agreed. "Can I have it for Christmas? I've been good, haven't I been good? It's the only present I want. You don't have to get me anything else. I have lots of clothes this year; grandma bought me new socks. I don't need anything else. I *need* the doll's house," she finished. "You don't need it," Sarah said, "you want it. We'll have to see. It's very expensive. You can't always have everything you want." "But that's all I want!" Elizabeth was beside herself at the injustice of this. "Arthur has electric trains!" "That has nothing to do with it," Sarah said, "Arthur is very good." "I suppose he's much better than me?" Elizabeth cried. "We'll see, we'll see," said her mother. They arrived home in a gloom of fog, not speaking. "How did it go?" Belle asked. "She didn't bite him this time, if that's what you mean," Sarah said. "Worse than a mad dog"; Belle turned around to Elizabeth, "keep that up and they're going to take you out and shoot you one of these days." "They're not going to shoot *me*," Elizabeth said meaningfully, going off to her room.

Every day she asked her mother about the doll's house; was she going to get it, it was all she wanted, she had been good, hadn't she been good, but all Sarah would say was that they would have to see: money didn't grow on trees. The night before Christmas, Elizabeth was out of bed every five minutes. For weeks, she had been searching through the closets and cupboards in the kitchen, climbing up on chairs, and inspecting the top shelves of books. "Do some dusting while you're up there," Belle called after her, "it shouldn't be a total loss." She fell asleep, exhausted. "What's that?" she demanded at six o'clock, having made enough noise to raise the dead, and having raised Manny and Sarah and Belle. She was pointing at a large cardboard box. "Open it and see," Belle suggested, "it's probably that cardboard house." "If it is, I don't want it," Elizabeth told her. "If you don't want it, we'll send it back," Sarah told her. Grumpily, Elizabeth went over to it. She pulled off the ribbon. "I'll take that," said Belle, retrieving it, "take the paper off neatly; I can use that too." Deliberately, she tore the paper from the cardboard house in shreds. Underneath was a giant white box with a picture of a doll's house on it; it looked just like the one in the store. Sarah and Manny were staring at her. She opened it: it was, it was the house! "You'll have to thank your grandfather for it," Sarah said comfortably. Elizabeth stared at her. "He got it for you," she said. "How did he know I wanted it?" "He asked us what you wanted, and we told him." "Why didn't you tell me before, then?" Elizabeth demanded; "why did you have to frighten me and say there wasn't any money?" "We wanted it to be a surprise," Sarah told her. "It's a surprise, all right, it's a surprise you'd get me anything I want!" "Elizabeth!"

Sarah exclaimed, shocked. "If you don't want it, you can always give it back," Belle suggested, moving in her direction. "Get away from it!" Elizabeth screeched; she picked it up and ran down the hall. "I don't know what's the matter with that child!" she could near Sarah's exasperated voice. Before she closed the door, she waited to hear more. "She's going to have to get used to disappointment; she's going to have to learn the whole world doesn't turn for her convenience." Elizabeth slammed the door as loud as she could. "Santa Claus just ruptured his appendix," Belle said sourly in the living room; "she's spoiled, that one." Manny sat on the couch watching Arthur playing with his wind-up truck. He wound it up; it drove into a chair; he set it off in another direction, wound it up again. Manny wondered vaguely if all this didn't have something to do with Elizabeth being a girl. In her room, Elizabeth was sitting on the bed holding the grandfather clock, a far off look in her eyes. "Bong bong bong," she said to herself. Then she got off the bed, and took out her box of doll's house furniture; it was the same mahogany color of all the furniture in the house, and she replaced the anemic pink plastic furniture with it. She sat in front of it, a church, an altar. "Lunch," Belle called imperiously. Elizabeth dragged herself away from the house, shutting the door behind her. She didn't want Arthur getting in and messing it up.

Elizabeth was looking out of the window. This was one of the advantages of having a last name beginning with "K." Now she could see a squirrel running along one of the gray branches from the tree in the yard. She never wrote her last name on her homework or test papers. Belle asked her why she didn't do this. Every paper she brought home had "Elizabeth" neatly spelled in the upper-right-hand corner. "Suppose there's more than one Elizabeth in the class?" Belle asked her. "There isn't," she said, "I'm going to make some eggs." She dragged the petit point stool out from under the kitchen table and over to the stove; then she got the little square pan out from under the sink, put a pat of butter in the pan, and turned on the fire. "Why do you have to make your own eggs?" Belle wanted to know. "Yours are too wet," Elizabeth told her. "Little Miss Fuss," Belle said. The square pan had become her pan. No one else used it. Elizabeth liked it because it made eggs just the right size for an egg sandwich, the size and shape of a piece of bread. When she got finished, she turned off the burner, and dragged the stool back under the table. "She does make good eggs, mother," Sarah said. "If you like them dry as a bone," Belle said, looking over at Elizabeth and her plate. "If you like those eggs so much, why don't you stop playing with them and eat them?" Elizabeth ignored her. She could spend hours dividing them into neat rows with the prongs of her fork, then eating one row at a time: "I might be a farmer when I grow up," Elizabeth said. "You can raise potatoes in your ears right now," Belle suggested; "as soon as you're finished, come into the bathroom; you're going to get a good scrubbing." Elizabeth plowed the field again; this was a smaller farm, just a few animals, a few chickens, one cow, and thirty dogs. "You're going to wash that dish yourself," Belle announced from the sink. "I'm not waiting for you all day." Elizabeth ate another row of egg. "Why don't you write your last name on papers?" Belle asked her again. "Because I don't feel like it," Elizabeth said without looking up. "Well, you'll have it long enough if you don't change your ways," Belle said cryptically.

Elizabeth wondered whether it was possible to get the squirrel to come closer to the window by staring hard at him, and thinking about how he should put first one foot, then another, along the gray branch tapping at her window like a hand. She was tired of those faces in the window, pumpkin after pumpkin. Her pumpkin was the only one whose mouth turned down at the corner, but Mrs Greenburg had pasted it on the window anyway because Elizabeth was the only one who had cut out the shape of candles in its eyes. The squirrel advanced a few paces, then retreated, and ran part way down the gray trunk of the tree. She wondered why they always had to draw the trunks of the trees brown; she couldn't see a single brown trunk out in the yard; the trunks were all wrinkled and gray, like elephant skin. There wasn't much hope of a fire drill. Already, she could hear the upper grades in the yard, recess, the shouts, the screams, the shrill, noisy laughs. They would never get out! How much longer did they have? She had begged for a watch; she had promised never to get it wet or wear it in the bath, or drop it, but everyone said she didn't take care of anything, and she was too young for a watch. "Elizabeth!" said the imperious voice of Mrs. Greenburg, "You are not listening!

Go to the board and do this problem." Elizabeth climbed off her chair, and went to the board next to Marty. "Forty-six times fifty-eight," said Mrs. Greenburg. Elizabeth was the worst one in class at math; she hated doing problems at the board even more than she hated doing them at home. Marty was the class prodigy; he did his problems very fast, and always got them right. Mrs. Greenburg always called on Elizabeth after she called on Marty; his last name was Kaminsky. Dutiful, Elizabeth wrote her problem on the board: forty-six times fifty-eight. Then she pretended to do some scratching with her chalk. As soon as she heard Mrs. Greenburg's voice busy with Brenda, she gave Marty a nudge. He looked over at her problem, and then in tiny numbers, worked the problem on his section of the board, keeping it hidden with his body. Elizabeth copied it over on her section in very big number. "Very good, Elizabeth," Mrs. Greenburg said; "sit down." "Now, Brenda," she continued. Elizabeth had no idea of what they were doing. She would have to give Marty the nickel she had brought for her egg cream. They had not gone to her grandparents' this week, so her grandfather had not given her a dollar. She had no allowance this week because she had kicked Arthur. It was too bad they had no compositions to do, or she could do Marty's, and then she wouldn't have to pay him anything. "And then, because his parents were so mean to him, he decided to run away," Mrs. Greenburg was saying. Elizabeth pricked up her ears. "He snuck on board a ship and went to a great many places. And when he came back, everyone thought he was dead, and he went to his own funeral!" Elizabeth was fascinated: running away from home! What book was this? "You look bored, Elizabeth," Mrs. Greenburg said acidly. Just then, the fire alarm bell rang. "All right, children, line up in pairs, no talking." Elizabeth slid out of her seat and stood next to Marty. They marched out and down the stairs. "Did you read that book?" she whispered to Marty, urgently. He shook his head yes. "What happened in the end?" she hissed. He shook his head; he wasn't going to be caught talking. "What happened?" she insisted loudly. "Quiet there!" boomed another teacher from another room. Elizabeth was insulted; this wasn't even her teacher, and it was her birthday; it was a surprise to her that someone would scold her on her birthday, while she was all dressed up in her best dress. When they got back to their room, Mrs. Greenburg had her go to the board and write fifty times, "I will not talk during fire drills." While she wrote, she tried to find out what had happened at the end of the story Mrs. Greenburg was telling them. "It was a very funny story," was the last thing she said. Elizabeth didn't see what was so funny about it. When she got back to her seat, she raised her hand and asked what was the name of the book. "Next time, pay attention," Mrs. Greenburg told her didactically. Marty hadn't been listening; he had forgotten by now, and didn't know either.

The next day, Mrs. Greenburg told the class they were all going on a field trip: Elizabeth expected it would be some place like the Bronx Zoo, and she could buy another of those wooden penguins that walked down inclines, books, boxes, hands. "We are going to the library, and everyone in the class will get a library card." The idea of a library card frightened Elizabeth. She didn't see why she needed a library card; they had plenty of books in the house. She complained to her mother; what a stupid trip, that Mrs. Greenburg was some kind of idiot. "Don't talk about your teacher like that," her mother said, angry; "you'll get a library card like everyone else, and you'll return the books on time, if you know what's good for you; we're not going to pay overdue fines for you; you'll have to pay them out of your allowance." "I'm not going to be taking out any books," Elizabeth said, "you don't have to worry."

The whole class went to the Sheepshead Bay Branch. They filled out their forms, and they got their cards, long yellow rectangles, with their names and addresses typed at the top. The librarian explained that each time they took out a book, the card in the back of the book would have their name on it, and she would stamp it with the date, and put it in her file, and each time they took out a book, the due date would be stamped in one of the blanks on their cards so they would always know how many books they had, and when to return them. They could not take out more than eight books at a time. Mrs. Greenburg informed them that they were each to take out two books, and then, in two weeks, they would read their book reports to the class. Elizabeth wanted the book Mrs. Greenburg had told them about in class, but she didn't know its name, and she was afraid to ask again. She wandered around in the shelves; finally, she came to a section called

Science Fiction. She had never heard of that. She found two books: *City Beneath the Sea* and *The Other Side of Green Hills*. Inside the front cover of *The Other Side of Green Hills* was a picture that looked like a black and white checkerboard; under the checkerboard was a little poem that said, "Look once, look twice, look thrice about, and in trice, what's in is out." She wondered what that meant; it seemed to have something to do with the picture. "Stupid poem," she muttered to herself. Then she saw it: the black spaces were changing to white, the white ones to black. Remarkable! She sat down on the floor and started to read. The book was about a little boy who could see the world that lived in the empty spaces between real objects in this world; there was a war going on in that world, and the little boy had to do something about it or the war would get into this world. "Mrs. Greenburg says to come right away, and you're not going on the next field trip," Marty announced importantly. Elizabeth unfolded herself from the floor. "What's the next field trip?" "The aquarium," Marty said. "I've been there," Elizabeth said. Mrs. Greenburg gave her a note to take home to her mother. "I'm in school more than she is," Sarah moaned; "when she gets out of there, they should give me half of her certificate." "It will be a miracle if that child lives to grow up," Belle predicted, gloomily.

Now Elizabeth spent most of her money taking the bus to the library. Every week, she took out eight books, and every Saturday, she took them back and got eight more. When she had spent too much money on egg creams or pretzels, she would walk one way to the library and take the bus back. Sometimes, she took the bus to the library and walked back. Then she would stop at Jacob's, whose house was midway between hers and the library. Everyone was always happy to see her. "Look at all those books," they would say admiringly. Sometimes, she would go home the long way, and stop at her Aunt Madelaine's. Madelaine lived in an apartment building, and before Elizabeth got off at the fifth floor where she lived, she would ride up and down in the elevator until she got tired. Madelaine fed her children something called "junket" which Elizabeth had never heard of before; she thought it had something to do with Chinese boats, and was very exotic. She would sit at the table very quietly, waiting to be offered some junket.

"Why don't you go out?" Sarah said one Saturday morning. "I am," said Elizabeth, "I'm going to the library." "No you're not," Sarah told her. "Why not?" Elizabeth demanded. "I go every Saturday." "Because you told Arthur to drop dead, and your father said you couldn't have any allowance." "But there's nothing the matter with Arthur!" Elizabeth protested. "That doesn't make any difference," Sarah said; "you shouldn't say things like that." Elizabeth went out, slamming the door. She looked around. No one was out. It was too early to go roller skating: the neighbors would call up her mother and say she was making too much noise. She decided to walk to the library. She snuck back up the stairs. Sarah was vacuuming the dining room, and she took her books and crept out; a stair creaked; she waited. Nothing. She trudged off with her books. "You're running out of science fiction books, Elizabeth," the librarian said, "soon you'll have to go to the big library. What do you like about them so much?" "I don't know," Elizabeth said; she had a vague idea whatever she told grown-ups was promptly reported to her parents; they might decide she ought to be reading something else. "Goodbye," she said turning around. She thought she could hear the librarian telling someone else she was a strange child. What was so strange about her, she wondered. She thought it was all her mother's fault; why couldn't her mother teach her to comb her hair like the other children? Why couldn't her mother teach her to be just like the other children? She didn't like the other children much, she thought, but maybe that was because she wasn't like them. She thought about Brenda who had told her they had "frozen" her appendix; if she liked them better, and talked to them more, she might find out more things.

She trudged up the steps to her grandparents' house. "You look tired," Irene said, taking a good look at her. "I have to walk to the library and back," she said. "Why don't you take the bus, it runs right by the house?" Irene wanted to know. "My father won't give me any money, so I can't," Elizabeth said. "Why not?" "He doesn't like me," Elizabeth said. Irene and Madelaine exchanged glances. "He'll get it now," Elizabeth thought to herself vindictively. That Sunday, when they went to Jacob's for dinner, she could hear an argument in the dining room. She pretended to be going to the bathroom and kept the door open. "Letting her walk all over like that, she's still a child," Irene was indignant. "I don't know what's the matter with you," Madelaine said; "you were the same way with Irene. I don't think you like her sometimes myself." "You don't know what you're talking about." Manny's voice was hard and angry. "She's a monster. You don't have to live with her, with that temper, she's going to wind up in a prison or an institution." "I suppose *you* don't have a temper," Irene said, sarcastically. In the bathroom, Elizabeth realized she wasn't breathing. She closed the door and sat down on the toilet lid, pressing her cheek to the plaster wall. She took a deep breath. In a prison or an institution! So that was what he thought! "Go out and play with the others," Sarah said the minute she caught sight of her; "look before crossing the street." A few minutes later, Arthur came back into the house shrieking. "She tried to hit me with a rock," he screamed, throwing himself into Sarah's lap. "I'm going to give that kid a heating she'll never forget," said Manny, getting off the swing, and starting down the stone stairs.

Chapter 4

One day, when Elizabeth was complaining about her life, or the lack of it, Doctor Greene told her it was time to get a job. "I'm in no shape to get a job," Elizabeth retorted angrily. "You *could* be in better shape," said the doctor, looking significantly at her mounding stomach; she could not believe he was serious: "I'm not healthy enough to get a job." "If you're not healthy enough to get a job, you're not healthy enough to be in analysis," Doctor Greene said. "Are you threatening me?" Elizabeth demanded. "I'm not threatening you; I'm merely stating a fact," the doctor answered. "You're *threatening* me," Elizabeth insisted. "I'd suggest you look into it," said Doctor Greene, unruffled.

Elizabeth went home and sat in her living room—which she was going to paint a dark red. Sometime after Mark's departure, it had occurred to her to paint each of the rooms in the apartment a different primary color, and she had always wanted a red room with white wooden trim. One day while Hettie, the cleaning lady, was poking

77

around with an unwound wire hanger at the insides of the vacuum cleaner, Elizabeth, who followed her around from room to room, finishing what Hettie forgot, ignoring Hettie's lectures on how "she could have let that fine young man go," happened to mention this idea. Hettie raised the clothes hanger prophetically in the air. It just happened she had a son who was a painter and he would certainly paint the room for forty-five dollars. "But does he really know how to paint?" Elizabeth wanted to know because, by now, she had a long acquaintance with Hettie's family; Hettie herself never could keep track of them. She was almost seventy, had had fifteen children, and lost count of the grandchildren. "Oh yaaaas," Hettie said, "he's real good." So they made arrangements that Hettie's son would come the next Saturday and paint the living room. Then Elizabeth went out and looked for the proper color paint. She discovered that the Hyde Park stores offered a choice of Chinese red enamel or fire engine red enamel. She decided she would have to go to the paint store all the way in Evanston.

When she went back in, she stared at the white walls, and then the squat phone; it looked like a half-melted, mutated animal waiting for the next reincarnation. The more she looked at the phone, the more it reminded her of the girl who sat next to her in a seminar, the same goggle eyes, the calligraphy notes preserving every scrap of the dead past falling from the white lips, preserved in absolute accuracy, providing nothing for the next generation of scholars to debate, this variant, that variant. The eyeholes even had numbers in their center, and she was sure if you could get close enough to Nancy's eyes, the perfect student's eyes, to look into their pupils, there would be the numbers in their center, and a dial tone buzzing between her ears. Nancy had a job at one of the city's junior colleges. She thought that there were still jobs open, and promised to talk to the chairman of her department about it. The next day, she called Elizabeth back to say that a job was open, and could she come down for an interview the next day? Elizabeth felt a strange sensation, unnameable. What was it? Excitement. She decided she had better say yes. Then she called another friend and asked how she should dress. "Normally," her friend said. "Any other suggestions?" she asked. "Wear perfume. It will make you seem older."

The next morning, Elizabeth set three alarm clocks

and was half-dressed before the first one went off. When she finished assembling herself in her one black skirt and one yellow sweater, she put on her one pair of black shoes. ("What will you do when that pair needs heels?" asked her friend, who still lived with her mother. "Buy another pair," said Elizabeth.) Then she looked for her one bottle of perfume, applying it like paint. This was Elizabeth's first trip on the inter-city highway, four lanes moving at maniacal speeds in each direction. She pulled out into the right lane, marveling at her accomplishment. Promptly, a truck blared its horn like the last trumpet, and Elizabeth swerved. By the time she had reached the exit for the college, over twenty-five miles away, Elizabeth had learned to cope with the trucks. Then she found she had another twenty miles to travel going west. With a premonition of what this trip would be like during a Chicago winter, and feeling like Christopher Columbus, Elizabeth pulled into the parking lot and parked the car in a "Faculty Only" space. She was a half hour early. The school was large and shaped like an L; it was made of mustard yellow bricks and looked like a high school penitentiary. From one of the windows, Elizabeth could hear what sounded like a minor riot. Finally, her watch said ten minutes to eleven, and she began her search for the office.

The English office turned out to be down in the basement, and looked very much like the Medical Order Department of the publishing house in Boston. Everything was painted Ex-Lax brown, and desks were separated from each other by pocked panels of glass which reached part way up to the ceiling. Above them, miscellaneous voices were meeting like smoke. The chairman turned out to be a pale blond, who, Elizabeth had been told, was once enrolled in the University's English department where he had had a tenuous future, and now, none at all. He seemed primarily interested in explaining the nature of the physical exam Elizabeth would have to take. She would have to go downtown and be examined by a Board of Education Doctor; also, she would have to have an X ray for T.B. Also, she would have to sign in every day, whether or not she was teaching a class. When Elizabeth agreed to these conditions, the chairman told her she had a job.

Nancy came out to congratulate her. Elizabeth wondered whether they might share a cubicle and a desk. "Oh no," Nancy said, aghast, "everything here goes by seniority. I'm number twenty-six. You will be number fifty-eight. You get to choose your desk after the first fifty-seven pick out theirs." "Great," Elizabeth said, "I saw a chair out there by the elevator." "You could always use mine," Nancy said importantly. Nancy introduced her to some of the people who were there. There was a woman who looked twenty and twittered like a bird. Nancy told her she was almost forty, and divorced: "Something about her husband not being normal." "And this," said Nancy, "is Dapper Dan." At first, she seemed to be addressing an empty chair. Gradually, something doing an experienced job of slumping began uncoiling from the gray swivel chair. Dapper Dan stood up and shook her hand; he was at least six foot three. For some reason she never could quite catch, Elizabeth expected any man of interest would manage to rise above six feet. He was dressed impeccably, a Brooks Brothers' mannequin, and there was not a drop of dust to be seen anywhere on his well-tailored shoulders. He had the appearance of royalty dispensing largesse. "And who do *you* share a desk with?" Elizabeth asked. "With Henry," Nancy answered. "And who is Henry?" "Henry is number nineteen. Dan is number eighteen." "Are they friends?" asked Elizabeth. "They hate each other," Nancy said. Dapper Dan was grinning uncomfortably. "She loves to tease," he said. His face looked like a well-oiled moon, a full moon with its night cream on. "It's a desirable office," Dan said, "lots of shelves, near the front." "In case of fire," Elizabeth said. "Right," said Dan, laughing heartily, as if she had just told a joke. Elizabeth was reminded of March, her neighbor's daughter. "Ask her to tell a joke," Emily would say. "Tell a joke, March," Elizabeth said, and March would burst into laughter. Elizabeth looked at Emily. "That was it," Emily said, "she thinks that's how you tell a joke." "Well, number eighteen," Elizabeth said, "it was nice to meet you. I am number fifty-eight." "Separated by a wall of digits," Dan responded gallantly. "A partition," Elizabeth said, and left with Nancy. She thanked her for talking to the chairman. "What are they like, the students?" she asked Nancy. "Morons," Nancy said. "Then why do you like teaching them?" "I like watching them become semi-morons."

When Elizabeth got home, she had a roll book, and a set of health forms, and a salary of five thousand dollars. It seemed an enormous amount of money. She began to make immediate plans for acquiring a wardrobe. Her upholstery shifts had been pushed to the back of the closet, and her respectable clothes hung, lonely, like lost children in a department store.

On the first day of school, the painter arrived with his mother in tow. "You do good now," she said, and went off to the kitchen to address Christmas cards; she had an incredible list and would start days in advance, and sometimes would get Elizabeth to help her. While they were sitting in the kitchen, Hettie's son came out to get more paint from the back porch. They both smiled up at him, and then bent their heads back over the cards. Suddenly, Elizabeth noticed a little trail of red footprints following him out to the porch. She got up and followed the prints. His heel was lifting from the linoleum, and under it, was another bright red shoe mark. "You! Alex!" Hettie called. For the next four days, the painting went on. Little pools of red paint would collect on the gray carpet under the white window sill; Alex brought in vats of turpentine and after work, his mother, who would arrive with a brush, and steel wool. At the end of her first week of teaching, the room was painted.

That Friday night, Dan drove her home. They had formed a kind of aristocracy of disgust. "Come in," she said cheerfully, and opened the door. The red paint was still wet; it glowed and reflected the light from the naked dangling bulb, sad embryo, aborted. The walls seemed to move in and out, internal organs of a square god. "It's because it's wet. When it dries to a flat finish, it won't look like that," Dan said. Then he told her about the houndstooth wallpaper he was putting up in his bathroom, and the glass bookshelves lining his entrance hall in Carl Sandburg Village. "Houndstooth?" asked Elizabeth. "Oh yes," Dan said; "it is *the* thing." "How about some red towels?" she asked. "That's a good idea," said Dan, looking around, "I was thinking of covering the chairs in mattress ticking." "Why not?" Elizabeth asked.

When he left, she called Armand. "Armand," she said, "I've drunk two glasses of red paint and swallowed fourteen yellow Dramamines. Feel free to hang up." "Let's go out for coffee." he said.

"My analyst would love it," Armand said when he came in. "What do you mean?" Elizabeth asked, trying to focus on the hall, still neutral gray. "Blood, he goes for blood,

81

he goes for the jugular." "Let's not start that again," Elizabeth said. When they got to the delicatessen, Armand wanted to know how she intended to write a dissertation and teach. "I will divide my day up into pieces, like the Red Sea," Elizabeth said. Armand didn't think it could be done. Elizabeth asked him how she was going to live if she didn't work. She asked him how he lived. "On reparation money from the German government."

One night, the phone rang late and woke Elizabeth up. "What now?" she mumbled groggily into the phone, trying to sound as poisonous as possible. "Elizabeth, it's Ralph," an unfamiliar voice said, "did I wake you up?" "Yes, that's all right," Elizabeth said sitting up; "how are you?" She wondered what was going wrong with Ralph somewhere in Cambridge. Ralph was an old friend of hers. She had met him when she rented a room in one of the white frame boarding houses surrounding the Harvard campus, and it turned out he was the son of an old friend of her mother's, the same Ralph who had gone to the University when they both were undergraduates; every vacation, Elizabeth's mother would tell her that she *had* to get in touch with Ralph; he was a wonderful catch; he had wonderful parents; they were very well-off; and somewhere on his spine was a little name tag saying "Jewish." Elizabeth would have nothing to do with him, and one day, when she heard someone introducing him to someone else in the Lounge, she had picked up her books and gone to study in the library. But, meeting in Boston, renting a room in the boarding house to keep the truth about her apartment with Mark from her mother, they became the best of friends, conspirators. Elizabeth would sit on the edge of Ralph's double bed for hours, and they would exchange interminable lists of complaints concerning their parents. Elizabeth remembered how her mother used to describe herself and Ralph's mother, both pregnant, journeying down Coney Island, two little boats, and how everyone laughed, because she was round as a matzoh ball, and Ralph's mother came to a point in the front. Gradually, Ralph's bed became a community meeting place for the crowd that met in the kitchen, and Ralph took to sitting in the wooden chair in front of the desk, while the rest of them sprawled on the covers, listening to music, idly remarking to whichever one was having the romantic crisis of the moment, how they deserved better, how they should get rid of whomever they were now seeing. Ralph had a girl friend who loved cats: her clothes were printed with cats; she had even managed to find sheets covered with cats. Her only trouble, said Ralph, was that she didn't know how she felt about him and would drink only orange juice and eat only hamburgers. Edna, the psychologist of the group, would remark that she seemed to have juvenile eating habits; Ralph would say that if Edna had to hide in broom closets wearing negligees to get attention, she was barking, ha ha, up the wrong tree herself. Elizabeth would begin to complain about Mark, who had just rented an untuned upright piano which he had moved into their bedroom; he was now practicing Bach's two part inventions. "He does it deliberately to torture me," Elizabeth said with conviction. "You are getting paranoid," said Edna from the foot of the bed. "I am not paranoid," Elizabeth said; "he's practicing Bach because he knows Bach is my favorite, and I get a splitting headache listening to him slaughter him." "How much does he play?" "Two hours at a time." "Two hours at a time is a lot," Edna agreed; "why don't you cut the strings, or whatever you call them?" "It's a rented piano," Elizabeth said gloomily. "It is also an untuned piano." "I know a piano tuner," Ralph said. "Does he make emergency calls?" Elizabeth wanted to know. "He probably does; I think he's starving." "Good," Elizabeth said; "he can eat my oatmeal cookies. I thought butter would be better than shortening, and they taste like round car-lubricants." The piano tuner came the next day, and ate the oatmeal cookies, which he pronounced delicious. "I hope his ear is better than his mouth," Edna said graciously. "Bach is still pinwheeling in his grave," Elizabeth reported, "and I am going out of my mind." "I think you should get rid of him," said Ralph, putting down his recorder. This was where the conversations always ended. Within fifteen minutes, Mark would come back from the lab to pick up Elizabeth, and take her back to their apartment on the back of his bicycle. Edna and Ralph would stand on the porch and watch her waver off into the darkness as if they were watching the departure of the Titanic. "She should get rid of him," Ralph said again. "Well, we can't afford to talk," said Edna, turning around, hugging herself, and stepping back into the warm square of light, and the yawning hall.

"I'm coming to Chicago, for a conference. Can I stay with you?" Ralph asked. "Sure," said Elizabeth. "I'll have a party." Ralph seemed such an old friend that Elizabeth was privately convinced they had become acquainted, belly to belly, as their mothers sat over coffee and taught each other to knit, to crochet. "How's La Belle Dame of the Cats?" "I don't see her any more. She decided she didn't know how she felt about Harvard and went back to Iowa." "I hope you're still drinking your juice," Elizabeth said, yawning. "I never had so many colds in my life until I met Julia," Ralph said, depressed. "Do you know anyone interesting out there?" Elizabeth took a quick survey of her friends, and decided she couldn't do anything like that to someone she knew so well. "You can look them over at the party," she said; "don't get your hopes up."

After Elizabeth hung up, she realized she had not given a party, or thought about giving a party, for almost two years. When she and Mark had been engaged, his thesis director had predicted that she would be another Perle Mesta, and that had confirmed what Elizabeth had always suspected, that she hated parties, especially giving them. The night of the party, Ralph arrived late. He had taken three busses and a train to get to Elizabeth's apartment. "He hasn't changed," Elizabeth thought to herself, remembering how he used to buy a box of six cupcakes for the four of them, thirty-seven cents, and then patiently wait until each of them forked over the nine cents they owed. "I'll absorb the extra penny," Ralph would announce, munificent. While Elizabeth was putting out the potato chips and the sour cream dip, Ralph turned on the air conditioner. "Don't do that," Elizabeth told him; "it isn't hot." "I believe in turning on air conditioners whenever the temperature goes over seventy-five degrees," Ralph said, switching it back on. Furious, Elizabeth went into the kitchen. Ralph was not offering to help. She thought about the time in Cambridge when she had been making dinner, and left the kitchen, and come back to find the water gently lapping at the foot of the sink. "Why didn't you *call* me?" she demanded of Ralph, who was sitting at the table with his feet up on the bottom rung of the chair. It hadn't occurred to him. Ralph now stationed himself in front of the air conditioner, and commented on the way Elizabeth was arranging the food. "Do you have any milk?" he asked her. "Milk? What for?" Elizabeth asked. "I always drink milk for breakfast," Ralph said. "No, I don't have any milk," Elizabeth said. "I better go out and get some," Ralph said, putting on his sweater, disappearing out of the front door. "Twenty-nine cents," said Ralph when he came back, setting down the brown paper bag, holding out his hand. "Take it out of my pocketbook," Elizabeth told him, enraged. She began to notice she was doing things too quickly; she knew when she felt like this she became accident-prone. "Ridiculous," she said to herself, opening the refrigerator, and, as if in slow motion, a quart bottle of beer, resting on the crack between the refrigerator back and door, began its slow journey to the kitchen floor, exploding as it hit. Elizabeth's foot was suddenly cold. When she looked down, she saw a triangular piece of amber glass protruding from the skin above her arch. She pulled it out. The blood streamed broad and flat over her arch onto the floor, broad and flat and smooth, shiny as the Amazon. "Ralph," Elizabeth called, "bring me a towel." Ralph arrived with the towel, and then saw her foot. "I cut it," Elizabeth said, wrapping the towel around the cut. Ralph didn't say anything; he stared at her foot; the towel was turning red and beginning to drip, sweating blood. "I don't think that's going to stop, Elizabeth," he said. "It will stop," she told him, "just get my brown shoes. They're under the bed." When Elizabeth put on the shoe, she could feel her toes beginning to get wet and sticky. "I think you had better go to the hospital," Ralph told her, puckering. "What about the party?" Elizabeth asked, staring stupidly at her shoe. The bell rang. It was Nancy. "Nancy will let everyone in," Ralph said, and called a cab. The whole way to the hospital, Ralph lectured Elizabeth about how much more expensive cabs were in Boston than they were in New York; suddenly Elizabeth realized that she didn't have any money. "That's all right," said Ralph, "I'll lend it to you until we get back."

Elizabeth got out of the cab, and as she closed the door, saw a dark little pool on the floor of the cab. As she walked into the Emergency Room, she left a trail of sticky red footprints. The nurse took a look and rushed her into the treatment room. "You can fill out the form lying on this," she said, spreading a paper sheet on the steel couch and helping Elizabeth up. "The doctor will be here in a minute." A few minutes later, the doctor appeared with her file. He peered at her suspiciously. When Ralph explained what had happened, he looked relieved.

There was a commotion at the door which turned out to be Benita. "Can I stay with her?" she asked the doctor. "Do you want her to?" the doctor asked. "I certainly do," Elizabeth said. "What happened?" Benita asked. "I slashed my ankle," Elizabeth said. The doctor jerked around. "Joke, joke," Elizabeth murmured, reassuring. "Will it have to have stitches?" "Unless you want to bleed to death," the doctor said. "His best morgue-side manner," Benita whispered, squeezing her hand, reassuring. The sewing hurt less than Elizabeth expected. The light was brilliant; the instruments clattered like knives and forks. She was mostly unnerved by the thick black thread and the strange, curved needle. "Come back in a week," the doctor told her, "they'll take the stitches out. You can walk on it now."

When Elizabeth got to her party, it was in full swing. Everyone was dancing and having a good time. A small group was sitting on the couch, one of them a nun from their seminar. Armand was asking her all sorts of questions about her wedding ring. "Is it true what they say about the nun's wedding night?" he demanded imperiously. "Armand!" Elizabeth called. He ignored her. "That Christ comes to them, and, um *takes* them?" Elizabeth seized Benita's arm and ordered her over to Armand. Benita, who took all metaphors literally, clung to Armand like a vine; she seemed suspended from his emaciated frame like a plant in leaf. "Elizabeth wanted me to meet you," she told him, widening her eyes. Armand got up, hypnotized. "Tell me about your divorce," he demanded. After an hour, they left together.

Elizabeth began to talk to Robert, whose girlfriend was spending the year in France "to think things over." Robert had been dating her since the ninth grade. Elizabeth was amazed at how nice he was; he was also very handsome. She noticed this abruptly, and for the first time. His head was very large, slightly hydrocephalic, giving him a vulnerable, exotic look. When he asked her to dance with him, Elizabeth was dizzy with gratitude. She danced with Robert five times, slowly, forgetting her fear of dancing, her fear that she had forgotten how to dance, not caring about her foot, about the little black stitches, knotted and precise, each with their two ends rising from the raw cut like two clipped animal ears. Before the party was over, Elizabeth knew Robert would never do this again.

That night, Benita came back to the apartment, and decided to sleep on the couch. Ralph turned on the air conditioner. Soon the apartment began to feel like the inside of a refrigerator. She and Benita began to complain about the cold. "Seventy-eight degrees out," announced Ralph, oblivious. Finally, they got blankets from the bedrooms and wrapped themselves up in their chairs like Indians. Elizabeth wanted to talk to Ralph; she had not seen him for three years, but her teeth kept chattering, and her exhaustion was turning to nausea. "Ralph," Elizabeth said, "I have to go to bed. Where do you want to sleep?" "Right here," Ralph said, "on the couch." "It isn't very comfortable," Elizabeth warned him. "I can't sleep when it's hot," he said; that settled it. Elizabeth looked at Benita; she had pulled the covers up over her nose, and her eyes looked mutinous. They both got up. Elizabeth limped off to the bedroom. In a few minutes, Benita knocked at the door, pointed at the living room, and started to laugh. "Very funny," Elizabeth said, "that's my Intended you're laughing at." "Does your mother still want you to marry him?" Benita asked. "Not since she's seen him," Elizabeth said.

That night, Elizabeth stared a long time at the French tapestry on her bedroom wall. In the tapestry, two women were watching two children who looked exactly like them, but smaller, dancing an intricate dance, as a man in a powdered wig played a violin. Cupids flew over their heads on the ceiling and wall. Pictures in thick gilt frames leaned in. The chairs were rounded and tufted and plush. French windows opened out. The buckle shoes of the little boy rested on a carpet, intricately patterned. Nothing moved; nothing changed. A smaller child sat on the floor next to a chair, holding a donkey with a basket resting on each of its sides. Two dolls leaned against his hip. Elizabeth loved this tapestry, in which life went on and on, and no dust collected and fell to spoil the perfection of their lovely, china lives. "Good-night," she said to it, and switched off the light, putting her foot up on the pillow Benita had placed at the foot of the bed.

That night, Elizabeth had a dream. She was in Arabia, visiting the country. There were acres and acres of sand and no water. In her pocket, was a tapestry of an oasis, which she could take from her pocket, and spread out on the ground, and immediately, there would be water and palm trees and shade. Elizabeth understood from this that she did not have to worry about canteens or the sun, or the strange, rippling heat. Then she came to a small house made entirely of mud. When she knocked at the door, a woman came to the entrance holding a child. "I have come to see Robert," she said. "I'll call him," the woman told her, and Elizabeth saw the woman was foreign. Robert was very happy to see her. "This is my wife," he said, "her name is Vida." Vida smiled at her. They were both dyed brown by the sun. Elizabeth was suddenly aware that she was white, terribly white. Robert put his arm around Vida, and he and Vida and the child began to spin away from her rapidly, as on a rapidly ascending globe. Elizabeth felt a terrible sense of envy, and a terrible sense of cold. She spread out her tapestry of the oasis, but when she bent down to drink, a snake reared its head out of the dust. Elizabeth felt a terrible pity for herself and a deep happiness for Robert and the woman who belonged to each other beyond beauty and ugliness, happiness or unhappiness. Their lives were woven together like threads. Her life was unraveling, like the tapestry she held, the oasis unraveling, leaving the sand. She felt she could reach out and touch them, the rough texture of their clothes.

Before she ate breakfast, Elizabeth emptied the top drawer of the little cardboard chest she had painted yellow in the fall. Already her fingermarks were forming black halos around the handles, the little stub suns. She sorted out all of Mark's letters. They filled a shoebox, and Elizabeth tied it up tightly with string, and, with pinking shears, cut up a large brown grocery bag from *Mister G*, addressed it, and covered it with stamps. "Do me a favor and mail this when you go out to get some milk," she said to Ralph. In the afternoon, she hobbled into Doctor Greene's office and told him about her ankle, and the party, and the dream. He pointed out that she had returned Mark's letters, one year to the day, after his departure for Boston. "The year of mourning is up," Doctor Greene said. Looking down at her body floating on the couch, Elizabeth saw she was entirely dressed in black, black sweater, black skirt, black tights, black shoes, in which shone two black bordered suns, the shined shoes of the dead. As she was leaving, he said quietly, "You were lucky about that ankle. Another quarter of an inch, and the glass would have hit an artery." "Am I hopeless?" Elizabeth asked. "You like to think so," he said.

The winter wore on, heavy gray flakes falling from the sky, a sodden, wet snow. Gradually, the faces in the class detached themselves from the square brown and black mass they composed together with their desks. Faces attached themselves to names. When students came up to the desk after class, Elizabeth no longer had to keep herself from saying, "May I help you?" The only other job she had had where people came and talked to her was in Gimbel's coat department in the summers, and in the winters after school. In the summers, no one came in, and Elizabeth and the other girls would practice the art of looking busy. If a customer came in, all of them fell upon her like vultures. Slowly, Elizabeth lost her fear that she was bad for the students, that she would do them some harm. The class that met late at night was full of older men and women; the younger ones had jobs during the day, and did not like them; they were not resigned, and wanted something better. The last class was a 90's class, a remedial class. There were students from Africa, and China, and Puerto Rico, and Cuba. They had all failed the stop-watch multiple choice test given at the beginning of the semester: Should there be a) a comma, b) a semicolon, c) a period, d) a colon following "parted" in sentence number three? Other students were here, having failed to pass the regulation section of the same composition course. Many of them were failed because of poor attendance or poor behavior. One night, Elizabeth came in after her thirty-five mile drive through the snow, the trucks going by, depositing a thick sheet of slush on her windshield. She had learned to look hard at the road, memorizing it, from the instant she sensed their approach, and then she would drive blind until the snow cleared off with the swipe of the blades. She saw some students sitting on the windowsill. All of the seats were filled. Two of the students came up and asked her if it was all right, they had brought their wives. The wives sat beaming throughout the session. The next week, the night was as clear as glass, the roads as smooth as ice. As she passed the blocks to the school, she counted the electrified reindeer on the lawns. The number of crèches. Three families had added themselves to the Christmas spirit of the block. When she got in, there were even more students sitting on the windowsill. Elizabeth put down her books, and peered at them a long time before saying anything. The department rigidly prescribed books for its courses, and this course had a required workbook, tiny four paragraph essays on the difference between rugby and football, and then pages of multiple choice questions, and lists of sentences full of grammatical errors to be corrected. The school bookstore would not order any books for the required courses which were not on the department list. When two students came up and asked if it was all right they had brought their girlfriend and boyfriend, she made up her mind. She asked the class what they thought of their book. They thought it was boring, they said after some prodding, but they liked coming to class to talk. Elizabeth explained to them, that legally, this was the only book she was permitted to use, but they were a good class, and she would like them to use something more interesting. The only trouble was, how would they get it? They would all have to agree to buy it before next week, somewhere near where they lived, or worked, or at another school. Everyone wanted to buy the new book. They looked happy and mischievous. Even the sullen row in the back had a new light in its eyes.

The next week, Elizabeth drove through the Santa Clauses and the reindeer and Jesus in crib after crib with a sense of dread; she felt guilty. Probably everyone was right: the 90's students were hopeless: they would not have bought their books, they would have complained to the department chairman about her peculiar ways. When she got there, everyone had his copy of the new book; she could see the red and gold square on everyone's desk. The class had an expectant air that was entirely new. They began their discussion of *The Minister's Black Veil*. One of the wives kept raising her hand until Elizabeth had to call on her. She had a theory that the woman in the box had been murdered by the minister. Elizabeth told them Edgar Allan Poe had had the same idea. Immediately, a silence fell over the class like a blanket. She realized they all assumed Edgar Allan Poe would have to be right. They had all had to memorize his poem, *The Raven*, in high school, and that very week, *The Fall of the House of Usher* was playing in all the neighborhood movie houses. Elizabeth said it was always possible Poe was wrong; everyone made mistakes. After that, someone raised his hand, waveringly, like a foreign flag, and wondered if it was important that a superstitious old lady had said the dead body moved. Elizabeth said it certainly was, and then asked them why. In a little while, they were all raising their hands, interrupting each other. The classroom was very noisy, and she did not have to say anything for a long time; finally, they asked her what she thought. She explained the basis of their disagreement, and asked the rest of the class what they thought could be done about it. Immediately, pandemonium broke out again. The door opened, and a male teacher poked his head in. He listened for a moment, and closed the door. Last week, Elizabeth's friend, Nancy, had been locked out of her room by students; the physics class was still throwing balls of paper at their instructor whenever he turned around to write on the board. Noise in a class was a danger signal; here, like the police, the teachers stuck together. By the end of the hour, the whole class was convinced the minister had committed murder. Elizabeth told them about *The Scarlet Letter*, where a minister had committed a crime, a sin, and suggested that perhaps the author might have another idea in this story; they would have to read it again and see. She could hear them arguing outside the door and down the hall. Occasionally, she could hear one of them asking the other his first name. It was twenty after ten. Elizabeth would not get home until twelve. She was more astonished than the students by what had happened.

On Monday, Elizabeth got a note asking her to see the department chairman. She went, expecting the worst. Instead, she got a long lecture on how she had not filled out her Personal Data Sheet on time; the chairman said he was worried that her Ph.D. work was interfering with her teaching. She lost her temper. She told him that she was a very good teacher, and none of her students were complaining to the Dean; none of her students were repeating courses over and over, like rats in the wrong maze. She told him that if he thought a Ph.D. disqualified her for teaching in a junior college, he should definitely write that up for the Dean of the school. The next week, the class did *The Lottery*. They were beginning to wonder what would make them act like the characters in the stories. Their writing improved; the exercises vanished, permanently. Elizabeth learned that the whole department had heard about her argument with the chairman. There was one man in the department who had a Ph.D., and, in the distant past, he had published an article on Shakespeare. Because of this, he had become the mild and somewhat unwilling champion of academic standards at the junior college. He, and everyone else in the office at the time, had heard Elizabeth's argument with the chairman; they had even talked to some of her students. After that, they told the chairman that if anything was done to fire Elizabeth, the union would take the matter up. "She hasn't been here long enough to be a member of the union," the chairman said, defensively. *"That* is the whole point," said the famous author of the Shakespeare article, "she will not be here long enough to join if the department discriminates against higher education in its faculty." Nancy told Elizabeth that this rebellion against the chairman was the first of its kind in the department. The next day, Elizabeth brought her cup of coffee and her five candy kisses—which she lined up on the desk like five silver pagodas, this was her dinner—to Professor Martin's desk. They had a long conversation about Shakespeare, while Elizabeth peeled one of her candy kisses at a time. She explained why she ate them for dinner; the sugar kept her from getting hungry and she had to lose weight. He nodded, and asked her about the last act of *Measure for Measure*. They never once mentioned the disagreement with the chairman, or his defense of her. She told him about her use of illegal books, and he seemed pleased. They talked some more about Shakespeare. At the end of their talk, Professor Martin jabbed at the bowl of his pipe. "You probably wonder what I'm doing here," he said. Elizabeth saw no point in lying; she nodded her head. "Too many children and too little self-respect," he said. "How many children do you have?" "Six." "Life has a way of changing things," Elizabeth said. Professor Martin looked at her, quizzical. "For the better," she said in a hurry. "Not my life," he said. "I don't know about that," she replied, crumpling the silver papers from the candy kisses into one tiny ball. A little strip of paper protruded from one end. "Look," Elizabeth said, holding it up, "it looks like a bomb." "I wish it were," Professor Martin said, staring at his bookshelf.

That night, Elizabeth went home and typed up letters requesting interviews for the position of Instructor for the fall of the following year. Three days later, she got a call asking her to come down to the Institute for Technicological Studies. Three people interviewed her, and asked her about her thesis, her thesis director, how far she had gotten in her course work. They seemed surprised to hear she was almost finished because she was teaching. The next day, the chairman of her department at the University called to tell her she would have the job, the people at the Institute were very impressed with her. "I'll believe it when I see it in writing," Elizabeth said. The next day she told Doctor Greene. He didn't seem surprised. "Every time you poke your nose out of a door, someone offers you a job," he said. "What are you talking about?" she demanded; "I'm just very lucky." Near the end of the semester, she told Professor Martin she was leaving. He said he had expected it. "Then why did you defend me?" she asked, surprised. "Principles," he said, looking surprised himself. He asked how much she would be paid at the Institute. "That's not much," he said, "we'll have to get you an extra course here." "Can I have one on Friday night?" asked Elizabeth, overjoyed. "You'll have it," he said; he sounded grim.

The last night Elizabeth taught, she wanted to bring something special for her class, but at the last minute, she could not make up her mind to do it; she wasn't sure it was "professional." But when she got to her desk, she found a black and white iced cupcake sitting in the middle of it. Then she saw a black and white cupcake sitting on each of the red and gold books. "What's this?" she asked, and the class started to laugh. "Integrated cupcakes," said Mrs. Tattham, a black woman who sat in the back. Elizabeth had hardly noticed her all semester, though in the last weeks, she had begun to talk. Everyone laughed again. "She made them," volunteered the sweet-faced girl in the front row. "Then let's eat them," Elizabeth said; her diet would have to wait. After Elizabeth told them what a pleasure it had been to have them in class, and after they all came up to say goodbye, some just hovering in the back, and staring, and not saying a word, she went out in the hall. A warm wind was blowing through the open windows. The green leaves were uncoiling in the steely, fluorescent light. She saw the drinking fountains that came up to her knee. They had been installed when the school was still an elementary school, and no one had thought to replace them. She was very sorry to leave. She thought to herself that she never knew how much she would miss something until she had to leave it. She was very happy that she would have to come back next year, every Friday night, for a three hour class, over the slush-covered roads, after a full day of teaching at the Institute. Next year, she would be teaching during the day. She would not be able to sleep until two, and cancel out a feeling of existence. She would miss this place very much. As she was looking for her keys to the locked office, an enormously fat woman tapped her on the shoulder. Elizabeth recognized her as one of last semester's students. The woman had heard she wouldn't be here next year; she wanted to tell her how much she had learned in the class: she was going to study English; she was going to be a teacher herself. She had never understood what it meant to read a story. She would never forget the class, she said. Elizabeth told her she would be back next year, on Fridays, and hoped the woman would come to see her. The woman said she would: she was emphatic about it; her chins rippled.

In the office, Elizabeth, number fifty-eight, with the latest schedule, sat listening to the hum of the air conditioner, on until June fifteenth, regardless of the temperature outside. She had thought the woman who stopped her in the hall had been bored. She had sat still all semester, barely saying a word, staring at Elizabeth as if she could not believe what was going on. Elizabeth had thought she was too well-mannered to complain. And all the time, she had been changing; she was going to teach; she was changing her life. Elizabeth wondered what unseen influences were acting upon her this way; she felt as if she had not moved an arm or a leg since Mark had left the apartment and set off for Boston and Doctor Fromm. "Why this is serious!" Elizabeth thought to herself, amazed. All along, she had been pretending, she was not really teaching, the students meant nothing to her, nothing was changing, but the noses of the reindeer had winked out, the buds had opened, her arms were bare, she had no coat; a year had passed. Next year, she would be one of a department of fifteen. When she had asked about required books, the committee had looked insulted. "You choose your *own*," they said, as if talking to a backward student. But things could not change, Elizabeth told herself. Could they change? Even in the spring, the parking lot was purple and black and blue. Hints of green buzzed around the street lights like wasps. The year had come to an end. Something was over.

Chapter 5

Sarah and Manny had rented the second floor of a two-family house on Avenue X. It was a red brick house, identical to every other house on the block, except for the color of its door. The door was painted bottle green. The house was attached to the one next to it, and in between the attached houses, was a narrow driveway leading to the garage and a tiny, square backyard. Sarah thought they were lucky because they had rented the top floor, and the rooms were full of light, even on dull days, and the children had the porch to sit on in the sun when they were recovering from the chicken pox, and the measles, and the mumps. Several of the neighbors had cemented over their little backyards, but in back of Sarah and Manny's house, the little yard was still filled with brown dirt, glinting with bits of bright glass. Every fall, Sarah would plant some new bulbs which would miraculously straggle up out of the grass and grit. There was also a giant pussy willow tree which grew in a corner of the yard and shadowed the whole patch, in the summer casting its endless shadows on the whitewashed wall. Elizabeth loved the backyard and would sit on the newspaper Belle gave her to put down on the grass so she wouldn't catch cold, and stare at the shadows for hours on end. She called the tree the kaleidoscope tree. When she knew Belle and her mother were busy with their cooking, she and Esther, the girl from across the street, would spend their time sliding down the bottle green cellar door which was forbidden to them as full of splinters and nails.

One afternoon, Elizabeth refused to go out in the yard. She would shut her window tight, and push up one slat of the venetian blind in the window overlooking the square plot of earth, but when Belle told her to go out in the back and play, she would not go. The pussy willow branches were covered with fuzzy green things; Elizabeth was sure they were caterpillars. She could not understand why her parents were not frightened of the tree, and why they would allow her, even encourage her, to play there under all those worms. She had heard her grandmother tell a story about a woman who stepped on a bee, and even though she had made a plaster of soda and put it on her foot, her foot had swelled and swelled, and the veins in her foot had turned blue, and red, and black, and when they took her to the hospital, she had died.

Elizabeth was sitting on the floor with old newspapers; she tore them up into shreds and soaked them in a pot of water, and, then, methodically, covered the shining darning egg her mother had bought for her at the five and ten with layer after layer of wet paper, and after she finished applying each layer, she would smear on a paste of flour and water. "How do you make a plaster out of soda?" asked Elizabeth, curious. "You mix it with water," her grandmother told her. Later, Elizabeth took some of her Pepsi-Cola and held her glass under the faucet, then waited for it to harden. Nothing happened; when she drank it, all the bubbles were gone. "There's something wrong with this soda," she thought to herself, pouring it down the sink. She wondered if the woman who died had had the wrong kind of soda, too.

"Hurry up and finish that thing," her mother said; "we've got to clean up the kitchen for company." "I've only got the nose left," Elizabeth said, staring at the darning egg head, and chewing on her thumb with concentration. "Stop that chewing," said Belle, "you'll have four fingers in the morning." Hastily, Elizabeth pulled her thumb out of her mouth and inspected its side. It seemed larger, not smaller. Where she chewed on it was a large, yellowish transparent patch; it looked like a bubble. She stared at Belle, and then pinched some wet paper together until it looked like a nose. She smeared on some flour paste, and gave the nose a good push. "I'm finished," she said; "I'm going to have to put it away to dry." "How many of those things does she have now?" Belle asked irritably. "Who knows?" Sarah said. "Her eyes are going to fall out of her head," Belle complained; "if she's not reading, she's busy with this."

Elizabeth came back in carrying another darning egg covered with a grotesque papier-mâché head: "This one's dry now," she said, "will you cut it off?" "Not now," Sarah told her, "I'm busy." "But I have to start painting it," Elizabeth whined. "All right, bring it here," Belle told her. Belle went into the bathroom and got the razor; she took out the blade. Elizabeth watched it with dread, lying on the table, sharp, blue-black. Suppose someone forgot it, and baked it in the bread? "Which is the front, Elizabeth?" Belle asked. "The front is the side with the *nose*," Elizabeth complained. "Some nose," said Belle, picking up the razor; she slit the head down the center from the top of its scalp to its darning egg neck, as if she were making a part. "*I'll* take it off, grandma," Elizabeth said, grabbing it from her. Each time her grandmother slit the papier-mâché head, she half-expected to see a real brain, real blood; she was always sorry when it was empty, when it refused to come alive under her hand. Very carefully, she peeled the head from the darning egg. Then she went off into the bathroom to get more wet paper and glue to seal up the seam. "This is a good one," she said when she came back to the kitchen; "this one is going to be the witch. I'm going to paint her green." "I wish you'd spend this much time on your homework," Belle said. "Leave her alone, mother," Sarah said, crabby. "Don't start painting now; wash up for dinner." "Daddy's going to build me a stage for the puppets," Elizabeth announced importantly. "I hope he builds it faster than he's shortening my coat," Sarah said. At dinner, Elizabeth asked Manny about the puppet stage. He said he would build it as soon as he got some wood. "Don't make promises you're not going to keep," Sarah said, not looking up. "He never does anything when you want him to," Belle commented. Manny got up from the table, pushing back his chair. "Where are you going?" Sarah asked. "For a walk," Manny said. "Let him, maybe he'll lose some weight," Belle said placidly. She was glad he was gone. "Daddy isn't fat, grandma," Elizabeth said. "Are you going to finish your peas, or are we going to have to save them for your breakfast?" Belle demanded harshly.

After dinner, Elizabeth got out her book and started to read. "Go out and play, Elizabeth," her mother said, "get some fresh air." "Her eyes are going to fall out of her head," Belle said automatically; "she'll have glasses as thick as his mother's." She never referred to Manny by name. "I don't want to go out," Elizabeth complained, "I want to read." "Go out, *now*," her mother ordered, imperious. "How do you expect to make any friends if you stay cooped up in here all day?" "I don't care if I don't have any friends," Elizabeth said, reading about the bodies. "That's too bad: out!" Sarah said, taking her book, and holding out her coat. Just then they heard Esther's voice in the alley calling out her name. "She's coming," Sarah shouted down. "You see, everyone's outside," she said, propelling her toward the door.

"I wanted to read," she announced sociably, when she got out. "Did you see Pinhead and Foodini?" Esther asked. Then they talked about Pinhead's trip to the moon, and if he would really get there, and how he would get back, since he didn't know how to fly the spaceship. In the alley, they could hear the sound of the television and Milton Berle pouring out of the window like dust on their heads. "Let's slide on the cellar door," suggested Esther. "Let's run down from the top this time," Elizabeth volunteered, "I'll be first." She and Esther did that a long time. Then Elizabeth decided to try it even faster; she lost her balance and fell. She fell forward and her knee caught on a nail, but her body kept falling. When she got up, there was a long gash across her knee traveling down onto her leg. Her leg was completely covered with blood. "You'll get it now," Esther said, horrified; "I'm going home." When Sarah and Belle saw Elizabeth's knee, they picked her up and slammed her down on a chair. "*What* did we tell you?" demanded Belle, "stubborn as a mule; it's a miracle she's still alive." They took a clean kitchen towel and wound it around her knee. The towel turned red. "You'd better call the doctor, mother," Sarah said, holding the towel in place, her lips clamped. The doctor and Manny arrived at the same time. "What now?" said the doctor. "She cut her knee," Sarah said. The doctor unwound the towel. Elizabeth didn't know she held so much blood. "Two legs too many for you, Elizabeth?" the doctor asked. "I think we're going to have to sew this up," he announced to the air. Elizabeth began to cry, and then to shriek. Manny was called in, the family straight-jacket. When the doctor came near her, she tried jumping off the chair, but her father held her down. "Maybe it will heal without stitches; we'll see," said the doctor. Elizabeth whimpered quietly on the chair. The doctor took some gauze and adhesive tape out of his bag; he cut the tape into strips and hung them from the edge of the table. Then he bandaged the knee up, tight. "See she stays off her foot tonight," the doctor said, leaving. "How are we supposed to do that?" Sarah wanted to know. "Try tying her to the bed," the doctor suggested, "if she's this bad at her age, what's she going to be like when she grows up?" Manny picked her up and carried her off to the couch; tonight, he was going to let her stay up and watch Arthur Godfrey with the rest of them. "Don't drop her," Belle admonished from the hall. "I forgot the tetanus shot," said the doctor, trudging back up the stairs.

A week later, Manny came home early on Saturday; he usually worked in the city until after dinner time. By this time, Elizabeth had a much smaller bandage on her knee, and every night, when they took off the bandage, she admired the thick crusty scab. "Leave it alone," Belle told her, "you'll get an infection; they'll have to cut your leg off." Manny had come home early because he and Sarah were going downtown to pick out a hat for his new suit. They decided to take her with them since she couldn't go out to play. Elizabeth sat in between them on the front seat of the Hudson. "Can I sit on your lap, mother?" she asked. She liked to do that because she could see out more. Otherwise, she would sit up on her knees and stare over the back of the seat, out the back window, watching things as they passed. On the whole, she preferred seeing them before they were already half-gone; that way, she had a second chance.

"Why not?" Elizabeth asked, "I can't see. All I can see is the clock." "Because there's not enough room in my lap," Sarah told her. She and Manny exchanged secret, knowing smiles; this always annoyed her. She wanted to know if they were going to the store with the bridge; her mother said they were, and they would go over it. "She means the passage between the two buildings," her mother explained to Manny. When they got to the store, they went up escalator after escalator, and came to a floor where there were hardly any people at all, and everyone moved in a thick, shaggy silence. On all the counters, were forms resembling heads, featureless, and on each head, was a gray hat, or a black hat, or a brown hat. She thought she had never seen anything as beautiful as the gray hats; they looked like velvet, smooth cat fur. The salesman would pick them up carefully, as if handling glass, and carry them one at a time over to Manny, where he sat on a chair. He would place each hat on his head, careful and ceremonious, as if they were crowns; it was a ceremony: a coronation, and everything was hushed, people spoke in whispers, as in a church. Elizabeth thought there was some secret under all this, some secret she could not understand. There were mirrors all over the room, multiplying the gray hats, the figure of her father, crowned in his gray hat, the hundreds and hundreds of featureless faces under their new, spotless, perfect, elegant, expensive hats. Elizabeth wanted desperately to try on a hat, but she knew she could not even touch them: they were not for children. If a child touched one, he would leave his fingerprints on the smooth texture of the hat above the beautiful band; the hat would be ruined, spoiled. Finally, her father picked out just the right hat. Elizabeth wondered how he knew this was the right one: to her, they all looked the same. Manny looked at Sarah, and Sarah smiled, inward, nodding. Then they both turned to the man in black, nodding. The man picked up the hat with both hands and carried it across the floor, careful, as if carrying a cake. When he got to the counter, he took out an enormous round box; Elizabeth had never seen a box like that before: it was covered with red and white candy stripes; it looked like the picture of the magic coach in *Cinderella*. Elizabeth jumped off her chair to get a better look at the box, and as she stood up, she felt something warm spreading down her knee. She looked down, and pulled at her mother's hand; Sarah turned and looked at her. The happiness went out of her face like a light. "Manny!" she said, "she's bleeding!" The blood was reaching her shoe, and some drops were falling onto the thick gray rug. *"Do* something," Sarah cried, frantic. Elizabeth was terribly embarrassed; she started to cry. She felt as if she had done something horrible, and she would never, never be able to make up for this. The salesman came back with the box, and saw Elizabeth's foot. "I cut it on a nail, it started to bleed," she wailed, disgraced. She wondered if the man could put her in jail for spoiling his room. "Well," said the man, "well, that's a bad cut you have there." He picked her up and put her on the long table that traveled down the center of the long, silent room. Then he went to the desk and came back with several sheets of tissue paper and some packing string. "What's your name?" he asked her, "my daughter's named Rochelle." He folded the paper over and over into a pad, and pressed it against her knee; then he tied the pad in place with the candy-striped string. "You sit there while I wrap the package," he said, "by the time I'm finished the bleeding will stop." Sarah and Manny kept looking at Elizabeth, worried, and then at the man, embarrassed. "I'm very sorry," Sarah said; she looked distraught. "Nothing to be sorry about," the man said cheerfully, and to Elizabeth, "too bad we don't have a box big enough for you, we could wrap you up all the way." But Elizabeth looked at her mother and father. She saw they were very upset; she felt she had spoiled something very important and they would never take her with them, anywhere, again. There was her blood, lying on the carpet, in spots. The man in black came over to her with the striped, round box. "Hold this, little lady," he said, as he lifted her down. The paper stuck to her knee, making it stiff; her knee had stopped bleeding. She felt she was being lifted down from a terrible height: the gray floor was far away; she was very dizzy. She could sense a rage in her mother; she knew her mother thought she must have done it deliberately. "But I couldn't help it," she kept saying to herself, as they drove home in the car, "I couldn't help it." All the way home, she didn't say a word, she didn't look out the back window, she didn't ask to sit on her mother's lap. When her father asked if they should stop at her grandfather's and get her a soda, she shook her head no. Her father looked puzzled. "I hope this teaches you a lesson," Sarah said, "the next time maybe you'll listen when we tell you to stay away from that cellar door."

The next morning, Elizabeth got up early and heard the mail arrive through the bronze slat in the door. She hobbled down the dark, steep flight of stairs to the pile of mail at the bottom. She liked to get the mail first, and see which envelopes were large and square and looked like they were cards; then she would ask whomever the envelope was for if she could keep the card when they were through with it so she could add it to her card collection in her shoebox. If anyone got a postcard, Elizabeth would stand around until they had finished reading it, and then make off with it at once. Elizabeth hobbled back up the steps, leaning heavily on the bannister, keeping her injured knee stiff; when she got back up, her mother was in the kitchen, scrambling eggs. "Why don't I get any mail, mother?" Elizabeth asked. "You don't get any mail because you don't write any letters." "Do *you* write letters?" Elizabeth asked her. "Of course," Sarah said. "I also get bills asking me to pay for things." "Like the hat?" Elizabeth wanted to know. "That's right." Sarah said, scraping the bottom of the pan. "Will I get letters when I get older?" Elizabeth asked her. "If you write them," her mother said, impatient. Elizabeth stared at her knee. She was not sure what she thought about this world. She had bled bright red blood on the carpet of a beautiful gray room. When they came home, they had had to soak her knee in warm water to get the paper loose of the cut before they could bandage it again. "What was she doing, climbing on the shelves?" Belle asked, disapproving. "I was sitting still," Elizabeth protested. "I'm *sure* you were," her grandmother mocked, sarcastic. Elizabeth started to cry. "Leave her alone, mother," Sarah said; "she wasn't doing anything." "No, she's *never* doing anything," Belle said, "you're spoiling her rotten." Manny came in and picked her up. "*You* spoil her," he said to Belle, "she shouldn't be sleeping in your room; you don't listen to us, she knows she can get away with anything." "What should I do, hit her with a strap when she gets into the bed?" Belle asked. "You and your strap, you think you're a big man, hitting a little girl." "Mother, keep out of it," Sarah said, angry. "He beats her up, and then he complains when she sleeps with me," Belle said, addressing the frying pan. "An animal, no better than an animal." Manny carried her into the living room, and put her down on the couch. "Where are you going?" Sarah asked him. "Out," Manny said. "Good for him," Belle said to the hamburgers. Elizabeth turned over on her side, and began to cry. The dust from the seams in the cushions filled her nostrils, and she started to cough. "He's making her sick," Belle called out from the kitchen, reproachfully. "Oh, mother," Sarah's voice said, fading, and somewhere down the hall, was the slam of a door.

Elizabeth, looking at her knee, thought about the letters, how you had to write them to get them; she had thought somewhere behind the little plot in the back was some vast force in charge of the grandmothers and grandfathers and arguments, who saw to things, saw to the mail, saw no one was left out, whether they were good or whether they were bad. A dark gong sounded deep in her mind. In the middle of the silence, was the fall of blood. In the middle of the kitchen and the warmth and the sputtering pans, were the raised voices and the slam of wood doors. There was something important she didn't know, that no one would tell her. "Mother," Elizabeth called from the depths of the couch, "mother, my ear hurts."

When the car pulled up at her grandparents' on Sundays, Elizabeth would run out first, and up the brick steps. Her grandparents' house was just like theirs, but all the houses on their block were connected, and in the front of their house, was a little square garden filled with rose bushes which Elizabeth thought were the most elegant things she had ever seen in her life. Above the front door bell, was a large square stone which sparkled like diamonds in the sun; Elizabeth thought it must be very precious, and was always surprised when it was still there; she could not understand why someone did not come to steal the stone, to pry it out of the wall, in the middle of the night. She had a fixed idea that there was something wonderful behind that stone, and before the rest of the family would come up after her, she would chip at the mortar holding it in place, waiting for it to move, pressing on it with the palm of her hand; would it swing inward, or out? "Ring the bell, Elizabeth," her mother would say from behind her.

Inside the house, it was always dark. If she wanted to read, she would have to take her book out onto the porch and read on the slatted rocker, but even there, there wasn't much light because the dark green awning shaded the porch all summer long. "Why is it so dark in here, grandma?" Elizabeth asked, and her grandmother told her it was so dark so nothing would fade. "But what do you care if it fades if you can't see it anyway?" "I can see it," her grandmother said, "do you want a cookie?" "Is Aunt Irene up yet?" she asked. Irene was still in college, and most of the time, when they got there, Irene was still asleep. Elizabeth thought this was very glamorous, sleeping half the day, worn out entirely by the drama of the day before. "Go up quietly, and take a look," Sarah told her. She tiptoed up the stairs. Irene was propped up in her bed, an island, supported by books. She was very impressed at how hard it must be to go to "college," if this is what happened; you were worn out all the time, and the books stayed with you in bed in case you should happen to wake up and have the strength to turn a page here, a page there. "Hi, Aunt Irene," Elizabeth said, climbing up on the bed. "Hi, Elizabeth," Irene said, smiling. Lately, Irene didn't seem to smile much. "Are you

103

going to teach me about Frisky today?" she wanted to know. Frisky, the family dog, had never acquired a taste for children. "Thank God," Jacob said, taking the metaphor literally. "As soon as I get up," Irene told her, "why don't you go down to the basement and say hello to Mrs. Guilini?" "Is Frisky out there?" asked Elizabeth, thinking of the black dog lying in wait under a rosebush. "He's there, but he won't bother you," Irene said. Elizabeth went into the kitchen and pretended to be getting a cookie. The cookie jar was an enormously fat woman dressed in voluminous skirts with a turban on her head. She knew the family didn't like her going down to see Mrs. Guilini; they told her this was because she shouldn't bother Mrs. Guilini; it wasn't nice, but Elizabeth knew Mrs. Guilini was glad to see her and always gave her green soda and cookies, and showed her the new toys she was making for her, a baby elephant, a new mother elephant, anything. So after she would ask about going to see Mrs. Guilini, Elizabeth would lurk in doorways and listen. She heard someone say something about Mr. Guilini and how he "drank." She didn't know what was wrong with drinking; everyone she knew did it. She couldn't understand why Mr. Guilini always seemed to stay in a dark room in the back of the basement part of the house; he hardly ever came into the living room, but Elizabeth began to think there was something sinister about him; he was very white and thin and his hands shook, "faded," Elizabeth thought to herself. He looked like an old sheet. Mrs. Guilini always seemed very uncomfortable when he came into the kitchen where she and her brother were sitting on stools drinking their green soda. She would take him out into the hall, and talk to him, and when they came out, they could hear him moving quietly, in the dark room, its door slightly ajar. After Elizabeth had been there awhile, someone in the family would notice she was gone, and someone, a brother, a cousin, would be sent down to get her: "Your mother says to come upstairs right away." Then she would kiss Mrs. Guilini goodbye and as she left, try to see once more into the dark room.

When Irene got up, she began to "teach" Elizabeth about Frisky. She took a wooden slat chair and put it in the middle of the kitchen. Then she sat Elizabeth down on it. "Don't move," she ordered her. Then Irene called Frisky, and stood next to the chair. Frisky circled the chair like a shark, eyeing Elizabeth's leg. "He has to get used to you," Irene said. "Is he getting used to me yet?" Elizabeth asked about a half hour later. "Not yet," Irene said, "sit still." "Can I try patting him now?" she asked Irene; the clock was chiming: a long time must have passed. Elizabeth stuck out her hand. Frisky pulled back his lip over his teeth, and growled. "He's not used to you yet," Irene said. The clock chimed again. Finally, Irene picked Frisky up and put him on Elizabeth's lap. The dog struggled, trying to get down. "What are you doing to that child?" demanded Jacob on a round through the kitchen. "She wants to play with the dog," Irene said. "I do, grandpa," she said. "Better she should play with the stove"; he walked out muttering. "Pat him," Irene commanded. Elizabeth patted the dog's head. He twisted around viciously. "Do it again," Irene said. Elizabeth patted him again. Frisky began to look interested. "I think he's getting used to you," Irene said. After that, Elizabeth took Frisky out with her into the backyard and they would sit on the slatted bench outside Mrs. Guilini's kitchen window. Elizabeth loved the dog, and would hug him as if he were stuffed; "She'll get fleas," her grandmother predicted gloomily. "As long as he doesn't take off an ear," Jacob said. Manny and Sarah watched nervously; they were both terrified of animals. Elizabeth came into the living room carrying Frisky who was dangling his hind legs in mid-air; she had grabbed him under his front paws. "Manny, make her put that dog down," Sarah said, "it's going to bite her." "It's not going to bite her," Irene said, "Frisky likes to be carried." "Since when does Frisky like to be carried?" Manny demanded. "Since Elizabeth started carrying him," Irene said, "no one ever tried it before." "Not after they saw those teeth," said Jacob, giving the dog a wide berth. "And put *on* your shoes, Elizabeth," Sarah said. "That's why she's always sick," Manny said. "It's my ears, not my feet, daddy," Elizabeth said. "You don't know anything about it, put the shoes on *now*," he commanded, "and put that dog down; you're going to get germs."

When they got home, Elizabeth asked her mother what was the matter with Irene. "She wants to get married," Sarah said. "Is that why she stays in bed?" Elizabeth asked her. "She stays in bed because she's unhappy." "Why is she unhappy, mother?" "She's unhappy because she's fat." "What's the matter with being fat?" Elizabeth wanted to know. "What's the matter with being fat?" Belle snorted in the background. "Men don't marry fat women," Sarah said. "If *I* were a man, I'd marry Aunt Irene," Elizabeth said. "Oh no you wouldn't," Belle said. "That's enough, mother," Sarah said, cutting off discussion. Elizabeth asked her father if it was true that no one would marry Irene because she was fat. Her father said Irene was going to get married, and very soon, and Elizabeth would be able to go to the wedding. "Who is she going to marry?" Elizabeth asked, curious. "A good-for-nothing who knows a good thing when he sees it," Belle said, bitterly. "Mother, if you say one more thing about it, there's going to be trouble," Sarah warned her. "But Aunt Irene is a good thing," Elizabeth protested. "That's not what she means," said Sarah, going back into the kitchen. From the living room, she could hear Belle and Sarah arguing; she could hear "divorce" and "fortune hunter," "tragedy," and then, "they always spoiled her, they never should have given her that car." "What car?" Elizabeth asked, materializing. "I told you to drop it, mother," Sarah said, disgusted. "The car they gave her when she promised to lose weight. Your grandparents gave Irene the car so she would get thin, and then she didn't get thin at all; all she did was drive around on her bottom." "Is it so bad that Aunt Irene's getting married?" Elizabeth asked. "It's not good," Belle said, prophetic. "Mother!" Sarah said, slamming down a pot on the stove.

Now, when they went to visit Manny's parents, there were endless conferences in corners; they all seemed to have something to do with Irene. After they talked for awhile, they would call Irene, and after a few minutes, she would start to shout and cry, and then she would run up the stairs and slam the door. Elizabeth would start to go up after her. "Don't go up there, Elizabeth," someone would call after her, and she would trail back down. When no one was watching, she would sneak back up to Irene's room; Irene's eyes were always red. "What's the matter, Aunt Irene?" Elizabeth asked, climbing onto the bed, and holding her hand. She thought maybe Irene was sick and going to die. "They hate me," Irene said, "they don't want me to be happy." "Why not, Aunt Irene?" she asked. "Because they're mean miserable skunks, that's why," and she would burst into tears again. "My parents hit me with hangers and straps; sometimes they hit me with a wooden hanger," Elizabeth told her, "do they hit you, Aunt Irene?" "They don't hit me," Irene said, "they're just trying to ruin my life." When Elizabeth wanted to know why they were doing that, Irene said it was because they didn't like the man she wanted to marry. They said he only wanted to marry her for her money. "Do you have a lot of money?" Elizabeth asked, astonished. She thought only parents had money. "My father does," Irene said, sobbing. Elizabeth pointed out that no one could take his money away from him. "That's what I said," Irene told her, turning over and crying harder. "Why is marriage bad, Aunt Irene?" "What?" "My grandmother said marriage is bad," Elizabeth told her. "Don't listen to her, she doesn't know anything about it," Irene said. "Marriage is the best thing there is. A woman has to get married, and have children." Elizabeth wondered why, if this was true, Irene was always crying and never came out of her room. "You'll get married, Aunt Irene," Elizabeth said. "Not if they can help it," Irene said bitterly.

When Irene finally got married, the wedding was very fancy. It took place in a big marble building, and inside, the walls were marble, and shining. There were little white cups with paper frills and candies in them on everyone's plate. Irene came out dressed in a shiny white dress that gleamed like the walls; her mother told her it was satin. Then a man came and stood next to her. "Who's that?" Elizabeth asked in a whisper. "That's her new husband, Arthur," Sarah told her. "What's wrong with him?" Elizabeth whispered. "Will you keep quiet?" Sarah hissed. After they finished standing there, and the man in black finished singing over their heads, everyone danced with Irene, and Irene kept drinking wine, and her cheeks were bright red, and she looked very happy. Elizabeth was beginning to get very sleepy, and finally she wandered off from the table. Sometime later, someone picked her up and she saw she had fallen asleep on a pile of coats. "Well, that's that," said her mother, looking around at the empty tables, "she got what she wanted." "And now we all have to live with it," Manny said.

The next Sunday, Irene was there with Arthur. No one seemed very happy. "He's going to be working for daddy," Irene announced. Jacob looked uncomfortable, and went off to the kitchen to get some schnapps. Elizabeth missed not having Irene up in her room to visit. She went upstairs herself. She had gotten interested in "asthma"; a friend of hers in school had it; he said when he got it, he couldn't breathe. Elizabeth had a notebook and took it with her when they went to other people's houses, and she would look for books that had anything about asthma, and copy the information down. She went upstairs, and found the *Merck Medical Manual*. It had a whole page and a half. With her pencil, Elizabeth began copying the information out. She would have to find out about "allergies." Then she heard Lillian's baby crying; she drifted out into the hall, following the noise. The baby was lying on Irene's old bed. Very carefully, she picked the baby up. It stopped crying, but then it started again. Elizabeth decided she had better take the baby down to its mother. She held onto the baby very tightly and carefully started down the stairs, one foot at a time. When she got to the bottom, Madelaine saw her, and jumped up, shrieking. Immediately, she was surrounded by people, pulling the baby out of her arms. She was terrified. "What's the matter with you? You could drop her!" Madelaine was screaming at her. Lillian snatched the baby from Madelaine and looked at it carefully. "I hate that baby, I hate it!" Elizabeth screamed, and ran up the stairs to Irene's room, and slammed the door. Sarah came up after her. "I hate that baby, I hate it!" she sobbed again. "I was being careful, I know how to carry babies." "I know, I know," Sarah said, "they were just frightened." "I hate them," Elizabeth shrieked, vehemently. She thought Sarah would slap her across the mouth. "I hate them! They're fat and they scream and they're horrible!" Sarah looked at Elizabeth, and Elizabeth waited to get hit. Instead, Sarah's mouth softened, and she bent over and kissed her daughter. "They shouldn't have yelled at you like that," Sarah said, "come downstairs." "I'm staying here," Elizabeth sobbed. "We'll call you when we get ready to go," Sarah said, standing up. Later, Irene came up. "Let's go out and see Frisky," she suggested. Elizabeth got up and went with her. When they got to the foot of the stairs, Elizabeth heard Manny saying, "She looks just like Irene." "God forbid," Belle said, emphatically. For the rest of the week, every time Elizabeth ate a cookie, Belle would tell her she would grow up to be just like her Aunt Irene, and then what would become of her? She would wind up with a good-for-nothing like Arthur; her parents would have to support her for the rest of her life; people would laugh when she went by on the street. "Stupid old witch!" Elizabeth screamed at her. "You take after the Kamens all right," Belle said, "you're just an animal, that's all you are." Elizabeth picked up a glass of milk and threw it at her grandmother. "I wish you were dead," she screamed. This time Manny got up from the table, and took off his belt. "I'll teach you to talk to your grandmother that way," he said, advancing on her. "But she said . . ." Elizabeth had no time to finish, the belt was cutting into the back of her legs. The world fell at her feet in bright pieces. She was sent to bed without supper, and the next morning, she took her notebook on asthma over to her friend Esther's house. When it was lunch time, she asked if she could eat lunch with Esther. "If your mother says it's all right," Esther's mother said; "call her up." Elizabeth called up and said she was not coming home for lunch. "Why not?" Sarah asked. "Because I don't want to," Elizabeth said, and hung up. "Give your father a kiss," Sarah said to her when Manny came home. "I have homework to do," Elizabeth said, and stalked off in the direction of her room. After that, when Manny came home, Elizabeth, who had already eaten dinner, would be locked in her room with a book, and she would not come out again, except to go to the bathroom, before going to bed.

Chapter 6

To get to the Institute for Technicological Studies, Elizabeth drove along the lake front, and then, halfway to the Loop, she would turn left, and drive another ten blocks west. She loved the drive along the bright band of water, blinding on sunny days, gray water flecked with white ice in the winter, water licking and splashing at the top of the rocks, reaching the road with their shiny, forked tongues. The wind from the lake drove the water; it drove the car; it drove Elizabeth. She had not had such a sense of motion since her last day on roller skates. She found herself thinking about her skates, all her old things, more and more as she drove. It was inconceivable to her now that she could not remember when she had stopped skating; she could remember everything about the neighborhood ritual

109

of the roller skates, how the wheels of the skates were relatively smooth when the skates were new, how, gradually, their flinty wheels dented with nicks, roughed against the thumb by the cement. She could remember putting on the skates, tightening their four teeth against the leather soles of her shoe, losing her skate key, trailing around with her skates hanging over her arm by their straps until she found someone else with a key, putting them on, setting off into the wind, stopping by sailing, arms out in front, into someone's low wall or gate. She could remember how each square of the block was part of a map of a country holding magnificent secrets, and how, at night, some of the blocks sunk down deep under the sidewalks of earth, taking whoever stood on them down to the hidden land below. But you had to stand on the right squares, and stand on them at the right time. Underneath was the perfect place Elizabeth thought about all day while the class was learning to read; she would draw pictures of it on the extra pieces of paper she put between the leaves of her notebook, when the class was learning long division. This perfect place was filled with swimming pool after emerald swimming pool; the whole place was tiled with green tiles, and everything shimmered and shone like water. Elizabeth could not imagine anything more perfect than a secret place under the ground, filled with pools, and gradually, she began to believe that every night, when she fell asleep, her bed sunk under the floor like an elevator going down, stopping when it got to the shining place of the pools. She even tried persuading some of her friends that they could come with her if they did special things, if they lent her their skate key, and they would always complain that if they had gone down to this place with the pools, they would remember in the morning when they got up. "Oh no," Elizabeth told them, "as soon as the bed comes back up into the room, you forget you were there." "Then why don't you forget?" they wanted to know. "Because I found it," Elizabeth said.

Every day, when it wasn't raining or snowing, she would put on her skates; when she turned the corner, she was in another country; when she went past stores, she was on a secret mission. When she came home, her knees no longer bore the ruby runes of blood, the maps of her journey, the encounters with the rough earth, her secret history. She was getting better. And then one day, the skates vanished as completely as if they had been dropped into the water. When Elizabeth and Mark went to the skating rink, Elizabeth could hardly balance; to stop herself, she would have to coast into the railing, or into Mark. She was afraid to go around the track too fast. The wooden skates were smooth; nothing felt right. Mark always felt sorry for the "city kids" who had to skate on the sidewalk; they had not roller-skated at all in Wisconsin, where he lived; they had ice-skated on the frozen lake. Mark was very proud of this.

Several times when she was a child, her grandfather Daniel had taken Elizabeth to Rockefeller Center; he wanted her to learn to ice-skate at the rink. Elizabeth would stand for a long time looking down at the skaters; she was fascinated by their short skirts, the way they glided and twirled. They could not be real! The men and women approached each other slowly, gliding, and slowly, glided apart and away. Their motion was as magical and as strange as the trapeze people floating through the air under the flapping ceiling of the tent. Elizabeth could not wait to put on her skates with their gleaming blades, like knives. The Instructor helped her put them on; they led her to the rink. Elizabeth's feet collapsed inwards; she found herself standing on her ankles. No matter what she did, she could not stand up on her skates. "I think her ankles are weak," the skating Instructor told Daniel. "She's always spraining them," he said. She tried and tried. She could not stand up straight. Finally, she held on to the rail and watched her grandfather sail out into the middle of the circle of ice, and begin revolving, like a top. She began to be afraid the circle of ice was only a thin skin over black water; at any minute, it could open. There was no way she could get across the ice to her grandfather. He floated back to her, smiling. "I don't like it here," she said.

Now Elizabeth seemed to have forgotten her body; she seemed to have forgotten everything but work. She liked the new school where she taught, its rows and rows of engineers, their slide rules, neat and precise, the little cases of surgical-gleaming instruments the architects carried with them everywhere; she liked the lost look in their eyes when she said, "I am Miss Kamen. This is English One. Is everyone in the right class?" Their fear of books amused and touched her, and she liked to teach them to read in

111

ways they understood, sorting out facts, making inferences, choosing the simplest, most elegant "hypothesis," the one with the least contradictions, rejecting theories in the absence of verifying procedures. They learned very fast. At the end of her first semester, when she collected her papers, she found a note from one of the students. He had crossed out six lines and then written, "that's all I really know about the man, 'the stranger.' It seems to me though, that there's a little bit of him in everyone. Too many people are unwilling to get involved with others, and want to keep things on a strictly physical basis. From what I've seen, that's about all engineering and physics and chemistry amounts to. It's just trying to understand everything physical; and it's implicitly assumed that nothing more exists. The 'scientists' in my dorm—the only people I've been able to observe—have been drawn to the physical world because they've failed or been rejected everywhere else (human relationships). I said failed, I meant hurt. By putting labels on everything, there is little chance of being hurt again. Engineering is so secure because it lets one understand all things. I guess I came here for the security which it offers. To conclude, I want to say that your class has been the most enjoyable and educational course I have ever taken here. It's certainly been the only interesting one. I want to thank you for the intelligent comments you have made on the subject material, because I believe I have learned from them (the comments)."

When Elizabeth handed back the finals, she pretended to have misplaced this one, and she put it in the box where she kept her special papers. Before the term was over, she asked Mr. Archer, the student, what he was going to major in. He told her he was transferring to the State University, and he thought he was changing his major. He said his parents were very upset, but he couldn't study to make them happy. Elizabeth had never seen anyone look so miserable. "Well," she said, "good luck. You're very intelligent; you should do whatever you decide to do very well." He smiled and stood up; neither of them said anything. "I'm never going to see him again!" Elizabeth thought to herself, horrified. "I will never know how this is going to turn out!" It has to be like that, it has to be like that, she kept saying to herself, incantatory. When he left, she felt as if he had gone out the door and fallen into the dark air like a stone. She sat down at her desk, and took out her pen. She had a lot more papers to grade. Some of them were going to have a lecture on the evils of irresponsibility, poor planning, lack of self-discipline, the works. "Dylan Thomas' *The Force That Through The Green Fuse Drives The Flower* is a poem about time. In the poem, the poet links his life to time. Time is only a force; it is neither good nor evil, only necessary." Well, she thought to herself, this one was in danger of getting an A. Around here, students came in when they got A's or B's to find out what had gone wrong—they expected C's; they were resigned from the first day of the course. "Time is only a force; it is neither good nor evil, only necessary." Elizabeth stared at the sentence again. It was true; in the middle of it there was a semi-colon; used correctly, it looked rare as a jewel. In the beginning of the course, Mr. McLean used to use the semi-colon as a substitute for an apostrophe, and when Elizabeth demanded to know what he thought he was doing, didn't it at least *look* peculiar to him, he had said desperately that it was the closest thing to what he wanted that he could find on the keyboard. "Then *write* out your papers. Or correct them with a pen. This is ridiculous." Miserable, Mr. McLean nodded. "Well, that's the bell," Elizabeth said, "what now?" "Chemistry," Mr. McLean beamed, "that's no trouble." *"Please,"* Elizabeth said, "you are talking to an old pre-med major. If you can use those scales, you can use the semi-colon."

On Saturday, Armand met her for lunch. "How can you stand it there?" he wanted to know. "What do you mean, Armand?" she answered. "All those crazy scientists, they can't even read." "They can read, Armand," she said, "they're very intelligent." "They don't have *souls,* Elizabeth," he insisted, sounding upset. "Who told you," she asked, "Sister Saint John? Divine Revelation?" "They can't think," he insisted gloomily, poking at his ice cream. "Armand, eat that, for Christsake," Elizabeth exclaimed, "what do you need, a knife?" "They are all very stupid," he added, staring at her copy of *The Wasteland* where it lay on the white tablecloth. "Oh God," Elizabeth said, "I think I'm going to have some dessert. Call the waitress." "Aren't you on a diet?" Armand asked. "I *was,*" Elizabeth said, glaring. She ate half of the hot fudge sundae; then she put the spoon down on the plate. "All right, Armand," she said, "tell me what you don't like about scientists." "They experiment on people," he said, making circles on

113

the tablecloth with his spoon. "Not at the Institute, they don't." She sounded much sharper than she intended. She could see the blue numbers marching down Armand's arm, like the stock numbers on the coat tickets at Gimbel's. "You have got," she said, "to stop feeling sorry for yourself." "Easy for you to say," he said gloomily, eyeing her sundae. "That's what you think," Elizabeth said, pushing her plate across.

The next day, Elizabeth gave her class a lecture on irresponsibility and the evils of self-pity. It was a good day for a lecture; she was still enraged with Armand, and it was easy to give lectures when she was already angry. She stared menacingly at the thirty white faces nervously peering in her direction. They looked as if they were afraid to move a muscle; in lack of motion, there was safety. In the middle of the lecture, Elizabeth began to hear her own words. She remembered a conversation she had had with Nancy the previous month; she had insisted *anyone* could write a thesis in six months if they picked the right topic. She had become positively messianic. When she hung up, the exaltation bled into the walls. "I am not anyone," she had thought to herself, bleakly. Now, hearing herself lecturing the students, she was ashamed. How could she give them lectures on self-discipline when she went home and graded papers and read Edgar Rice Burroughs' *Fighting Men of Mars?*

The English Department was in an old building; it looked like something out of a Charles Addams cartoon. Elizabeth loved it. The rest of the campus was new and raw and the ghost of Mies Van der Rohe floated in the trees, disciplining the disordered leaves. But the English department was on the third floor under the gables, and the wooden stairs were so narrow that only one person could go up and down at a time. Halfway up, someone would have to wait on a landing until the other had gone down and past. It reminded Elizabeth of a ship going through a lock. The secretary was a little old lady who Elizabeth thought was a biddy; then she found out she had worked for the Army during the war, and lived in China for years. Elizabeth fell in love with Mrs. White and her wrinkles, her cheek which pleated under her hand when she leaned her head on it. She loved sitting in the department lounge, which was a shabby little room opening out from the office, furnished with hand-me-downs from faculty apartments. They would all sit on the gray couch from John Greenberg's house, and sooner or later, someone would move abruptly, and the couch would slide out from the wall, and everyone would grab at each other to keep from falling backwards onto the floor. There was a remarkable absence of disagreement. There seemed to be very little to fight about. Elizabeth noticed that she was getting very fond of John, who looked like a cross between Edward G. Robinson and the enchanted frog waiting to be turned into the prince. Whatever he sat on began to look like a lily leaf. Then, one afternoon, she saw him sitting on the couch in Doctor Greene's office, but when she said hello, he didn't answer her. She asked him about it later, and he was very apologetic; he said he just hadn't expected to see her there; he didn't realize who it was. He asked Elizabeth which doctor she was going to see, and she told him. He wanted to know how long she had been going, and she told him it had been a year and a half. Then she asked him how long he had been going. "Seven years." When he saw her expression, he added, "But I'm much better." Elizabeth looked at John now as if he were the Ghost of Christmas Future. That night, she went home and typed up her dissertation proposal. Before it was approved, she began the first chapter.

Now the days became homogeneous. She would get up at a quarter of seven, earlier if it had been damp the night before, because her 1950 Plymouth would not start in damp weather; her students called it the "Blue Bomb," and all of them seemed to enjoy watching it oxidizing from dull blue to iridescent purple. She had not washed it since Mark left: the purple glaze was its badge of independence. Before getting out of bed, she would swallow the two aspirins she had put on the windowsill the night before, and then lie in bed waiting for them to take effect. If she got up too quickly, the cold and the pain in her joints would make her sick to her stomach, and dizzy. "That's shock," Doctor Greene told her. "Eat some of those candy kisses with the aspirin." She would get dressed in the bathroom where it was warm. Her hair was her main concern. By now, it was down to her waist. She didn't have any idea of what to do with it. When she woke up in the morning, a long strand would have gotten into her mouth, or tangled itself around an arm, or she would turn over on it, jerking her head backwards. She never thought about cutting it. She wore it permanently now, braided, the braids wound around the top of her head like a crown. "You look like my Polish grandmother," Doctor Greene commented. "I'd rather look like your Polish grandmother than a superannuated Alice in Wonderland," Elizabeth said, but she wasn't happy about it; she loved her hair when it was down, and one day on campus, the wind had disentangled it all and it had fallen about her face and down, and there she was, a cone of hair. She had fled into the Ladies Room, savagely jabbing the long steel pins into her hair and against her scalp. "I didn't know those were the only two choices," commented Doctor Greene.

When she finished with her hair, Elizabeth got dressed. She rarely looked at her body, and dressed expeditiously. She had no interest in jewelry, or clothes, or shoes. Then she would get in the car and drive to the school and eat breakfast in the student cafeteria. She would pick a table in the corner, and face out through the metal and glass. While she ate the same pecan roll and cup of coffee she had for breakfast every day, she would read the book she had to teach, or grade papers. But she liked the noise of people around her, the company of the sleepy, stunned students at their tables, clumping closer together as exams approached, predicting disaster. After a few months, one of her students, who was older, began to join her; at first, she was annoyed, and then she was angry with herself for looking forward to it. One day when he didn't come, she was terribly disappointed.

After breakfast, she would teach. By lunchtime, she was finished. Then she would drive downtown to see Doctor Greene. When she got home, she would grade papers until dinner time. After dinner, she would watch "The Bullwinkle Show," and then "Batman," and as soon as "Batman" was over, she would turn off the television and start writing the thesis. She wrote at least eleven pages a night. At three o'clock, she would stop, and get into bed with Edgar Rice Burroughs. The books dragged her into sleep like bricks. Every few months, she would be so exhausted that she would have to stay home a few days and sleep. She would feel terribly guilty, but she began to feel less and less so. Now, every time a note arrived from the chairman, she no longer expected it to be a note of dismissal. Armand would call up and ask her if she wanted to go out for dinner; did she want to go to the movies.

"I can't; I have to work," she said. "There are other things besides work," Armand informed her. Elizabeth didn't say anything. "Maybe I'm not one of them?" Armand asked nervously. "Armand," Elizabeth said, "I have *got* to finish this, I can't be a baby forever." "What a horrible thought," said Armand, crabby. "Are you avoiding me?" he asked next. "I'm not avoiding you, I'm busy," Elizabeth said; she had the phone scrunched between her shoulder and ear, and with her free hand was grading a paper. "I shall ever have the fondest memories of you, Armand," she said, getting ready to hang up. "Of *me*," Armand said, *"I'm* not going anywhere." "As long as you like it where you are," Elizabeth said, abstracted, hanging up. Ten minutes later, the doorbell rang. "Well, well," said Elizabeth, "faster than a speeding bullet, jumping over small buildings in a single bound." "Do you think the Institute might hire me?" Armand wanted to know. "How should I know?" Elizabeth asked. She knew if she showed the slightest enthusiasm, he would change the topic to his doctor and how the doctor would leap upon his emaciated frame from his trampoline chair. "Well, I thought I'd write the chairman a letter; what's his name?" "Sloane, for the four hundredth time," Elizabeth said; "do you want me to deliver the letter for you? don't you trust the mailman?" "What are these?" Armand asked, picking up a stack of papers. "Papers," Elizabeth said. Armand sat down on the couch and started reading the graded ones. He asked her about some of her comments. "You sit there and read and I will go type," Elizabeth told him. When she was through, Armand was still on the couch reading the papers. "Sloane?" Armand asked. "Sloane," Elizabeth said.

Elizabeth heard about the interview a week later. When she got to the Faculty Club, there was a ghastly silence hovering over the hamburgers and pickles. "What's going on here?" she asked. "Do you know an Armand Waterman?" John asked her. She said she did. "We interviewed him," John said; he looked as if he had come from a particularly vivid automobile accident. "And?" Elizabeth asked, curious. "He had very good letters of reference, evidently he's very bright." "How was the *interview?*" Elizabeth demanded. Robert Sloane coughed. "Speak freely," said Elizabeth, "I've known him for years. I am beyond surprise." John looked at Robert, who nodded. "Well," he began, "first, he told us what the exact budget of the FBI was, and when we asked him how he knew, he said he knew for a fact." "Why were you talking to him about the FBI?" Elizabeth asked, puzzled. "That was after he told us not to trust anyone over thirty," Robert put in gloomily. "Why were you talking about that?" Elizabeth wanted to know. "He didn't seem to talk about his thesis. Is his thesis about drugs, Elizabeth?" *"Dreams,"* Elizabeth said. "I thought it was about drugs," Sloane said, befuddled. "He kept talking about opium, how opium affected creation, he went on and on." "Did you ask him about teaching?" *"Of course* we asked him about teaching." They stared at her, disapproving. "What did he say?" "He said he wanted to teach because he had a special philosophy of teaching." "Which was?" "Which was that he would strip the masks of social convention from his students and liberate them into themselves. Robert asked him what would happen if the students didn't want to be liberated, and he said *everyone* wanted to be liberated. We also noticed he was very thin." "He's stripped off a lot of masks, I guess," Elizabeth said, "are you going to hire him?" "Do you think we should?" Robert asked her. Elizabeth thought about her students and their semi-colons; "no," she said. "We're not," said Robert, "someone should talk to the chairman of your department about him." "I'll do it," Elizabeth said.

When she got home, she parked the car and went to the supermarket. Armand was wandering lonely as a cloud among the fruits and vegetables. "I want to talk to you, Armand." It turned out Armand thought he had gotten the job. "You didn't want the job," she insisted, "you wanted to go there and carry on and you had a captive audience." Armand feebly insisted that he did want the job. "If it ever occurs to you that you will have real live students in your room, you'll get a job," she said, furious. "Maybe it's because my thesis isn't finished?" Armand said, hopefully. Elizabeth walked away abruptly. When Armand tried to get on line behind her, she told him the other line was shorter. "What nonsense!" she exclaimed, apropos of nothing. She wouldn't talk to him for almost a week. "You're acting just like your father," Doctor Greene pointed out. "Armand is not my child," Elizabeth retorted. "I know that," Doctor Greene said, "but do you?"

By the end of the year, Elizabeth could not believe she had once had so much trouble about calling the men by their first names; they had seemed octogenarians to her at first, and she had felt disrespectful when she called them Robert, or Allan, or John. Now they seemed her age, or no age at all. She was very comfortable with them. Her thesis had finished itself one night in the spring, and she had piled two towers of books on her desk to be read for the Special Field exams. She sat in the middle of them like an offering on an altar. She was beginning to be intensely jealous of people who had nothing to do, who could go to parties and meet people, who could go to the beach and meet more people, browning in their skin, and stare at the water, and pages with the light rippling on the print like water. She began to think that if she stopped going to see Doctor Greene, she would have much more time; she would have much more money; she would not have to teach an extra course. She began to discuss it. One day, she said she had gotten over her world's greatest unpublished critic syndrome. The next day she came home and found a letter in the mail telling her an article from her thesis was going to be published. When she went downtown, she brought the doctor flowers from the flower stand in the subway station. "We'll have to discuss this," he said, peering at them, but he looked pleased, and began hunting around for a vase. A week before the exams, Elizabeth began to feel as if she was going to die of isolation. Armand came over and mumbled about how he was going to work on his thesis this summer, and how it was just as well he didn't have a job, or he wouldn't be able to do it. Elizabeth glared at him balefully; did he think she was a sheet of glass? but she was glad he was there.

The day Elizabeth finished her exams, it was ninety degrees. She came home and turned off the air conditioner. Then she took off all of her clothes and stood in front of the full length mirror and inspected herself carefully. Her stomach was flatter than she thought. Her bottom had an odd shape. Her breasts were very large, and her face was very pretty. Her hair was impossible; she would have to cut it. A person with a Ph.D. could not have hair like that. "Doctor Kamen," she said to herself, trying it on, tucking the hair under her hand to see what it would look like short, "Doctor Kamen." Benita rang the bell. "Come on over," she said, "I'm having a party." "I'll be right there," Elizabeth called from the bathroom, "who's coming?"

A few days after she got her hair cut, Elizabeth put on her new dress and high heels and went to see her thesis director. She sat down, and crossed one stockinged leg over another. She was surprised to see how thin they were. "Well, Elizabeth?" he said, smiling. "Well," she said, "I've decided to go back to New York." "Why New York?" he asked. "I want to find a Jewish husband," she said. He stared at her, then at his pipe. When he looked up, he looked ten years younger, and mischievous. "In that case, I'll have to write you some letters of recommendation." "I'd appreciate it," Elizabeth said. "And about time, too," he said, as he saw her to the door.

Although it had not seemed possible, the spring semester was coming to an end. The tower of papers on the lid of the black phonograph had shrunk from a leaning tower of Pisa to a mere five or six, which lay there sloppy, with no purposeful look. It was Sunday, and it was after twelve, and the bell would be beginning to ring. In the last three years since Mark had left, Elizabeth had found apartments in the building for five or six of her friends; on Sundays, they would drop in on each other as soon as they saw the shades on the back porch kitchen windows go up. Elizabeth was sitting in a rattan chair counting her papers, thinking she spent more time counting them than grading them, when the bell rang. It was Armand. He looked vaguely green. He wanted to know if she wanted to go for a walk to the lake. Elizabeth said she did, but first she had to grade six papers; in the meantime, why didn't he go over to Benita's and see if she wanted to come with them. "*I* could grade the papers," Armand said, hopeful. "No you can't, Armand," Elizabeth said, "I have to do it." "But you don't like grading them, and I've never done it." Armand was whining; he sounded about six years old. "Look," said Elizabeth, "*I* have to grade the papers; if the students complain about the grades, I have to know what they're talking about. If they don't complain, I still have to know who's learning what, so *I* have to grade them. Why don't you get Benita, and we'll leave in an hour?" "Do you think I'll get a teaching job next year?" Armand wanted to know. "Not if you walk in and tell them your secret theories about who set fire to the Hindenberg dirigible and who really sunk the Titanic, you won't," Elizabeth said. "You're always exaggerating," Armand mourned, "can I go make some coffee?" "Go ahead," Elizabeth said, "make some cookies while you're at it; they're in the refrigerator." "Cookies?" "They're the kind you slice from a roll of dough, just put them on a piece of aluminum foil, and put it in the oven." "How do you light the oven?" Armand asked her. "I don't know," Elizabeth said, "I've never done it myself. Why don't you find out and come back and report?" "Very funny," said Armand, trudging off down the hall.

Elizabeth and Benita walked out to the lake. Elizabeth knew Benita and Armand had been sleeping together during the winter; Benita had kept her posted during her marathon calls. She would call Elizabeth late at night and tell her all about Armand's history in Belgium, how he had been separated from his parents during the war, how he had been in a concentration camp, gotten out, and been taken care of by some nuns in a convent. Benita wanted to make sure Elizabeth knew all about his history, but Elizabeth had never let Armand talk much about it; the last thing he needed, she thought, was to take daily inventories of previous disasters. Still, when Benita kept telling her more and more about Armand, she couldn't stop her from talking; she wanted to know more.

When they got to the lake, it was bright blue. The radar tower the army had built on the Point was revolving, and they could see all the way down to the white and gray skyline of the Loop on the left, and to the right, traces of Gary, Indiana. Benita wanted to know if they remembered the time the three of them and Mark and their friend Robert had stuffed themselves into Mark's Porsche and driven to Valparaiso where the sand dunes were, and the lake, and Robert had found a vine hanging from a tree next to a soft canyon in the sand, and had swung on it, and half-way across the canyon, the vine had broken, and he and the vine had tumbled down into it, Costello wrestling a leafy snake. "It's a good thing he's a doctor," Elizabeth had said, and they scrambled down, sliding down the sandy incline to see if Robert had broken any bones. "You Jane!" Robert had boomed, springing up as Elizabeth got to him, and hugging her hard. Elizabeth had not pulled away, but had stayed, pressed against Robert's chest for a long time. "Come on, come on," Mark called from the top of the hill. The ground was sandy and covered with leaves; he had been sure Bob had not been hurt. "We're coming," Bob said, "aren't we,

121

Elizabeth?" He looked at her, questioning. "We're coming," Elizabeth echoed, solemn. "Monogamous maniac," she said to herself now, remembering. When they got to the top of the hill, Mark insisted they all race to the top of the dune, the highest, overlooking the lake. "I am not racing," said Elizabeth, taking off her sneakers, feeling the damp sand squeeze between her toes, "you go ahead." "I'm not racing, either," Bob said, putting out his arm to steady her, wobbling on one foot like a gawky stork. But Mark had already whipped the others on up the hill. Bob sat down next to her, and took off his shoes. "Elizabeth?" he said. "What?" she asked, not looking at him. "How can you stand him?" he asked. "I don't know," she said, feeling very endangered. "I used to think he was, sort of, well . . . my Platonic ideal . . . that we were fated together, destined, or something." Bob didn't say anything for awhile. "And now what do you think?" he asked. "That he's a bloody ass," Elizabeth said. "We'd better climb that hill."

As they climbed, she remembered again the trip to Maine, she and Edna and Mark and Ralph camping on Mount Desert Island. Mark had decided that they were all to climb a mountain. Edna had decided that she was staying in her tent with her psychology book. But Elizabeth was afraid to refuse, and so she had gone. She had never climbed a mountain before, and now she kept wanting to turn around and look down, on the valleys, the trees, the rivers winding, the cars contracting to stones. "You can look when we get to the top," Mark kept saying, and she had to hurry after him, or she would get lost. As they climbed, the mountain got mistier and mistier. Finally, all she could see was her hand; she could not even see Mark in front of her: all she could hear was the sound of his voice. *"Wait,* for God's sake," she called out to an animated cloud, and gradually, his form emerged from the mist, gray and black and damp, like a wet, twisted stick. When they got to the top of the mountain, the whole site was shrouded in a thick, white, wet mist, and when Elizabeth put her hand out in front of her, she could not see her fingers. They were all freezing cold; it had been hot at the foot of the mountain, and they were wearing shorts and T-shirts; Elizabeth had on a sleeveless blouse. "We'd better get started down," Mark said, "there are two trails, one is difficult, and one is easy. The difficult one looks more interesting." "I am taking the easy one,"

Elizabeth said, "and so are you." She had never been angrier in her life. When they got to the bottom of the mountain, Elizabeth was exhausted and furious. Mark decided he wanted to climb the smaller mountain nearby. "You go ahead," she said, watching him trail off with Ralph. She drove one of the cars back to the camping site. "Where are they?" Edna wanted to know. "Running up and down another mountain," Elizabeth said.

Edna had come out on this trip with high hopes; in the romantic woods, she was sure she would be able to seduce Ralph. They would have to share a tent; things would be easy. But on the first night, Ralph had taken his sleeping bag and trotted into the clearing saying there was nothing better than sleeping under the stars. As she fell asleep, Elizabeth could hear Edna's muffled sobs sifting out of her tent. "What did she expect?" Mark asked. Elizabeth pretended she was already asleep. When they woke up in the morning, it was raining; it rained all day. Edna's hopes rose as the drops fell. Ralph would *have* to sleep in the tent tonight. That night, Ralph told Edna they should sleep head to foot the way they had when he was in camp; that way, she wouldn't catch his cold. In their tent, Mark and Elizabeth could hear them arguing. "This is turning out just great," Mark said. "It certainly is," said Elizabeth, "it certainly is."

In the morning, Edna refused to come out of her tent. When Ralph came out, he said she had been talking about taking all her sleeping pills, and when he tried to talk to her, she told him to leave her alone. "What's for breakfast?" he wanted to know. "Nothing," Elizabeth answered. "What do you mean, nothing?" asked Ralph, outraged. Last night, Mark had insisted they save all the sweetrolls for breakfast along with their eggs; they had to be economical. Elizabeth and Edna had protested; they were hungry *now*. But Mark and Ralph had prevailed. Elizabeth motioned to the far end of the camp site. A trail of paper and cellophane marched into the woods. "Raccoon," Elizabeth said, spiteful, "I'll go talk to Edna." She picked up the dripping flap of the tent and went in. Edna was lying in a tangle of wet blankets and sleeping bags; her tent had leaked. Drops of water clung to the tent walls like liquid bees. She made a great many self-pitying remarks, the gist of which was that when everyone left her alone, she was going to take all of her sleeping pills. "Don't be so selfish," Elizabeth said, snuggling down

123

on the other sleeping bag, "you're ruining the trip. If you don't come out, I have to go and talk to Ralph and Mark." "Who's making breakfast?" Edna asked, almost audible. "The raccoon made it and ate it," Elizabeth said. "Good for it," Edna said viciously, "I wish they'd starve to death." "So do I," Elizabeth said, "but I'm hungry myself." "Let's make them take us into town and *buy* us breakfast, it serves them right," Edna suggested, stirring embryonically; her blonde head was beginning to emerge from under the pillow and blanket. "We're going into town," Edna announced as they emerged. When they came back, it was still raining. Ralph and Mark strung ropes from tree to tree, and hung the wet blankets and sleeping bags from Edna's tent around the fire. The rain stopped, and the four of them sat around the fire, frozen, watching the smoke rise from the wet clothes like ghosts, disappearing, helpless, released, into the trees.

Two weeks later, Elizabeth found out she had gotten her fellowship back; Mark found out his thesis advisor was going back to the University after his leave. They began packing to return to Chicago.

"I remember the sand dunes," Elizabeth said, "sometimes I think that's my trouble, I don't forget anything." "Well, it comes in handy for exams," Armand said. "True," Elizabeth agreed. They began running into people from their seminars. Everyone wanted to know what the Special Field exams had been like, was Elizabeth really finished? "She's really finished," Armand said proudly, like a parent. "Let's eat some lunch," Benita said, and they all trailed off to the local delicatessen. "We should rent a room here," Armand suggested; he looked around for a waitress. "Waitress!" Armand boomed in his cavernous voice, striking the table with his fist. Two came running toward the table. Elizabeth and Benita hid behind the winged menus, grinning.

On Monday, Elizabeth went to the Institute to turn in her grades. Mrs. White wished her a happy vacation, and Elizabeth told her she would see her in a few weeks because she was teaching during the summer. As she went down the stairs, Elizabeth thought how she would never see Mr. Archer again, she would never see Mr. McLean again; she wouldn't know whether they would end up living in houses like the little pasteboard ones near the junior colleges that had plastic reindeers with red noses on their lawns, plastic dwarfs climbing their walls. "But you will have *new* ones," she thought to herself, "you will forget all about these in a few weeks. Whenever Elizabeth was upset, she found she was lecturing herself like a strict mother. The bottom landing was already flooded by the brilliant blue day. Elizabeth wondered again about the conservatism of the campus; at the University, the students were rioting: they had kidnapped the Dean, whom they were holding for academic ransom, and occupied the administration building. Here, if five students stayed after class to ask questions, the campus guards suspected a riot. Even the modern, mirrored buildings were defeated today: they had gone under, reflecting the riot of spring, their black ribs unnoticeable as trunks. "The end of another year," Elizabeth thought to herself, putting her foot down on the next to the last wooden step, when she stepped into the blue air, her ankle twisted, she found herself on her back, staring up into the unwinking sky, its pupil of blue. Elizabeth sat up, feeling for her ankle with her hand. Her books were scattered around her like cards from a deck. It was already swollen. "Oh no," said Elizabeth; she could not believe it; she was too astonished to cry. "Are you all right, Elizabeth?" it was John, his frog face completely concerned. "I think I sprained my ankle," Elizabeth said. John put his briefcase down on the top step and came down to look. "It's swelling up," he said, "it's turning black and blue." "I have to go to the doctor's," Elizabeth told him. "You want it X-rayed?" John asked, worried. "It's my head I'm worried about," Elizabeth said, "I was going downstairs, thinking about leaving, and how I was sorry the year was ending, and I fell, I used to do this all the time at P.S. 206." "Well, you can't go downtown like that," John told her. "I'll get the car and drive you down." When Elizabeth stood up, she found she could limp along. "I'm getting better at this," Elizabeth said, "when I was a child, I'd do such a good job they'd put my foot in a cast." She was looking closely at John, as if for the first time. He was a whole head shorter than she was; he was very ugly and seemed always out of breath. He also seemed very interested in her. Elizabeth wondered if that was what Mrs. White was smiling about when she saw them together. They did look ridiculous together, she thought. When they got downtown, Elizabeth limped out of the car and to the elevator. John had double-parked. "I'm going to wait for you," he said. "Don't be silly," Elizabeth said, "you have to work."

John had been writing a book on E. M. Forster for twelve years; she could not understand how anyone could work on anything for so long. He also lived at home with his father, who was even shorter than he was, and hard of hearing. Whenever she tried to call John to leave a message, she would end by shouting louder and louder, and in the end, losing hope, would finish by bellowing her name. "*Liz*abeth," she would hear the voice at the other end say with relief and satisfaction, and they would hang up. John always called everyone back immediately; he never had any idea of what anyone wanted. "I'll wait," he said.

When Elizabeth got into Doctor Greene's office, she did a lot of crying. She told him what she was thinking about when she fell down the stairs. "You *do* have a lot of trouble with partings," the doctor said. "I don't need you to tell me that," Elizabeth said bitterly. "Nevertheless, it's true," the doctor answered, "I think we should look into this some more." Elizabeth didn't say anything. The light fell through the room, floating its golden dust, Midas-touched. "What are you thinking about?" the doctor asked. "I'm thinking about how I'm never going to get any better," Elizabeth said. "That is, of course, possible," said the doctor, with his faint touch of an accent. "What, particularly, are you not going to get better about?" "I'm not going to get married that's what," Elizabeth said; she was trying so hard not to cry that her throat was beginning to hurt. "The only men I know are Armand, who's still waiting to be toilet-trained, and Robert, who's getting married, and John, who looks like the enchanted frog, and you, and you're already married. Would you marry me if you weren't married?" she wanted to know. "No," Doctor Greene said. "Why not?" Elizabeth demanded. "For one thing," Doctor Greene said, "I know too much about you. Romance needs some illusion, after all." "Excuses, excuses, you just don't like me, I can't say I blame you." Elizabeth focused on Doctor Greene's ceramic ashtray: "you and your ceramic amoebas," she said to the walls, accusing. "You *are* in an embryonic state," Doctor Greene said, "you will have to be patient." "I've been patient for two years, and where has it gotten me?" she demanded; she sounded whiney. "It's gotten you a Ph.D., some self-respect, quite a bit, I'd say." "It hasn't gotten me married," Elizabeth complained, querulous. "Well," said Doctor Greene, "let's think about that.

Who would have wanted to marry you with your braids pinned on your head like my Polish grandmother, refusing to get a job, insisting your life depended on Mark, convinced you were mentally retarded, incapable of finding two pairs of shoes, collapsing each time you passed a mirror?" "Armand would have married me," Elizabeth protested. "I think," said Doctor Greene, "it is a good sign you have not married until now. Before, you were not in a position to make a good marriage. Now you are." "There are people who don't get married, aren't there?" "There are," Doctor Greene said, "and that is very sad. You may have to face the fact that, at your age, the best men are already married; you may never find anyone good enough for you. One of my colleagues got married last week: she was sixty. She married a widower, also an analyst." "Why didn't she get married before?" Elizabeth asked, horrified. So this doom did befall people, perpetual loneliness! "Bad luck, maybe. She was also a brilliant woman, very successful. You may have to marry a divorced man, or a man with children. You cannot afford to be too casual about these things." "For every pot there's a proper little cover," Elizabeth muttered. "What's that?" "That's an old Estonian folk saying my friend's mother keeps saying. She says sooner or later, everyone gets married." The doctor didn't say anything. "She's been in this country twenty-five years and she hasn't remarried." Elizabeth thought some more. "Her daughter isn't married, either." "Your students are not your children," the doctor said gently. "I know that: I'm not always taking them home with me, the way some people are." She meant John. "When I get married, I want to be happy," Elizabeth said. There was a long pause. Then Doctor Greene said, sadly, "The last thing most people need is happiness." "*I* need happiness," Elizabeth insisted. "In that case, you may be in a position to make a very good marriage," Doctor Greene said. "I'll never get married," Elizabeth prophesied.

"We've been through that before, Cassandra," the doctor said, "what else happened today before you fell down the stairs?" "Nothing," Elizabeth said, looking at her watch. Ten minutes left. Then Doctor Greene would throw her out, drop her down the elevator shaft. She told him of her picture of him dropping her down the elevator shaft. "Like drowning a cat," he commented. "My mother would never let me have a cat," she observed.

"What else happened today?" he persevered. He had heard about her pet problems before. "Nothing," Elizabeth said, "I got a letter." The doctor didn't say anything. "I got a letter from Joshua. In California." "And who is Joshua?" Doctor Greene asked. Elizabeth realized she had never mentioned him. "I think I have been in love with Joshua for years," she said; "he said he was coming to visit me on Wednesday. I think he will be staying with me for a couple of weeks." "Well," said Doctor Greene, "tomorrow my vacation begins. I will be back in two weeks. I think we should talk more about this Joshua and why I have not heard more about him." "You may not have heard more about him because I have not thought more about him," Elizabeth said. "Have a good vacation," she told him, as if predicting the San Francisco quake. She hobbled over to the door. "Goodbye," she said, turning around. Doctor Greene was bent over his books. "Goodbye," he said, without looking up; "I will see you on the twentieth."

Elizabeth went into the office and said goodbye to Jane. Then she hobbled out to the elevator door, its blank face, she watched the numbers light up, thirty-four, bright green, thirty-three, twenty-five. The last thing most people needed was happiness. Then what *did* they need?

Chapter 7

When Elizabeth had first come to the University, she could not get over its size. Its gray walls rose up, towering, leaving little pieces of blue sky, jagged, like bits of a brilliant puzzle she had no place in. She had transferred here after one year at Simon College, where she had proved to herself and everyone else that she was a dismal failure at life. At that time, she had wanted to be a nurse, and Simon College had an excellent nursing school. For months after she had been admitted, her father had stormed through the house saying no daughter of his was going out of town. Sarah had trailed after her, red-eyed, asking her why couldn't she give in, look at all the trouble she was causing, she had two New York State scholarships, and Simon College—had she forgotten?—was in Massachusetts. Sarah insisted that if Elizabeth lived at home, no one would bother her; she would lead her own life. That night, Elizabeth asked if she could borrow the car to go to the movies with Esther, and her father, slicing his steak without looking up, said no. Elizabeth wanted to know why. "Because Esther's parents also have a car," he said. Elizabeth pointed out that Esther's parents were using it, and that they would not be able to go *anywhere* unless she could borrow the car. "Then stay home," her father said, forking a piece of steak into his mouth. She started screaming about what a monster he was, how he lived to make her unhappy, and ran into the living room crying. From the kitchen, she could hear Sarah pleading with Manny: why couldn't she have the car? They weren't using it anyway; what difference did it make? "Not after she opens up a mouth like that," Manny said, final. Elizabeth ran into the kitchen and told her father she hated him, she didn't know why her mother had married him, she was going out *now,* and she was going to college whether they liked it or not; she would stand on street corners and beg if she had to. Through this, she was tugging on her coat. Sarah stood in the middle; she told Elizabeth she could not walk around alone at this time of night; she told Manny Elizabeth could not walk around alone at this time of night. "You should never have married him: you're just a nonentity!" she screamed at her mother, flying out the front door, slamming it as hard as she could. She ran down the cement walk, and the sidewalk, toward the school, its dark yard. "Get back in this house!" she could hear Manny shouting from the yellow rectangle of light, but she ran faster, slipping between the school wall and its gate which kept out the cars. She walked as fast as she could to Esther's, her eye on every shadow, half-hoping someone would jump out at her, the white body, the slashed throat, the disgraced family, the monotonous funeral. Why were they always after her? She did nothing; she practically lived at Esther's; she was quiet as possible. She thought of her mother's master's thesis sitting up in the attic, the hem of Sarah's wedding dress brushing its cardboard box cover, in back the stacks of old photographs, and she was ashamed of calling her that, a nonentity, what her mother feared most. But her father! There was nothing bad enough she could think of to do to her father.

When she was ten, her brother had kicked her under the table. The first time he did it, she ignored him. The second time, she picked up a fork full of green peas and threw them at Arthur. He set up an impressive wail. Manny came into the kitchen, and without asking what happened, smacked Elizabeth across the face with the flat of his hand. Elizabeth seemed to lose her mind. She jumped out of her chair and tried to kick him, but he held her by the shoulders, and when she gave up, smacked her twice on the bottom, hard. She started to scream. Manny said, "I'll teach you to scream," and grabbed her by the collar, and dragged her to the head of the basement stairs. "Get down there!" he commanded, "and stay there until we call you." "I won't go!" Elizabeth shrieked. "Get down there," Manny ordered, "do I have to get my strap?" Elizabeth went downstairs and cried as loud as she could. She opened the little windows; maybe the neighbors would hear her. Nobody relented; no one came down. Finally, Elizabeth crept back up the stairs. She opened the back door quietly. It was cold; she had no coat. She shut the door gently; she was out in the backyard. She was going to run away. She walked down the block, and to the corner. The only place she could think of to go was the police station. They would understand; they would take her to an orphanage. She imagined the orphanage as a blank-walled place, where grownups came and went, the children raising themselves, and every now and then, two nice people with no children would come, as if to a store, and say, "I want *this* one," and they would take her home and they would not shout at her and hit her and lock her in her room. She was half-frozen when she got to the police station. A red-faced man in blue sat at the desk. Elizabeth told him she was running away, and, when he wanted to know why, she said it was because her parents locked her in the basement. She told the policeman she wanted him to take her to an orphanage. Instead, he told her to get in his car, and he would drive her home.

When they got to her house, Manny and Sarah had not even noticed she was gone. The policeman looked embarrassed when he had to explain what he was doing there with their child. Sarah began crying. She showed the officer her hands: "Look how red they are, from cooking and cleaning, all day long, all day! And she says we don't love her!" She burst into tears all over again. Elizabeth tried to tell the policeman Sarah's palms were always red,

130

that was just the way they were, but no one paid any attention to her. When the policeman left, he told Elizabeth to be a good girl and to listen to her parents. Then Manny came into the living room. "Get upstairs," he said, "you are going to get it for this." He followed her up, and slammed the door after her. She locked it after him, helpless. "No television for a month," he called through the door, vindictive.

She would go away to college; she had had enough of this for the rest of her life; she didn't think there would be much more of it if she tried to live at home. Two days before Simon College was scheduled to open, Sarah and Manny drove her up. Her trunks had been sent up ahead, her suitcase was in the back. Manny said nothing for the entire trip. Sarah tried desperately to keep up a conversation: allowances, courses, clothes. Elizabeth answered in monosyllables. When they got to Boston, Sarah wanted to eat at the famous delicatessen they had always heard about. Neither Manny nor Elizabeth said a word. Then they took her to the college. She had to get special permission to move into her room early, but she could not move in that night; she could only move in the next day. Tonight, she would have to stay at a hotel. "I *told* you, Manny," Sarah hissed, but Manny repeated that he couldn't afford to miss a day at "the place." They drove downtown and rented Elizabeth a room for the night. Sarah went upstairs with her, and sat on the bed while Elizabeth put some things away. "Goodbye," Sarah said, finally, "your father's downstairs, waiting." "Goodbye, mother," Elizabeth said. "Don't you want to come downstairs and say goodbye to your father?" Sarah asked. Elizabeth said no, and watched the door close, slowly. She felt like a shoe in a box. The next day she checked into the dorm. It was completely empty. "The housemother will be there in the afternoon," the Dean of Students told her. Downstairs, the phone was ringing. It was Belle. She wanted to know if Elizabeth was settled. "Yes, grandma," she said. "How many times does his only daughter go to college, he couldn't take a day off from work?" Belle asked rhetorically. "There's no point in talking about it, grandma," Elizabeth said. Belle told her to call her Aunt Frieda, who lived in Brookline, and then hung up. Elizabeth sat in the phone booth for some time, trying to think of a reason to move. The walls of the booth were covered with numbers. Surely she could call up one of those numbers and someone would come to get her: she went back to her room and started unpacking.

It wasn't long before she realized she had made a mistake. At Simon College, the girls were all given placement tests, and Elizabeth was exempted from all beginning courses. This seemed to annoy the housemother. Her roommate was attending school on a Blueberry Homemaking Scholarship: Elizabeth had never heard of such a thing before. Then she found out about the Group Guidance lectures. The whole freshman class was gathered together and shown films about the egg and the sperm; they were given lectures by the upper classmen about how a Simon girl always smiled when she met other Simon girls: in fact, she always smiled when she met *anybody*. When she stopped attending, she was called in by the Dean who gave her a lecture on her attitude and reminded her that attendance at these lectures was compulsory. Then, one night, the phone rang. It was a quarter of eleven. All the girls at Simon College were on the Honor System; they were not to answer the phone after ten-thirty. Elizabeth thought it might be an emergency and answered the phone. It was for her. Everyone assumed she had done this deliberately, and she was campused for the weekend. Mark came to see her, whispering through the front door, another violation of the honor code, and she began to think about transferring. Her Honors English class was supposed to be writing a story or poem—on command. She could not do it. Mark was graduating in the fall and going to the University of Chicago. One day, Elizabeth asked her Philosophy teacher if he thought she should transfer: "Get out of this hell-hole before it's too late," he told her. She went back to the dorm in a state of shock. The next day, the results of the Biology exam were posted in the halls outside the lab. Elizabeth had gotten an A; her roommate, Claire, had gotten a B. When she got back to her room, Elizabeth found Claire waiting for her. "It's not fair," Claire kept insisting to anyone who would listen, "she doesn't study at all. She goes downstairs to June's room, and June reads to her, and tells her things, and she remembers it, and the next day, she gets an A, it's not fair!" Elizabeth loved Claire, but now Claire would have nothing to do with her. Over the holiday, she went home with another girl from the dorm. She didn't even ask Elizabeth what she was going to do.

Elizabeth went back to the Philosophy professor. She

wanted him to tell her what schools were most unlike Simon College. He mentioned three, and one of them was the University of Chicago. Elizabeth decided she would go there if she could. The whole summer she worked at the Cerebral Palsy Center and waited for the letters deciding her fate. Her father said nothing; he punctuated his silences with the grand slams of doors. Finally, she was notified the University would take her. She still had six weeks to go, but she began to pack. Her father would have nothing to do with her. Her mother would come into her room and plead with her: she said she never finished anything she started, she had better stay where she was now, because they wouldn't pay for another school, that Elizabeth never could make up her mind about anything, her trouble was she had a one-track mind. Then she would begin worrying about her clothes: would she be warm enough in Chicago? The neighborhood was very dangerous. Would she be careful and not go out after dark? Did Elizabeth have any idea of how expensive it was going to be for them to send her out there? She would have to call every week and tell them how she was. Had she thought about what it would be like to get only C's, and maybe worse? The University was not an easy school, like Simon College. Sarah told her that when she had flown up to Simon to talk to the Dean of Women, the Dean had told her all about her bad attitude, how uncooperative she was: did she think they were going to stand for that at the University? Elizabeth went on with her packing. The Dean didn't think Elizabeth was all that smart, Sarah said, Simon College was good enough for her. "She's not half as smart as Arthur; Arthur's the smart one in this family," Manny shouted from behind the closed door to his room. When they day came for Elizabeth to go to the airport, Manny refused to come; he said he was going to stay home and do the crossword puzzle; he was too tired to hang around the airport.

Sarah and Belle and Arthur and Esther took her to the airport. "Which flight?" Belle demanded. "101," Elizabeth said. "Do they give you any lunch?" Belle asked, worried. "Yes, grandma," she said. "I don't know why you couldn't have taken the train," Belle complained. "Because I've never taken a plane," Elizabeth said, "besides, I want to get used to it out there." "If you think it's going to take so much getting used to, why are you going?" Sarah asked her. "Oh, mother," Arthur said, "leave her alone." The plane

133

was late. They all sat around on bright blue plastic chairs, not saying much. Esther kept promising to write. Arthur was large-eyed, frightened. He kept telling her he would take good care of the dog. She and Arthur had pooled their allowances to buy him, and they had named him Rex. When they brought it home, they told their mother, who had just come in with company. "What do you need with another stuffed animal?" Sarah asked her. And then she heard its yowl. They both knew that if there hadn't been company there that day, the dog would have been sent back. Now their mother was as fond of it as if it were a third child. She had bought it a red-plaid coat for its second winter. "It's still a puppy," she said as she and Arthur struggled to get the squirming animal into its coat. "I wonder about its feet," Sarah said thoughtfully, watching Arthur dance down the road into the snow, watching Rex leaping about in front of him. "Crochet him some boots, mother," Elizabeth suggested, helpful.

Elizabeth was terrified. All summer, people had told her about the University, how hard it was, how only geniuses went there, how everyone was eccentric, how everyone cracked under the strain. She was also terrified of planes. But she knew if she showed the slightest doubt, she would not be permitted to go. Even to Esther, she pretended supreme confidence. When she got on the plane, she pressed her nose to the glass, trying to see her family. She saw a little dark clump she thought might be them. She kept waving and waving. Even as the plane taxied from its place, she kept her nose pressed to the glass: she missed most of the take-off. At any moment, she expected the plane to crash, or explode. Instead, it felt like a long train ride through the Holland Tunnel. At the airport, she got off the plane, and took a cab to the school. Her trunks had been sent to the wrong dorm, the woman said, but they would send them over in the morning. Elizabeth went to her room: it had French doors that opened onto a fire-escape and faced into the quadrangle and the library. She was astounded by the gray walls, a distillate of cloud after cloud, centuries of them. She felt dwarfed. She sat down on the little iron platform, and read the notices in her box. Placement exams. "Here we go again," she thought; she felt as if the world had come to an end, as if she had sailed over the edge of the flat earth.

Every morning for a week, Elizabeth set the alarm and got up and took "placement exams." A week later, her advisor told her she had "placed out" of the first three years of the humanities courses, but she could take the third one if she wanted to. Elizabeth decided she wanted to. While she was waiting for her advisor to make up a schedule, she looked through her file. A red card was clipped to a letter. Furtively, she looked at it. It was a letter from the Dean of Students warning of her unconstructive attitude, her smugness, her disobedience, and general undesirability. When the advisor saw her looking at it, he took the folder away. "You're not supposed to see that," he said. Then he saw her face. "Don't worry," he said, "would you have wanted to be a good Simon girl?" Elizabeth shook her head no; her throat was tight and sore. "This is it, then," the advisor said, "Good luck." Later, she found out he was the Dean of the school.

It was in Humanities Three that she first met Joshua. She was already attached to Mark, whom she had met in Boston, and who had also come out to the University, having been spurned by Harvard. She noticed Joshua right away. He had the biggest head and the thickest glasses in the class. His face was very long, and vaguely foreign, and he had thick, drooping lips. His mouth seemed always to be open. He looked dazed, basset-houndish. Elizabeth knew, by normal standards, he was ugly, but she thought he was handsome. The second day of class she sat next to him. The third day she wrote him a note. The fourth day he bent over and asked her to come with him to the coffee shop. She thought about Mark, and nodded her head yes. Then she scribbled down everything the teacher was saying. She was determined not to get into trouble here. It was a long time before she realized it was almost impossible to get into trouble at the University: attendance was not required; there was no exams until the end of the year, and then there was a six hour exam in each course; and there was no curfew at all. At night, some time or other, they just had to sign in. Mark was settling in across campus in another dorm; Joshua lived off campus in an apartment. Elizabeth thought they would be very good friends.

Joshua was supposed to arrive from New York on Wednesday; he had gone home for the summer to visit his mother and younger brother, and now he was going back to California. He wanted to see Elizabeth, he said. He had not seen her for a very long time, and wanted to see her very much. Something about the idea of seeing Joshua again unnerved Elizabeth, and when he called on Tuesday night to say he would be in Chicago by eleven, she called Armand and asked him if he would mind if she came to study in his apartment for part of the night. She felt if she had to stay in her own apartment and wait for him, she could not stand it; she would be humiliated, betrayed. She could only imagine seeing him again, having him with her, if she came home to her apartment from somewhere else, somewhere secret Joshua did not know about; the secretness would protect her from him, would keep her whole.

She put Joshua's last letter away in the box with all his other letters; then she took them all out, and read them all over again, slowly. They dated over nine years. The first one was typed, in an archie-and-mehitabel style: "I think I've had enough of the golden sun. I'm going to wipe the milk and honey from my feet and come East. The Golden Gate Bridge sticks in my throat like a bone. I'm hungry for grime. What are you doing there, peering through Harvard's spiked gates? I don't think mathematics is for me. Remember Humanities Three, and Mrs. Jesselyn? I was in love with you both. I've got a new job at IBM. Are you married? Are you divorced? Can I come and see you?" At the bottom of the letter was a passage of poetry, something about Aunt Yetta making chicken soup in the Himalayas. She never knew if Joshua was quoting someone, or writing the poetry himself; she liked to think he was writing. She could remember how she had sat on Ralph's bed and answered the letter, without taking her coat off, immediately. "Dear Joshua, dear Joshua," she had written, "please come, milkless, honeyless. I am here working in a Medical Order Department. Everything is the same. I am still seeing Mark; my hair is longer than ever. Do you still have your maroon sweater? I have a pet white rat who plays with the tips of my fingers; he thinks my nails have eyes, and can see him: he hops out at them, taking them by surprise. I miss school: I have missed you for years. I ask everyone from the coast about you. I have a large square room in a boarding house, and the planks of the floor are painted black, and the whole thing lists, like a ship. Do you remember the day you were leaning out over the railing of your porch when Mark and I walked by? You asked us to come up. You were writing a paper on Auden's *In Memory of Sigmund Freud*; we talked about what had happened to the course since I had left it for the glories of Botany. I told you about Franz; he was also in love with Mrs. Jesselyn: I think we were all in love with her. He kept jumping up and down on the curb at the corner of Fifty-seventh and Dorchester; he had just seen her husband, and he was over six feet tall, and Franz was five foot three, and looked like Franz Kafka at the last. 'I come up to *here* on him!' Franz kept exclaiming, thumping his heart like a resuscitator, tragic as Marmeledov. You were laughing, and then you looked at Mark. I kept looking around the room to see if there were traces of anyone else there. After awhile, I said we had better leave because you had work to do. I've always thought there was a riddle in that day, and I've never forgotten it. Drive carefully; honey slips, Elizabeth."

Joshua had written back air mail, instant. "I am coming, neither wind, nor rain, nor snow. Don't cut your hair; we'll see what we will see. All this blue water, these sharks. I will probably be there on the tenth." Elizabeth looked at his signature: "Love Joshua." There was no comma after "love." She always wondered: was it a signature, a closing, or a request?

On the tenth, Joshua arrived. Elizabeth had informed Mark that she would be spending the weekend at the boarding house, and that Joshua would be there. Mark had nothing to say. That summer he had had an ostentatious affair with an older woman at the Research Institute, and Elizabeth had spent her weekends talking to a young Polish man on a National Science Foundation fellowship. They were both too frightened to get involved with one another, but for years afterwards, they wrote each other letters, and in the last one, he told her he still had her picture over his kitchen sink in the family house. "International fame," Elizabeth sighed. She wished he would get married; she did not think their meeting had done either of them any good. Whenever she got very depressed with Mark, she would find herself thinking about going to Poland, and finding Janick, and moving into the family kitchen. Still, she was upset when Mark was not jealous. "When will he be leaving?" Mark inquired, as if checking on a relative's intended duration. "Sunday night," Elizabeth said, "he has a new job starting Monday." "When should I pick you up?" "Monday night," Elizabeth said, and was gone.

All day Friday, she fidgeted and went to the window

and looked out. "Sit still, already," Edna said, "I can't concentrate." "It looks like you're reading the right chapter," Ralph chimed in, looking over her shoulder, "the manic-depressive psychoses." "What time is it?" Elizabeth asked. Ralph started to look at his watch. "Elizabeth?" a voice said tentatively. Elizabeth turned around slowly, afraid. It was Joshua. He looked no different. "How are you, Joshua?" she said softly, standing up. "Tired," he said. "You look just the same," she said; she wanted to cry. "You do too," he said, "your hair's just longer." "Come up and we'll put your things away," Elizabeth said, "I've rented you a room for the weekend." Then they went out for a walk; Elizabeth had never felt so shy. Joshua hardly said anything at all. They had walked three blocks before she realized they had been holding hands from the minute they left the house; she squeezed his hand, tight. "You know you're the only one who's ever called me Joshua?" he asked. "What do other people call you?" she asked, surprised. "Josh," he said. "Should I call you that?" "Please don't." She looked up at him, questioning. "This way I always know it's you when I hear you on the phone." "Is that important to you?" she asked. "You have no idea how important." They walked three more blocks, along the cobbled brick. Elizabeth could not catch her breath, but they were walking very slowly. Finally, Joshua said, "How are things going with Mark?" Mark's name hung in the air like a dead body on a gibbet. "Things are not going with Mark, I don't know why I stay with him; I don't love him anymore, we don't get along. He spends his time slaughtering Bach on a rented piano, and I read *The Good Soldier* in the kitchen with pieces of paper napkins stuffed in my ears. I think I have no moral courage, and I'm very unhappy." "And Mark?" "Mark is just the same, it's just that I don't think he knows how to be unhappy. Or happy either," she added. "Well," Joshua said, staring ahead of him, "that's a lot to say." "I haven't been talking to anyone for a long time," Elizabeth said, "I used to talk to Edna and Ralph, but now I've gotten too worn out even to do that. I think I'm just waiting for things to get over, to get back to Chicago, and school, and then it will all come to an end." As she said it, Elizabeth wondered if it could possibly be true, that she believed what she said. They walked along in silence. "And you?" She was having trouble with her voice; she could hear love pulsing in it, like the sound waves that broke

138

and broke whenever she and Joshua spoke to each other, one edge of one seared continent to the other. She had always imagined it was the noise of the oceans, the Pacific and the Atlantic, mixing their waters. "Me," Joshua said, "Nothing much has happened to me. I've fallen from mathematical grace. We can talk about me later."

Finally, they found an Italian restaurant and ordered a pizza. It tasted like strawberries. "They don't know how to make pizza here," Elizabeth said, apologetically. "Let's buy some food for breakfast," Joshua suggested. As they went down the aisles, Elizabeth was dazed with happiness. Soup cans beamed at her. She could spend the rest of her life doing this! She was doing something very important, looking for eggs, medium size. She opened the carton to make sure none of them were broken. When she looked up, she saw Joshua staring at her; she knew the same glazed expression was irradiating her face. "Let's get out of here," he said. That night, they lay together in bed. Joshua talked. Elizabeth knew that Joshua hardly ever talked. He told her about his mother, and how, when she had gotten divorced, her new husband had wanted to send him away, and for awhile, he had lived with his aunt. "Yetta?" she asked. "Not Yetta," he said smiling, "Faye." He had always wanted to meet his real father, who lived in Canada and directed plays. "Can't you go to see him?" Elizabeth asked. "I guess I'm afraid." Joshua wanted to make love to her, but Elizabeth suddenly drew back. In some way she could not understand, she felt she was married to Mark; she had never slept with anyone else. She told Joshua that. He seemed to close over himself, like a clam. Then Joshua told her he had never slept with anyone. They both lay very still. Then he began to talk about California, school in California, the endless math problems, how he didn't care whether he was good at them, how he didn't care whether his students learned to solve mathematical problems or not. He had to get out. "So now you are working at IBM?" asked Elizabeth, watching his body—in the moonlight, it was marble-white, stiller than stone. "Yes," he said. He seemed to have retreated somewhere, waiting for her disapproval like a slap. "It will give you time to think," she said, "why don't you go back into English? You were always one of the best in the class." "I wanted to ask you about that," he said, "do you think I could?" "Well, if you can't, I can't," she said, flatly. "I'd have to save up money first," he said considering.

Joshua started talking about his mother again, how she hardly had any money, how she always got involved with the wrong men, how none of them had wanted him around. "I had no idea," Elizabeth said. "Sometimes I think I didn't either;" he sounded very distant and sad. Elizabeth turned over, and put her arm across his chest, hugging him. "Joshua," she began. He pulled away from her. "I knew this would happen. I would start talking, and you would feel sorry for me, and then you would sleep with me: it's not a good idea." "It's a good idea," Elizabeth said, gently; "it has nothing to do with any of that. I've wanted to sleep with you since the first day I tickled you in Mrs. Jesselyn's class, really, Joshua, I really have." Saying it, she knew it was true. Joshua raised himself on an elbow and looked at her. "Then what were you doing with Mark?" he said. "Why were you always with Eileen?" "I wasn't with her long," Joshua said: that was true, too. "Well," Elizabeth told him, "if Mount Rushmore decided to move, it would look like Mark. I needed a great deal of safety. Also, I'm a prude."

After they made love, Joshua started to cry. Elizabeth held on to him tightly and he stopped. "I've missed you," he said, as if confessing a horrible sin. "I have every letter you ever wrote," Elizabeth said, confessing herself. "Would you like to see them?" She was ready to get out of bed. "Tomorrow." "Tomorrow you go back to work," Elizabeth said. "I'll come back. Go to sleep." They slept like stones. Elizabeth woke up first: on the single bed, they looked like Hansel and Gretel. The black crow floor was covered with crumbs.

After breakfast, Joshua asked her in a tight voice if he could come back the next weekend. "Please," Elizabeth said; she couldn't stop staring at him. The next weekend, Joshua arrived before lunch. He came in carrying a large bag of red apples, for Elizabeth, and Edna, and Ralph. He was under the impression none of them ate right around there. During the week, Elizabeth had asked Edna what she thought of Joshua. "He looks frightened," Edna said. "There she goes again," Ralph put in, disgusted, "she got an A in 'Jumping To Conclusions.'" "In *Projective Techniques*," Edna said acidly. "Same thing," said Ralph. "Frightened of what?" Elizabeth wanted to know. "Of himself, I suppose," Edna said. "*And*," she added, "he's probably jealous." "Of what?" Elizabeth asked, astonished. "Of Mark, of course," Edna said. "But he said he wasn't,"

Elizabeth protested. "Never mind what he said," Edna warned her, "he's only human."

Joshua knew Elizabeth was going back to school in Chicago that fall, but when she mentioned it, a black cloth fell down between them; it was as if they were about to be photographed for an old picture, a daguerreotype. Elizabeth thought about what Edna had said, and wondered if it was because he knew Mark would be driving her back. "But I'll be home for Thanksgiving and Christmas." "Thanksgiving and Christmas," Joshua repeated bitterly. "Joshua," Elizabeth said desperate, "I'll write. All the time. Really, it won't make much difference. We can't see each other that much here not now that you've started working." "Not much difference," Joshua said. "Will you stop doing that!" Elizabeth demanded. "Doing what?" "Repeating what I say." Joshua gave her a blank look. On the other side of the table, Edna was staring at them gravely. The rest of the weekend was strained. "Finish the apples," Joshua instructed her as he got ready to drive off. "Aren't you going to kiss me goodbye?" Elizabeth asked, desolate. She felt Joshua was shipping her back to Mark. Mechanically, he stuck his head out of the window. She bent down. "Take care," she said. "You too," he said, and the car started to move, and then it turned the corner, and was gone.

In Chicago, things were going from bad to worse. Elizabeth finished her Master's: she and Mark seemed to be finishing each other. The first thing she did when she got home from the airport for Thanksgiving was to call Joshua; she was dopey with Dramamine and aspirin and had to ask him to repeat things two or three times. Lying on her parents' bed, it was an effort to keep awake. "Thursday night?" she asked again. "Thursday," Joshua said, and hung up. Elizabeth couldn't tell whether it was her imagination, but he sounded very short.

On Thursday, Joshua came to pick her up at the house. Manny was sitting in the armchair reading a newspaper; the belt on his pants was unbuckled and he wore only a T-shirt. "Mother," Elizabeth demanded, "ask him to put on a tie." "I'm fine as I am," Manny answered from behind the depths of his paper. "I'll meet Joshua outside," Elizabeth said. "You'll meet him in here, like a normal person," Sarah told her. Just then the doorbell rang. "Manny, for God's sake!" she could hear Sarah whispering as she went to answer the door. When Joshua walked in, Manny didn't even get up. He nodded gruffly, then raised the paper again. Joshua looked around the house, stricken. Elizabeth knew this was something to do with her having a whole family, all in one place. She thought if he knew more about what it was like, he wouldn't envy it at all. They went out into his car. "I'm going to Canada," Joshua announced. "Why?" Elizabeth asked, shocked. "I want to see my father. He's promised to send me back to school, either here or there." Elizabeth still didn't say anything. "I'll see you when I come back." There was a silence. They looked for a place to eat lunch. She felt she was being punished, but she didn't know what to do, or say. Joshua brought her back early. "Well," she demanded, seeing Sarah's tragic face, "what did you think?" "Your father says," Sarah quoted, "he's either a gentile, or a fairy." "He's English," Elizabeth said, and went up to her room, locking the door. By Christmas, Joshua was gone. That spring, she swallowed sleeping pills.

Several months later, Joshua came back from Canada. Seeing his father had not solved much, he said. He wanted to stay with Elizabeth for the night, and he had his younger brother with him. "You're welcome to stay," Elizabeth said, "but I have to teach tonight. I get home late. I'll see you in the morning." In the morning, Elizabeth was up early, typing a paper on *Doctor Faustus*. Joshua came and put his arms around her and the chair; he was standing behind her. He wanted them to get into bed. "I don't think it's a good idea, not while your brother's here," she said. She wondered why Joshua's hands were always so cold before making love; sometimes, they trembled. When Joshua's brother got up, she made breakfast for the three of them. She watched them eat through a thickening fog. "Have a good trip," she said formally, as she watched them go down the stairs, "Be careful." Two days later, she got a postcard from the Grand Canyon reporting their progress. "That's that," she said to herself, tearing it in half. But then Joshua had started writing, and she found herself wondering if she shouldn't go out to California and have him take care of her: she even asked Doctor Greene about it. "What makes you think Josua could handle it?" Doctor Greene asked. "Has he seemed ready for a permanent relationship before?" Elizabeth remembered his telling her about the last girl he had loved, how she had sat on his lap the night before she got married and told him she wasn't sure she wanted to go through with it; she wasn't sure she really loved him; what should she do? And all the time she was sitting on his lap, caressing his head, caressing his ear. Elizabeth had to admit there was a parallel. She wrote Joshua and asked about coming to California. He wrote back that he was living with a girl, but he wouldn't mind if she came, though he thought it would be hard on Elizabeth and the other girl. After that, she didn't answer any of his letters for a long time. And now, he was coming, again, just like that. This time, Mark was gone; she was on her own. Joshua was on his own, she could tell that from his letter. But something was frightening her. Armand said she could study at his place; should he make something to eat?

When she got to Armand's, she could hardly find him at his desk. "What is this, home of the Collier brothers?" she asked, picking up a stack of papers and dropping it on a table. "It's a good thing you don't smoke." Armand watched her, and didn't say much. At ten o'clock, she went home. "I feel like General Sherman on his way to Atlanta," she said, picking her way out through the papers. "It's not House Beautiful," Armand sighed.

When she opened the door, Joshua put his arms around her before she had time to let him in. "You cut your hair," he said. The next thing she knew, they were in bed. The light fell through the slats in heavy golden bars. They walked out to the lake. They held hands; they had nothing to say. When they got back, Joshua sat on the couch, Elizabeth on the floor in front of him. "I don't want you to be just some girl I see in Chicago," he said. "It's not your fault," Elizabeth said, therapeutic; this was not what she had wanted to say at all. She was afraid of committing herself; she was afraid Joshua would decide he had to go see his father somewhere in Japan. "I don't understand why you haven't met any suitable men in Chicago," Joshua said; his voice had changed character completely. Elizabeth was very angry. "That's none of your business," she said, haughty. The bell rang. It was their friend Robert; they had met him before on the street going out to the lake. He stayed for a long time, finally for dinner. When he left, Elizabeth was at the end of her rope. She felt she had been waiting for years, and now Joshua would be gone in the morning. She couldn't stand it. She went

143

into the dining room, and lay down on the plush Victorian couch, and started to cry. Some time passed: Joshua came into the room. When he saw what was happening, he told her to stop. She kept crying. He told her if she didn't stop, he was leaving. Then she got up from the couch; she started screaming about how unfair he was to her, why had he kept Robert there for so long, she wasn't interested in his explanations about how Robert was his friend, she wanted to know why he was doing this to her, why had he come this far to do this to her? Joshua said he was leaving, Elizabeth pleaded with him to stay. But she kept crying, and choking, and finally, he hit her. She kept on crying; she had waited and waited, and now this, she couldn't understand it. They went to bed in silence. She woke up very early. She watched the sun lighten the stained-glass window; she got angrier and angrier. When Joshua got up, she told him not to call her again, or write her again, or try to see her again until a psychiatrist gave him a certificate pronouncing him officially cured. Joshua said nothing; he had told her he intended to go to a psychiatrist when he got back to California. "Is it because I have my Ph.D. and you don't?" Elizabeth asked. Joshua didn't say a word, just started putting on his socks and shoes. They walked over to the campus like two strangers. "Sit down and talk for a few minutes," Elizabeth said after they ate lunch, "We may never see each other again." "There's nothing to say," Joshua said. Elizabeth felt a smug satisfaction: he would go back to California; he would suffer. But when his car turned the corner and fell off the edge of the earth, winking its lights, her stomach fell. "My God," she said to herself, "My God, what have I done?"

The next morning, Doctor Greene was back. Elizabeth was dry-mouthed with exhaustion. She described what had happened. "It sounds," said Doctor Greene, "as if you took out on him your anger for my having left you. What he did was not unreasonable." "But he hit me," Elizabeth reminded him. "Most people would have, under the circumstances. I think he showed admirable control." "But I think I love him," Elizabeth said in a small voice. "Then what happened is very sad," Doctor Greene said. "I don't think he will forgive me," she added. "That is sadder yet," Doctor Greene said. Finally, Elizabeth said, "I think we should talk about when I stop coming to see you. I think I should stop coming in nine months, on my birthday." "Do you want to make that a definite termination date?" the doctor asked her. "I think so," Elizabeth said. "Think about it some more," the doctor told her, "once we set a date we will stick to it, whether you weigh nine-hundred pounds and are climbing my pole lamp, or are engaged to Armand, or swallowing your Dramamine cocktails." Elizabeth could not understand why; she felt like an orphan threatened with the loss of the world. "Because," said the doctor, "as these weeks have so amply demonstrated, the issue of separation is so important as to take precedence over everything else." "Is nine months enough?" Elizabeth asked, hoping he would say no. "Nine months is enough to create a child, and you are no longer a child," Doctor Greene said. "I think it is enough. You must think it over, and make up your mind."

The next two days Elizabeth spent driving all over Chicago looking for a small stained-glass window; she wanted to send it to Joshua. Finally, somewhere on the northwest side, she saw one exactly like her small one in the window of a florist's. She went in and bought it. Then she drove back to campus and posted a note asking for someone driving to California who would take the package to Berkeley and deliver it. Two days later, a graduate student arrived and went off with the window. When he came back to the city, he told Elizabeth he had given the window to Joshua. "What did he say?" she asked. "Just thank you," the student said. Elizabeth checked the mail every day all year, but Joshua never wrote, not even a card.

Chapter 8

The next day, Elizabeth arrived in Doctor Greene's office outraged. Usually, she left her coat on one of the hooks in the waiting room, and her books on one of the end tables, but today she came in with her coat still on, thumped her books down on the chair with a crash, took off her coat and threw it on top of them. The coat fell on the floor, dragging two books with it. "Damn!" Elizabeth

145

said, bending down to pick up the books and the coat, and throwing the whole disorganized heap on the chair where one arm dangled brownly toward the rug like Camille. Doctor Greene watched with slightly raised brows. "Getting here is impossible!" Elizabeth announced before she was even on the couch, "the traffic is impossible; no one stays in one lane for more than three feet; there was an accident on Michigan Avenue; all the public lots were full; I'm amazed I got here at all, I might as well have stayed home. I almost turned around and went home three times! And," she said, "I think I'm coming down with a cold." She sniffed dramatically, then felt her forehead. "Tsk," said the doctor from the depths of his chair, "what is it this time? Malaria? Spotted fever? An untreatable virus of unknown origin?" "I'm sure I have a fever," she said, feeling her head again. "It must be nice," she said, squirming around to look at him, "to be healthy as a horse." "Well, it does allow one some peace of mind," Doctor Greene said equably. "I run into traffic every day, I spend half of my life getting here, and a lot of good it does me; I'm worse than ever." "Is this the first time you've run into traffic?" Doctor Greene asked. "I just told you it wasn't," Elizabeth snapped at him. "Might this have anything to do with Joshua?" "Why should this have anything to do with Joshua?" Elizabeth demanded. "Does he tie up traffic? Is he stalled on the Outer Drive? As far as I know, he's somewhere near the Grand Canyon, probably fallen into it, with his luck." "I thought you said he was a very good driver," Doctor Greene said. "He is," Elizabeth answered gloomily; she was thinking of three years ago when they had driven back to Chicago together, her parents at the living room window watching them go, two of Poe's Ravens; they had stopped at a pancake house in front of a cemetery, and from the window, they could see the tombstones, and in front of the little gray and black squares, a traffic sign saying "Dead End." "Look at that, Joshua," Elizabeth said, pointing. "I used to write things like that down," he said, "in the days when I thought there was still a master plan;" he went on chewing, "even if it was one like that." The whole trip seemed to have taken three hours. When they got back, Benita had come over to inspect him; she had sat down on the floor, and thrown her arms over the couch, and her breasts floated in the air, two balloons. Joshua was polite; when Benita left, Elizabeth asked him what he thought of her. He seemed

146

not to hear. "Well, now we can talk," he said. "Wherever you are, so there are people," he said, stroking her hair. "Two gray hairs," he said, pulling one out. "Silver," he said holding it up to the light. He looked at it again. "No point in pressing hairs, I guess," he said, "the next person to get the book would just think I'd been tearing my hair out." He wound it around his finger like a ring.

"I have not thought about Joshua all day," Elizabeth said. "Congratulations," said the doctor. "Just this morning when I got up," she added, grudgingly. "I wondered what it was like to drive all the way back to California alone, what kind of personality was warped enough to *like* driving back to California alone." "You don't seem to like driving at all," Doctor Greene observed. "What's there to like about it?" Elizabeth asked, "crowded streets, last week, my brakes failed, Mayor Daley was on the radio asking people not to use their cars except in case of emergency, which my neighbor thought meant taking her laundry around the corner, all night long cars were honking horns under my window while they tried to dig her out; you never know when some maniac is going to drive through the windshield and into your lap, what's there to like about it?" "I don't notice you taking the train," the doctor observed. "Tomorrow I will take the train," she said, "or the bus. Not the bus, the train," she said, thinking it over. "Actually, I don't mind driving so much when *I'm* driving; at least then I know what to expect." "Do you think nothing can happen to you when you're driving?" the doctor asked. "That's not it," Elizabeth said, "when I drive, I go where I want to go." "You didn't want to come here today," the doctor commented. "I never said that," Elizabeth protested, nettled. "You gave a good performance, then," said the doctor, looking at her coat and her books. "That chair looks like it's ready to go to the laundry." "I'll clean it up before I leave, don't worry," Elizabeth said, sarcastically. "I have no doubt you will," said the doctor. "And suppose I didn't?" Elizabeth asked. She knew she was behaving horribly, but she didn't care. Doctor Greene didn't answer her. "You know," she said poisonously, "you analysts are all crazy. You are always talking, you are always talking when you have something to say I don't want to hear. When I ask you a question, you answer sometimes, and sometimes you don't." Elizabeth paused didactically, "Doctor Spock says that parental figures should always be consistent." Doctor

Greene still didn't say anything. "You are not consistent at all," Elizabeth complained, her voice rising, "you probably have no reason at all for doing anything. If I miss an appointment, I have to pay you, but if you miss an appointment, you don't have to pay me, I'd like to know what's consistent about that." "I'm not sure I understand the nature of your objection," Doctor Greene said, "why should *I* pay *you* for missing a session? Do I ordinarily pay you for coming to the office?" "You *should* pay some kind of penalty for missing appointments; *I* pay twenty-five dollars whether I come to one of mine or not." "Do your students penalize you when you miss a class?" Doctor Greene asked. "It's not the same thing," Elizabeth said. "Is it?" She waited for an answer. Silence. From the street below came the honking of a horn, then another, and another. "Those stupid horns!" Elizabeth exploded, "a person can't think around here! You would have to get such a noisy office." "I don't remember you complaining about the noise before," the doctor said. "You don't remember anything, but then why should you, busy giving papers, having vacations, colds, God knows what. You'll be observing All Hallow's Eve this year; how about the Saint Valentine's Day Massacre, that's a good one," Elizabeth suggested. "Don't you think a psychiatrist is entitled to a holiday?" Doctor Greene asked mildly. "No," Elizabeth said, adamant. "I see," said Doctor Greene, "then you would not mind if I fell asleep exhausted while listening to you, or mixed your case history up with some other patient's, or had little bouts of amnesia while talking to you?" "You already read your mail while I'm talking," she accused him. "Where did you get that idea?" the doctor asked. "I can hear all those papers rattling," Elizabeth said, "you must be rattling them for some reason." There was a long silence. "What are you doing now," Elizabeth asked, "reading Donald Duck?" "I never read Donald Duck," said the doctor. "Too bad," Elizabeth said, "it's very interesting. Although not as interesting as Chicken Man." "What is Chicken Man?" asked the doctor. "A radio serial, a parody of Batman. Have you heard of Batman?" No answer. "Well, you never know," Elizabeth said, "for all I know, you live in a cave." "Do you think that's likely?" the doctor asked. "How should I know?" Elizabeth said. "How do you get to work?" Silence. Elizabeth contemplated the ashtray and the bare walls and finally settled on the painting at the foot of the couch.

"That gray shape looks like a dead rat," she said. "I hadn't noticed," Doctor Greene said. "What is all that smoke?" Elizabeth demanded. "All that smoke is coming from my pipe—as usual," said Doctor Greene. "When I was a child," Elizabeth volunteered, bored to death, "my father always used to smoke cigars in the car." From where she lay on the couch, her coat looked like a decapitated body. "Every Sunday, we used to drive out to the Island and go 'house hunting.' Arthur and I sat in the back seat, and we would start out, and after an hour or so, we would get out and go look at a house. Usually, the house was completely empty, no furniture, nothing. It was very depressing. We would get sent outside to play, and my mother and father would go whisper in a corner, and then they would come out and tell us to get back in the car. It took them years to find a house, years," she said accusingly. "I used to pretend to be carsick so they would leave me with my Aunt Irene. You should have seen the imitation of incipient vomiting I could put on," she said. "You sound like it's still going on," Doctor Greene commented. "What," she asked, "the vomiting?" "No, the looking for a house." Elizabeth had a sudden vision of her apartment, which seemed very empty. She decided not to mention it.

"My father also smokes," she said, "like a chimney. I can still see all that blue and gray smoke filling the car. 'Manny,' my mother would say, 'open a window, they're getting sick.' He would just ignore her and keep on driving. Then I'd roll down the window. 'Close that window,' he would command, without turning around. 'It's not open,' I'd say. 'It is too open,' Arthur would pipe up, and then my father would want to know if I wanted a smack. After a while, I would get carsick. A wonderful way to spend weekends. Finally, they thought they found a house. My mother ordered some dining room furniture. Then it turned out every time it rained, the basement filled up like the Atlantic Ocean, and everything was washed back where it started from." "But I thought you said you were left with your Aunt Irene?" "Only afterwards," Elizabeth said. "After what?" asked the doctor. "After Arthur and I started fighting in the back seat. He would kick me, I would hit him. This isn't very interesting; I'm sure your children *never* fight." "Why do you say that?" asked the doctor. He actually sounded interested. "They're probably *afraid* to fight," Elizabeth said, accusing. "What do you think I would do to them?" "Who knows?" Elizabeth said,

"Maybe nothing, maybe you wear yourself out here, torturing patients." "By taking holidays," Doctor Greene suggested. "When you and Arthur fought, how did they punish you?" "First they would tell us to stop fighting. Then they would threaten us. First, they would threaten us with no ice cream. Then they would threaten us with no television. Then my mother would tell my father to pull over. Then my father would say that if he had to pull over to the side of the road, we would get a beating we would never forget. Then he would pull over to the side of the road and I would get a beating I would never forget." "Didn't Arthur get a beating?" the doctor asked. "Every now and then," it was hard to remember, "but he was the younger one, he had a nice pumpkin face, angelic as a cabbage; they assumed I started it; he always did the loudest screaming." Elizabeth thought a minute. "I must say he was a good screamer," she said with some admiration. "That doesn't sound like torture," Doctor Greene commented. "That *wasn't* the torture," Elizabeth said, "I'm sure I've told you about this, you've probably just forgotten—as usual." "What was the torture, exactly?" "Sometimes, after they had pulled over to the side of the road once or twice, my father would start smoking, and the windows were closed, and I would start getting bored, and Arthur and I would start fighting again. Then my mother would say, 'Manny, if she doesn't stop, pull over to the side of the road and put her out.'" "*Did* they put you out?" the doctor asked. "They certainly did," Elizabeth answered, nettled. "One day in the winter, the sky was gray and we were coming to the part of the road where you could begin to see the ocean on the left and the marshes to the right. 'Stop the car, Manny,' my mother ordered, 'put her out.'" Elizabeth stopped to catch her breath. "My throat hurts," she complained. "Go on," said the doctor, "what then?" "Are you sure I didn't tell you about this?" demanded Elizabeth. "What then?" Doctor Greene repeated. "*Then,*" Elizabeth said, as if reciting *Goldilocks* to a child, "my father got out of the car, and some cold air hit me in the face, and he came around to my side, and opened the door, and pulled me out." She stopped talking. "I hope you're happy now," she said, "I'm crying for a change." "And then?" "And then," she said, crying quietly, "he got back in the car and they drove down the road. I could see the car getting smaller and smaller; I used to wonder if anyone would stop and pick me up. The second time they did it, I was getting ready to go off into the marshes and drown myself, but by that time they had backed up, my mother's head was sticking out of the car. 'Get in,' she ordered. I ran away, she had to chase me. When she got me, she slapped me across the face." Then Elizabeth said, "that wasn't the worst part," but now she was crying convulsively. "What was the worst part, Elizabeth?" the doctor asked gently. "The worst part was Arthur. Arthur was terrified. He was terrified the same thing was going to happen to him. I'm going to take one of your tissues," she said, sitting bolt upright on the couch and grabbing one of the giant Kleenexes the doctor kept for the head of the couch. She blew her nose, loudly. The doctor didn't say anything. "Arthur is all my fault," she announced. "What do you mean?" the doctor asked. "I don't know," she said, sounding confused. "Do you mean he was afraid of being deserted because of you?" "Maybe," she said, "I don't know. Once, I hit him on the knee with a baseball bat, and then he had a tumor of the hip, and I thought he got it because I hit him with the bat. It's funny," she said, "but until right now I thought I hit him on the knee with the bat, and that was where he got the tumor, but that wasn't how it was." "And Joshua?" the doctor asked. "What about Joshua?" she demanded, "he has nothing to do with this. You are obsessed with Joshua. Joshua did not hit Arthur with a baseball bat. Joshua doesn't smoke." "What about Joshua and desertion?" the doctor asked. "What about it?" Elizabeth asked, as if daring him to something. "You know, Elizabeth," the doctor said, "for a very intelligent woman you can be very obtuse sometimes. Does Joshua have a great fear of desertion?" "He does," Elizabeth answered, mechanically. "Did you desert him this weekend?" the doctor asked. *"He* deserted *me,"* she protested. "Well, that's a moot point, isn't it?" the doctor asked. "Who told who not to come back until they had a certificate from Good Housekeeping testifying to their mental health?" "He was impossible," Elizabeth said. "So were you," Doctor Greene said. "He was *more* impossible" Elizabeth insisted. "Well, I wasn't there," the doctor said, "but he was the one who said he didn't want you to be just a girl he saw in Chicago, and instead of paying attention to that, you responded to your wish to stay with him permanently. And then, when he wanted to talk to an old friend, you thought he was deserting you for someone else, and you decided to throw him out." "*He* said he was leaving," Elizabeth argued. "Did you give him a choice?" Elizabeth yawned. "I'm getting very tired," she said, "I can hardly keep my eyes open." "Something you don't want to see?" the doctor asked. "You and your stupid interpretations," Elizabeth said, bitterly. She looked at her watch. "Isn't the hour up?" "Are you in a hurry to leave?" "Always answer a question with a question, rule one page one, psychiatrist's medical manual." "I will tell you when the hour's up," Doctor Greene said, "as always." "Usually, you can't wait to get rid of me," Elizabeth observed.

"I could go out to California and talk to Joshua," she said. "I don't think he wants to see you," Doctor Greene said, "and besides, do you think he's ready to give you the security you evidently need?" Elizabeth shook her head no. "I could wait until he got better," she suggested hopefully. "Then he would definitely have nothing to do with you," Doctor Greene warned her. "Why not?" Elizabeth asked, astonished, "If I waited like that it would *prove* how much I cared about him." "If you waited like that, without being asked by him, when very possibly he might meet someone else, or change in unexpected ways, he would have every reason for asking to see *your* certificate. And if he were 'cured,' why would he want to have anything to do with someone who was crazy? Besides," the doctor added, "what guarantee do you have that Joshua is going to change, that he's curable? He may never change." "He hasn't changed much so far," Elizabeth murmured, flipping back over the days like index cards. "Be that as it may," Doctor Greene said, "right now Joshua is a closed book—unless he reopens it himself." "He won't." Elizabeth was positive. "I've ruined everything." "Then there you are," the doctor said. "Contemplating the ruins," she said. "Not if you've learned something from this." "What did I learn?" Elizabeth was too tired to talk. Her lips felt like iron. "Not to think every man you meet is going to put you out of the car on the Belt Parkway." "It's a little late for that now," Elizabeth said. "Better late than never," said the doctor; "by the way, I will not be here for my Monday appointment. I have a conference. I believe I told you about it before." "I can't *believe* it," Elizabeth said, picking up her coat and books, "why don't you just retire?" "You exaggerate," said Doctor Greene, opening the door, "I'll see you on Tuesday." "I certainly *hope* so," said

Elizabeth, dropping a book, picking it up. "Want to bet?" asked the doctor. "Not more than a quarter," Elizabeth said, "I can't afford it, you'll do anything for money." "Next Tuesday, Elizabeth," Doctor Greene said again.

The next Tuesday, Elizabeth arrived at ten minutes to eleven. "Where were you?" Jane demanded. "What do you mean?" Elizabeth didn't have the slightest idea of what she was talking about. "Weren't you supposed to be here at ten after ten?" "Oh God," Elizabeth gasped, collapsing on the couch.

Sometime in the fall of the following year, Elizabeth definitely decided to return to New York; as she drove along the lake, leaves blew onto the road, dry and shriveled as brown sarcophagi, clicking and clacking like beads. When she tried to remember how many times she had seen this before, she was amazed: nine times; nine years, since she had left Simon College and come to the University. When she had first come to Chicago, she had felt she would never get used to anything, the enormous buildings, the intricacies of courses and students; every time she sat down at a table, she expected surprise. Now the dry leaves, the glitter of the lake, were familiar and routine as old albums, their black pages turned over time after time, occasionally a shining square working its way loose from the four black triangles holding it in its place, missed for its absence, the unfamiliar gap. She knew every stop on the commuter train; she could fall asleep and wake up before the train pulled into the Loop. The students, too, were becoming familiar; their problems fell into patterns; her own life was familiar; it fell into a pattern; everything had become predictable. She would get home, would eat dinner, Armand would call, Benita would call, she would read, she would go to bed, in the morning, it would begin all over again. It was hard for her to remember, leaning into the mirror, to draw the neat brown line under and over her eyes, that she had once had such trouble getting dressed; the whole problem had solved itself a few months ago when she had gone shopping with Benita. Nothing she tried on fit right. But the clothes Benita tried on were so pretty! Finally, Elizabeth tried on one of the dresses to get an idea of what it looked like, and it fit: she tried on another one, and it also fit. She was mystified. "Well," the saleswoman said, "you're a perfect nine junior petite." "But I have very large bones!"

Elizabeth protested, tugging at the dress to see where it was giving at the seams. "You have a small frame," the saleswoman said, stepping back, eyeing her critically, "and a short waist; you've been wearing the wrong size." It had never occurred to Elizabeth that she could fit into something as small as a size nine. Now, she thought to herself, she had become a clothes fanatic. In the morning, she would get up and decide what to wear; she found she could go into a store, and tell whether something would fit her without trying it on. Then, one day, she decided she would not make much progress if she continued to stay with Doctor Greene. He was right: all of the goals she had had when she had come to see him were reached. She had not gotten married. As she thought about it, it seemed to her that Doctor Greene himself was the reason she was not likely to do so now; if she married, what reason would she have for continuing to come? And she could talk to him; he was the first person she had ever been able to talk to. She talked to him an hour a day, four times a week. When she got lonely, she had Armand to amuse her, or John, who would come over on the slightest pretext; could he proofread an article? help paint a room? But she was becoming less and less satisfied with this, with the growing homogeneity of her hours with Doctor Greene: she would describe what had happened during the day, what she was afraid of, always the same thing. The main thing she feared now was, that when she stopped, she would get worse, time would reverse, like a car, things would go back to where they were. She remembered an old story she had read somewhere about an oriental guide who would take clients to fabulous castles in fabulous lands, and the castle would be the one they had always dreamed of, had always desired, and they could have it: there were no conditions. But when they looked more closely, there would be a thin beam of light between the castle and the cliff, a tiny, razor-cut strip, and when the visitor asked how the strip came there, the castle and the guide would vanish as if in a dream, and the visitor would be left on an arid plain, the castle receding before his eyes, the castle of health, a soap bubble in a wind.

When she talked to Doctor Greene about leaving, he agreed with her. Her main fear was that she wouldn't be able to come back if she wanted to: when she got worse. He pointed out that she would not be able to commute to

Chicago from New York, and besides, there was no reason to assume she would get worse. "But suppose it turns out that you're like a giant tranquilizer, and when I leave, I go back to being a nervous wreck." "That's always possible," the doctor said, "then it would turn out our work had not been complete." "Suppose you find out I'm going to a doctor in New York, what would you think?" "I'd want to know what had happened before I thought anything," Doctor Greene told her. "And," he said, "seeing a psychiatrist is not always a sign of regression, or relapse. You may find yourself in new situations which bring new problems to light that were never touched here because of your manner of living." "Well, that's a brand new wonderful way of thinking about progress," Elizabeth said grimly. "That's neither here nor there," the doctor said, "the thing is, do you feel you are covering new ground?" Elizabeth thought this over for a while. "No," she said, "this is like a pleasant habit." "And how do you feel now when I go away for vacations?" "Relieved," she admitted guiltily; "however, I hate to admit it, I'm afraid you'll cancel the rest of my remaining appointments." "Without asking you?" the doctor wanted to know. "What else?" asked Elizabeth. "I can't imagine not coming to see you; I feel terrible if I even think about it. It would be different if I were married," Elizabeth went on, "then I would have someone else, I wouldn't mind so much." "You're wrong there," the doctor said, "you would feel just as bad, married or not." "That's hard to believe," she said softly, "that must be hard on the husband, or wife." She still had trouble thinking of males as patients. "It is," said the doctor, "very hard." "I saw the surgeon in the waiting room the other day," Elizabeth said, "he looked just the same. He must have been coming here for a long time. He used to tell me that he had nothing to say when he went in to see his doctor; that he just lay there or sat there for hours, not saying anything. I told him my problem was that I could never shut up." "Then you are evidently not the sickest person in the world," Doctor Greene commented. "Sick enough," Elizabeth sighed. "A garden-variety neurosis, I'd say," he estimated, "but it will do, it will do." "He looked very surprised to see me looking like this—the surgeon," Elizabeth added, grudging. "You sound as if you want to hide signs of progress," said the doctor, "why is that?" "Well," Elizabeth said, "I don't want you to get above yourself. Also, I don't want you to take away my pink plastic pulmotor and give it to someone else." "Like the surgeon?" "Like the surgeon," she said, "probably you're already painting it blue." "I think we will have enough to keep us busy until your birthday," Doctor Greene said, "there is this problem of the pink versus the blue pulmotor, and your idea that I cannot wait to get rid of you." "Why shouldn't you want to get rid of me; I want to get rid of you," she said. "You make it sound as if you're about to take out a Mafia contract," the doctor remarked, amused. "Do you want to rub me out? Replace me with another doctor?" "But there should be *something* I could do," Elizabeth wailed; then she was quiet; "My throat's starting to hurt," she said. "Like what?" "Like I should be able to do something for you," she said, "I don't really want to talk about this," she finished, "I'll just start to cry." The doctor didn't say anything. "It just seems as if it's all been one way," she cried, "I hardly know anything about you: when I came here I was like some kind of stupid plant that couldn't learn to use its trellis, and now look what's happened. I want you to know I blame you entirely for my success—such as it is." "I know you find that success frightening," the doctor said. "But I should do something for *you*," Elizabeth insisted. "You seem to forget," Doctor Greene said, "that I have been very well paid for my services; you were not a charity case." "Money has nothing to do with this," Elizabeth insisted. "Well, perhaps not everything," the doctor conceded, "but just what is it you want to do for me?" "I don't know," Elizabeth said, "that's the whole trouble. I was thinking of getting you a present, but I couldn't think of anything to get you. The only thing I could remember was your saying that when you were a child, the elephant was your totem animal, and last week, I saw a museum replica of an Egyptian elephant with a person on it, and I thought about getting that." "It's true I used to love elephants when I was a child, but I've gotten over it," the doctor said; he sounded amused. "Why do you feel you have to get me something?" "Why can't you understand why I want to get you something?" Elizabeth demanded, angry. Now things seemed on a familiar footing, the materialistic doctor, the misunderstood patient. "I think there's more to it than meets the eye," the doctor said. "It occurs to me," said Elizabeth, "that I've never really looked carefully at those diplomas of yours. God knows who certified you." "You're welcome to look any time," the doctor said, "there's an even fuller listing of my credits in the Directory." "Last year, they left your name out of it," Elizabeth reminded him vindictively. "So you *have* been checking," the doctor said, triumphant. "You told me, you told me," Elizabeth said; she was too tired to move, "you are becoming senile." "It appears," said Doctor Greene, "as if you think I will perish the instant you set foot out of this door." "I am so sick of the way things appear, you have no idea," she said. "Time's up," she announced, looking at her watch. "And you are already taking over my duties," he observed, "since in my weakened state I can't see the big hand is on the five, is that it?" "The point is that it's five o'clock, that's all," Elizabeth said, annoyed. "How true," said the doctor, "how good of you to tell me. We will have to look into this some more, your idea that I will take revenge on you for getting better and leaving me: evidently by dying myself." "*Is* that such an odd idea?" Elizabeth asked, looking at her watch again. "Only if you think a surgeon would see his patient recovering after a dangerous operation and celebrate by running him through with a sword," the doctor said. "There's good security in those hospitals," Elizabeth said, crabby. "I see," said Doctor Greene, "otherwise, only the terminal cases would be permitted to escape alive." "It is true," he said, standing up, "that you have been a most successful case. Now we must find out why you think that should make me angry. I would imagine it would make more sense to imagine someone angry if they thought they had failed." "You are not an architect; you deal with people," Elizabeth was getting very confused. "We will talk about this next time," said the doctor, looking at his watch, "I'll see you tomorrow." "Tomorrow?" asked Elizabeth, "I thought my next appointment was Friday." "And that I had given your pink pulmotor away to the surgeon, perhaps, for Thursday, a day at a time, then you won't notice; is that the idea?" "You have a one-track mind," Elizabeth said, picking up her coat. "Thursday at four," said the doctor.

Chapter 9

"I won't be here next Tuesday," Elizabeth told Doctor Greene, "I'm going to New York for an interview. But I probably won't get the job," she added, reassuring, "they didn't sound too encouraging in their letter." "They must want you to run around the corner for some reason," the doctor suggested. "I don't want to get my hopes up," Elizabeth said. "By no means," the doctor said, "I'm disappointed to see you are still so superstitious." "Superstitious, nothing," Elizabeth retorted, "I'm just not sure I want to go."

"To New York?" Armand asked, flabbergasted. "That's right," Elizabeth said, gnawing on the remains of a stale bagel. "You look like Bertrand the Beaver; why are you eating that thing?" "Because, by the time I get finished eating it, I'll be too tired to eat anything else," she told him. "I eat all day and get thinner all the time;" he observed his hand gloomily: "a shadow of my former shadowy self." "You exaggerate," Elizabeth said, "the sun is falling on you, and I can see you quite clearly." "And count my bones if you wanted to," he said, depressed. He brightened. "Has it occurred to you that your *family* will be there?" "Where, at the interview?" Elizabeth asked. "No, in New York," Armand said, "they will call up every day to find out why you haven't called, who you're going out with, is he Jewish, why didn't you come home for the holidays, when are you going to see your grandmother; they'll be close enough to sit in on your classes." "I'll take out an injunction," Elizabeth said thinking. "I've thought about it, I don't want to think about it at the moment." "What about San Francisco?" Armand suggested. "What about the University of Nagasaki?" Elizabeth asked, "that's even further away." "So you're going to let yourself in for all that again, voluntarily no less; you must be crazy," Armand said. "I'll give you my doctor's number: call him, he needs a consultant," Elizabeth said; "besides, I should learn to cope with my family." "Why?" Armand demanded. "Why not learn to cope with smallpox

158

by going into the contagious ward at the hospital?" "It's not the same thing," Elizabeth told him. "It is, you'll see," he predicted. "Look," Elizabeth said, "I'm going. Stop trying to make me more nervous." "You'll have enough people to do that for you when you get there," Armand predicted, "if they meet you at the plane, you'll probably be sent back in a straightjacket." "I thought you were going to help me with some books," Elizabeth said, glaring. "I don't see why you're packing things *now*," Armand said, "you don't even know if you'll get the job." "I'll get some job, Armand, I'm going to New York even if I have to sell ribbons at Macy's" "With your family, you'll never lack for customers," he predicted, direly. "Get the door, please," Elizabeth said.

"She's going to New York," Armand announced to Benita in his best tragic voice. Benita looked around the apartment. "Are you going to move all this?" she asked. "All what?" "All this," Benita said, "it isn't everyone who has three couches; how many people do you know with a couch in the bedroom and dining room," she asked Armand. "There are *seven* rooms of furniture in this apartment," Armand announced like Balboa discovering the Pacific, "and most of it is solid oak. Probably that sideboard weighs four hundred pounds." "In other words, I can't afford to move," Elizabeth elucidated, like a textual commentary, "just what my mother said." "Well, it won't be cheap," Benita agreed. "Why don't you let me worry about that?" Elizabeth asked. "I don't have to move every stick and stone." "But you will," Benita protested, "the only thing you throw out is the garbage, and you put that off as long as possible." "Thank you, Sanitation Commissioner," Elizabeth said, wearily; "What do I need parents for when I have the two of you around?" "All right," Benita said, "do you want to start with the filing cabinet?" "Good idea," Elizabeth said. "How do I know what to throw out?" Armand asked. "Don't throw anything out," Elizabeth told him. "I *told* you," Benita announced, victorious. "What are these?" she said, pouring an armful of letters into her lap. "Letters from Joshua," Elizabeth said shortly. "If I were you," Armand said, "I'd rent a helicopter and scatter those ashes over the city." "Put them in a box, Benita," Elizabeth told her. "A black box," Armand added. "But you'll be upset to go, won't you?" Benita asked later. "I certainly will not," Elizabeth announced, emphatic. "Let's get this over with so we can go to the party." "What party?" Armand asked, injured. "Irene's party; she asked you last week." Armand looked disappointed; he had sniffed an insult, a rejection.

Irene was another girl in the building, "one of those crazy socialists," Armand reported. She was in one of their seminars. "She hasn't actually joined the party yet, but she probably will," Armand said. "I didn't know she was interested in politics," Elizabeth remarked. "She isn't," Armand said, "but she's interested in men, and for some reason, most of the socialists here fall into that category." "More onion soup and sour cream," Benita said grimacing. "What do you expect at a socialist party," Armand asked, "caviar and cream cheese?" "Are you going like that?" Elizabeth wanted to know. Armand had a black streak bisecting his face; he looked like he was being prepped for surgery in some version of *Frankenstein*. "I shall wash my face," Armand announced, grandiloquent. Benita bent over him, and, using her dusty finger as a pencil, drew the stripe into a swastika. Elizabeth stared at her. Armand looked pleased as a peach. Then they heard the water running in the bathroom. "I think I'll go home and change," he said, not looking at either of them when he came out; he was white as a sheet. "Why did you do that?" Elizabeth asked after he left. Benita shrugged. "I don't know what's the matter with you sometimes," she said. "What's there to know?" Benita asked. "I'm just a bitch. Let's get going."

The party was fully assembled when they got there. Clouds of cigar smoke, cigarette smoke, pipe smoke, swirled in the room as if the clouds had come down, personally, for a visit. "Come on, I'll introduce you," Irene said, grabbing each of them by the arm. "Where's Armand?" she asked, looking around, greedily. "Changing," Benita said. "Into what?" Irene asked, witty. "Have a drink," she said, leading them to the punch bowl: "I'll be right back." "Oh God," Benita said, "strawberries." There was a large punch bowl in the middle of the table, and in the center of its red sea, was a package of frozen strawberries, gradually decomposing. "It's delicious," Irene said, materializing and dematerializing at their elbows. "Have a potato chip," Elizabeth suggested, "it will make you thirsty enough to drink anything."

It turned out most of the people at the party were musicians. After everyone had been there for some time, a group of them gathered around the piano and began playing familiar things in slightly strange ways. Elizabeth understood that these were musical jokes, and the crowd around the piano roared with laughter every time something not-quite-odd happened to Schubert, or Beethoven, or Bach. Armand was sitting greenly on a couch staring at Benita. "Where did you find all of these?" Elizabeth asked Irene. "He knows them," Irene said, pointing to Fred, who was a physicist and also reviewed concerts for a magazine of some kind. "Are they socialists?" she asked. "Musicians don't seem to care about politics," Irene said, "we've tried."

Someone standing near the piano was beginning to sing. He sounded like an opera all by himself. "Who's that?" Elizabeth asked, curious. He was extremely handsome, and very large. *"That,"* Irene said, "is the celebrity; he's going to be an opera singer; he's having a concert next week." "What's his name?" Elizabeth asked. "Van Hassel." "No kidding?" Elizabeth asked. "Who could make up something like that?" Elizabeth gravitated to the piano. When Edward stopped singing, he smiled at her, and when he started again, he put his arm around her. When the group at the piano broke up, they started to talk. She was mostly interested in how he liked singing in front of an audience; anything vaguely involving acting had always seemed mysterious to her, and terrifying, standing in the center of a stage, raised, on a platform, as if a sacrifice, all those eyes, as many as pins in a pin cushion, riveted on you. Edward seemed to like explaining about performing, what it was like. He asked Elizabeth if she had come with anyone, and when she said no, he asked if he could take her home.

When they got to her apartment, she asked Edward if he would like to come up for coffee; he said yes. Elizabeth could remember when she wouldn't have known what to do: naïve idiot, she had thought someone should be asked up for coffee only if he actually wanted some; it had taken Doctor Greene to alert her to the system of codes and signals. When they got upstairs, Edward didn't want any coffee; they sat at the kitchen table and talked. Elizabeth told him she thought she was leaving during the summer. He said he never knew where he was going to be from one minute to the next because of the tours. Elizabeth found this profoundly reassuring; the next thing she knew, both of them were in bed. She had always been a fanatic about "protection," but this time it didn't even

161

occur to her that there might be "complications." In the morning, when she woke up and found Edward still there in her bed, she didn't know what to do with him; she didn't really like him; she was mostly interested, in a detached way, in her own motives. Edward woke up, looking pleased. "I have to go to work," Elizabeth said, getting out of bed, "make yourself something to eat." "Shall I call you?" Edward asked, looking mystified. "Well, I'll be in New York for a week," Elizabeth said, "I'll call you when I get back." Edward got dressed slowly. "Goodbye," he said tentatively, holding on to the doorknob. "Goodbye, have a nice concert," she said, closing the door with relief. The phone rang. "Well?" Benita asked. "Well," Elizabeth said, "today I am an adult. I feel as if I've smashed myself over the head with a bottle of champagne. By the way," she added, "he's on the lose again." "That was fast," Benita said, admiring. "When do you want to leave for the airport?" "At three. I'm going back to sleep for awhile." "See you later," Benita said, hanging up.

The minute her head touched the pillow, Elizabeth was sound asleep. She was in an empty room; the walls were painted white, but the plaster was cracked, thin hairline cracks, like old china, and there were thick streaks of dust which seemed about to sift loose from the walls. The wooden planks of the floor listed, and bits of dust blew across the floor like embryo souls. The room was filled with a gray light, but when Elizabeth looked for its source, she saw there were no windows or doors. "The light must be coming in through the cracks," she thought to herself, but she had no time to check this, because she saw the figure of a man in the corner. The more she looked at him, the more vague he became. "It's like trying to remember someone from the past," she thought to herself, "first you have a vivid picture, but when you try to look at it too closely, it begins dissolving like cloud." She thought she could see the face out of the corner of her eye, but when she turned to him, his face seemed to fall out of her eye like a tear. "Should I be afraid of you?" Elizabeth asked. "I don't think so," he said; his voice sounded familiar. "Someone sent me this to bring to you," he said. "I don't know who would send me anything," Elizabeth insisted. The man didn't listen, but moved toward her, and Elizabeth could see he had no body at all, but was a series of boxes connected by string, and each box was the color of one of her rooms. When the man got near her, he stared over her head at the wall. Elizabeth turned to look at it, and it faded to fog, and the fog faded to sea, and the sea was the color of prison, slate gray, and floating on its waters were spool after spool, emptied of their thread. "What are those spools?" Elizabeth demanded. "People," the man said, as if surprised by the question, and as she watched, they all sank under the wave. "What people?" she asked. "What people?" he mocked, sitting down on a slatted chair. "What did you bring me?" she asked, "I have to get ready to leave." "This," he said, getting up and holding out his hand; in it was a pearl-gray globe of water, and when she took it, it was cold to the touch, and when she looked into it, it grew large as the sea, and in the center was a face she could not name, and she felt all the salt in her blood drawn to the salt in that drop. "I don't want it," she said, her voice spiraling into the ceiling, and tried to shake it loose, but it clung to her palm, magnetic, and in some lights, silver. "Take it away," she screamed, but the man was fading into the pattern of the cracks on the wall. "Take it away," she called again, desperate, but he was gone, and she whispered in a voice like flame that gray water puts out, "I don't want it," but now the face in it seemed clearer, and when Elizabeth looked into it, it stirred on her lifeline like a live thing, and she was very afraid. "What a stupid dream," she said to herself when she woke up, "obvious. Sperm, that's what the gray drop was," but even as she told herself this, rinsing her face with cold water for the fifth time, she knew she was wrong.

When Elizabeth got off the plane at Idlewild Airport, her mother was waiting for her, neat in her red coat. Immediately, she felt a surge of resentment. Sometimes, her mother looked so clean she thought she used Ajax for face powder, Clorox for perfume. Automatically, she checked her mother's face for the look of disapproval, of disgrace, that this was her daughter, her only daughter, and this was what she looked like, her hair! her clothes! But the look was not there. "You look wonderful!" Sarah gasped, genuinely astonished. It seemed real enough. "Let me look at you," Sarah said, stepping back. "You really are a beauty," she said, shaking her head in disbelief. "You look pretty good yourself," Elizabeth said, through

163

the fog of resentment. She didn't know what she was so busy resenting; if her mother had been late, she would have resented that, but she was on time, early. Elizabeth resented that, the implication that Sarah had to be there or Elizabeth would get away. "The interview's tomorrow morning, but I don't want you to drive me there; you'll make me too nervous." "But it will take you two hours to get there by train," Sarah protested. "If I get the job, I'll have to get there myself all the time," Elizabeth said, "I'm going alone, that's that." All night, Sarah and Manny talked to her about the advantages of New York: New York had everything, how if you could make it in New York, you could make it anywhere. "I've got a headache; I better go to bed," Elizabeth said.

The train trip to the college seemed interminable; the last twenty minutes frightened her to death: she was not used to trains that ran underground, or trains that had two people per car. "It will be just my luck to get killed on the way to the school," she thought to herself, nervous. When she surfaced, she asked directions. The school enchanted her. Everywhere, students were talking, animated. She sat on a bench and listened to one boy telling another, "There's nothing the matter with you; you're not even neurotic. You flatter yourself. What you're suffering from," he said with great authority, "is existential anxiety." "I don't think so," the other one argued back. "Then what *do* you think is the matter with you?" the first one demanded, the aggrieved, the exaggerated patience of a saint. "I'm worried about whether I'll get into graduate school," the first one answered. "*That's* existential anxiety," the first one announced, triumphant. "So what isn't, according to you?" the worried one asked as they drifted off. Next to her, a girl was making notes, evidently for a paper. At the top of the page, was the single word "marriage." Beneath it were three headings: "as death, as security, as independence." Elizabeth thought the girl had a very yellowish skin, not in good condition. Every other student seemed to be carrying a petition. This was not at all like the Technicological Institute, and the buildings were old, and brick, with a vaguely colonial air. Suddenly, a carillon struck the half hour. "That settles it," Elizabeth thought to herself.

The interview was extremely formal. Seven men sat at the table, three on each side, one at the head; she sat at the other end, facing him. They asked her all the usual questions. When they asked her about her thesis, she went through it all again, hoping they would not notice the mechanical sound, the sound of the needle scratching in the groove. Then one who looked like a wise old owl asked her what she thought she would do next. She thought perhaps she might write a book on modern writers she didn't like, examining their faults. He said that was a dangerous idea, because if she really didn't like the writers, she might not have the patience to finish the project. Elizabeth agreed, politely. Her smile felt shellacked. The man across from her, whom the Secretary had told her was the Chairman, looked like he was suffering from a particularly acute attack of appendicitis; he had looked like that ever since she had come in. Then they asked her how much of a salary she would expect; she told them what the school in San Francisco had offered her. She thought she could see seven smiles, curved, sliding from their faces like half moons, onto the table. Then one of them asked her if she was interested in poetry. She said she was not. He observed that that was odd, considering her choice of a thesis topic. Elizabeth said she supposed it was, and then everyone stood up and shook her hand.

As soon as she got back to the train station, Elizabeth called her father in his place, and told him she had not gotten the job. He wanted to know how she could tell. "I could tell by looking at the Chairman," she said shouting over the noise of a passing train, "and besides, I think I asked for too much money." "If they want you, they'll pay it," Manny said. "They don't want me," Elizabeth said. Then, more hopeful, she added, "I did tell them I might be willing to take less, considering the advantages of coming to the city." A train roared by. She thought for a minute in the shaking booth. "But I don't think it will make any difference." They had a gloomy supper. Arthur said, "What do you want to come back here for, anyway?" "What's the matter with you?" Manny demanded, outraged, "what kind of a thing is that to say to your sister?" "She knows what I mean," said Arthur, staring at his plate.

The next morning, Arthur and Sarah drove her back to the airport. "I have to go back to work, mother," she said. Everyone was grim, in a fog. "Call and ask for yourself so we know you got there all right," Sarah said. "I will," said Elizabeth, picking up her bag.

The next morning, as she was getting ready to leave for work, she found a telegram in her mail. It was from the college; they were offering her a job, and they were offering her exactly fifty dollars more than the school in in San Francisco. She dropped her books on the floor and ran up the stairs to call her father.

The day before she was ready to leave Chicago, there was a horrible banging on the front door. "What the hell is that?" Elizabeth thought, crawling out of bed. It was her next door neighbor, Emily, hysterical. "He's going to shoot me, he's going to shoot me," Emily kept saying, "you've got to let me in." Elizabeth let her in, and Emily ran to the phone and called the police. Elizabeth sat down on a chair and watched her. Emily told the police her husband was threatening to kill her, and had a gun. In ten minutes, there was the sound of sirens, and the whole street was blocked off, blue and white. Megaphone voices called for him to come out with his hands up. The phone rang. "What's going on?" Benita demanded. "I'll call you back later. Emily's husband is threatening to kill her, or anyone else; you better stay inside," she said, hanging up. There was a lot of indistinct shouting. "They're going to kill him, they're going to kill him," Emily kept saying over and over. Elizabeth didn't know what to say: she didn't know how these things worked. "Don't worry," she said weakly. All of a sudden, there was a terrible smell; her eyes began to burn. "Tear gas!" Emily shrieked, jumping up. Suddenly, they were coughing and choking; Elizabeht's eyes were red and streaming with tears. "Don't rub them," Emily ordered her, flying over to the window. It was over in a few minutes. James, Emily's husband, was out on the street; when he disappeared into one of the cars, black and angry, a malignant pearl, Emily did not seem really upset. A policeman came up to talk to them, and *he* seemed terribly upset. He kept telling them to put out little bowls full of vinegar and water; the vinegar would absorb the gas; they would be able to breathe. The policeman was shiny and black. Emily was white, so fat her flesh folded like sagging socks over her ankles, obscuring the tops of her shoes; she kept her daughter pressed to her side, little baby March, the color of milk in coffee. "He hit me because I braided her hair," Emily said, pointing to the child's head. The policeman shook his head. He looked at March; she looked back at him.

He saw the braids, each fastened with a striped, gros-grain ribbon. There were at least thirteen of them. At the back of the child's head, one stood almost straight up in the air, like an antenna. The policeman kept swallowing, as if there were something terrible stuck in his throat. "I think we should all go out on the back porch," Elizabeth said, "it's easier to breathe out there." They trooped out through the apartment. March wanted to know where they were taking her daddy. The policeman didn't answer; he turned his back and walked to the railing on the edge of the porch, spreading his legs. He looked as if he were facing a urinal. Emily told March her daddy was sick, and they were taking him to a doctor. "Is he sick because of the gas?" March asked. "Because of the gas," Emily said; she smiled apologetically at the policeman. Elizabeth was getting very upset herself. Why on earth was this going on when she was leaving in the morning? She hardly knew Emily, having said hello to her as she fumbled with her keys and shifted her groceries from hip to hip. "March is a ridiculous name for a child," she said to herself, "no wonder they took him away." She was trying to get back her balance.

Later, they had coffee out on the porch. March asked for candy, and Emily took some raisins out of her pocketbook and gave them to her. Elizabeth asked if the child thought they were candy, and Emily said she did. Then she hesitated. "I don't want her to get fat," she said, starting to cry. "I'm a nurse," Emily said. Elizabeth wondered where Emily found uniforms to fit. She wondered what patients thought when they saw those two huge breasts inclining toward them; she wondered if they thought this was how God answered their prayers for a soft place to cry on, with this parody of their last, white, innocent hopes. "Where?" Elizabeth asked. "In the University hospital," Emily said, "they hire a lot of practical nurses because the cases are so depressing. In the experimental unit, anyway. You should see my patient." "What's the matter with her?" Elizabeth asked, wishing she hadn't. "She has psoriasis, all over her body, under her hair; it's even under her toenails. It was, I mean, it was." Emily sounded confused. "How is she now?" Elizabeth asked. She wondered momentarily if someone had arranged this so she should have no regrets. The graduate student in Evanston already had her car; he would be driving it back to New York in a week; she was flying home in the morning. The anonymous woman, covered with scales, seemed to hover before them, a recumbent cloud, filling the room. They both turned to her with relief. "She's almost better," Emily said mechanically. "Why couldn't they fix her up before?" Elizabeth wanted to know; she knew, somehow, the woman must be old. "They didn't know how, every day we wrap her in Saran wrap, she stays in it all the time." In the spring air, the mummy crinkled, tore at the thin film over her eyes. There was a long silence. The floor tilted. "She's happy," said Emily, abstracted. The words fell on the porch slats like stones. "I want more raisin candy," whined March.

Late that night, they moved in with her, into the shell of an apartment; the landlord said they could stay until the tear gas thinned in their rooms. It hung in the corners for months, old enemy, bent on revenge, getting thinner and thinner. Benita wrote her in New York and told her it was three months before the hall got back to normal. In the morning, Benita and Armand came to get her. Emily and March were sleeping on the floor of the other bedroom; there was nothing else but a giant oak filing cabinet she was leaving for the next tenant. "The tear gas comes on little cat feet," Armand said, looking around, trying not to rub his eyes. "Let's get out of here," Elizabeth demanded.

Years later, in New York, Elizabeth would find herself thinking about her last days in Chicago. Benita kept her posted over the phone. The judge had called Emily's husband a paranoid schizophrenic. Evidently, James had told everyone he was something else: a graduate student, a medical student, a lawyer. He was always happy when people asked him questions about one of his lives. He would answer meticulously. He had always smiled at Elizabeth on the stairs; he had always looked happy. Then Emily braided March's hair, and the threads of the web pulled and gave. Elizabeth found herself thinking about them, living their lives out in her empty apartment, seven rooms full of hot, stinging air. Had March gotten fat? More and more now, she found herself looking back into those days, nine blocks from the blue lake that looked like the ocean, and everything was in its same place, the dust was where it was, the curtains dispensed the same light, careful pharmacists, the same imitation crystal chandelier was screwed into the socket in the bathroom, the cement chipped between the tiles and came loose as if someone had started a house of cards, the radiator humped like an old cat, its coils up, its paint chipped, she could see it all through the thin veil of wrap, and then it began to burn, it began to burn like paint, it bubbled and scorched like skin, but when she closed her eyes, it was there. "See what you're missing?" Benita said.

Chapter 10

Now Elizabeth was back in her old room under the attic, with its small ceiling that slid down into the wall at an angle. The ceiling and back wall were wallpapered with quilted paper, patterned with small roses. At first, Sarah had been reluctant about papering a ceiling, but then Elizabeth had said, "It will make the room look larger, mother," knowing perfectly well her mother felt guilty about the tininess of the room, and Sarah had given in. Then there had been many expeditions to Macy's with Belle to find a desk small enough to fit into the room; the room was about fifteen feet long, and nine feet wide, "coffin-shaped," Elizabeth said. "God forbid!" said Belle, "cross your heart!" They had finally found a desk which was also a chest of drawers on the bottom. It had a wooden lid that came down, forming a desk, revealing a shelf and a great many cubby holes. It was the discovery of the secret compartments on either side that made up Elizabeth's mind. The salesman had carefully not shown them to Belle. "We'll take it," Belle said, "when will it come?" "Next Thursday," the man said. "Next Thursday!" Belle exclaimed, "when is the child supposed to study?" "Don't worry, grandma," Elizabeth told her, "I'll work on the card table." "You'd better use that desk once it gets there," Belle said severely, "no more doing homework in the basement in front of the television set; how you get anything done is a miracle to me." "I'm used to all that noise," Elizabeth said. "What noise?" Belle demanded, "the house is always quiet when you children study." "From the playground in the back, grandma," Elizabeth lied. "I don't know what your father was thinking of, buying a house facing a playground. How are any of you going to concentrate with all that noise?" "They go home at night," Elizabeth reminded her, "and I like it." "I hope you'll also like selling ribbons at Macy's," Belle warned her. "Look around, Miss Know-It-All, this is where you'll wind up." "Quiet, they'll hear you," Elizabeth hissed. "So what if they hear me?" Belle said, stentorian, "*they* didn't study in school, and this is what they get."

In the years she had been gone, ten years, almost nothing had changed in the room. Sarah had moved a chest of drawers into her closet; when Elizabeth went through it, it seemed to be filled almost entirely with linen napkins. "All those family dinners," she thought to herself, sighing. Her end table had the same number of cracks it had always had, no more, no less. They were covered by a thick layer of wax. Elizabeth pulled out the top drawer and looked in it. An old diary, its band broken, inscribed in her tiny hand, better than a code, every page with a picture stapled to the top: Mary, Esther, Rhoda, everyone. It revolted her to look at it: like a cemetery where the graves slid slightly down and little white hands snaked up, tugging at your feet. A Lady Sunbeam electric razor. "Now that you've got it, you never use it," Sarah had said, "you certainly carried on enough." Four old style silver hair curling pins, opening their mouths when pinched in the back like crocodiles. An army of hair pins. Old photographs, letters, dust. An old picture of Mark, wearing his beard. "Every time I come home I decide to throw that thing out," Elizabeth thought to herself, closing the drawer. "What am I doing here? the burnt child dreads the fire." She looked down at the blue linoleum. Before they had moved in, the room had been a child's nursery. "I must have a Joan of Arc Complex." She tried to imagine tear gas in this house, and got off the bed and went downstairs. She knew absolutely nothing about the city of New York. "Esther?" she said into the phone, "when are you coming with me to look for an apartment?" "Maybe Tuesday," Esther said tentatively. "I thought we were going today," Elizabeth protested. She was beginning to realize that Esther was afraid to leave the house. She tried to think how this could have happened. She and Esther had been friends as long as she could remember, but Esther had gone to the neighborhood college and she was still living with her parents. Esther would boast that she could keep track of the last fifteen years of soap opera plots, that one character who had just had twins, she claimed, had had a hysterectomy twelve years ago. "Marvelous," Elizabeth said, "but what am I going to do about an apartment? These addresses don't mean anything to me. For all I know, they're in the middle of the Bronx, or somewhere in Harlem." "How about Tuesday?" Elizabeth asked her again. On Tuesday, Esther called up and said she couldn't go with her because she had to go to the dentist. "You know you haven't changed at all," Elizabeth said furiously, "it was always impossible to count on you. Call me when you think you can spare the time." She slammed down the phone. Esther had not had a full-time job yet; she was a psychologist, and when she saw her patients starting to get better, she would quit, and go home and catch up on the soap operas. Her mother, who was a secretary, did all the cooking and cleaning. On Saturday, Esther called her back. "I've been reading the paper," she said. "What does Ann Landers have to say?" she asked coldly. "I found three apartments that look good." Elizabeth still didn't say anything. "Do you want to write down the addresses?" "All right," Elizabeth said, grudging. "Where are these places?" she demanded when Manny got home. "You have to look," he said, "the streets change from block to block." "Will you come with me tomorrow?" she asked, "you promised you'd help before I came home." "I don't see why you can't live here," Manny said, grumpy. "I thought we had been over that already; I want to live alone; I am moody and not fit to live with. Will you come with me tomorrow or not?" "We were going to your grandmother's," Manny said from behind the paper. "I'll go myself," Elizabeth said. "Manny," Sarah said, "we have to go with her, God knows what she'll find. She doesn't even know about the subways." "I thought she knew everything," Manny said.

The first apartment they looked at was in the East Eighties. "If you take this, you'll have to sleep on top of your oak table," Sarah said, "and you can forget about a double bed." Elizabeth went off to look at the bathroom. "Let's go, Elizabeth," Sarah said urgently when she came out. "What's the matter? I haven't made up my mind," she said. "Come out on the stairs; I'll tell you," her mother said in the stentorian family stage whisper. "The previous tenant just told me they don't heat the place in the winter; you're a fool if you take it." "I don't *want* it, mother," Elizabeth said mechanically. The next apartment they looked at was a fifth floor walk-up on West Eighty-sixth Street; it was the only brownstone on the block, sandwiched in between two big hotels. With satisfaction, Elizabeth noted that there was a small restaurant on the corner. "I hope you're not going to eat there," said her father, noticing the direction of her glance. Elizabeth started to get out. "Stay in there," Manny ordered her, getting out himself. "Your father is going to talk to the doorman," Sarah said. "About what, for Christsake?" Elizabeth asked. "About whether or not it's safe here; you saw that other street we drove down." Manny came back. "Let's go," he said. "What did he *say*, Manny?" Sarah asked. "He said it's a good street." They started climbing the five flights of stairs. "They'll never get your furniture up these steps," Manny predicted. "You were an idiot for shipping all that junk; it'll cost you a fortune." "It would cost me more to replace it," Elizabeth said, gasping for breath. "What's there to replace?" Manny asked.

The minute she saw the apartment, Elizabeth fell in love with it. It had high, carved ceilings, flying with cherubs. The floors were good, shiny wood. The bathroom was tiled, and her favorite color; the bedroom was long and narrow and reminded her of home. "It's much smaller than what you had in Chicago," her mother observed sourly. "Maybe I should move back?" Elizabeth suggested bitterly, "I'm taking it." "You should think about it first," Sarah said, distressed. Elizabeth made arrangements with the boys doing the subleasing to come see the landlord on Monday. "What are you doing with the couch?" she asked them. "We're leaving it, you can have it." "Good," Elizabeth said, "I can sleep on it until my furniture comes." Manny looked at the car as if he had just seen a giant brown plush snake. "She'll never learn," Sarah sighed aloud.

"So I'll be moving in today," Elizabeth said. "There's no hurry," Sarah told her. "There is, there is," Elizabeth said monotonously. "I want to get used to it before school starts." That night, she wanted to go with Hilda to see her grandmother in the hospital. Her mother wanted to know why she couldn't wait until later and go with her. Elizabeth said she would. That night, Esther came over with the car and they drove most of Elizabeth's bags over to the new apartment. When she got back, her mother was crying. "What's the matter now?" Elizabeth wanted to know. "Belle just died," her mother said, "I think you better come with me to Hilda's." At Hilda's, everyone sat around the table in a state of shock. "We knew it was coming," Hilda said, "it's better this way; she didn't know anyone anymore; she was just skin and bones." Then the phone rang. "Answer it, Elizabeth," her mother said. It was their next door neighbor. "Sarah?" she asked. "No, Elizabeth," she said. "Oh, Elizabeth." Mrs. Epstein sounded relieved. "Call your mother. There was a fire in your house; the engines are here, but we can't find the dog." "Thank you," Elizabeth said mechanically, hanging up. "Mother," she said, going back to the kitchen, "I think our house burned down. Mrs. Epstein just called up. We better go home. They can't find the dog." "We'll go with you," Hilda said, getting up. The house was still steaming when they got there. A fireman said he was sure he had seen a dog shoot out of the house and down the street. Sarah went off in the direction he pointed calling the dog's name: "Rex, Rex." Elizabeth could hear her mother's voice getting smaller and smaller. "I'm going to go in," Elizabeth said, "I want to look." "You're not going anywhere," Manny said. "It's all right, she can come with me," one of the firemen said. Inside, everything was black and streaked with smoke. The stairs were mostly burnt. The rail was gone. "Can I go up?" Elizabeth asked. "Yes, but be careful," the fireman said, "it probably was a bad lamp, you know, bad wiring." "Yes," Elizabeth said, picking her way upstairs. Her room and her mother's were badly burned. Arthur's room was blackened with smoke, but none of the furniture seemed hurt. She went over to the closet in his room. Her 1920s raccoon coat, her most priceless possession, was in it; it had kept her safe for nine Chicago winters; it was like a second skin. She had spent what little money she had saved to get its square shoulders rounded. She could hear one of the men at the Institute saying, "If you go to New York you won't be able to wear that coat." "Why not?" Elizabeth asked. "Things are much fancier there," he said knowingly. She had to force herself to open the closet. She felt as if she were opening a grave. Inside, nothing was touched; her coat was safe, her shoes, all her dresses were safe. She felt as if this was the last thing her grandmother had done for her; she had done this; she had kept back the hands of the fire. She was sure the lamp had sparked, like a candle, when Belle drew her last breath. Elizabeth buried her face in the shoulder of the raccoon coat, and thought about her grandmother, burnt house, burnt house of her childhood. Outside, she could hear a car sputtering into life. "You better come down now, Miss," the fireman said gently.

"Where's mother?" Elizabeth asked when she got outside. "She took the car to look for Rex," Manny said. They stood around shivering; it was very hot. "They didn't find the dog inside," Elizabeth volunteered. Everyone stared in the direction of the car. Finally, the car came into view. "I've got her," Sarah shouted before she pulled up, "she was hiding in the Levin's backyard." She got out of the car carrying Rex in her arms. "Put that thing down; you'll hurt yourself," Manny ordered. Sarah paid no attention to him. "You'll come back and stay with us,". Hilda said. Her parents nodded. "Just drop me at the station," Elizabeth said, "I'm going back to the apartment." "Get in, then," Hilda said, and then there was complete silence.

It was July; the heat was intolerable. Elizabeth was waiting for her brother to help her move her air conditioner from her parents' garage and then she would have to wait for someone to install it. She would sit at her window and stare into the lit windows of the hotel across the street. One night, she saw a man, fully dressed, neat in a black business suit, spread-eagled on his floor. Elizabeth watched him for a long time, and then he got up and wandered into a back room, out of her sight. He immediately became a symbol of the city for her. She felt as if she lived on a platform, five stories up, a flagpole sitter with three rooms, no way to get down. "It's the heat, the heat that makes me feel like this," she kept thinking, but she felt rigid as ice, so stiff she felt if she bent, she would crack. The day before she had gone to Belle's funeral. Outside, in the parking lot the air was rippling off the tops of the baking cars like pure liquid. She kept circling the brown sofa, the only piece of furniture in the apartment besides the folding chair and card table she had brought from Sarah's; finally, she settled by the phone.

"Edna," she said, "how would you like a visitor?" An hour later, she was on a plane to Boston. Edna's husband met her at the airport; did Elizabeth know Edna had just had a baby the week before? Elizabeth certainly did not. She began to feel better the minute she caught sight of their house in the trees. Whenever she saw her parents' house, it was as if someone had rolled all the old time up like strips of a lawn, about to be moved and planted somewhere else, and a new grass she could not quite place carpeted the entrance to the familiar door. Now, if she visited her parents, she had to visit them in a motel where they were staying while their house was being remodeled. "I don't know what's the matter with me," Elizabeth said after she got in, "I think maybe it's psychiatrist withdrawal symptoms." She still could not get rid of the fear, the hard feeling, the pane of ice. All through dinner, she tried to be cheerful. Finally, she admitted she had a bad headache, and asked Edna if she would mind if she crawled off to bed for a nap. "Go ahead," Edna said, busy with the baby. In bed, she uncurled like a root in the dark. She remembered how, in the spring, she used to plant seeds in little earthenware flowerpots and put them on the railing of the old porch ("Don't drop them on anyone's heads," Belle warned), and how they would come up, little and pale, like tiny green flames tipping the edges of candles. She hugged the blankets tighter; it was very cold, she was very cold. She heard a faint stirring; she listened, she realized it was Edna's oldest daughter, Marie. "Can I get in with you?" Marie whispered, conspiratorial. "Come on," said Elizabeth, sliding as far over to the wall as she could. She was lying on her side. Marie snuggled into her belly as tightly as she could. "Are we going to sleep?" Marie asked. "Yes," Elizabeth said. She could hear Marie trying to breathe deep and regular, pretending to be asleep. Then she heard Edna's voice calling Marie, wavering up the stairwell like smoke. "She's up here," Elizabeth called. "Come on, Marie," Edna said, standing in the doorway, the light forming a halo behind her, "it's time for bed." "Sorry," she said to Elizabeth. "That's all right," Elizabeth said, "I enjoyed it." In the dark, she began to cry softly, then she fell asleep; when she woke up, it was already morning.

"Do you want us to call Ralph? We could invite him over for dinner," Edna suggested. "Not really," she said, "I don't think I'm up to it." "Get the phone, Marie, please," Edna said. Marie held the receiver out to Edna. "It's for you, Elizabeth." "How the hell did they know I was here?" Elizabeth hissed, furious. "I'm never going to

175

have any peace, I never should have come back." "Well?" she demanded, taking the phone. It was Sarah. "It's your grandfather," she said, "he died last night." "I thought you said he was in Florida." Elizabeth thought this had to be some kind of joke. "He was," Sarah said, "but he didn't feel well, so your grandmother flew him home." "What did he die of?" "No one knows; he came home with something the matter with his stomach, but Irene says she thinks he was scared to death." "What do you mean, mother?" Elizabeth asked, shocked. "He was always terrified of hospitals," Sarah said in a weak, drugged voice; "he died two hours after they left him there." There was a pause: "Your father's very upset." "I'll be back on the next plane, when's the funeral and what's the address?" Her mother told her. "Do you want Arthur to meet you at the airport?" "No, I'll go home to the apartment first and drop my things off." "My grandfather died," she said turning around to Edna. "So I gathered; we'll take you to the plane. Come back next week." "I probably will," Elizabeth said, "if I'm not in the Neponsit Home for the Aged myself."

Elizabeth got back to the apartment. She looked around: she was surprised at how much she hated it; she had been refusing to admit it, that was half the trouble. Then she took out the directions for taking the trains into Brooklyn and the funeral parlor. There were a good many changes to be made. Finally, Elizabeth found herself on the QJ Brighton Beach line. "This must be the train we used to take to Coney Island," Elizabeth thought to herself, remembering how she and her friends used to go down to the beach themselves, take off their dresses, go swimming in their slips, and, when their slips dried, put their dresses back on, and go home; they were forbidden to go swimming without their parents around. President Street. That was where her grandmother had lived after her parents had thrown her out. Elizabeth could remember Belle leaning out of the window of her red brick apartment house, as they were coming, or going—again. By the time she got to the funeral she was late. She slid into the back row and listened to the Rabbi, but she couldn't understand a word he was saying. Everyone was crying. "Your grandfather had a lot of friends," the woman sitting next to her whispered at the end of the service. Elizabeth wondered who she was.

176

A few days later, she took the train into Brooklyn to see the family; everyone was sitting shiva at Irene's. "The first time she's worried about him," Sarah whispered, looking over at her grandmother, sitting on the plain wood chair, rocking back and forth. "Sit here," Madelaine said, scrunching against one of her children. Elizabeth sat down. "How is she taking it?" she asked Madelaine. "How should she take it?" Madelaine said philosophically, "no one likes it when things like this happen." "There'll be trouble with Irene now," her mother predicted, gloomily, "and your father will get the worst of it, the Head of the Family, some honor!" Elizabeth asked her what she meant, but Sarah just shook her head: "You'll see," she said.

Four or five days later, Elizabeth called Sarah. "What happened with Irene?" she asked. "Just what we expected," Sarah said bitterly. "It turned out your grandfather had been supporting them all along; of course, everyone knew that, considering the way they were living, and what he earns for a salary, so there was trouble with the will." Elizabeth remembered how Sarah and Hilda had prided themselves on the lack of arguing done over the wills left them by their parents; whenever there was some kind of conflict, they just flipped a coin. "What kind of trouble?" "Irene wanted all the money in a lump sum, but the will said it was supposed to be some kind of trust, and your father was to take charge of it. Irene thought she should get all the money right away because she had debts to pay." "So?" Elizabeth asked. "So," Sarah said, "everyone told her she couldn't have the money right away, because she would just spend it, and then she'd have nothing left, and then your grandmother would try to give her money, and then she'd have nothing left, and then we'd all have to support *her*." "So?" Elizabeth asked again. "So we all thought it was settled, but Irene ran out on the street screaming that we all hated her, and she wished she was dead, and what kind of family did she have, the works." "What's Daddy going to do?" Elizabeth asked. "Just what he said, operate the money as a trust fund. But it's what your grandmother is going to do that we're worried about." "This really is a mess," Elizabeth said, comforting. "She never grew up," Sarah said, "they spoiled her rotten, and now they have only themselves to thank. I don't know where this is going to end. They'll have us all in the poorhouse."

"Did Daddy co-sign my application for a loan yet?" she asked. "Yes, he did Elizabeth, but I'm warning you now that if you don't pay that loan back and we have to take over the payments, I'm going to deduct the amount of money from what we're leaving you in the will; it wouldn't be fair to Arthur." Elizabeth had borrowed fifteen hundred dollars to pay for moving, new furniture, a month's advance rent on the apartment, and the debts she had left over from paying the last year's doctor bills herself. "You're just like Irene," her mother said, "and you're not getting any younger. Why can't you find someone who likes *you* for a change?" "Drop dead," Elizabeth said slowly, and hung up. Two minutes later, the phone rang. It was Manny. "Why did you talk like that to your mother?" he demanded. Elizabeth looked at the phone, and replaced it on its hook.

Chapter 11

The last day she had gone to see Doctor Greene, Elizabeth didn't have much to say. She had repeated her fears about going back to New York, having to deal with the family, being swallowed up, backsliding. When she got up to leave, she asked Doctor Greene if she could kiss him goodbye. "No," he said, "I do not think that would be wise." She had nodded her head and left. Then she went down the hall to the bathroom, and let herself in with her key. She sat down in the locked bathroom stall and started to cry. After a half hour, she stopped and dried her eyes, but as soon as she had blown her nose, she started crying all over again. At last, she heard another key turn in the lock. "All right," she said, talking to herself, "let's go." As soon as she sat down on the train, she started to cry. She pressed her face against the window glass and stared out at the lake. The man sitting next to her took one look, and, petrified, turned to his paper, comforting himself with the front page story: RICHARD SPECK KILLS 8 STUDENT NURSES. "Fine world, fine world," Elizabeth thought to herself. For the next few weeks, she would find herself going downtown to the

Art Institute at the very same time she used to have her appointments; finally, she got worn out by the trips to the museum and stayed home, sleeping. When she got up, she sat down at the desk and wrote out a poem. Doing that upset her so she had to lie down on the floor; she felt she was falling into pieces, shattered by fright. In the next few weeks, she got used to it; she had not done any writing in eight years. After awhile, she called Doctor Greene: "I wanted to say goodbye," she said, "guess what I'm doing?" "I'm not good at guessing games," the doctor said. "I'm writing poetry again," Elizabeth told him. "Good," he said, in a neutral voice, sounding unimpressed. Elizabeth realized she had never discussed the subject of writing, other than her thesis, with him. She wondered why this was. "I'd like to see you once before I go," she said lamely. "I'll put my secretary on the line," he said.

After school had started in New York, Elizabeth was shopping in Bloomingdale's, when she ran into Jane, Doctor Greene's secretary. They fell upon each other like long lost friends. Jane had quit her job and opened a gallery on the North Side and it was doing very well; she wanted to know about Elizabeth: "I'm fine," she said, "just not married. And I miss Doctor Greene. I'm tempted to call him, or something." "Don't," Jane said, "he'll think more of you." Elizabeth made some excuse to get away, promising to visit Jane's gallery the next time she was in Chicago. She left immediately and took the train back. Walking home, she stopped at the muffin store for a doughnut and coffee. There was a policeman waiting at the counter for nine coffees to go. He had the harried look of a mother of ten. He kept on explaining, this one with sugar, this one with sugar and cream, this one black. The woman in back of the counter was losing her temper; grease spluttered and burst. She wiped her hands on her black nylon apron; it streaked with confectioners' sugar, in long scrapes, as if white, powdery hands had clawed at her abdomen, trying to get in. The innocent doughnuts, lay, little witnessing eyes, in their trays. The trays were not aluminum, but something else; rusty patches showed through. The policeman was in despair.

Finally, what turned out to be a secretary from the precinct office pushed in behind him; a square pane of cold air swung in with her. She suggested he make a list and offered him a piece of paper she tore from a pad in her pocketbook. The woman behind the counter pushed back her hair in relief. A floury streak covered her forehead like a bandage; it traveled up through her hair, aging her ten years. She turned her back on the world; she began the ritual of the cups. A bus swung out from the curb; a truck honked its horn.

The policeman and the secretary began to talk about the latest rash of cop-killings. Elizabeth was surprised to hear them talk about it that way, but then she remembered Irene telling her about how, after her first baby, which took days to be delivered, her surgeon was so upset he landed in the hospital with pneumonia. "Don't complain Doctor Graham is so gruff," Irene had advised her. The secretary said she had known seven of the nine men from the precinct who had been killed so far this year. "No, you knew eight of them," the policeman said. "Why eight?" she asked. "Eight," he said, "you forgot the Sergeant was killed last week; he was the eighth." "Oh," she said. "The eighth," he said again to himself. Elizabeth looked at him again. Probably the first two numbers on his badge were twice his age. A red light burned in his cheeks. He looked as vulgar and as stupid and as plain as the red light on the reindeers' noses that used to cover the lawns of the houses near the junior college from the beginning of December to late January. Now Elizabeth wished she knew him better. She had no sympathy for her students' simple hatred of the police: "Pigs," they would shout, pointing at their fat necks caught cruelly in their tight collars. She had the feeling she didn't know the first thing about the effects of danger, death, responsibility. Responsibility, that's the important thing, she thought to herself, getting up to pay the check. She smiled at the policeman as she left, and he pinked with pleasure. Outside, the clouds were scudding over the tops of jagged buildings in a clear blue sky. It seemed to Elizabeth she never had any answers; her answers were always turning into questions, still, still. Why would Doctor Greene think more of her if she didn't call him? Yet the process seemed as repetitious and inevitable as the pendulum ticking in back of the clouds, swinging them across the face of the day sky, the night sky while she slept, the ever-present, constantly moving clouds. The night sun, the setting sun, was an oven, melting the answers down; if you followed a road long enough, it drove into the sun, and everything you knew melted and went out. The incandescence stayed after; for a moment, it burned behind closed lids; then it went out. Today, the moon hung in the sky like a second sun; it was impossible to tell which was which. "I haven't gotten anywhere, not anywhere," Elizabeth thought to herself, depressed. Then the bottom fell out of her bag of groceries, and began falling down three flights of stairs. "Damn!" she said, hearing the janitor, suspicious, unlocking his door.

One day, Arthur arrived at the apartment to help her put up bookcases, but the ordinary drill bit would not penetrate the bedroom walls, and they had to go out and get a special kind. Finally, Elizabeth could unpack her cases of books; she was beginning to cheer up. The sight of her books on the walls gave her some premonition of order. She had also acquired a small gray kitten at Edna's: "maybe if you had something to keep you company, it'd keep you from getting involved with the wrong kind of men," she had said, handing it over, and sadly Elizabeth had to agree there was something to that. She had flown him home in her Mexican shopping basket, and he had been too terrified to make a sound. The whole time they were drilling holes for the bookshelves, Sammy, the cat, hid under the bed. After Arthur left, he began climbing from shelf to shelf, practicing jumping down on the bed. Elizabeth had nothing to do and alternated going to museums with going to stores; she was getting desperately bored. Her only male friend in the city, David, Mark's old roommate, finally introduced her to an old friend of his from his days in Washington. Ira had evidently worked for the CIA, but now he worked for a Manhattan bank. He would stand in David's backyard throwing knives at chalk marks on trees, never missing. There was much mysterious, cloudy talk about the days he had spent hopping along the Ho Chi Minh trail in Laos: "But the United States isn't supposed to be in Laos, is it?" Elizabeth asked, thinking she had the names of the countries mixed up: all conversation came to an end. She and Ira were steady visitors at David's house that summer, along with another physicist who had known Mark—this one was currently out of a job, his top security clearance having been canceled when the security force found out he was propping the door to his top-secret lab open with his Banker's Trust card. That way, he explained, no one knew whether he was late or not; they didn't even know whether he was there or not. The other member of the group that gathered at David's, fleeing the city, the cultural opportunities, the challenge they all claimed to love, was Saul, another ex-member of the CIA; he had the distinction of having been arrested in a foreign country; a distinct picture of his rear end had appeared as he bent to retrieve a document behind a door, or a wall; he was selling stocks for a large, New York company. But Ira was the focus of everyone's attention. "Ira is a poet," David told Elizabeth in an awed voice one afternoon while Ira was throwing his knife at a tree. "Has he published anything?" she asked. "No," David said, looking offended, "but he won a prize when he was in college, the same one your precious Sylvia Plath won." "She did go on from there," Elizabeth pointed out. "Have you ever read anything of his?" David said he had, and he thought they were good, but, of course, he was no judge, and Ira was very secretive. They all seemed to agree that Ira was a sensitive soul who had suffered terribly from the sights and sounds of the CIA: "but maybe it will be good for his work, he's writing a novel," Saul told them, hopeful. Ira began to pay attention to Elizabeth. He wanted to know if she had read any Richard Wilbur, and when she said no, he said he would bring her his copy. Had she read Wilfred Owen? He would bring that too. The next weekend, when she and Ira were both staying over at David's, she wondered about the books, but no one mentioned them. Then she went into her room and found them on the little table next to her bed. She was beginning to see what the others meant. During the week, Ira called her and asked her for a date. He had gotten tickets for *Man of La Mancha;* it was clear from his tone that he thought Elizabeth would be impressed; afterwards, they went to an espresso house in the Village; Ira kept telling her how beautiful she was, how intelligent she was, and gradually, it began to dawn on her that she was going out with a man with "a line." She had never met anyone with a line before; slowly, her first flash of contempt faded away, and she was dazed with delight. This must be what it was like to lead a normal life. Elizabeth was drunk with a desire to lead a normal life, this talk about the subways, the overcrowding, the high rents, the ins and outs of finding apartments, in and out neighborhoods, and, whenever it had gone on too long, Ira would invoke Richard Wilbur as if talking about a secret saint; his soul, his true soul, floated above the D train and brownstones, and Greenwich Village and art fairs, drinking with the boys and endless recitals of how much of what each one had drunk, and how, dead drunk, he had managed to put himself on a train for Washington and had woken up sober at the other end, unaware of having gotten on. In five weeks, she saw seven musicals. She forgot how she hated musicals; this was how normal people lived; she would learn to like them. When Ira called to say he had gotten tickets to *Fiddler on the Roof,* she managed to sound enthusiastic. Sarah and Manny went into paroxysms of delight: she would love it: it was a marvel, a wonder. After *Fiddler on the Roof,* she and Ira and a group of the boys from the bank all went out drinking; when Ira got back to her apartment, he fell asleep on the couch, and Elizabeth couldn't wake him up. Finally, she set the alarm for six o'clock and went to bed herself. He got up at six, all apologies. Then for two weeks, she didn't hear from him. She was sitting over her typewriter like melting butter, expecting to see the metal beading with sweat, when the phone rang. "How are you, gorgeous?" he asked. "Not so good," Elizabeth said. There was a long pause. "My grandmother died, my house burned down, and last week, my grandfather died: I'm depressed," she said into the black worm-holes of the phone. "Can I come over?" he asked. "Sure," she said, hanging up. When he got there, he complained about being cold. "Cold?" Elizabeth exclaimed, "it's ninety-six degrees out." Her apartment was right under the roof on the fifth floor and when they sat on the couch, they were baking, like waffles on an iron. Nevertheless, he was shivering. "I have malaria," he informed her in a matter-of-fact tone. "Shouldn't you do something about it?" Elizabeth demanded, worried. *"You're* the one we're supposed to be worrying about," he said in a slightly oily, patronizing tone. She asked him what he wanted to do. "Let's take a walk and have a drink," he suggested. They marched off down Amsterdam; Elizabeth was terrified of the neighborhood; just yesterday, someone had told her it was the worst street in the city, and looking around, she believed it. Finally, they found a bar with green shades on the lamps and a lot of pinball machines. "Two gin and tonics," Ira ordered, without asking her. It was part of his manner of command. They didn't say much. Ira seemed sunk in some depression of his own. "I saw you were writing poetry," Ira said at last. "Yes, I could use some help; it's been a long time since I did anything," she said. "Some night, we'll go over them and work on the structure and meter," he said importantly, and then lapsed back into silence. "Every now and then I get a letter from Isabella Gardner, she was the one who gave out the prizes, asking what I'm doing." "That's impressive," Elizabeth said. Ira stared into his drink. Then they walked back to her house. "I guess I didn't cheer you up much," Ira said grimly. "You did, you did," Elizabeth lied. "I just needed to get out."

The next day, she called Esther and told her about Ira. She was sure she was getting too attached to him, out of boredom if nothing else. When she got to the malaria part, Esther got hysterical: "You must be kidding," she said, "it sounds like some dialogue out of a Leslie Howard-Jennifer Jones movie." She didn't think there was much in it for Elizabeth. "You know how you get attached to everyone," she reminded her. Elizabeth protested that Ira was interesting. "So was *Gone with the Wind*," Esther said, sarcastically, "just malaria, but don't mind me, stiff upper lip and all that," she mocked. "And you don't mind the delirium tremens?" Esther asked. "What are you talking about?" Elizabeth asked, annoyed. "Hasn't he passed out yet?" "He certainly hasn't," she said, seeing the picture of his waxy face sleeping beyond shakings and alarms on the brown living room couch. "I don't believe you," Esther said, "what do you need that emotional cripple for?" "Oh, he's not *that* bad," Elizabeth said. "If you mean he's better than staying home alone, you may change your mind yet," Esther told her. But then the question became academic, because Ira did not call her again. "So what could he do to follow the malaria act?" Esther asked, "I'm not surprised."

Then Sarah called. Did Elizabeth realize how bankrupt she was, that she hardly had a penny to her name, that she was borrowing from Peter to pay Paul? She should get a job for the rest of the summer, the family couldn't afford to support her for the rest of her life. Elizabeth pointed out that she would be employed by the beginning of September. "But in the meantime you could save *something*," Sarah insisted, "you'd have something for clothes." "Look, mother," Elizabeth said, "I've

184

worked very hard for three years, I've been teaching extra courses, and in the summer, doing a thesis; I deserve a vacation." "Money doesn't grow on trees," Sarah said, "we all have to work hard. When are you going to grow up?" There was a long hostile silence. "Have you met anyone yet?" her mother asked. "I'll meet someone when I get to school," Elizabeth said, "I'm hanging up." "Get a job," her mother said, as she put the receiver down. When she hung up, Elizabeth wondered how her mother still managed to make her feel so guilty after all these years, as if her loan was taking money out of their mouths, disgracing the family name. But, she thought, she was depressed and lonely: maybe she *should* get a job. The only thing she could think of was to go to a temporary agency; when they heard about her degrees, they looked hopeless. "Can you type?" they asked. She said yes. The woman looked dubious, but checked off the appropriate box. "Can you use a dictaphone?" Elizabeth said yes. Now the woman was sure she was lying. "How about an electric typewriter?" "I haven't used one for a long time," Elizabeth said. "Go practice," said the woman, smiling under her varnished lips, "and then we'll give you a test." "Seventy words a minute," the woman said admiringly, "no mistakes." "I learned at a publishing company," Elizabeth volunteered, "when I started, I typed twelve words a minute, so at four o'clock, I used to distribute the contents of my wastepaper basket in everyone else's so no one would know how terrible I was." The woman looked appalled to even hear of such goings on. "So, are there any jobs?" Elizabeth finished, squelched. "We can send you out this afternoon," the woman said, "to a television studio."

The television studio turned out to be a large religious building near Columbia, and Elizabeth was given the job of typing scripts for pastors of religious programs in the deep South: there was an enormous backlog of them: none of the other secretaries had managed to learn which word went in italics, which in capitals, which were underlined. "Why is it so important, what happens if you make a mistake?" Elizabeth wanted to know. "If you make a mistake," her boss, who was a young, bearded man, not much older than she was, told her, "the Minister reads his lines like this: 'and God looked at the world and saw it was good significant pause, and the dove flew back from the mountain message from the sponsor occurs

185

here.' " Elizabeth laughed, hearing it, the stunned face of God, the fundamentalists puzzling it out. "They get *very* angry," her boss said, smiling. "Where's the script on baseball as a religious activity?" he shouted, running out of the room.

Elizabeth and Bill, her boss, got to be friends very fast; for one thing, she was the only secretary he had ever had who could type the scripts properly. He basked in the absence of outraged telegrams from the Ozarks, the Everglades. The very thought of her leaving in the fall filled him with despair. One day, he came in and announced since she was going back to school, *he* was going back to school. "And here is my wife, Cinny," he said, producing a small blue-eyed woman with dark hair from behind his back. "She works upstairs." "For a witch," Cinny said in the high drawling voice of the Southern Belle, "you see, I'm pregnant and that's not *ryught*, even for a married lady." Cinny and Elizabeth and Bill became a kind of unit, a family. Elizabeth found out that Bill had intended to become a minister, but then he had volunteered for one year's work on the terminal ward at the city hospital, and he had lost his faith. Now he had decided to become a minister anyway: "You don't need faith at all," Cinny said, "you need *character*." He really was going back to the seminary in the fall, but they were going to go back South. Elizabeth said she would really miss them, and she wrote their address down everywhere, even on the wall. But the work was upsetting her, its monotony. She was beginning to suffer from headaches and stomach aches and sleeplessness. At night, she would call David to erase the thick gray sludge of the day hardening behind her eyes like newly poured asphalt. After a week of phone calls, she realized they were long distance calls, and she would be lucky if her salary at the studio covered them. She quit in the morning. *"Poor Bill,"* Cinny wailed. "We understand though," he said; "I knew it was coming, I knew it, we never should have left Sewanee, I knew it, those damn scripts." *"Dayum,"* Cinny said archly, "what a word for a minister." She reminded them they were going back in the fall. For Elizabeth, Cinny and Bill had become a touchstone couple, a happy marriage. She saw them standing in a little glass globe, the seasons inverted, the snow swirling over them where they stood, then settling, hidden, the lovely floor of the crystal globe, the air turning to spring. They tried to tell her it hadn't been so easy in the beginning. "For instance, he didn't want a baby," Cinny said. "The first six weeks we were married, I had a migraine from the stainless steel scraping on the Melmac," Bill put in. "But you never hear the scraping on the paper plates," Cinny said comfortably. "I really did have those headaches, though," Bill said dreamily, "I had to go to a doctor." "He did," Cinny agreed, "but he's better now. All those dying people, that was what it was." "It was the Melmac," Bill insisted. And so they left, and exchanged addresses again, and the summer, like a bad movie, came to an end, the audience asleep, or dazed in its seats.

The night before school started, Elizabeth was woken up at three in the morning by a horrible crash. Sammy's claws were digging through her nightgown into her breast-bone. She had a horrible feeling the third world war had begun, and was wondering if she should turn on the radio. Then she realized she was weighted down. She stuck out a hand. Books, she realized, she was covered with books. She switched on her nighttable lamp; the bookshelves had fallen out of the wall, and were thrown all over the bed and the floor, flung open randomly as if someone had rifled them in a terrible hurry, looking for a very important secret. "All right, Sammy, all right," she said, stroking him automatically, wondering if this is how people got heart attacks, and pushed the books off the bed with both hands. God only knew what the people downstairs thought: Family Quarrel. Probably nothing. This was not Chicago. In the morning, she woke up, sniffling. When she got to school, which was an hour and a half train ride away, she was impressed by the size of the classes and the noise they generated. This was not like the Technicological Institute where the students sat in their rows, good as lettuces. She remembered her training as a counselor and gave them the most frightening talk she could think of and sent them out to get their books. She was beginning to cough. When she spoke to Esther that night, Esther recommended a patent cough medicine, which, she said, not only cured the cough, but made you feel like you didn't care if you had it. Elizabeth bought the largest bottle she could find, and put it in her pocketbook. She felt perpetually hot, but the days were getting colder; she had no time to get a winter coat now that school had started, and she hadn't gotten to the crate where her old clothes were packed. Between classes, she would go to the student coffee house, and order a cup of black coffee and take her cough medicine chaser. By the third week of this, she was beginning to feel horrible, as if she could barely drag herself around, and if she started to laugh, she couldn't stop coughing. One day, she was sitting at the secretary's desk making a phone call, and Frieda looked at her and said, "You don't look well to me." "It's just a cold," Elizabeth said coughing. "Colds don't go on this long," Frieda said, "you better see a doctor." When she got home, she called Arthur and got the name of one. "Why can't you use Doctor Blaustein?" Sarah wanted to know. Doctor Blaustein was the family doctor and lived out where the family lived, on the Island. "Because I don't have the time or energy to trundle out there, I need a doctor where I live." "What does Arthur know about doctors?" Sarah asked rhetorically, and hung up.

The next morning, Elizabeth felt so dreadful she began to think Frieda was right, but she didn't have an appointment to see the doctor until the next day. She went to school. She noticed her hearing was distorting, and there was a constant sound, like waves breaking, in the classes. That night, she had a splitting headache, but she forced herself to go to a meeting of The Poetry Organization of the English Speaking Countries. "I have to do something, I can't be a hermit," she said to herself, as she poked herself out of the door with an imaginary cattle prod. The Poetry Organization was showing a film on Theodore Roethke, carefully skirting the mention of any of his problems. It seemed composed primarily of old women in cut-velvet coats and rusty veils. "I had no idea there was so much money in poetry," Elizabeth thought to herself, shivering, looking at the cut-velvet coats; she would have loved to borrow one and put it over her lap. Then they had a contest to pick the poem of the week. At first, Elizabeth thought this was a joke; then she realized it was a treasured tradition, the highlight of the evening. The official presiding had a quavering voice, and looked like The Ghost of Christmas Future. One poem had something to do with a concentration camp. The audience fell upon it like hawks. At last, one man got up, and, in an emotion choked voice, said he could not understand, he could not, he would never understand, why everyone felt so sorry for the Jews. Were the Jews the only victims of the war? What about the gypsies? Didn't anyone know about the gypsies? Here he struck his breast. *Six thousand* gypsies had died during the war, but what did people care about them? There was a museum in New York commemorating them, but what did anyone care, tragic, tragedy. People were beginning to complain, and hiss. What did this have to do with the poem? Elizabeth's head was beginning to swim. Gypsies? *"Poem, poem,"* the man said, tragically, tears in his eyes, sitting down. "Yes, Mrs. Lusterwood": the chair recognized the next speaker. Elizabeth got up. Outside, it was freezing cold. Her head ached as if its bone plates were being pulled apart by granite hands. She took a cab and went home.

The next day she went to the doctor. He took her temperature; he shook his head. "Breathe in," he said, "Hold it, now breathe." When the ritual was completed, the doctor said, "You have crackles in your lungs, a mild pneumonia. Shall we put you in the hospital, or is there someone who can do your shopping for you?" Elizabeth told him a friend of hers from Chicago was coming in the morning, and would be staying with her until she found an apartment of her own. "Fine," the doctor said, writing out a prescription, "take these every four hours, do any shopping you have to do now, get in bed with a vaporizer trained on your nose, and call me in the morning and tell me your temperature." "I don't have a thermometer," Elizabeth said, weakly. "Then get one," said the doctor, "this is important." Elizabeth looked at him questioningly. "If we aren't very careful," he said, "you will be in the hospital by the end of the week."

Chapter 12

The next three weeks, Elizabeth spent in bed inhaling the hot white mist from the vaporizer. She became attached to it, and thought of it as a domestic Casper the Ghost. Once or twice, Ira called "to cheer her up," but when he made her laugh, she couldn't stop coughing, so she started rationing her calls. Whenever Nancy was there, she would tell people Elizabeth was asleep. When she got bored, she would get up and go to the typewriter, typing up final versions of the bits of poems she scribbled flat on her back on the torn remnants of envelopes from Chicago; they were mostly about the heat, or the cold, or the monotony, and she was not pleased with them. Usually, after she did this, she would crawl into bed, take her temperature, and find it had gone up. After two weeks, the doctor let her go out occasionally; she was still a fanatic about dieting; for a long time she had refused to take any cough medicine because it was very syrupy; she was sure it was full of sugar. Now, whenever she went out, she would make the same trip: stop at the drugstore to buy a new bottle of patent medicine Esther had told her about—three swallows and she would sleep for five hours, like the dead, she really could not remember when she had last had enough sleep; it must be five years ago, she thought to herself, calculating; then she would stop at the restaurant on the corner and buy a corn muffin, unbuttered, and a cup of coffee; she drank it as hot as possible; it seemed to make her feel better. She could cope with the drunks and the bums and the panhandlers now. It was mostly a matter, she thought, of carefully choosing your seat. She had learned it was folly to wait for evidence before acting suspicious; at the slightest indication of anything, a look sliding in her direction, an accidental brush with a knee, a "pass the sugar," she would turn and look at them poisonously, then ostentatiously move her muffin and coffee far down the counter, looking, she thought, as if she had every intention of screaming should she be asked for one more thing: "pass the ketchup, the salt." Now that she and the counterman were on speaking terms, no one seemed to bother her. This alone was phenomenal progress, Elizabeth thought.

When she had begun seeing Doctor Greene, she had still been phobic about public transportation, and would drive the Blue Bomb downtown and park it in an elegant parking lot on Michigan Avenue. The man who retrieved it, driving it like a new Porsche, always had something for her: a sneer, a heavy breath, a "what's for Saturday night, baby?" She didn't have the slightest idea of what to do with him, and the alternatives she considered were not practical: abandoning the car on the street, buying a gun, writing letters of complaint to the manager. She considered writing the letter for some time. Then she told Doctor Greene about it. He suggested she stop tipping the man. "But then I'll have no peace!" Elizabeth protested.

Still, she stopped tipping him. After the first time, he wanted to know why. "Because you won't keep your mouth shut," she said, "would you rather have no tip or have me complain to the manager?" She expected to be murdered where she sat, the well-dressed matrons looking on, the line of men waiting to redeem their coupons peering interestedly into the front seat. "Fuck you, lady," he called after her tailpipe, but the next time he retrieved the car, he was normal, polite. Over the years, they occasionally had cordial things to say to each other. "Have a nice weekend," Elizabeth said, the last time she left the lot. "Sure thing," he said, giving the windshield a swipe with his cloth: he had never done that before.

The first time Elizabeth had come to the restaurant, the man behind the counter had asked her did she have a boyfriend. She had to admit he was cute. She said yes, she did. He asked her if she would like to go out some time, maybe to a movie. She said she didn't think it would be a good idea. "Your boyfriend wouldn't like it?" he asked. "Nope," Elizabeth said, "that's *black* coffee I asked for." Now they were neighborhood friends; he watched the men who sat down next to her like a hawk. "Sit over here, what's the matter with you!" she heard him shouting one day. She looked up: he was shouting at a man about to sit down next to her. "Push, crowd! You want to be thrown out, we don't need your business, sit over there!" Elizabeth pretended not to notice what was going on; on her way to the bakery to get the pastry she ate for lunch, she left an extra quarter on top of the tip. Then she would climb back up the five flights of stairs with her little white bakery bag, put on her nightgown, plug in the vaporizer, plump up the cushions, cover herself with the quilt, and ceremoniously eat the rum ball she had brought back. Finally, the doctor pronounced her well enough to go back to school. "We'll try it," he said, "but you have to keep taking the medicine."

The first day back, it was raining; Elizabeth felt as if she had walked out of one gray bubble, into another. Three days later, she lost her voice. In whispers, she made three students panel leaders of each class, and from the front row wrote them notes objecting to this idea, or that, suggesting new ways of dealing with their story. Finally, her temperature went up, and she was back home. By the time her voice returned, her students were beginning to act oddly; they pretended they couldn't remember what they had been doing last; it had been so long since they had seen her. On general principles, she gave them a lecture, and things went back to normal. Except now she had a constant, splitting headache that kept her nauseous. She would make bets with herself before she got on the train regarding the success of her trip to the college. "Sinus," the doctor said, writing out a new prescription. The new year seemed to be a trip through the halls of the eye-ear-nose-and-throat manual. She had never been so depressed. "You will have to get those sinuses drained," her doctor told her, writing down the name of another doctor. The other doctor began seeing patients at six-thirty in the morning; when she got there, he explained that it was the city that caused all this trouble; if he didn't start early, he didn't finish. He took out a long wire. "Is this really necessary?" Elizabeth asked feebly, but he was already at work. There was much crunching and scrunching. In her dazed state, it seemed like some kind of childbirth; she mumbled something about Athena: "Not from the nose," the doctor said, poking. "This is worse than the Roto-Rooter," she gasped when he unclasped her jaw. "You have good bone structure," he said, falling on her again, "very good." "Now what?" she asked as she left. "You won't be having any more trouble," he said. She always wondered how they made these predictions: she was beginning to dread the doctors, their licensed, electrical hands, pale eunuch Cassandras, peering through time and space, where time and space spoke in tongues.

She met Jeremy, another teacher from the college, as she staggered down the subway steps in front of Bloomingdale's. "How do you feel?" he asked. "Like Persephone," she said. He laughed. His laugh seemed overly hearty to her, as if he were trying to show her that he understood the allusion. Why shouldn't he, for God's sake? Another of those effeminate English teachers. "I have good bone structure," she said. "So you do," he said, looking at her with interest. "I mean in my head," she said, annoyed: it was still hard for her to talk or listen; everything echoed, boomed, and distorted; the subway made matters worse. "That's some coat you've got there," he said in an odd sort of way. Elizabeth stared at his expression, trying to fix it. She didn't trust any of her impressions, not in this state. She was wearing her faithful raccoon, and a fuzzy mohair scarf, and high, shiny black boots. "I'd have worn a quilt if I thought they'd let me on the train in it," she said demoralized. But there was something: it occurred to her that he thought this was an expensive fur coat; he looked like he was wondering what she had done to get it. (She was reminded of the girl in the New School where she and Ira had gone to the movies before the malaria scare; they had both made some remarks about the man introducing the old films; he always made a point of giving away the ending, and telling the audience which sections of the film they were supposed to enjoy. Elizabeth had said the man reminded her of a character in Nabokov. Then they had subsided and watched *The Guardsman* quiet as mice. After the picture, a girl who was wearing jeans and a sweatshirt, pushed past them and hissed at Elizabeth, "You may be rich, but you sure haven't got any brains!") "Thank you," she said, testing, pretending she thought his remark was a compliment. "You're welcome," Jeremy said, but his look gave him away. "Vulgar, ostentatious, sin," it was written all over his puritanical face. He looked like a Jesuit priest—defrocked. He had very thin lips, a cruel mouth. The lower lip was surprisingly full, and Jeremy had a way of making it tremble with sensitivity when he talked. At the beginning of the term, Elizabeth had made a mental note to herself: *avoid at all costs.* "I'm having a party," she thought she heard Jeremy saying over the noise of the trains. "A party?" she asked: really, she thought, I ought to have an ear trumpet. "On Saturday?" he shouted into her inner ear. "Can you come?" "I'd love to," she said. She was horrified to discover she really meant it; she had had no idea of how lonely she had been.

At the party, Jeremy, who seemed to be playing the perfect host, managed to pay special attention to her. Elizabeth reminded herself that Doctor Greene had pointed out that all her affairs began with a mad passion and ended in disaster; perhaps, he had suggested, it was time to try something which began more slowly; time, he said, to give the man a chance, to let things develop. "But then he'll find out how horrible I am," Elizabeth had moaned. "Let him find that out later, there's no need to tell him right away; then, by the time he finds out, it will be too late," Doctor Greene finished. Well, Elizabeth thought to herself, poking at some sickly looking white dip, she certainly was not attracted to Jeremy,

193

that blonde hair, thin, those blue eyes, he looked like a superannuated choir boy. She bit into the cracker. Pineapple and cottage cheese! Was it possible? Did she still have her cold? She didn't; it was. Later, some friends suggested to Jeremy that the four of them go out to dinner. Elizabeth and the other woman started straightening up the apartment. Then they all sat down. They waited. "It can't be taking him *this* long to dress," said Edward uneasily. They waited some more. Finally, Jeremy emerged. "I lay down for a while," he told them, as if that explained everything. At the Japanese restaurant, everyone talked and laughed; then Jeremy put his arms over his head and pretended to fall into a sleep of ravished contentment. Elizabeth and Jan looked at each other and shrugged. Just then the waiter rushed over to the table and started shouting at Edward; for some time, they couldn't tell what was wrong. Then Jan noticed he kept pointing at Jeremy; "Oh!" Edward said, clearly relieved, "he's saying 'no sleep, no sleep.' " "Let me help you on with your coat," Jeremy said, with the same sly look she had noticed on the train. They divided the check up four ways.

Gradually, Elizabeth didn't know how it had happened, they began to date. One day, she was sitting in the Faculty Cafeteria sorting some poems from the Xerox room. "What's that?" asked Jeremy, picking them up without asking permission, as if he had all the nerve in the world. "Poems," Elizabeth said. "May I read them?" Jeremy asked as if he were requesting something sacred, an audience with the Pope. They began to have long conversations about her work: was it possible she was writing as a reaction to having finished her thesis? Elizabeth sensed something cruel in the question, but she wasn't sure; she was following Doctor Greene's instructions, withholding judgment.

One night, they accidentally took the same train home. After some awkward silence, he asked her if she would like to come up to his apartment for dinner. The shadow of the day's one thousandth stranger fell across their laps like a car blanket. "But will you have enough?" Elizabeth asked. When she got there, she realized how foolish the question had been. Jeremy had fourteen hamburger patties, all neatly frozen, divided by strips of wax paper: "two for each day," he explained, didactic and shy. Every night, he told her, he defrosted two, and made some vegetables; he ate yogurt for dessert, "except," he added, "when I have company." "Then what do you eat for dessert?" Elizabeth asked. "Then I defrost four," Jeremy answered, vaguely annoyed. After dinner, he pointed out all the beauties of his furniture. "Solid maple," Jeremy boasted, pounding on the arm of his chair. She was sitting on an old couch. "I built those myself," he said, pointing to the bookshelves, "it's my peasant heritage." Elizabeth looked at them; they reminded her of a particularly awkward erector set; shelf met shelf, but each section had the shelves set in at different levels; the whole thing was stained and varnished an unpleasant maple yellow. Jeremy, his legs crossed, floated on one side, smoking his pipe. "They match your chair," Elizabeth told him; it was all she could think of to say, but he evidently expected more. She was somehow touched by his pride in these innocent and stark objects, in his pride at having built the shelves, the pride of a mother for a baby only a mother could love. Perhaps he was softer than he seemed; perhaps solider; perhaps he needed taking care of. "While I'm getting dinner," he called, "you might like to look at these." He appeared with a pea green pamphlet of poems: the cover was made of oak tag, and it was stapled; the title was *Coffin Nails*. Elizabeth turned the pamphlet over; on the back cover was printed "150 copies of *Coffin Nails* were printed, by hand, at the Self-Destruction Press, Iowa City, Iowa, of which this is copy 49." Underneath it was the signature: Jeremy McAllester. Elizabeth began looking through the poems. "Don't you want me to help you with the dishes?" she called through the hand-built partition separating the living room from the kitchen. "No thanks," he called back, expansive; "I like to get these things over with, air hardens, and so on." Elizabeth sank back into the couch; its age took her in. She could never remember Mark offering to help with the dishes. She could remember Joshua trying to help, with one arm around her waist: they had smashed two plates. Perhaps here was the possibility for some balance. The first poems she read made almost no sense at all; they seemed entirely wordplay, a monstrous kitten batting an over-sized ball. Then she came to the love poems. They were surprisingly good. Curious, she turned to the inside front cover. "To Catherine," the dedication read. "Who was Catherine?" she called out. There was a silence, while the water fell from the faucet into the sink, a small Niagara Falls. "My wife," Jeremy called, "my ex-wife." He emerged from the kitchen, forehead puckered, holding a towel. "I think they're very good," she told him, meaning it. "They're very derivative, very influenced by Frost," Jeremy said. "I think they're better than Frost," she told him. "Do you write any more?" "Not since I got divorced," he said; his whole attitude implied the one was the cause of the other. "Can I take these home with me?" Elizabeth asked, reluctant to give up the book. "A present, my dear," Jeremy said, bowing from the waist.

After that, Jeremy took Elizabeth out to dinner several times. Each time, he would see her to the door, kiss her chastely on the cheek, and then leave. Then, one day, she found a note in her department mailbox asking her to come to dinner at his place. The hamburgers slid from their wax wrap. "I'll set the table," she volunteered; she was getting used to the routine: the loneliness was lifting, like a horrible fog; she could see the bright ribbon of blue between the field and the sky; anyone, she concluded, impinging on her consciousness, was a blessing.

Inevitably, they found themselves in bed afterwards. She was amazed at the nude body, discovered again, like a continent, his, hers, the primal embarrassment, the blessing. Then Jeremy rolled over on his side, facing the wall. "What's the matter?" Elizabeth asked after a while. "I don't know," Jeremy answered in a muffled voice, "maybe I still feel guilty." "About what?" "About my wife." "How long have you been divorced?" Elizabeth wanted to know, somewhat nettled. "Three years," he said; his voice came to her through cotton. "Wait a while; maybe I'll feel better." After some time, he turned to her: a few minutes later, he turned back to the wall. Finally, he got out of bed; he came back with a book bound in black and plumped it down next to her on the bed. "Here," he said, "read these; it looks like they're the only things you're going to see tonight." Elizabeth was impressed by his look of torment. "Poems?" she asked. Jeremy had already disappeared into the bathroom. "I like the others better," she said, when he came back wrapped in a towel, "these are too miserable." "I wasn't very happy then," he told her, "but it was nice of you to say that." "What?" she asked, startled. "That I was too miserable," he said, "it's been a long time since anyone seemed to care." "I think I'll take a shower," Elizabeth said, getting out of bed. Jeremy stared at her as if he had seen the Medusa. "He really is a complicated person," Elizabeth thought to herself, "I will have to be careful." "Do you mind?" she asked, surprised. "Go ahead, the towels are on the rack," he answered stiffly. She was standing in front of the mirror when Jeremy walked into the bathroom; the dampness had made her hair curl in little black corkscrews. "Something about your ancestry you didn't tell me?" Jeremy asked in an odd voice. "I'm a mulatto," Elizabeth answered, pulling a comb through her hair. What on earth was she getting into?

The dates went on, and the season began cracking, like the shell of an egg, first the white, then the yoke cracking through. On Saturday, one would sleep at the other's apartment; then they would have breakfast together, and go home to, as Jeremy put it, "work." One Sunday, Elizabeth woke up and found Jeremy staring out of the window. "How about a picnic?" he asked, his voice surprisingly gentle. "In the city?" Elizabeth asked, astounded; she was still half-drugged with sleep; neither of them had a car. "There's a way of getting to the park by train," Jeremy told her. "But the parks are always so crowded," Elizabeth protested, "not even room to sit down." She would rather stay where she was than go to Central Park again, waking that thirst for the country, that parody of green. "Not that Park," Jeremy reassured her, "there's one near the Cloisters." "If you say so," Elizabeth said, climbing out of bed, obliging. They descended into the tunnel of blown papers and glass grit, the city's universal carpet, city, street, and park. "This is it," Jeremy said, as they got to a stop whose number was surprisingly high, in the two hundreds. "Are we still in Manhattan?" she asked, disoriented. They surfaced between high apartment buildings, all cream-colored. Little store fronts, delicatessens, clothing shops, restaurants, lined the level of the street. Jeremy went into a delicatessen and bought three sandwiches, some bottles of soda, and then went to the fruit stand and bought a bag of apples. "This way," he told her, leading her along as if she were a child. They came to a playground. Elizabeth wanted to use the Ladies Room; she went in; all the doors had been removed from the stalls. "The city!" she thought to herself, but from the window over the tiny sink, she could see a thicket of trees; emphatically, they were green. In back of the playground was a path: they began to climb. Elizabeth didn't

197

have much hope. Gradually, the city began falling away like dark, sunburnt skin. They were on a forest trail; it was soundless; there was not even the sound of a car. They kept on climbing, in silence. Finally, Jeremy asked her if she would like some soda: Elizabeth had not even noticed the heat, the melting of the ice-cubes in the blood. It was lovely. A squirrel ran in front of them, unconcerned. "There must be other animals," Elizabeth thought to herself, wondering. Then they got to the top of the path and a brilliant green field; it looked like a rug, thrown down. Elizabeth threw herself down on it, flat. Jeremy sat down next to her, resting his hand on her stomach, his other hand still holding the packages. They could see the Palisades, the river a bright fabric of blue constantly rolling back and unraveled, back to the ocean, Penelope's spool. One early fly was buzzing somewhere, invisible. It was a long time before they wanted to eat. When they finally got up, they found a large stone and sat on that, watching the river. There was not a person in sight, not a piece of paper in the grass. Then they went back to the green carpet, the magic rug. After some time, Jeremy said he had a question he wanted to ask Elizabeth: would she like to rent a house with him in the country for the summer? "In the country" Elizabeth repeated mechanically. Coming back to the city, every building like sour salt, had given her a thirst for the country, unquenchable. "We could rent a farm," Jeremy told her, taking something out of his pocket. It was an envelope full of pictures, of farm buildings; in some, little people smiled out of gray lawns. "I've been answering ads; some of them don't cost much," Jeremy told her. Elizabeth had not expected anything like this; she stared across the river, at the cliffs, and the buildings on the cliffs, and the bright sky behind them, reducing the skyline to ash. "I think I'd like that very much." It was getting colder, and dark. They went back; they had dinner at a restaurant near her apartment. After they finished eating, Elizabeth noticed Jeremy kept making sucking motions with his cheeks: it reminded her of something: sucking a bottle. "I feel strange," he said softly, covering her hand with his. The salads went uneaten. The next day, he came to her apartment straight from his psychiatrist. "She said what I was feeling was happiness," Jeremy told her, befuddled, "she said perhaps it was the first time I had felt it since I was a very little child." Elizabeth was elated; for the first time, she was taking care of someone properly! "I love you," she said slowly, "because you know where to find all the grass in the city." Jeremy beamed back at her. Elizabeth felt cared for, perhaps, she thought to herself, also for the first time.

But after that, things seemed to go less well. Jeremy always seemed to rush; she had never seen him walk at a normal pace, and Elizabeth was annoyed at herself that these little things bothered her, that there was something in her, she was sure, that was never to be satisfied. Still, he was beginning to remind her of The White Rabbit. "You'll get too attached to him, you'll see," Esther warned her. "Why do you say that?" Elizabeth asked, fed up. "Because you get too attached to everyone," Esther informed her, her professional manner showing like a slip, "you have the reverse of the male psychology: you think if you sleep with a man, you have to make it up to him by marrying him." "Don't be ridiculous," Elizabeth told her, icy, but she was beginning to wonder. More and more, she was wondering what it would be like to be married to Jeremy. She wondered what kind of father he would make; she had noticed how stingy he often was ("Cheap," corrected Esther, who had taken on the responsibility of one of the fates, "he thinks Dutch treat at Chock Full o' Nuts is a night on the town"). He was thinking of suing his father because his father had threatened to cut him out of his will. "How much money is involved," Elizabeth asked, amazed, imagining Jamesian happenings, fortunes, golden bowls. "A couple of thousand dollars," he said, "but it's the principle of the thing." "And," he added, "if we have to rent a car this summer, it will be very expensive." "I'm not sure I want to rent a car that way," Elizabeth said, almost in a whisper, but Jeremy did not answer her. At the same time, she noticed he was carrying his tuna fish sandwiches to school in a little brown bag; every night, he would slice a carrot into thin strips; then he would add one piece of fruit. "No point in throwing money out on that cafeteria," he said when he saw her eyes on him. Elizabeth began teaching in the new Black studies program; she suggested Jeremy try it since he was so interested in experimental things. He seemed uncomfortable. Finally he said, "I'm not sure how I feel about Blacks. Yet." They had long talks in which he described his psychoanalysis and his psychoanalyst. His psychoanalyst was a woman, and Elizabeth began to be jealous of her. Before he had gone to see her, he had suffered from bouts of amnesia, and he seemed to tell Elizabeth this with a certain degree of pride. "Blackouts," he remembered, "I couldn't remember anything." "Can that be normal?" she asked Esther. "What do you think?" Esther asked. One day, she told Jeremy that she really wanted to have children; she had not wanted to before. That night, Jeremy asked her if she would consider taking the pill. There was something imperious beneath the humility of the request, and without really considering what she was doing, she said yes. It seemed a normal, modern thing to do, taking the pill.

But now Elizabeth found herself living in a constant state of anxiety; she could not imagine what was the matter with her. First, she thought it was some side effect of the pill, but then it went on too long; it was as if she were wrapped in a kind of cotton batting and could not get out. The anxiety was almost physical, a painful sensation in the stomach. She began to wonder if she was really in the right field; more and more, she thought she had made a mistake: it was still possible, she told herself, to go back to graduate school and become a psychiatrist. She consulted with Esther, and wrote to the head of her department; he wrote back, inviting her to come for an interview; it seemed perfectly possible. She told Jeremy about her idea, and he seemed pleased. She had expected he would be angry, tell her to leave well enough alone. But even this did nothing; she still felt as if she were about to crack, like glass; the city streets reminded her of fold-out pictures from a children's book, about to be folded back in, flat, with her caught somewhere in the scenery, gray and black. At last, Elizabeth had what to her was a dreadful thought; perhaps she did not really love Jeremy; perhaps that was the source of this misery, this need to escape. The farm in Vermont was moving closer, its door open like a threatening hand. They began to spend a great deal of time in Central Park; Elizabeth noticed they were also spending a great deal of time on the Staten Island Ferry. Whenever she bought food, Jeremy never contributed a penny. It was impossible to doubt any longer; he really was cheap. She said something about moving to be closer to the college; it took her an hour and a half each way from where she lived now, but Jeremy disapproved. She questioned him about it, and he said something about how much more time he would have to spend on the train if he had to come uptown and then go all the way back to see her; this way, he pointed out, he just took the Crosstown Bus.

Then he asked her if she would like to take him to meet her parents. "I've been seeing this all the wrong way," Elizabeth thought to herself, "he must want to get married; that's why he's making all these demands." But she still didn't know what to make of herself, all folded up like a carpet, stiff and awkward at the edges. "Should I call my parents tonight?" she asked him. "We'll be here," Sarah's sleepy voice said, and the next morning, they went out. The whole time, Elizabeth felt as if Jeremy were taking citings for Dun and Bradstreet. "I must be out of my mind," she said to herself. She felt that her anxiety was dangling from her ears like earrings, getting icier and more elaborate with every minute and day, stalactites. The longer they were in the house, the more depressed Jeremy seemed to get, so Elizabeth suggested they drive down to the beach. "Maybe it's bringing someone home to the house," Elizabeth thought to herself, remembering her visit with Joshua. Jeremy wasn't saying much; yes, she had been through this before. When they went back to the city, things seemed even more strained.

"I think I'm going to see Doctor Greene in Chicago," she told Jeremy the next day; she could see him in the bathroom shaving; she had not gotten up. "Won't that be expensive?" Jeremy asked her. "Tax deductible," Elizabeth said, feeling foolish, "Arthur tells me I can deduct the plane fare to Chicago as transportation to the doctor." "All the way to Chicago?" Jeremy asked through his lather. "It's not my fault that's where he works," she answered. Later in the day, she called Doctor Greene. Jane was gone; a new girl answered. Doctor Greene called her back within an hour; afterwards, she was surprised when she realized he had not called her collect. She made four appointments for the next week, part of her Easter vacation. She called the airport and made the arrangements. "Do you want me to come with you?" Jeremy asked from the bed on Saturday morning, watching her pack. "Yes," Elizabeth murmured, inaudible into the clothes. "But there's no point," Jeremy said, "take a cab, and I'll meet you when you come back, or you can take a cab straight to my place." She didn't answer him: hair curlers, toothpaste, she had to wrap the top of the tube in tissue, she had lost the cap. "Sloppy," Jeremy commented, disapproving.

The minute the plane landed in Chicago, Elizabeth began to feel better. She beamed at the back of the cab driver who took her to International House. It was strange being back here, no longer a student, dressed—as Doctor Greene would put it—like a person. She spent the rest of Saturday and all of Sunday walking over every inch of the old ground, no better than a cocker spaniel, she thought to herself. She ate all the things she always used to eat. She went to the library, the coffee shop, everyone was there, the old group, discussing the thesis, why it was not finished, how they had to work, how the children made noise. She walked with Armand to the lake. "How's Rossetti?" she asked. "Still dreaming," he said. "You're sure it's Rossetti, not Sleeping Beauty?" she asked, laughing. "Sometimes I'm not so sure," he said, mournful. They walked to the lake like two ghosts from an old movie set. It wasn't the same.

She felt strange and out of place. In the morning, when she trailed down to the bathroom, she was absurdly conscious of her grown-up nightgown in a world of flannel; she dressed carefully; she drew on her eyes, she took the train to Doctor Greene's. Everything there was exactly the same: the tortoiseshell paper on the walls, the tortoiseshell frames over his eyes. When Doctor Greene shut the door behind her, Elizabeth wanted to know if she should lie down on the couch: "You're beyond that now," he told her, motioning to a chair. She felt a horrible sense of loss; she wanted to cry. Instead, she began talking about Jeremy, her problems with him, how she couldn't make up her mind about anything, whether he was the right person for her, whether she had picked him because she was still punishing herself. Doctor Greene listened, impassive and unimpressed. Near the end of the first hour, she began to tell him about her plans for changing fields, how she had written to the Chairman of the psychology department in New York and been given an appointment for an interview. Doctor Greene sat up straighter; "we will have to discuss this further," he said, something of the old severe tone creeping back into his voice like water through plaster. "But you always said I would make a good psychiatrist," Elizabeth complained, piqued. "So you would," Doctor Greene told her, "but the question is why you want to do this. Here you are at the pearly gates, writing poetry, and teaching, and you want to exchange it for this; I don't understand why." "But *you* like what you're doing," Elizabeth answered, accusing. "So I do," Doctor Greene said, "but neither do I have the time to change my life, nor the talent to write. I should think it would be a great joy to feel your mind operating as it does when you write poetry." "I could still do that," Elizabeth protested. "You underestimate the amount of energy this work takes," Doctor Greene told her. "Teaching takes energy," Elizabeth protested, confused. "Not the same kind," Doctor Greene said, getting up. "No, I think the real issue is why you wish to identify with me." "What are you talking about?" Elizabeth demanded, the old fury with this obstinate person returning as suddenly as a blown-open door. "I am a psychiatrist, a psychoanalyst," Doctor Greene answered, "and now, six months after you leave me, you decide you wish to be one too. Perhaps it is your way of keeping me with you." "I don't understand how you can be so egocentric; I can deal with my career; I want to know what to do about Jeremy." "My dear Elizabeth," Doctor Greene said, eyebrows traveling into his hair, "at this point, any advice I could give you about that would be no better than any you could give yourself. You will probably make the right decision. If you don't, you will change your mind. You painted your bedroom blue two years ago, and didn't like it, then you painted it green. The world did not come to an end because of those blue walls." "This is different, for heaven's sake," Elizabeth gasped, exasperated. "Not much," Doctor Greene told her, "tomorrow at nine." "I remember, I remember," she said crabbily, leaving the office, closing the door.

The next day, although Elizabeth tried valiantly to talk about Jeremy, Doctor Greene talked about her desire to be a psychoanalyst. "Perhaps it is a form of paying me back," he said finally, "you will take care of others as I took care of you." "But *I* want to be taken care of," Elizabeth insisted. "What better way of being taken care of than by having me on the premises in person, in your person?" Doctor Greene asked her. A switch flicked; Elizabeth could see her anxiety dropping as visibly as mercury in a thermometer. "You may be right," she said, none too gracious. "It was very hard for you to leave me," Doctor Greene reminded her. "I cried all the way home." "As I remember, you said you cried for a week,"

Doctor Greene put in. "For a week," she repeated softly. "You may have to go through this many times before it is finally over," Doctor Greene said, somewhat sadly. Elizabeth did not understand: "Through what?" "Through leaving me," he clarified, "you have come back, and in a few days you will do it again. There are many ways of leaving," he elaborated, "you may go through one dreadful relationship after another until you tire yourself out; you will do this to prove that no man is any good, that they will all desert you as I have done." "But I decided to leave," Elizabeth reminded him. "I doubt if you really believe that," Doctor Greene said, standing up. "If you believed that, you would not feel it necessary to incorporate me body and cell by becoming my shadow, another figure in a chair behind The Couch of Sorrows. And," Doctor Greene added, "I will say this about Jeremy. It sounds as if you look upon him as your first patient; he feels happiness for the first time; he rents a house in the country; he progresses so well, just as you did." "It's not going that well," Elizabeth said, grim. "That's the trouble with first cases," Doctor Greene said, grinning, "you don't have much experience. It shows. And from what you say, your fees are much too low."

The next day, which was the last, they talked much more generally. "Do I look better," she asked, fishing for a compliment. "Much," he said promptly. "But I've gained weight since last time," she announced, triumphant. "You look much better integrated," he replied. "Oh," Elizabeth muttered, wondering what she had looked like before, an unassembled collection of clothes, the youth collection at Marshall Field's. "Will I cry all the way home on the plane?" she asked, as she was getting ready to leave. "Probably," he said, smiling. "You know," he told her, "last week my old analyst died. I went to his funeral. I hadn't seen him in ten years." A cloud went over his face, a fogged glass. Elizabeth accepted the comment as a gift. "Stay well," she said. "You too," he said, and they shook hands. Elizabeth cried all the way home on the plane. Everytime she tried to stop, she could see Jeremy's face at the end of the tunnel, and she began again. What was she going to do? When the stewardess brought lunch, she settled it on her lap. She no longer had any desire to apply to the graduate school in psychology.

She called Jeremy from the airport, and went straight to his apartment. "I can tell you feel better," he said, almost irritated. "Can you?" she asked queerly. The earth was still crackling under her feet. Then, one day when they were in Central Park on the swings, she could feel herself hemorrhaging. "Let's go back," she called to Jeremy, "I think I'm bleeding." "Those damn pills," she thought to herself. She could see Jeremy was annoyed at having his idyll interrupted, but he got off the swing. When she called her doctor, he thought it had something to do with the pills, but it was "nothing to worry about." Certainly, Jeremy didn't seem worried. "I'll make us some bologna sandwiches," he said. The next week, the semester ended. Jeremy took Elizabeth home with him Friday night, and then again Saturday; he seemed to assume she would be staying again. "Are we living together?" she asked. He said he guessed they were. "I think," Elizabeth said slowly, "that we should not see each other for a few weeks. Tonight is Tuesday. Let's see each other two weeks from Tuesday." "Why do you say that?" asked Jeremy, alarmed. "I don't know; I just think it's the best thing," she answered vaguely. "I'll take you home," he said, suddenly solicitous. "No, I think I'll go myself," Elizabeth said, stuffing her nightgown and brush into her huge bag. "I'll call you in two weeks?" Jeremy asked. "Tuesday," she said, leaving; "I'm going to Boston; that's when I'll be back." When she got to Edna's, she told her all about Jeremy; they discussed the matter for some time, and she and Elizabeth came to the conclusion that perhaps Elizabeth was afraid of commitment. This seemed possible. "But perhaps I was lonely?" she asked Edna. Edna didn't think that was it; "that might have *started* it," she said, wisely. "Why did you decide to go away for two weeks?" Edna asked, curious. "I don't know," Elizabeth said automatically, "isn't that how long a psychiatrist takes for a vacation?" "Something you didn't tell me about your job?" Edna asked, sarcastic. "Only joking," Elizabeth said, tired.

When she got back to New York, two days earlier than she expected, she called Jeremy. "Would you like to come over?" she asked. "I thought you said Tuesday," he answered in a flat voice. "I did, but I'm back early," she said, feeling idiotic. "I think it would be better if we waited until Tuesday," Jeremy said, final. On Tuesday, things seemed to resume. They made plans to rent the house in the summer; then Elizabeth decided perhaps they should take separate vacations; she couldn't understand what was wrong with her: Edna must be right. What was wrong with Doctor Greene that he couldn't fix her: after she had flown, like a demented duck, all the way out to Chicago, transcontinental homing pigeon. When Jeremy was ready to leave on his vacation, he insisted that Elizabeth, who had Arthur's car, drive him to the airport—he was going to Japan. "Japan!" exclaimed Elizabeth, "I thought you didn't have any money." "You could go to Japan too," he said, sour, "if you didn't spend so much money during the year."

Every day he was gone, Elizabeth got long, eight page letters; they were filled with photographs, picture postcards, pressed flowers. They were also curiously impersonal. Then she got a letter saying he was coming back a week later than he expected. Every day, she called his apartment. She had moved, and had no phone, and would go down to the supermarket, and dial from the chrome booth, her face peering back at her, mocking, distorted. Finally, he answered. "It's nice to hear your voice," he said. "Why didn't you write and tell me when you were coming back?" she demanded. "I got in late, but I'll come to see you this afternoon. I have a doctor's appointment first." "Why can't you come *here* first?" Elizabeth demanded; waiting for him, she had decided to commit herself: she would be committed; these were unnecessary obstacles. "I need more sleep," he said, hanging up. When Jeremy finally came in, she knew everything had taken a turn for the worse. Never had she seen anyone look like the Reverend Dimmesdale. "I think it would be better if we stopped seeing each other," he said after a long pause. "Just like that?" Elizabeth demanded. "I guess so," he said, feeble. "I was an *idiot* ever to get involved with you," she stormed to the walls, "What the hell were all those letters about?" Olympian, he refused to answer: "When you have time to think about it, you'll understand." "I won't understand if I live to be one hundred," Elizabeth raged, "What were you doing, writing a diary and sending it to me to keep? I suppose you want them back?" "I wouldn't mind," Jeremy said. "You miserable creep," Elizabeth exploded, "why didn't you give me any warning? I waited for you all summer." In the back of her mind she could hear Doctor Greene, the voice of the toad: tit for tat. Suddenly, she had an inspiration: "Did you sleep with anyone else this summer?" Jeremy said he had. "Are you going to see her again?" He said he didn't know; she lived in California. "Now it makes sense," Elizabeth said, thinking out loud, "you've discovered you can actually sleep with other girls, and you've decided to get rid of me." Jeremy didn't say anything. "You really are a selfish bastard," she said with a certain amount of admiration, "you'd be a lot better off if you stopped suing your father for a few thousand dollars and stopped spending all that money on yourself; you really are a miser!" Jeremy started to shout about how she should leave his father out of this, and she had a sudden impulse to run around shutting windows in her new apartment; it occurred to her that this latest inconvenience, her having moved, was his last straw. She didn't know her neighbors, and she didn't want this to be her introduction to them. If she lived long enough, she thought to herself, she would begin to understand her parents. "I'm sorry you feel cheated," Jeremy said patronizingly. "I *do*," Elizabeth said, "who else knows every waitress at Chock Full o' Nuts by name?" "Did *you* sleep with anyone this summer?" Jeremy asked her. She said yes; it had somehow slipped her mind. A filmmaker she knew from the Institute had come into town, and they had both felt so sorry for themselves, they wound up in bed. Jeremy looked visibly deflated. But still Elizabeth could not understand it. "Why *did* you go out with me?" she asked, "wasn't there anyone else?" "That's not flattering to either of us," Jeremy said severely; suddenly, he reminded her of Doctor Greene. "So what?" she shrieked, beyond politeness.

"What is going to happen to me?" she asked Jeremy, suddenly quiet and sad, as if he could answer. She felt as if her life were slamming shut, like a book; she was pressed, like a flower. "Good things," said Jeremy, suddenly kind, "you're a vital person, talented." "But you are too," Elizabeth said, the bitterness returning to her voice. "I'm not so sure," Jeremy said, genuine sadness stamping his words; she would never forget them. In that instant, their defenses lay, windshields shattered, glittering and dangerous, under their feet. But then she was sure he would be lucky; she would not; she would meet him at the movies with his date; she would be alone.

Once Jeremy had told her, mournful, that he would never be all hairy, or big, like Jewish men. "And so the token Jewess leaves the picture," she said, shaking herself, "you are leaving, I take it?" "I have to go to school," he said, picking up his briefcase. "Of *course,* I forgot, school doesn't start for two weeks, but then you always have so much to do." "I think I better go," Jeremy told her, more dignified than a tree, "you'll be sorry about this afterwards." "I doubt it," she said, slamming the door, quaking the lobsters in Sheepshead Bay. She jerked the door open again. Jeremy was walking away under a canopy of green leaves. "Break a glass," she called after him. "What?" he called back, and then he turned on his heel, and was gone.

Elizabeth flung herself down on the bed and burst into furious tears. How *could* she have been such an idiot! And she had considered marrying him! Mark was a bleeding heart by comparison. Promptly, she fell into a depressed sleep, and in some confused dream, she heard a voice telling her, infinitely reassuring, "Even *he* would forgive you for loving him." When she sat up, she wondered what that meant. Where was her Freudian Dream Decoding Ring? Broken. Smashed. She understood that she was still not willing to give anyone the satisfaction of seeing her happy; she was still angry at Manny and Sarah; she remembered Jane, met in Bloomingdale's, telling her Doctor Greene would think more of her if she didn't get in touch with him; surely, if she married, if she was stamped "Happy" by *Good Housekeeping*, he would have no reason for letting her in his office. She had a vision of herself, trying to slide under his door like a letter. Could something that stupid be behind it? Ruefully, she decided it could. She had just been through another parting. She thought back over the days she had spent with Jeremy: they divided in half, black half, white half, blue mornings, gray afternoons. He could not permit himself happiness either, and so they had been perfectly cast. In the morning, she could not believe what she was doing, she called him. Was he sure he didn't want to change his mind? Then she took a cab to his house, but he wouldn't answer the door, or else he wasn't in. She straggled back to her own place. Hadn't she worn herself out? Was she still retrieving the bone of misery, trained, like the family dog? She threw the square cardboard pack of pills into the garbage bag, and then carried the bag down the stairs and out. She didn't want the cat to eat them by mistake. Sammy the Cat had not been the same since Jeremy's arrival; he had suddenly become a man hater. One night, he had sunk teeth and claws into Jeremy's ankle, and whenever she was there, and Jeremy passed, Sammy would swipe at his thigh. She wondered now if Jeremy had kicked him, done something to him. She didn't know why she hadn't thought of this before. Now she had, she was sure. "Poor cat, poor baby," she said, picking Sammy up, carrying him through the house. A heavy depression settled on her, like a damp camping blanket, and it was getting dark.

The next day, Elizabeth found herself giving herself lectures in a voice sounding suspiciously like Sarah's; "I will think one more thing about Jeremy, and then I will not think about him again." This was Elizabeth's fall resolution: she always made hers before the start of school; by midyear, she was confirmed at her worst. She searched: this had to be a memory, a photograph, definitive. Jeremy's book! Jeremy had written a book, *Coleridge's Influence on the Lyrical Ballads,* and then had sent a chapter of it to a journal called *Contemporary Fiction.* The journal had returned it with a little icy note to the effect that, as their title implied, they were interested in novels, and modern ones at that, and the section Mr. McAllester had sent was not suitable for their purposes. Jeremy was infuriated! "Those stupid editors!" he bellowed, banging the returned envelope down on the breakfast table; the surprised mugs jumped an inch in the air. "But Jeremy," Elizabeth said mildly, soothing as cough syrup, "what would *Contemporary Fiction* want with an article on Coleridge and Wordsworth?" "That's just the point," he explained triumphantly, puffing himself up like the king of the frogs. "If they had *read* the article, not *too* much to ask in an editor is it?" (his voice dripped sarcasm; it hung in little icicles from the oilcloth tablecover), "they would have seen that my last paragraph revealed the impact Wordsworth and Coleridge had on the contemporary novel! Idiots! I don't know where they get their reputation!" "People make mistakes," Elizabeth pointed out, pouring out two more cups of coffee, "you could write a letter." "A letter!" Jeremy snorted, "Oh *noooo.* Look at this." He slammed the manuscript down on the table; the coffee sloshed over the cups and onto the checkerboard pattern, melted chessmen, melting game. "This is your book," Elizabeth said, puzzled. "Open it!" Jeremy commanded, imperious as any lord. "Is it wired?" Elizabeth asked; she couldn't understand what else could cause such a fuss. "Open it, open it," he insisted, his voice tragic and mechanical; he looked like a caged mouse. "So?" Elizabeth asked, having opened it. "So," Jeremy said impatiently, yanking it away from her and turning a page, slamming it down again, "look at the dedication!" "Dedicated to *Contemporary Fiction*," Elizabeth read out loud. "Jeremy," Elizabeth asked, "when did they first return this article?" "Three years ago," he said viciously, "but I thought I'd give them another chance." "I see," said Elizabeth, who didn't. But she did now. The afternoon Jeremy left, she had asked him whom he was going to dedicate his poems to now. First he had dedicated them to Catherine; then he had crossed out her name, and dedicated them to her. "I'm through with dedications," Jeremy said, stepping through the door.

"We are going to think this over, Elizabeth," she said to herself, turning down the covers. "Am I going to live the rest of my life like a character in a comic book?" She felt like a character in a very bad play, always running in to the King with the same stupid line, the bad news. At least in Greece, they heard the bad tidings, and cut off the messenger's head. "We are going to think this over, Sammy," she said, putting the cat down on the bed. Sammy jumped down, and having convinced himself the apartment was free of intruders, came back and curled himself around her head, on her pillow, her silvery gray half-moon. She was silver haired, like a grandmother. "Good-night, all," she said to the walls, "good-night, last gasp of masochism, good-night, Sammy," she whispered to herself, a footnote of breath, and then, obliging, night dropped its curtain; the depression winked out, blessedly, for twelve hours, like a light.

Chapter 13

Arthur was getting married. It was no surprise to Elizabeth; she had always said that he would be the first one to get married. Sarah called her up and announced the news in gloomy, sepulchral tones: "Nothing good will come of it," she predicted. "Look, mother," Elizabeth said, "every time someone in town got married, you would tell us about it like it was another nail in our coffins. So what's the matter now?" "I don't know, it's just something about the girl." "Like what?" Sarah thought. "She doesn't make the bed when she stays over." "My God," Elizabeth exclaimed in mock horror. "And she wears the same pair of jeans, all the time, and the same T-shirt." "Everyone dresses like that in college, I went through a beatnik phase," Elizabeth reminded her. "Don't remind me," Sarah said, "and besides, you're not doing so well either." "Just what do you mean by that?" Elizabeth asked. "Are you still going out with Adam?" her mother asked in the dread-filled tone of a policeman disarming a bomb. "I am," Elizabeth said. "Is he divorced yet?" "How could he be divorced yet, mother, he just got separated from his wife last week." "There are ways of arranging these things," Sarah said, "if he really wanted to, that is." "I think I'll wait and see what happens," Elizabeth said; she was thinking of disfiguring herself by pulling clumps of hair out of the side of her head. "Nothing is going to come of this," Sarah said, "he's just interested in you because he's lonely; the minute he gets his divorce, he'll drop you like a hot potato." "Thank you, Ann Landers," Elizabeth said. "Thanks for telling me, you do wonders for my self-confidence." "Who else is going to tell you," Sarah demanded. "Your friends, you think they care? They're delighted to see you going out with a married man, they can work on the single ones." "I better hang up," Elizabeth told her. "What about your job?" Sarah asked provocatively. "What about it?" Elizabeth asked; should she call the operator and tell her she was getting obscene calls from Sarah's number? "You teach at a public institution; if there's a scandal, you'll get fired, and then you'll have nothing, but if that's the way you want it. . . ." "No one's going to fire me, mother," she said, but she hung up and worried.

Sarah called up the next day. "What am I supposed to do about inviting you to the wedding?" "Don't do it if you don't want to," Elizabeth suggested, "just tell Arthur that his only sister, the scarlet woman, can't come because of the scandal in the family." "Be serious, Elizabeth," Sarah complained. "I mean about Adam, should I invite Adam?" "That would be nice," Elizabeth said. "Then you are serious," Sarah pounced like a hawk. "Serious enough," Elizabeth said. "How's his divorce coming?" Sarah demanded. Elizabeth said Adam was having trouble with his wife. "If he really wanted a divorce, he could fly down to Mexico and get one," Sarah informed her.

"The divorce wouldn't be legal here without his wife's consent," Elizabeth told her, suppressing a scream. "That's not what Florence said," Sarah said reproachfully. Florence taught at her mother's public school. "Has Florence gotten divorced recently?" Elizabeth wanted to know. "Don't be so smart," Sarah told her. "Mother," Elizabeth said, "why don't you just call a lawyer and ask him; I can't seem to convince you about anything." "You'll never convince me that man is going to marry you, if that's what you mean." Sarah hung up. Adam was perpetually astounded at the way Elizabeth and her mother shouted at and hung up on one another. Evidently, perfect decorum reigned in his house. "Would your mother like to rent me a room?" she asked him wistfully. "We have enough here of our own," he said, pulling her over toward him. "And should *I* worry now?" he asked. "What?" she demanded, alarmed. "About whether you'll want me now that you've gotten what you want from me. Maybe you'll just toss me aside like an old bone, why should you want to get married, now that you've had your will of me?" Elizabeth could not believe she was laughing only ten minutes after talking to Sarah.

Sarah arrived at her apartment on Sunday, unannounced. Elizabeth had been studying in the front room; Adam was typing his dissertation in the study. She took one look at her daughter and hissed, "Is he here?" "Is who here, mother?" Elizabeth asked. "You know who I mean," Sarah said, "anyone could have pushed through that door after me, a photographer, a lawyer, anyone, and then where would you be?" "I wouldn't let the photographers in," Elizabeth said reassuring. "How would you know they were there?" Sarah demanded. "All right, from now on, I'll answer the front door with a bag over my head," Elizabeth said, controlling herself. "You won't think it's so funny when you can't get a job," Sarah went on. "Are you coming up or not?" Elizabeth asked, tired of standing in the draft. "And don't think I don't know what you were doing," Sarah went on, enraged. "We were studying, mother," Elizabeth said; her voice was beginning to rise. "Studying, look at yourself, *studying,* my foot!" "I think you're disappointed you didn't find us copulating on the welcome mat inside the front door," Elizabeth burst out, losing her temper. "I just wanted to bring these books back, and now I'm leaving," Sarah said, petulant. "Where's daddy?" Elizabeth asked, "why don't you bring

212

him in for some coffee?" "And let him see this?" Sarah demanded, aggrieved. "It would break his heart!" Elizabeth gave up.

Now, whenever the phone rang, Elizabeth jumped three feet in the air. "I'm getting paranoid," she thought. Then Adam's wife started threatening suicide. Her mother began calling regularly, warning her about private detectives, photographers. Adam tried to laugh her out of it: "Smile for the cameras," he would say as she climbed out of the car to go to the Poetry Institute, but she was getting more and more nervous. She began eating compulsively. "Why shouldn't he live there, the rent's free?" her mother asked. "He pays rent on his own apartment, will you leave me alone, you're driving me crazy." "You're driving yourself crazy," Sarah retorted. "You've been this way from the minute you were born; it's in the genes; I had nothing to do with it." Elizabeth hung up.

Elizabeth had met Adam in the Faculty Lounge. He was the largest person she had seen there in some time. She sat down next to him, and they started to talk: what was his field, what was hers. She said she wrote poetry. "You can't be a real poet and teach full time," Adam said gravely. Elizabeth got up and walked away. She didn't talk to him again. Finally, her friend Gina told her that her husband had met Adam and he was very intelligent. "He's an idiot," Elizabeth replied, categorical. "You underestimate that one," Gina told her, "I'd look again if I were you." One afternoon, she was having coffee with Gina and her husband Frank, and they caught sight of Adam eating alone. "I think I'm going over to join him," she said, getting up. Gina looked faintly irritated. Adam looked delighted to see her: "have an oyster? a french fry?" She said no, she had already eaten, she was just wasting time getting ready to go to the city. So was he. "I'll give you a lift," he suggested, smiling. "Are you sure you wouldn't mind?" she asked gingerly. "I'm sure," he said, "want some roll?" They talked most of the way into the city, and when they got to the New School and the old movie, Elizabeth was amazed that she would have to get out; she must have expected to stay in the car, drive home wherever he was driving, and that would be that. After that, he drove her into the city regularly. She invented errands for herself, movies, shopping, everything; he never asked her to go out, for a date, but things seemed hopeful. One day she mentioned him to Gina.

"Isn't Adam married?" Gina asked. A bright pane of glass seemed to splinter in front of her. "I don't know," she said, "it never occurred to me." Gina said she had looked him up on the Faculty List and there was an asterisk after his name. Elizabeth knew that Gina thought her "pursuit" of Adam had been, in her terms, "unaesthetic." "Why should he like me anyway?" she asked herself, crossing the street. Then she thought to herself, "Why shouldn't he?" The next day, she let him drive her into the city. On the way to the car, he touched the tip of her coat: "pretty," he said. She asked him up for coffee, and he came up. The subject of his wife never came up. Then one day, he mentioned "our cat." "Our?" Elizabeth asked. "I've been meaning to tell you," Adam said, uncomfortable, shifting in his seat, "we're separated." Elizabeth didn't say anything. "My wife needs to use my insurance policy," he explained lamely, "it has a psychiatric provision, she goes to a psychiatrist." But three weeks later, he decided he wanted to get divorced. Adam and Elizabeth were parked in his car in front of her apartment; she was painting it, one room at a time; it still had no curtains; the blank black square eyes stared down at the little blue car. "You'll have everything you want," Adam said to the silence, "we'll have children, everything." He kept playing with the furry hem of her coat. Elizabeth remembered how, one night when Adam had driven her into the city, he had stopped for a light, and then changed his mind and pulled over. "I'd like to come with you," he told her, "but while I'm still living there it wouldn't be fair." Elizabeth sat quietly. "Thank you for telling me," she said finally. A few weeks later, they were both invited to a party. Adam asked her if she would be going, and she said yes. He told her he would like to go, but it didn't seem right, leaving his wife alone while he went out. She said she understood, but she resented it. When she complained to Esther, Esther asked her what she would think of him if he didn't have those scruples. "That's one way of looking at it," Elizabeth said, very tired. She let her friend Paul pick her up and take her to the party. Sitting on the couch, her legs in lace stockings, crossed, her lavender plush dress with the short skirt gleaming, trying to look interested, she saw the door open and Adam walk in. She felt sure her excitement was showing, indecent, like a slip. He was dressed, as usual, in his black suit, perpetually dressed like someone, his father, for Rosh Hashanah services. She didn't move a muscle; finally, she patted the space Paul had left on the couch when he stood up to greet the newcomer. She and Adam left early. She had a momentary fit of mourning for his perished scruples. "Prude," she told herself, telling Paul that Adam would be driving her back; "now you won't have to go out of your way," she said, hypocritically, trying not to notice his expression. Driving home, Adam said he thought the divorce might take a long time; his wife was taking it badly. "I'm not sure I want to get married yet," Elizabeth told him; she had learned something, after all. Now they spent a great deal of time talking about houses, babies, furniture, how he would support her, she could stop working, and she listened, it was the most wonderful story she had ever heard. Then her mother would call: Mexican divorce, scandal, photographers. But she had it, folded up in a corner of her mind, his promise: she would have everything she wanted. Later, thinking back, she would remember: this was the only marriage proposal she was ever to get.

In the meantime, the preparations for Arthur's wedding went on. "What preparations?" Elizabeth asked. "Don't ask me," her mother said, tragically, "they're not telling us anything; evidently, it's going to be very high class." "She means cheap," Manny volunteered from behind the paper. "What kind of wedding will it be?" she asked. "A garden wedding." "That's nice," Elizabeth said. "I'm glad someone thinks so," Manny put in. "She's making her own dress," Sarah said. Elizabeth thought this was a little bit odd; after all these years of insisting she didn't want a proper marriage, she was hunting through the offerings of *Modern Bride*. "I hope it looks as interesting as it sounds"; Manny's words emerged from behind the paper like a smoke signal. "Well, people make too much fuss over these things anyway," Elizabeth said, wondering if this were really ture. "That's what you think," Manny said. "You'll have a chance to find out," Sarah told her. "And what are *you* going to wear," she demanded, as if she expected Elizabeth to come dressed in the mattress ticking of her double bed. "An antique chinese robe," she said. Sarah looked as if she had fallen on a spiritual sword. "Tell Adam to wear a suit," she reminded her. "I'll tell him, but I don't know whether he'll do it," she said, leaving. "What does she mean, Manny?" she could hear Sarah asking as she shut their front door.

The day of the wedding was perfectly clear. It was also ninety-five degrees, "in the shade," Adam said grimly. They got to Rebecca's house early; "I'll go up and see her," she said to Adam; "she's had a hard time with my mother; I don't think she would like anyone Arthur married." She found Rebecca in a tiny attic room that looked like a parody of her old one. It didn't seem to have been painted for fifteen years. Elizabeth kept looking around for Cinderella's sisters, but there were only three very pretty maids of honor. "Where's the dress?" Elizabeth asked. Rebecca produced it; it was extremely plain, off-white. "Beautiful," Elizabeth said admiringly. "She made it," said Rebecca, beaming at one of the long haired blonde girls. In the hall, Rebecca's mother was dancing around in her underwear like a child just let out of its swimsuit. "He's seen me this way before," she called out gaily, retreating into her room. "See you later," Elizabeth said, drifting downstairs. When she saw Adam, he shook his head. Irene had taken a look around the kitchen and was trying to persuade everyone in the family to go out to the White Castle while there still was time. "There's not going to be anything to eat," she said with the voice of authority. Everyone was melting in the heat. "I didn't eat all morning." Madelaine said, "I didn't want to stuff myself." "Here, stuff yourself on a nut," Irene said, handing one over, "it's the last one." In an atmosphere of impending doom, they draggled out onto the lawn. A bearded boy was taking pictures. "Only the very best," Eleanor said, "I hope he remembered to take the cover off the lens." Then the ushers began to line them up; the bride's family on this side, the groom's on the other. Everyone complimented Elizabeth on her robe while Sarah listened, looking puzzled. After fifteen minutes of standing under the sun, blinding as a flash, there was a strange sound. Rebecca's mother had not yet appeared. Elizabeth and Adam were standing with Hilda and her daughters. Suddenly, the triumphal march from *Aida* blasted among the leaves. Everyone's head jerked around, yanked, as if by rope. "It's the bride," everyone whispered. Someone diaphanous and brilliant white was floating out of the house. "No, it's her mother," someone whispered; and it certainly was. Mrs. Goldbarth was floating down the aisle in what was evidently a designer original, pure organdy, layer on layer; she looked like a living cake. "I don't believe it," Hilda's daughter gasped. "Believe it, believe it," Elizabeth hissed. "There's the bride," Sarah said, with relief. Rebecca came down the aisle, plain, in her off-white dress, her sensible heels, her veil obscuring her face, her hair blowing out from under. "Oh God!" said Sarah to the winds.

The ceremony was monotonous, and hard to hear. The Rabbi seemed to be predicting all the disagreements they would have in the future, the disillusionments they would have to look forward to, and how a good marriage could be built from such bricks. "Do you think they'll go through with it?" Adam whispered into her ear. "After her mother spent all that money on the dress?" Elizabeth asked. When it was over, Arthur and Rebecca were pink and giggly and looked about thirteen. Elizabeth thought they looked adorable; privately, she was dreaming up some way of pushing Mrs. Goldbarth into the wedding cake. "Icing to icing," she thought; it was only just. "Don't do it," Irene said, "it's all we have to eat." "Her friend made it," Sarah volunteered. "The whole wedding must have cost them a big fifty dollars," Manny said, "you know what really hurts? Last night, they got me to take everyone out for a champagne supper; she read about it in *Bride's*. It cost over three hundred dollars. If I'd known, I would have had the Rabbi yanked in then." Irene dispatched her youngest daughter to hunt for food. She came back with four stuffed mushrooms; "The Red Cross," Madelaine said, grabbing one. "Let's sit down." "Where?" Eleanor asked. They looked around. There were ten chairs scattered under three trees. "It's a good thing I took my pressure pills," Madelaine complained. "Where did you say that White Castle was?" "Have some punch, there're some strawberries in it; you can chew on them for a while; they're still frozen," Eleanor said, mopping her head. "I'm glad they're frozen," Irene said, lobster-red, "how long before we can decently get out of here?" "Poor Manny," Madelaine said, "he's going to get it from mother." Sarah was already walking around with her head slightly tilted, as if anticipating the morning's phone calls. "They promised to support her next year, but I don't believe it for a minute," she whispered in Elizabeth's ear. "Don't borrow trouble," Elizabeth whispered back, "at least they mowed the lawn." "*Arthur* mowed the lawn," her mother wailed softly. "A tray, a tray! after it!" Irene shouted, as if she were riding to the hounds. Her children rounded up an army of melted cheese crackers on toothpicks. "Eat the toothpicks too," Madelaine said, "they may have some salt, you shouldn't drop dead from the heat." Adam was leaning against a tree, his arm around Elizabeth. "Do you think your parents would have a wedding like this?" he asked; he was very hot, but very amused; it's a Renaissance Comedy to him, she thought to herself. "Well, we'd better be going, Sarah," Irene said, coming up. "The kids have to be up early in the morning." Miserably, Sarah nodded. Elizabeth looked at her watch. It was only three o'clock. "We'll be going, too," said Eleanor's husband, shaking hands with Manny. "Got to put the kids to bed?" Manny asked, a strange sad expression on his face. "No, got to take the baby-sitter back," her uncle said; then he looked at his daughters; it wouldn't be long now. Soon almost everyone was gone. "I'll have to be going, mother, Adam's got work to do," Elizabeth said; she felt guilty, abandoning them on a sinking lawn. "When are you leaving?" she asked Rebecca. They were spending their honeymoon in Russia because that was what Rebecca had been studying. "In a few days," Arthur told her, "we had to wait for the student flight." "Have a good time," she said, kissing them both. It was a long time since she had put on fashion shows for Arthur, making costumes out of blankets, when he had the chicken pox, the mumps. She felt like something was coming to an end herself.

The next day, she called Manny and asked him what he thought about the wedding. "Did you ever see anything like it?" she wanted to know, "you would have thought they could have rented some chairs." She refrained from mentioning the triumphal march from *Aida;* when she and Esther had been convinced, in high school, that they would forever be old maids, they had joked that at *their* weddings, they would have either the triumphal march or the chorale of Beethovan's Ninth. Now someone had done it. "They managed to rent a lot of mosquitoes," Manny said, "maybe they ate all the food." "Aren't you mad, daddy?" Elizabeth was surprised at how her anger at him had evaporated over the year. "What's there to be mad about; it's done, it's over with." She listened to the noise of the men in the shop. "What's done is done," he said finally, "let it lie." When she hung up, she asked Adam if that was a normal reaction. "I doubt it," he said, "I'd have tried to kill them." That night, they were watching *Star Trek* when the phone rang. It was Arthur. "Daddy had a heart attack." "A what?" She thought Arthur was joking. "Put mother on," she said. "What happened?" she asked Sarah. "Your father had a heart attack," Sarah said. "How is he?" Elizabeth wanted to know. "I don't know," Sarah said; her voice trailed off. "Is Irene there, put her on." "What's going on?" she demanded. "It was a heart attack," Irene said in her soothing tones, "but he's not in much pain, and the doctor hopes for the best; he'll know more tomorrow. When are you coming out?" "As soon as I can," Elizabeth said, knowing she was lying. The next day, she called the doctor herself. He told her all heart attacks were cataclysms, but the first forty-eight hours were the most important. Then she spoke to Sarah. Sarah said it was a blessing in disguise, now maybe Manny would stop smoking and lose weight. "What's the matter with her?" Elizabeth wailed to Adam; "She can't face it," he said, "and neither can you. Why aren't you going to the hospital?" "I'll go tomorrow," she said. "Well after the forty-eight hour limit expires," Adam pointed out. "I think I have some idea if I go I'll kill him," she said desperately.

The next day, she drove out with Irene. Why hadn't her father ever practiced law? He had gone to school, he had graduated with honors. Irene thought about it, but she was only eight at the time; she remembered him calling after he won his first case: "I won my first case!" he had shouted into the phone, "make kreplach!" "But your father had a hard time," she said, "he saw his father wiped out in the depression, and then, when your mother was pregnant with you, she was sick and had to lie on the couch all the time; he would have gotten paid five dollars a week; if he was lucky and didn't have to pay someone to let him work for the experience. Maybe he didn't want to be a lawyer," Irene said, thinking out loud, "maybe he did it to please his parents; maybe he thought money was the most important thing." "I can't believe my father was ever that agreeable," Elizabeth told her. Irene laughed. "He was very small once, believe it or not; your grandmother's still got his teddy bear."

When they got to the hospital, Manny did not seem at all happy to see her. She told him to behave, not to leave, not to turn up at Irene's still wired to his machine. When she left with Irene, she told her she didn't think she would come back: he didn't want to see her. "He treats

219

me the same way," Irene said, "he's frightened." Elizabeth was crying. "You've got to understand," Irene told her, "he worries about you, he always has. That's why he scolds. You're not married; you're not provided for." Elizabeth started to object, but Irene cut her off. "It hasn't happened yet, that's the important thing, and now he doesn't know what's going to happen to him. When he sees it, he'll believe it. He's a worrier, all the Kamens are worriers; your Aunt Madelaine is the Champion. Also," Irene went on, "he has his own problems, he's not perfect. Why should a parent be perfect?" Irene asked her. "Are you perfect? Are you just what he wants?" She looked over at Elizabeth. "Here, have a tissue." She thrust it under her nose. "He'll be all right, the Kamens are stronger than horses." Elizabeth choked on a sob. "He's mellowing," Irene said, " you'll see."

"It was that damn wedding!" Elizabeth said to Adam furiously: "I told you yesterday; he was fit to be tied; he wouldn't admit it; it's the first time I've ever heard him pretend not to be angry. That damn wedding!" she burst out again, starting to sob. Adam stroked her hair. "He'll be all right, he'll be all right." "And he wasn't even glad to see me," she wailed. "What do you expect, a catered heart attack?" Adam asked her, gentle. He kept stroking her hair, and she stopped crying; she fell asleep.

A spring and summer had come and gone. The Faculty Lounge had blossomed with a new carpet and chairs, new tables made of genuine wood grew starkly out of the mushroon colored wool. The basic color scheme, however, had been kept: orange and green. A strange pale salmon and lime green mural covered one wall: it was a design of intersecting circles, and made the room look like a 1930s movie set. Elizabeth kept expecting to see Greta Garbo and Robert Montgomery walk out of the wall, arm in arm. Half of the room had also disappeared, and partitions now marked off the space where the lounge had originally extended into spaciousness; that space had became the President's "sitting room." "Around here you never get something for nothing," Jeremy said bitterly, looking around the room. Elizabeth hardly ever talked to him; a few weeks before, he had come over when she and Adam were sitting on a couch. "How is your cat?" he asked her. "Cats," she corrected him, "I got Sammy a companion." "*I* got a cat," he announced importantly, "but I had to get rid of it; it broke my balloons." "Do you have a lot of balloons around your apartment?" Adam had asked innocently. It had been inconceivable to him that anyone could find a cat so distracting. "It always wants attention," Jeremy explained. "What did you do with it?" Elizabeth asked. "I gave it back," Jeremy said, "I told it's owner it wasn't good for me after all." "Too bad," Elizabeth mumbled, turning her back on him; embarrassed, he had gotten up and gravitated to another couch. "Balloons!" she said out loud, scornful.

A key turned in the lock. Mindy walked into the room, hesitated when she saw Elizabeth, and sat down. Mindy did not have her Ph.D.: Elizabeth did. Mindy belonged to the Union; Elizabeth did not. These things seemed to have an enormous importance to Mindy, who seemed to use them as markings on her moral slide rule. "Your cousin is in my class," Mindy told her. "I know," Elizabeth said, "how is he doing?" "Oh, he's a little freaked out, but otherwise he's fine. I just finished grading his first essay. Would you like to see it?" "Not particularly," said Elizabeth, who had a brand new batch of her own. Abraham was Irene's son; he had left home swearing he would never came back, that his parents had ruined his life; they had mistreated his girl friend; they had never cared for him. On the first day of school, Abe had arrived at Elizabeth's office, distraught, babbling about some battle-ax who came on like gangbusters, raving about grammar. "How can I get out of there?" he asked, wringing his books. Elizabeth had seen this teacher before; she spent a great deal of time talking to herself in the halls lately, and she agreed something should be done. "I'll find out who else is teaching at the same time," she told him, "and see if I can get them to let you in as an extra, what they call a red card." "It sounds like a red blanket," Abe said, grinning with relief; on his off nights and weekends, he worked in the hospital emergency room: he wanted to be a doctor. Mindy agreed to take him in. But then Elizabeth couldn't find him again, and so she called Irene to leave a message. Irene's daughter answered, and said they didn't even know where Abe was living; it had been weeks since they had talked to him. She sounded extremely depressed. "That was such a close family," Elizabeth mused, bewildered. "But we have his friend's number,

221

you might try him; you could leave a message there," Rachel was saying. "All right, thanks," Elizabeth told her, "do you want me to say anything to him if I find him? do you want his address?" "No," Rachel said evenly, "but it's nice of you to help him." "Don't mention it," Elizabeth told her. "I'm sure *he* won't," Rachel said, bitter.

"Freaked out?" Elizabeth asked in a neutral voice. Mindy was one of the "new emphasizers," which meant that if she didn't use one student word in each of her sentences, she had to go back two Monopoly spaces on the Monopoly Board of her childhood. There, at the start, her Brooklyn name waited for her like a pink ribbon. "He's very mixed up about his parents," Mindy elaborated, "he doesn't seem to know where they leave off and he begins." "He's moved out of the house," Elizabeth told her. "I know," Mindy said, "that's what the essay's about." "Can I read it?" Elizabeth asked. "Sure," Mindy said, "that's why I asked you." "She's enjoying this," Elizabeth thought to herself, taking the paper, thinking it wasn't really ethical, "she's enjoying finding out something about the Kamen family; she thinks I'll be upset." "I feel like I'm talking to the FBI," Mindy said, a guilty tinge coloring her words salmon and pale green. "Don't worry about me," Elizabeth said, not looking up, "I've been through it all before; I'm bulletproofed."

"How does one explain the disappointment one feels," the essay began, "when one realizes that a nineteen-year relationship you thought was perfect turns out to be nothing but a ridiculous farce?" "Good God," Elizabeth thought to herself. "Why should it be hard for parents to tell a child they can't afford to send him to college or to give him a car? My parents couldn't do this." Elizabeth thought about the version of the story she had heard from Irene: how Abe had changed, how his girl friend had changed him, how she had taken him away from all his friends, how she had poisoned his mind, turned him against the family, made him lose all respect for his father and mother. They had poured their whole life into their children; their children had been their life. "Wherever he wanted to go, I took him," Irene lamented, "to me, he was a God, we used to sit and talk, we were closer than any mother and son." "We were never wealthy, but thanks to wealthy grandparents, we lived very comfortably," the essay continued. Resentment of Jacob, of Jacob's support of the family, percolated up through the lines of the theme like coffee. "The three of us shared a room, but we had a color television set. There always seemed to be money for clothes and movies. Then my father's business failed. I had been working since the eighth grade, and helping out in the house. Everyone assumed this was expected, but my sisters never had to work; they could just lie around in the house. Nothing was expected of them. If one of them gained a pound, the whole world came to an end. My mother would not work either. Then, when the business failed, my father borrowed one thousand dollars from me which he never paid back. It is not the money I resent, but the lack of appreciation for my efforts.

"It is not easy to be on one's own, knowing you have only yourself to rely on. Next month, I will have to have an operation, and I will have only my friends to rely on. But it has become clear to me that I will never amount to anything unless I break away from the family. I know what I want to do, and I will have to do it myself. What I thought was my parents' love for me was only possessiveness. If I did not do or say exactly what they wanted, they would throw me out. My mother tells me, as far as she is concerned, I am only one more mouth to feed. Yet, in spite of the fear I have of living alone, I know it is something I must do when the only alternative is complete possession. I now think that my parents did not understand what love was; they confused it with possessiveness, and wanted me to do the same. I cannot live with such hypocrisy. For this reason, I am living alone, and doing the best I can. Only time will tell whether my efforts will be successful."

Reading the essay, all Elizabeth could think about was Irene, Irene, the baby of the family, taking care of everyone; it was Irene who had come to see her in the hospital when her bandage had come loose and she had begun to bleed; Irene who had called her doctor at his home and gotten him to come back to the hospital to look at her. She could see Irene, it was not hard to picture, not at all, lying, a white shape felled in her darkened room, no books on her bed, crying for hours over this son who had left, for reasons she simply could not understand. "I know I'm not perfect," she had said to Elizabeth, "I don't mind his moving out. But does he have to do it this way? You can't imagine the terrible things he said to his parents." When she spoke about Abe, Irene seemed to talk about herself and her husband in the third person archetypal.

"He lies, he exaggerates, he calls names. I don't know where we went wrong, I go over it all day, our lives revolved around him, our whole lives," she said, her voice dropping like the last act, its dark velvet curtain. "Look," Elizabeth told her, "you remember the trouble I had with my parents; we get along well now. This sounds semi-normal to me; most kids go through this in high school; Abe is just starting late. Sooner or later, this will end, you'll see, Irene, the same thing happened to me." "But I don't want it to take that long," Irene protested, starting to cry. "Of course you don't," Elizabeth said, "but what can you do about it? Nothing. You can't go out and get him with a net. You have to take care of yourself. How's your blood pressure?" she asked, catching her breath. "Two hundred and sixty over one hundred and thirty; the doctor said it was in the stroke range." Elizabeth winced inside, frightened. Abe would not want to know about this; he would not understand that Irene could not decide to shed her weight simply, as if stepping out of a fat suit; a brilliant student, he would not see the connection between her weight and her high blood pressure and her problems in getting a job. "There you are," Elizabeth told her, "you have to take care of yourself." "That's what I've been telling myself," Irene answered without conviction, "I have two other children and a husband to live for; I can't kill myself for him." "I'm glad to hear you say that," Elizabeth told her. "The doctor says my pressure's gone down since he left." "There you are," Elizabeth said positively, "you both need time to cool off. This may turn out to be a good thing yet." This was the family doctrine, the family line, the silver lining in the black tornado. And all the time Irene talked, she had not mentioned money as an issue, not once. So she had no idea what was at the core of this. Abe was proud, he was afraid if he stayed home, he would lose his independence; he would not be able to support himself; he would be on the dole. There was no way she could tell Irene this. It was not hard for her to understand Abe's fear; her own father had given up law and taken up cutting suits; arm after arm down the rows of time, all of them empty, a faint dust settling on the gaberdine shoulders. She would permit no interference with her career, with her life! Not even now.

"This is very sad," she said to Mindy; she was conscious of having a remarkable opportunity; Irene had helped raise her; she had grown up with Irene, and then she had grown up with Irene's child, Abe. Now, at thirty-one, she was seeing the parent at the throat of the child, the child at the throat of the parent. She could see both pictures; time was double-exposed. She could see no right or wrong; it was impossible to assign blame. "Once you know in back of every parent, there's another parent, you have to forgive everything," Irene had told her, after she and her mother had had a particularly bitter battle over Belle's ring. "Did I give you your grandmother's ring?" Sarah had asked her at dinner. When Elizabeth said no, Sarah got up, and Elizabeth, sitting at the table, waited happily for the ring to be produced. Unexpected bounty! Life from the dead! Instead, she heard her mother dial Hilda's number and tell her, yes, she still had the ring, and her daughter could have it for her birthday. "She'll have a sentimental attachment to it," Sarah said, sitting down, pleased with herself. Elizabeth didn't say anything, but looking at Adam, she could see he was also very upset. But she could not say a word: her throat was beginning to hurt. The next day she called Manny: "How could she do that?" she demanded, bursting into tears, surprising herself, "How could she give that ring away? She knew I would have wanted it. What kind of mother doesn't even ask her daughter about something like that first?" Manny was genuinely puzzled and upset. "Your mother means well," he said, "she doesn't have a mean bone in her body." "That's what you think," Elizabeth interrupted vindictively, "she does these things to hurt me. She knows how attached I was to Belle." "It wasn't an expensive ring," her father volunteered. "Expensive enough for Hilda to give her a painting in exchange for it!" Elizabeth shrieked. "I don't know anything about that," Manny said in a small voice. "And besides," Elizabeth said, "money has nothing to do with it, it was Belle's ring; that's why I wanted it." "I'm sure your mother didn't mean anything, I don't think you should be so upset," Manny said.

"It was *my* ring to give away," her mother said as Elizabeth picked up the phone that night. "Give away whatever you damn please from now on," Elizabeth said, "I'm surprised you didn't give me away." "And you always wear costume jewelry," her mother said, as if that settled things. "Did it ever occur to you," Elizabeth asked her, "that one reason I wear costume jewelry is that I don't have much money? *I* am your daughter, Ellen is your niece. You should have asked me." "It was my ring," Sarah repeated, "and besides, you never knew I had it until yesterday." "Why did you tell me about it then?" Elizabeth demanded, "just to let me know I couldn't have it?" "Sometimes, I think you're crazy," Sarah said, "you're always imagining things." "I know that's what you think, mother," Elizabeth hissed, furious, "but I am not crazy at all. *You* are the one who can't admit you do anything wrong." "You never wear your grandmother's earrings," Sarah accused, switching the subject. "I wear them *all the time*," Elizabeth retorted; it was true; she wore them whenever she was upset, and, when she didn't wear them, would spend hours looking into their aquamarines, their beautiful aquamarines that reminded her of the old marble stone glinting near the bell at Jacob's house. "Well, *I've* never seen you wearing them," Sarah told her. "You can take my word for it," Elizabeth said, "I'm not going to forget about this for a long time." And she hung up. She didn't want to give her mother the satisfaction of hearing her start to cry. Manny called her the next day. "Why are you making such a fuss, it's too late to get the ring back." "It may be too late to get the ring back but I wanted you to know how I felt," she said, starting to cry again. The ring, the round circle, her grandmother, given away, to someone else; she could not believe it. "I'll never understand you, Elizabeth," her father said, sadly, "your mother means well." "I'm glad *you* think so," she said, "you have to live with her." At night, the ring would rise and revolve in her dreams like a planet, a great hollow planet. "Behind every parent is another parent." Irene was right. Elizabeth realized she had "gotten over" the ring episode; she wasn't sure this was the same as forgiving, but she hoped it was. It was going to take some time before Irene and Abe were friendly. It had taken her fourteen years.

"I made him write it over," Mindy said. Elizabeth was glad to hear it; Mindy was tougher than she thought. "It wasn't well-organized," she explained. "It's so sad," Elizabeth said, more to herself than Mindy, "there's no one to blame." "I don't know," Mindy said, "it looks like the parents are to blame to me." Elizabeth looked carefully at Mindy; Mindy was four years older than she was and divorced. She was wearing what appeared to be house-dresses to school. Adam said he expected her to come in some day with a pail, from which she would produce her corrected papers, and begin handing them out. "The parents are always to blame," Elizabeth said, testing. "I think so," Mindy responded, and that was the end of that.

When Elizabeth saw Abe in the hall, she told him to come have coffee with her sometime; he said she probably knew what this was like. "I certainly do," she told him, "my mother hit me on the head with a high-heeled shoe for talking back." "My mother hit me with one inside," he said, gloomily. "Well," Elizabeth said, "someday this will work out." "Not for a long time," he predicted, "she's turning everyone in the family against me." "Your mother," Elizabeth said, "she's not so bad, but I don't expect you to believe that. These things take a long time: that's what I told her; I told her to take care of herself." Abe looked slightly shocked. "You don't know what it was like at home," he said grimly. "I've been through it," Elizabeth said, "and I'm not impressed. You'll survive, but if you have any trouble, come around. There's always the psychiatrist; don't let anyone in the family convince you that's the end of the world." He started to protest. "I don't mean you should go to one because you left home," Elizabeth told him, "I don't think that was crazy, just if you find you can't live up to what you expect of yourself, that's when you might want to think about it." Abe nodded, turning it over: "Did you go?" "I certainly did," she said, "do you want to see my certificate?" "No, I'll take your word for it," he said solemnly, looking at her. "Come see me when you don't have a class," she called after him. The Department Secretary was standing in back of her, looking astonished. "My cousin," she elucidated, and cheer returned to Frieda's face. Parents and children. It was an impossible riddle. No wonder the sphinx had taken it up. He had gotten to the heart of the matter; a few words, and he had destroyed the whole cousin's club at Greece. Who thought they knew anything? Blinded, the father was led by his children. "These things take a long time," she said to Irene again, that night. How did it begin? How did it end? She had wanted the ring; the ring had had the answer. She still believed in magic.

Falling

Chapter 14

Elizabeth was getting married; her parents had made all the arrangements; they had rented the hall, hired the photographers, chosen the menu. At the last minute, her mother had decided that a room with paneled wood walls and red drapes should have pink tablecloths and red napkins and called the restaurant to find out the additional charges. Horrified, Sarah agreed. The wedding cake was under construction, layer upon layer: it would have sugar jack-in-the-pulpits, Elizabeth's favorite flower; it was growing, floor after floor, a skyscraper, iced, ascending into a gray sky of clouds, cigar smoke clouds, where she and Adam would stand at the top like dolls, lightning rods struck and struck again, electric with the current of three generations, and tables like red moons, fringed with their friends. Her mother had a pink brocade dress; her father was making tuxedoes, her grandmother was having her hair tinted ice-blue. It occurred to Elizabeth that she didn't know her grandmother's name; she had never called her anything but "grandmother." "What's grandmother's name?" she asked Manny, surprised. "Jenny," he said, "Jennifer?" He didn't know himself. Elizabeth wanted to tell him that was the name she had always wanted to call a daughter, but a lump formed in her throat; she kept quiet.

All Elizabeth had to do was buy the dress, because, in two days, she was leaving with Adam on a cross-country trip, and when they got back, his divorce decree would be final, and they would marry. "The cart before the horse, as usual," Sarah muttered, despairing, handing over the sample wedding invitation, its beautiful gothic letters, each one little and pointed like a home. But now that Elizabeth was really getting married, the fights and arguments had fled from the house like birds from a cage. Elizabeth went with Esther to pick out the dress; she would not let Sarah come with her. She still had too many memories of shopping expeditions with her mother; four years ago, she and her mother had gone together while she bought a winter coat, and Elizabeth, who still had trouble with her ears, wanted one with a hood to protect their halls from the white Chicago winters. Sarah didn't like such a coat; she thought they looked too juvenile. She was so upset that when Elizabeth bought the coat, she started screaming at her the minute they got into the car in the parking lot, and she drove the car right into a pillar. They sat there in silence, listening to the crunching glass. They had two more levels to get down before the street. "Now I hope you're satisfied," Sarah said. "The trouble with you, mother," Elizabeth answered, "is that you can't imagine anyone loves you who disagrees with you."

She wanted her wedding to be normal, like everyone else's in every respect, but at the last minute, she decided she could not endure them playing *Here Comes the Bride,* so she arranged to have them play Purcell's *Trumpet Voluntary.* Immediately, Manny was storming around the house: "I never heard of such a thing, *everyone* plays *Here Comes the Bride.*" Nevertheless, Elizabeth was adamant. With Esther, she found the dress she wanted in less than an hour. It cost one hundred dollars more than her mother wanted to pay, but Elizabeth decided that was all right, she would make up the extra herself. When she came back, she was vaguely dissatisfied. She wanted *something* to be different, special. Then she saw the hat: it looked like a medieval wedding hat, at least nine inches high, embroidered with pearls; it looked like the hat in her picture of a medieval wedding, where all the family, and the furniture from all the houses, and everyone who had ever lived or died, lined up on both sides of the bridal procession. "We'll have to order it specially from Boston," the saleswoman said, "I'm not sure we can get it." "Try," said Elizabeth, unusually imperious. The woman called the store long distance: "They think it will get here, but it will cost fifty dollars extra." "Fine, fine," Elizabeth told her. With that hat, she would be safe; the hat would conjure up the past and the present, the living and the dead; it would gather them all under the veil; there would be all the faces under the veil; none of them would ever be lost. She remembered a line from a poem: "I have come, bringing the dark in a tiny white pot." She would make up her cheeks with that pot; she would make up her eyes. Things would go on. When she wrote out the check, more than she had ever paid for a year's wardrobe, it felt like a celebration.

The night before she got married, Elizabeth worried mostly about her hair. "But the hat will hide it," she reminded herself, reassured. That night she had a dream. She was with her mother and Arthur at the beach. For a long time, Arthur, wearing his little sun hat, dug in the sand with his shovel and pail. Then he ran off toward the ocean, fast, on his little fat legs, the white triangle of his diaper flashing before them like a sail. He sat down at the water's edge and began playing with shells. Elizabeth was sitting near her mother's chair, building a sand castle. She had hauled pail after pail of water back to wet the sand, turning it to clay, until Arthur demanded the pail; it was *his* pail. "Give him his turn, Elizabeth," Sarah told her. Suddenly, Sarah was on her feet. "Where's Arthur?" she demanded. Then she saw him; he was knocked over by a wave, and the wave was pulling him in and down. Sarah flew across the sand; Elizabeth had no idea her mother could run so fast. Sarah ran into the water, her eyes riveted on Arthur. "But she can't swim!" Elizabeth realized suddenly, a scream growing in her throat, "she can't swim!" Sarah ran into the water, deeper than she ever went, and snatched up Arthur, hugging him to her chest. She carried him back to the blanket. Elizabeth sat there transfixed. When Sarah put him down, she gave him a good whack on the bottom. "I *told* you not to go in alone," she said, and started to cry. Then Sarah began to fall: she was falling through blue space and black space, holding Arthur. "She can't swim, she can't swim," Elizabeth said over and over, seeing her mother falling through air like a black stone, her white face a moon, her child's face a moon. "What can I do?" Elizabeth cried out loud, but her mother was falling and falling, like a cloud, or a world, or a stone, and as she fell, her face changed: it was Elizabeth's face, it was Irene's face, it was Belle's face, it was Madelaine's. The baby's face changed: it was Elizabeth's face, it was Arthur's face, it was Abe's face. "Where is the bottom, mother?" Elizabeth cried out, terrified. "There is no bottom," her mother called to her, "there is only this falling," and she fell and fell and at the bottom Elizabeth could see something like a blue water, but though Sarah was falling, she was not getting closer to it. "I am the salt bead," Sarah called to her, falling, "hold him, you are

233

the salt bead, the salt of your blood is falling now." "But you can't swim!" Elizabeth screamed again; she wanted to wake Sarah up, to stop her, to take her away from this column of blue air and black air. "But I have him," said Sarah, "I have him," and she held him out to Elizabeth. Elizabeth took him from her mother, and when she woke up, she had settled on her bed at the bottom of the world, holding the salt bead in her hand, the gray, iridescent, mysterious pearl. The dream still seemed to hover in the corners of the room. "Can you swim, Elizabeth?" her mother was asking her. "Yes, mother," she said, "you hold me, and I'll kick." Sarah, who was terrified of the water, held her, and she kicked. Waves of time broke against the white walls like surf. She leaned over and woke up Adam. "We better get going" she said, while somewhere behind her eyes, the woman and child were falling and falling, like a feather, or stone.